Dear Readers,

Many years ago, when I was a kid, my father said to me, "Bill, it doesn't really matter what you do in life. What's important is to be the *best* William Johnstone you can be."

I've never forgotten those words. And now, many years and almost 200 books later, I like to think that I am still trying to be the best William Johnstone I can be. Whether it's Ben Raines in the Ashes series, or Frank Morgan, the last gunfighter, or Smoke Jensen, our intrepid mountain man, or John Barrone and his hard-working crew keeping America safe from terrorist lowlifes in the Code Name series, I want to make each new book better than the last and deliver powerful storytelling.

Equally important, I try to create the kinds of believable characters that we can all identify with, real people who face tough challenges. When one of my creations blasts an enemy into the middle of next week, you can be damn sure he had a good reason.

As a storyteller, my job is to entertain you, my readers, and to make sure that you get plenty of enjoyment from my books for your hard-earned money. This is not a job I take lightly. And I greatly appreciate your feedback—you are my gold, and your opinions *do* count. So please keep the letters and e-mails coming.

Respectfully yours,

William Johnstone

WILLIAM W. JOHNSTONE

HEART OF THE MOUNTAIN MAN

JUSTICE OF THE MOUNTAIN MAN

PINNACLE BOOKS
Kensington Publishing Corp.
http://www.kensingtonbooks.com

PINNACLE BOOKS are published by

Kensington Publishing Corp.
850 Third Avenue
New York, NY 10022

Copyright © 2006 by Kensington Publishing Corp.
Heart of the Mountain Man copyright © 2000 by William W. Johnstone
Justice of the Mountain Man copyright © 2000 by William W. Johnstone

All rights reserved. No part of this book may be reproduced in any
form or by any means without the prior written consent of the Publisher, excepting brief quotes used in reviews.

If you purchased this book without a cover, you should be aware that
this book is stolen property. It was reported as "unsold and destroyed" to the Publisher and neither the Author nor the Publisher
has received any payment for this "stripped book."

This novel is a work of fiction. Names, characters, places, and inci-
dents are either the product of the author's imagination or are used
fictitiously. Any resemblance to actual persons, living or dead, or
events is entirely coincidental.

All Kensington Titles, Imprints, and Distributed Lines are available
at special quantity discounts for bulk purchases for sales promo-
tions, premiums, fund-raising, and educational or institutional use.
Special book excerpts or customized printings can also be created
to fit specific needs. For details, write or phone the office of the
Kensington special sales manager: Kensington Publishing Corp.,
850 Third Avenue, New York, NY 10022, attn: Special Sales Depart-
ment, Phone: 1-800-221-2647.

Pinnacle and the P logo Reg. U.S. Pat. & TM Off.

First Pinnacle Books Printing: June 2006

10 9 8 7 6 5 4 3 2 1

Printed in the United States of America

HEART OF THE
MOUNTAIN MAN

1

Smoke Jensen came fully awake, his heart hammering as he sat up straight in the bed, his hand automatically reaching for the Colt .44 that was never very far from his grasp.

Sally opened her eyes, blinked twice, and asked in a sleepy voice, "What is it, darling?"

Smoke shook his head, forgetting for the moment she couldn't see him in the darkness. "I don't know," he answered, the hairs on the back of his neck stirring at some as yet unexplained noise or movement.

He turned his head toward the window, where a light breeze was billowing the curtains, bringing into the room the sweet scent of mountain laurel and pine needles along with a hint of ozone that foretold of fall showers on the way.

Sally glanced at the glint of moonlight on the barrel of Smoke's gun and sat up herself, reaching for the Colt Navy .36-caliber pistol on the table next to her side of the bed.

"Something wrong, dear?" she asked.

Smoke slipped out of bed and pulled on his buckskin trousers, which he'd flung over the back of a chair the night before. "I'll let you know in a minute, sweetheart. Go back to sleep."

"Not on your life, Smoke. I've learned never to ignore your instincts." She threw the covers back and grabbed a robe from the foot of the bed. "If something woke you up, then I'm going to go with you to find out what it is."

She could see his teeth gleaming in the semidarkness as he grinned at her. "Well, there's no need for both of us to lose sleep. Why don't you check it out and I'll go back to bed?"

She put her hands on his shoulders, turned him around, and pushed him toward the door. "I'll be right behind you."

"So that's the way it is, huh?" he whispered over his shoulder. "I take all the risks and you stay safe behind me."

"That's why God gave you such big shoulders, dear, so I could hide behind them," she answered with a chuckle.

Smoke snorted. "That'll be the day."

They walked through the darkness of the cabin and stepped to the back door. Smoke eased it open, eared back the hammer on his Colt, and stepped outside. Sally followed him out the door and stepped to his side, her Colt Navy held in front of her.

The night was typical for early fall in the high lonesome of the Rocky Mountains where they had their ranch, Sugarloaf. The sky was crystal clear with millions of stars shining down like diamonds on a field of black velvet. The moon, though not full, shone with brilliance through the thin air, illuminating the area around the cabin with a ghostly yellow light. Lightning danced in dark, roiling clouds over distant mountaintops and the faint sounds of thunder could be heard.

Smoke's eyes stopped their movement and he pointed to the hitching post off to the side. "There's a horse," he said.

Sally followed his gesture and could see a solitary horse standing next to the hitching post, its head down as it calmly munched on nearby grass. Its reins were hanging loose, as if it'd wandered to the post by itself.

"It's wearing a saddle so there must be a rider somewhere close by," Sally whispered back.

Smoke reached inside the cabin and grabbed his Greener ten-gauge short-barreled express gun off a rack next to the door. He stuck his Colt in his waistband and held the Greener in both hands as he stepped off the porch and approached the riderless horse.

"Be careful, Smoke, there may be more than one of them out there," Sally called softly, her eyes flicking back and forth as she tried to cover his back. Since Smoke had once been a notorious gunfighter, she knew there was always the possibility of men tracking him down, looking to get revenge for some perceived wrong Smoke had done them.

"There's something familiar about this horse," Smoke said, a puzzled expression on his face as he turned back to look at Sally. "I've seen that blaze on his forehead before."

Sally took a closer look at the horse and realized she knew who its owner was. "Wait a minute, Smoke," she said, putting her hand on the barrel of the shotgun and pushing it toward the ground. "I think that's Monte Carson's horse."

Smoke walked over to the horse and examined the saddle. "You're right, Sally. It is Monte's mount."

Monte Carson was the sheriff at Big Rock, Colorado, the closest town to the Jensen ranch, and a dear friend of Smoke and Sally.

When Sally got to Smoke's side, she noticed the look on his face. "What's wrong, Smoke? You look like you've seen a ghost."

He pointed at the side of the saddle. The leather was covered with a large stain, looking almost black in the moonlight, that ran down the sides of the saddle onto the fender skirts of the stirrups. Smoke put his finger on the stain and held it under his nose. The coppery scent brought back unpleasant memories of times he'd been shot. "It's blood. Something bad's happened to Monte."

He eased the hammers down on the shotgun and laid the barrel on his shoulder as he looked around, searching for his friend in the semidarkness. "I guess I'd better get some of the hands up and we'll do a search. If this blood's his, he's injured pretty bad. It won't do to leave him out here too long."

Sally pulled her robe close around her against the chill of the mountain air. "I'll get some water on the stove to boil and have my medical kit handy."

Smoke nodded his approval. "Put some coffee on too, please. We're gonna need it if we spend too much time out here in the cold."

Sally walked back toward their cabin and Smoke proceeded to the bunkhouse across the wide yard. He opened the door and moved to the wood stove in the corner, which was still warm from the evening before. He lit a lantern on a shelf and picked up a coffeepot and banged it on the stove a couple of times.

His foreman, Pearlie, sat up in his bed, yawning and rubbing sleepy eyes, a puzzled expression on his wrinkled, sunburned face. "Pearlie, get everybody up!" Smoke said. "Sheriff Monte Carson's horse showed up here covered with blood. I think Monte may be out there in the night bleeding to death. We need to find him."

Pearlie scrambled out of bed, clapping his hands and shouting, "Off yore butts an' on yore feet! We got work to do and we got to do it fast!"

The cowboys, most of whom knew Monte and liked him, didn't argue. They swung out of their beds and began to pull their clothes on.

"Sally'll have coffee ready over at the cabin. Report there when you're finished dressing," Smoke said as he left the bunkhouse.

By the time Pearlie had the hands gathered outside the cabin, Sally had biscuits and sausage patties cooked along with a large pot of fresh coffee.

Pearlie, a renowned chowhound, made sure he was at the front of the line for food. "Havin' some of your fresh-cooked biscuits and sausage almost makes gettin' up at this ungodly hour worth it, Miss Sally," he said, as he grabbed a handful of the sausage and biscuit sandwiches.

Cal Woods, Pearlie's best friend and unofficial son to Smoke and Sally, spoke up from behind the foreman.

"Hey, go easy there, Pearlie. Anybody'd think you ain't eaten for days the way you grabbin' those sinkers."

Pearlie puffed out his chest. "The man who has to do most of the work gets the most food, Cal, my boy. That's the way it's always been and that's the way it always will be."

"Huh," Cal snorted through his nose. "The only time you move faster'n molasses in January is when you're rushing toward a mess tent."

Pearlie shook his head. "Boys! You just don't understand the difficulty being in charge of a bunch of lazy galoots like you causes a man. Why, I get plumb wore out just thinkin' on ways to get you to earn your salary."

He paused to stuff another sandwich into his mouth as Smoke stepped up on the porch to address the group of men.

"Boys, we need to get moving. Monte is out there, so let's go find him." He glanced at Pearlie. "Pearlie, you organize the men to cover all the territory between here and the gate to the road to Big Rock. If we don't find him there, we'll move on down toward the town."

"Yes, sir, Smoke," Pearlie said, and he turned and began giving orders to the men on where to search.

Sally put a hand on Smoke's arm. "Perhaps we ought to send someone to Big Rock to fetch Doc Spalding."

Smoke nodded. "Cal, hold on a minute. I want you to saddle up and ride as fast as you can to Big Rock and get Doc out here. And tell him to bring what he needs for a bullet wound."

Cal nodded once and sprinted toward the barn to get his mount.

It took the men less than thirty minutes to find the wounded Monte Carson and carry him to Smoke's cabin.

"Put him on the bed," Sally said.

She tore open his shirt and looked at his wounds. She glanced up at Smoke. "Looks like he's been hit twice, once just below the left shoulder and once in the chest."

"Is it in his lung?" Smoke asked.

She shook her head. "I don't think so. He doesn't have any bloody froth on his lips and he seems to be breathing all right."

As Sally took cloths and dipped them in hot water and began to wash his wounds, Smoke bent over the bed, his lips close to Monte's ear.

"Monte, can you hear me?"

Monte's eyes flickered and opened, his lips curling in a half smile. "Of course I can hear you, Smoke. I've been shot, but I ain't deaf."

Smoke grinned. It was a good sign his friend could still joke in spite of having two bullets in him. "Who did this to you, pal, and why?"

Monte's eyes moved to look at Sally, then back to Smoke. "Big Jim Slaughter and his men."

"I thought Slaughter was up around Wyoming, near the hole-in-the-wall area."

Monte nodded, then groaned with the pain the movement caused. "He was. He decided to pay me a visit and talk over some old times."

Smoke pursed his lips. He hadn't been aware that Monte used to ride with Slaughter, who was one of the most vicious and bloodthirsty killers still roaming the countryside. Before he could ask any more questions, the door opened and Doc Cotton Spalding walked in, followed by Cal.

Sally stepped back from Monte's side and she and the doc began to discuss his wounds and what to do next.

Smoke grabbed Cal by the arm and led him out to the kitchen. "Let's let the doc do his work in peace, Cal."

Smoke went out on the porch and told the men waiting there he thought Monte was going to be all right and they could go back to bed if they wanted.

Pearlie laid his hand on the butt of his Colt pistol. "Who did this to him, Smoke? Me and the boys'd like to have a talk with them galoots."

Smoke held up his hands. "There'll be plenty of time

for that later, Pearlie. Soon as we find out what's going on, we'll do whatever is necessary to help Monte."

Pearlie scratched his chin, a glint in his eye. "Any of Miss Sally's sausage and biscuits left?"

Smoke laughed, "Cal, go in and get that platter and hand 'em out before Pearlie faints from hunger."

"Man ain't allowed hisself to get hungry in ten year at least," Cal muttered as he went back inside the cabin.

2

Monte had just finished the lunch of beef broth Sally had prepared for him when Smoke sat down next to his bed. "Hey, partner," Smoke said, "you ready to tell me what happened last night?"

Monte's face changed and he got a faraway look in his eyes as he glanced out the window. Smoke followed his look, observing the distant mountaintops already covered with snow down to the tree line, the bright yellow leaves on the grove of aspen just down from the cabin, and the deep green of the evergreens mixed with the reds and yellows of maple trees on the mountainsides. Fall was as beautiful as ever in the high lonesome of the Rocky Mountains, but Smoke knew Monte wasn't seeing the scenery so much as he was looking into his past.

He and Monte Carson had become very good friends over the past few years. Monte had once been a well-known gunfighter, though he had never ridden the owl-hoot trail. Or so Smoke believed.

A local rancher, with plans to take over the county, had hired Monte to be the sheriff in Fontana, a town just down the road from Smoke's Sugarloaf spread. Monte went along with the man's plans for a while, till he couldn't stomach the rapings and killings any longer. He put his foot down and let it be known that Fontana was going to be run in a law-abiding manner from then on.

The rancher, Tilden Franklin, sent a bunch of riders in to teach the upstart sheriff a lesson. The men killed Monte's two deputies and seriously wounded him, taking over the town. In retaliation, Smoke founded the town of Big Rock, and he and his band of aging gunfighters cleaned house in Fontana.

When the fracas was over, Smoke offered the job of sheriff in Big Rock to Monte. He married a grass widow and settled into the job like he was born to it. Neither Smoke nor the citizens of Big Rock ever had cause to regret his taking the job.

When Monte didn't speak, Smoke leaned back and crossed his arms, signaling he was there until he got some answers. "Why don't you start by telling me how you know Big Jim Slaughter?"

After he picked up a glass of fresh milk from the tray and took a deep draft, Monte began talking, still without meeting Smoke's eyes.

"It was a lot of years ago, Smoke, when I was still in my teens and thought I was a big man with a gun. It was just after the big war, when the country was still wild and gangs were on the prowl everywhere. Slaughter's bunch, Slaughter's Marauders, invited me in when I didn't have a whole lot of other choices. All the men were back from the war and there just wasn't much honest work to be found. Anyway, I began to ride with 'em, doin' little jobs at first, stealing a few horses or cattle or boosting a wagonload of freight here and there. Then, Slaughter decided to hit it big in one job. He found out from a drunken sergeant in a bar that an Army payroll was coming in on a train in a few days. After he got all the details, he planned out how to rob the train."

"How many men did he have riding with him at the time?" Smoke asked.

"'Bout ten or so, countin' me. Well, we pried up some tracks and hid nearby. When the engine ran off the rails, we spurred our hosses and charged that old train like Pickett did in the war. We managed to get the payroll out of the boxcar pretty quick, and then Slaughter had me put the money in my saddlebags. He'd divide it up later, he said. We rode off free and clear. Only, somehow an Army patrol managed to catch up with us."

"What did you do?"

Monte grinned, his eyes looking inward as he remembered the day. "Slaughter told me to git the hell outta there. He said we'd all meet up in two weeks down at Del Rio, and split up the money and head on down into Mexico. Then we all rode off in different directions with the blue-bellies coming on like dogs on a coon's trail."

"Did you meet up later?"

Monte shook his head. "No. I waited around Del Rio for almost three weeks, spending most of my time in bars and cantinas, drinking myself to sleep every night. You see, Smoke, I'd never done anything that serious before. Now I knew that I'd never be able to stay in the country, not with the whole government after me. I didn't much like the idea of spendin' the rest of my life tryin' to learn to speak Mexican."

"What did you do when Slaughter didn't show up?"

"I heard from some men in a bar that he'd been shot and killed and his band of Marauders was broken up and scattered across the whole territory, so I packed the money in my saddlebags and headed north. I drifted for a while, but never spent any of the money. Finally, I came to work for Tilden Franklin and ended up with you offerin' me the job as sheriff in Big Rock."

"So you still have the money?"

Monte wagged his head. "You remember, after you offered me the job, I told you I'd need a week or so to think it over?"

"Yeah."

"Well, during that week, I rode over to the U.S. marshal's office in Denver and traded that money in for a pardon for the robbery. The government was right proud to get the money back, and they knew Slaughter had been behind the whole thing, so they let the little fish, me, go. That way I was free to take the job you'd offered with a clear conscience and not have to live my life lookin' back over my shoulder at my back trail."

Smoke nodded. "And then you met Mary."

Monte smiled for the first time since Smoke came into the room. "Yeah, Mary saved me, Smoke. She showed me what life is all about. Fallin' in love with her and marryin' her was the rightest thing I've ever done in my life."

"So, that brings us up to last night. What happened and what does Jim Slaughter have to do with it?"

Monte cut tortured eyes toward Smoke, eyes that were wet with unshed tears. "I got home late from the office, 'bout eight o'clock. As I rode up to our house, I saw three men sitting on their horses out front . . ."

Monte pulled back on the reins, letting his right hand fall to his side and unhook the hammer-thong on his Colt pistol. "Howdy, gents," he called. "What can I do for you?"

As he spoke, he let his eyes flick to his house, trying to see if Mary was in sight, or if the door was shut. There were no lights on in the house, which worried him, for she always left a lantern burning on the porch when he was late getting home.

"Carson, we came to give you a message from Big Jim Slaughter," one of the men said. He was tall and skinny, with a beard hanging down to his chest and scraggly hair sticking out from under his hat. He wore two pistols, butts forward, on each hip. They were tied down low, so Monte knew he wasn't a cowboy but made his living with his guns.

Monte's heart beat faster when he heard Slaughter's name. "I heard he was dead."

One of the other men laughed, and then began to choke on his chaw of tobacco. "Pardner, you gonna wish he was dead 'fore all this is over, that's fer sure," he finally managed to say.

"Before what's over?" Monte asked, his hand drifting down to rest on his thigh next to his pistol.

The third man heeled his horse closer to Monte and stared at him from under the brim of his hat. "Slaughter wants his money, Carson, the whole fifty thousand."

Monte recognized the man. He'd ridden with Slaughter back when Monte had. His name was Boots Malone, and he was as nasty a specimen of humanity as Monte had ever met. He liked to slice up bar girls with his Bowie knife, just for fun, and Monte had seen him gun down women and children for no reason other than they were in his way.

"What if I tell you, Boots, that I don't have it?"

Boots shifted the toothpick in his mouth from one side to the other, his dead eyes never leaving Monte's. "Then I'd say it's too bad for that pretty little wife of your'n."

"What do you mean?"

Boots leaned back against the cantle of his saddle. "Slaughter took her on over to Robber's Roost, near Jackson Hole, Wyoming. He said to tell you he'd keep her there for four weeks, free from harm, to give you a chance to bring him his money. Then, he's gonna start handin' her out to the men there in the hole-in-the-wall area. You know the type, men on the run who ain't seen a woman in months."

"You bastard!"

Boots started to rein his horse around. "You got thirty days, Carson. Then if you want to see your wife, you're gonna have to stand in line."

Monte's pistol appeared in his hand as if on its own volition. His first slug took Boots in the chest, knocking him backward off his horse to land spread-eagled on the ground, his eyes wide and surprised until the life slowly winked out in them.

The second man had his pistol half out of his holster when Monte shot him in the face, the bullet entering his mouth and blowing out the back of his head, showering the third man with hair and brains and blood as he pulled the trigger on Monte.

Monte felt the bullets tear into him, twisting him sideways in his saddle. As his horse danced and whirled, trying to escape the explosions of gunfire, Monte snapped off a shot at the man as he rode away. The man flinched and leaned over his saddle horn, but Monte couldn't tell if he'd hit him or he was just ducking.

Monte tucked his useless left arm into his belt and ran to search the house. Mary was gone . . .

Monte looked up at Smoke, his voice hoarse from the tale. "All I could think of was to get to you, Smoke, and see what you thought I should do."

Smoke thought for a moment. "A lot will depend on whether you hit the galoot that was running away, and how hard you hit him. If you planted him forked end down, we've got some time to plan what to do. On the other hand, if he made it back to Slaughter and told him you don't have the money, Mary's time is a lot shorter than I like to think about."

"Yeah. As long as he thinks there is a chance he'll get the money, he'll keep her safe. At least until I see her and hand over the payroll."

Smoke hesitated. "Monte, you know Slaughter and his reputation better than I do, but I don't think there's any way in hell you and Mary are going to be allowed to walk away from this."

Monte nodded. "You're right, Smoke. Even if I had the money, which I don't, I got to plan some way to get Mary out of there and put an end to Slaughter once and for all."

Smoke stood up. "First things first, Monte. Cal and Pearlie and I'll head out to your place and see if we find two bodies or three. If there's three men down, I'll go up into the mountains and talk to some friends of mine about the hole-in-the-wall area, see if there's some way we can get in without being seen."

"What if the man got away?"

"Then we don't have time to do it the easy way. I'll have to get moving right away and work something out on the way to Wyoming."

Monte started to get up, struggling to use his bandaged left arm.

"Hold on, pardner. Doc Spalding says you got at least a week in bed, and then another few days before you're gonna be able to use that arm."

"But I can't let you and the boys do this alone. It's my mess and I need to get myself out of it."

Sally, who had been standing in the doorway for most of their talk, stepped into the room. "Monte Carson, you sit yourself back down in that bed right now. You'll be of no use to Mary if you get those wounds to bleeding and end up killing yourself. You let Smoke and Cal and Pearlie do what they need to while you heal. After that, we'll see what the doc says about how soon you can go to Wyoming. All right?"

Though she said it as a question, Sally left no room for discussion. Monte knew she was right and he'd have to let his friends do the initial investigation into the happenings out at his ranch.

He flopped back down on the pillow. "All right, Sally. You win. Smoke, would you let me know what you find out at the ranch?"

Smoke nodded. "One way or another, Monte, we'll keep you informed. Now, you rest up and eat whatever Sally brings you, 'cause you got a lot of blood to make up for what you spilled all over the country between here and your place."

He turned to Sally. "Keep him down until we get back. We should know something by supper time."

Sally stood on tiptoes and kissed Smoke's lips. "You ride with your guns loose, Smoke Jensen. I don't want to have to call Doc Spalding back out here to patch you up, too."

"Yes, dear," Smoke said as he strapped on his Colt .44.

3

As Smoke and Cal and Pearlie approached the Carson house, Smoke pulled his Colt and eared back the hammer.

"You expectin' trouble, Smoke?" Pearlie asked, resting his palm on his own pistol butt.

Smoke shrugged. "You never know. Monte said he may've put some lead into the man trying to ride away. He may be wounded and lying around here somewhere just waiting to put a bullet into whoever might come looking."

Cal and Pearlie looked at each other and pulled their guns.

When they got to the house, they found the two dead men right in front of the porch. Both had been killed with clean shots.

"Jimminy," Cal said, "I remember you sayin' Monte was a gun slick 'fore he joined up with you and became sheriff, but he must've been pretty doggone good to draw down on three men and get 'em all."

Smoke nodded. "There isn't any back-up in Monte, that's for sure. And it looks like he hasn't lost much of his skill with a six-killer either."

He pointed at the bullet hole over one man's heart and the other in the center of his face. "Dead center with both shots," Smoke said with some admiration.

Pearlie shook his head. "And then, after gettin' hit

twice, he managed to possibly put some lead in the third man as he was ridin' off. That takes some *cojones*, Smoke."

Smoke looked at his friend. "I've never had any doubts about Monte's courage, boys. Now let's spread out and see if we can find the last man."

As Cal and Pearlie reined their horses off to opposite sides of the yard surrounding Monte's house, Smoke got off Joker, his blanket-hipped Palouse stud, and walked bent over, staring at the ground.

An experienced tracker, he could almost see what had happened from the way the horses' hooves tore up the sod around the bodies. Once he found the trail of the third man, he began to follow the hoofprints, glancing up frequently so he wouldn't be caught off guard if the man were still around.

About thirty yards from the original confrontation, he found spots of dried blood on the ground. "You did hit him, Monte," Smoke mumbled. He looked back over his shoulder at the distance. "And at thirty yards on the back of a moving horse. That was a hell of a shot, partner," he said, as he followed the trail of blood toward a copse of trees nearby.

As he approached the trees, he whistled shrilly through his lips to get Cal and Pearlie's attention. When they rode into view from opposite directions, he pointed at the grove of trees and held up his gun.

The men dismounted and approached the trees from different directions, guns drawn and ready.

All of their precautions were unnecessary. Smoke found the man lying on his stomach, a bullet hole surrounded by dark crimson stains on the back of his shirt. He was still alive, but unconscious.

"Pearlie, go get a wagon out of Monte's barn and hitch a couple of his horses to it. We need to get this man to town and see if Doc Spalding can save him."

Cal leaned over and spat in the dirt. "Why go to all that trouble to save pond-scum like that, Smoke?"

Smoke glanced up. "Because if he lives, he can give us

important information about Slaughter and how many men he has and where they're holding Mary."

Cal's face colored. "Oh, I didn't think of that."

"What if he won't talk, Smoke?" Pearlie asked.

Smoke looked at him with an expression on his face that made Pearlie glad he was the big man's friend and not his enemy.

"Oh, he'll talk, Pearlie. He'll talk or he'll wish he'd never seen either Big Jim Slaughter or Monte Carson."

Smoke took a slab of fatback pork out of his saddlebag, placed it over the bullet hole in the man's back, and tied it in place with a strip of cloth torn from the gunny's own shirt. When Pearlie brought Monte's buckboard up next to him, he bent and lifted the man off the ground as if he weighed no more than five pounds, placing him in the back of the wagon.

"We're gonna ride for town, Cal. You go on ahead and have Doc Spalding ready to do some cutting on this man. Tell him Mary Carson's life depends on keeping this snake alive!"

4

Big Jim Slaughter pulled his Winchester from its saddle boot and waved it over his head at the sentry standing on a nearby ridge. It was the third such sentry he and his gang had passed in the last few miles as they approached their hideout known only as the "hole-in-the-wall." It was a natural valley high in the mountains surrounding the small Wyoming town of Jackson Hole. Accessible only by a narrow pass that meandered between several higher peaks, it had been a hiding place for men on the run for longer than anyone could remember. Easily defended, it had simply never been worth the trouble or the many dead men it would take to roust the criminals out of the place.

Slaughter led a column of twenty men, all hard cases who were wanted by the law across the country for everything from rape to armed robbery and murder. Riding next to him was an attractive woman in her late thirties. She had long brown hair, tied loosely behind her neck with a small, silk ribbon, and was wearing a man's shirt and trousers. She rode her horse with practiced ease, as if she spent a lot of time on horseback. Her face was serene and composed and she showed no trace of fear or trepidation, a fact that bothered Jim Slaughter.

As they rode down a dry gulch, cut out of the surrounding mountainside by hundreds of years of seasonal snowmelt runoffs, he glanced at her, his face showing his puzzlement.

"Mrs. Carson," he said, his voice neutral, "excuse me, but all the way here from Colorado, you've acted like you were out for a ride in the park. Doesn't the fact that you've been kidnapped by a gang of men and taken from your home to a strange place bother you?"

Mary Carson turned her calm eyes to Slaughter and gave a half smile. "Does it bother me? Yes. Do I fear you? No."

Slaughter shook his head. He was beginning to admire this woman more and more. Monte Carson was a lucky man.

"Why not?" he asked. He'd raped and killed and beaten hundreds of times before, and he'd never failed to see the haunted look that appeared in someone's eyes the moment they knew for certain they were going to die or be seriously injured, the acknowledgment of defeat and terrible sadness. It was a look he knew well, and he had come in some perverted way to look forward to it and enjoy instilling it in others.

"Because I know my husband will come for me eventually."

Slaughter snorted. "Even assuming he tries, and assuming he is able to make it past the sentries and guards we have set up to discourage visitors, what makes you think you'll be alive when he gets here? How do you know I won't just turn you over to this"—he hesitated as he glanced at the scum riding with them, then back at her—"pack of animals ridin' along with us?"

She raised an eyebrow. "Are you trying to frighten me, Mr. Slaughter?"

"No, just wondering why you seem so unconcerned about your fate."

Mary looked away from him, her eyes taking in the mountains that surrounded them, the blue sky, and the grass-covered slopes still layered with wildflowers and blooming shrubs. Finally, she took a deep breath and spoke. "I've lived a good life, Mr. Slaughter. I was married to a fine man for five years, and when he was killed I was lucky enough to find another wonderful man. Out here on the frontier, we learn to accept death as just another part of life, and not necessarily the worst part either. So, if I die . . . if you kill me, then so be it. I've had more than my share of goodness, and I'll die knowing I've had more than you'll ever have if you live to be a hundred years old."

Slaughter nodded. There was more than a little truth in what she said. He stared ahead down the trail without answering, thinking back on his life. It'd been a hard-scrabble existence ever since he was a kid. After his mother died when he was no more than five or six, his father dove into a whiskey bottle and lived there until he died, at Jim's hands, ten years later.

Daily beatings became a way of life for the young Slaughter, until finally, one day when he was sixteen, he took the razor strap out of his father's hands, knocked the surprised man down, and beat him to death with an ax handle. Instead of burying him to hide his crime, young Jim threw his dad in the hog pen, figuring they had to eat too, just like worms or buzzards. When he saddled the plow horse and rode off to make his way in the world, he never looked back.

"All right, Mrs. Carson, you're right," he finally said. "I haven't got anything against you, so you have nothing to fear from me or my men, if your husband does what he's been told to do."

Mary stared at him for a moment, before asking in a low voice, as if she feared the answer more than anything Slaughter could do to her, "What about my husband, Mr. Slaughter? What business do you have with him?"

Slaughter laughed, a sound many of his men who'd ridden with him for years had never heard. "Old business, Mrs. Carson. A matter of some money he's owed me for a long time."

Mary's face showed her surprise. "Money? Why would Monte owe you money?"

"I suspect there's lots of things about your husband you

don't know, Mrs. Carson." He pursed his lips, thinking. "Perhaps I'll let him explain them to you . . . if he's got the *cojones* to come after you like you think he does."

Mary faced forward and put her heels to her horse's flanks, causing it to move forward so she wouldn't be riding next to Slaughter any longer.

He shook his head, thinking how lucky Carson was to have such a woman, and wondering if he knew it.

Smoke glanced across the operating table at Doc Spalding. "Doc, why don't you mosey on over to Louis's place and have a steak, on me?"

Doc Spalding looked up from where he was washing blood off his hands. He glanced at Smoke, then at the injured man on the table. He'd just taken two bullets out of him. "I take it you want to have a private word with this miscreant, Smoke."

"If you don't mind, sir."

Doc sighed and threw the dirty towel in a basket next to the table. "Try not to make any more work for me today, all right? The man's lost a lot of blood and his heart won't stand much more . . . grief."

"You got my word on it."

Doc stared at Smoke, his eyes narrowing at the expression on his friend's face. He shook his head. It went against everything he'd ever believed in to leave the gunman with Smoke looking like that, but Mary Carson was a good and kind woman and a dear friend of everyone in town. If a little judicious absence was what it took to get her back, then so be it.

After Doc left the room, Pearlie and Cal lined up on the other side of the table, hands on hips, waiting to see what Smoke had in mind.

Smoke reached down and slapped the man lightly across the face, causing his eyelids to flicker open.

"What's your name, mister?" he asked.

The man's eyes moved from Smoke to Cal and Pearlie,

and his lips tightened into a white line. Evidently he wasn't prepared to speak just yet.

Smoke nodded to Pearlie, and they both took leather straps Doc used to tie down unruly patients on whom he was doing surgery, quickly fastening the man's hands to rails alongside the table.

"Hey," he said, a look of fear entering his eyes, "what the hell do you think you're doin'?"

"I'm fixing to do a little surgery on you, pardner, and I don't want your hands to get in the way. And I don't intend to use any of that chloroform the doc used either."

Smoke inclined his head toward Cal. "Cal, shut that window over there, would you? I don't want any citizens to be scared by any hollering that might occur."

"Sure, Smoke."

"Smoke?" the man asked. "You're not THE Smoke Jensen, are you?"

"One and the same, pardner. Now," Smoke said as he pulled his Bowie knife from its scabbard on the back of his belt and held it up so the light from the lantern in the room sparkled off the blade. "I'll ask you a question, and you'll answer. For every question you don't answer, I'm gonna remove one of your fingers. After ten times, if you're still reluctant to answer, I'll start on your toes. *Comprende?*"

The man shook his head. "You can't do that," he cried, his voice trembling with terror.

Smoke grabbed his right hand, bent all the fingers over except the index finger, and held the knife against it where the man could see.

"First question. What's your name?"

"Blackie . . . Blackie Johnson."

"Who sent you to brace Sheriff Carson?"

"I . . . I can't tell you that. He'd kill me!"

Smoke stroked the finger lightly with his knife, the razor-sharp blade slicing through skin as easily as if it were butter on a July afternoon.

"Wait! Hold on!" Blackie screamed.

"Last chance, Blackie, or they're gonna start calling you Stubby," Smoke growled, his eyes glittering with hate.

"Slaughter, Big Jim Slaughter sent us," Blackie said, his voice hushed as if he was afraid to say the name out loud.

"What were your instructions?"

"We was supposed to tell 'im to bring the money to Jackson Hole an' Slaughter'd find him there and give him his wife back."

"And where is Slaughter going to take Carson's wife?"

Blackie shook his head, flinging fear-sweat off his forehead. "Please, Mr. Jensen, don't ask me that. Slaughter'd skin me alive if he found out I tole you any of this."

Smoke smiled, but there was no friendliness in his face. "How's he gonna find out, unless you tell him?"

Blackie licked his lips, his eyes staring at the blood oozing from his finger. "He's gonna take her up to the hole-in-the-wall."

"How many men does he have up there with him?"

Completely defeated now, Blackie made no more pretense of hesitation. He spoke in a low voice. "Anywhere from twenty to thirty, depending on the time of year and how many men are off spending the loot they've earned."

"Is there a back way in?"

"No. Only one way in and one way out, an' it's always guarded real well. Jensen, if you're thinkin' of tryin' to get in there without Slaughter knowin' it, you're crazier than he is."

Smoke looked at Pearlie. "Get this man a bandage for his hand. He's gonna draw us a map of the area around the hole-in-the-wall and Jackson Hole, then we're going to keep him locked up here until we get back."

"What . . . what if you don't make it back?" Blackie asked, sweat pouring off his face in a steady stream.

"Why, then the good citizens of Big Rock will hang you by the neck until you're as dead as we are, Blackie, so you'd better put everything you can remember in that map."

5

Smoke sat at the kitchen table in his cabin with Sally, Cal, and Pearlie, finishing a plate of scrambled hens' eggs, bacon, flapjacks, and sliced tomatoes.

Cal was watching Pearlie, who had his head down and was shoveling eggs into his mouth as if he hadn't eaten for days.

"I swear, Pearlie, you got to have a hollow leg," Cal said with some astonishment. "There ain't no other explanation for you bein' able to put away that much grub at one sittin'."

"Don't say ain't, Cal," Sally said without thinking about it. She'd been a schoolteacher when she met Smoke, and had tried her best, without much luck, to teach Cal proper English usage in the few years he'd been staying with them.

She glanced up at Smoke and he looked back, smiling, both of them remembering the first time they'd met Cal . . .

Calvin Woods, going on eighteen years old now, had been just fourteen four years ago when Smoke and Sally had taken him in as a hired hand. It was during the spring branding, and Sally was on her way back from Big Rock to the Sugarloaf. The buckboard was piled high with supplies because branding hundreds of calves made for hungry punchers.

As Sally slowed the team to make a bend in the trail, a rail-thin young man stepped from the bushes at the side of the road with a pistol in his hand.

"Hold it right there, miss."

Applying the brake with her right foot, Sally slipped her hand under a pile of gingham cloth on the seat. She grasped the handle of her short-barreled Colt .44 and eared back the hammer, letting the sound of the horses' hooves and the squealing of the brake pad on the wheel mask the sound. "What can I do for you, young man?" she asked, her voice firm and without fear. She knew she could draw and drill the young highwayman before he could raise his pistol to fire.

"Well, uh, you can throw some of those beans and a cut of that fatback over here, and maybe a portion of that Arbuckle's coffee, too."

Sally's eyebrows rose. "Don't you want my money?"

The boy frowned and shook his head. "Why, no, ma'am. I ain't no thief. I'm just hungry."

"And if I don't give you my food, are you going to shoot me with that big Navy Colt?"

He hesitated a moment, then grinned ruefully. "No, ma'am, I guess not." He twirled the pistol around his finger and slipped it into his belt, turned, and began to walk down the road toward Big Rock.

Sally watched the youngster amble off, noting his tattered shirt, dirty pants with holes in the knees and torn pockets, and boots that looked as if they had been salvaged from a garbage dump. "Young man," she called, "come back here, please."

He turned, a smirk on his face, spreading his hands. "Look, lady, you don't have to worry. I don't even have any bullets." With a lightning-fast move he drew the gun from his pants, aimed away from Sally, and pulled the trigger. There was a click but no explosion as the hammer fell on an empty cylinder.

Sally smiled. "Oh, I'm not worried." In a movement every bit as fast as his, she whipped her .44 out and fired, clipping a pine cone from a branch, causing it to fall and bounce off his head.

The boy's knees buckled and he ducked, saying, "Jimminy Christmas!"

Mimicking him, Sally twirled her Colt and stuck it in the waistband of her britches. "What's your name, boy?"

The boy blushed and looked down at his feet. "Calvin, ma'am, Calvin Woods."

She leaned forward, elbows on knees, and stared into the boy's eyes. "Calvin, no one has to go hungry in this country, not if they're willing to work."

He looked up at her through narrowed eyes, as if he found life a little different than she described it.

"If you're willing to put in an honest day's work, I'll see that you get an honest day's pay, and all the food you can eat."

Calvin stood a little straighter, shoulders back and head held high. "Ma'am, I've got to be straight with you. I ain't no experienced cowhand. I come from a hardscrabble farm and we only had us one milk cow and a couple of goats and chickens, and lots of dirt that weren't worth nothing for growin' things. My ma and pa and me never had nothin', but we never begged and we never stooped to takin' handouts."

Sally thought, *I like this boy. Proud, and not willing to take charity if he can help it.* "Calvin, if you're willing to work, and don't mind getting your hands dirty and your muscles sore, I've got some hands that'll have you punching beeves like you were born to it in no time at all."

A smile lit up his face, making him seem even younger than his years. "Even if I don't have no saddle, nor a horse to put it on?"

She laughed out loud. "Yes. We've got plenty of ponies and saddles." She glanced down at his raggedy boots. "We can probably even round up some boots and spurs that'll fit you."

He walked over and jumped in the back of the buck-board. "Ma'am, I don't know who you are, but you just hired you the hardest-workin' hand you've ever seen."

Back at the Sugarloaf, she sent him in to Cookie and told him to eat his fill. When Smoke and the other punchers rode into the cabin yard at the end of the day, she introduced Calvin around. As Cal was shaking hands with the men, Smoke looked over at her and winked. He knew she could never resist a stray dog or cat, and her heart was as large as the Big Lonesome itself.

Smoke walked up to Cal and cleared his throat. "Son, I hear you drew down on my wife."

Cal gulped. "Yessir, Mr. Jensen. I did." He squared his shoulders and looked Smoke in the eye, not flinching though he was obviously frightened of the tall man with the incredibly wide shoulders standing before him.

Smoke smiled and clapped the boy on the back. "Just wanted you to know you stared death in the eye, boy. Not many galoots are still walking upright who ever pulled a gun on Sally. She's a better shot than any man I've ever seen except me, and sometimes I wonder about me."

The boy laughed with relief as Smoke turned and called out, "Pearlie, get your lazy butt over here."

A tall, lanky cowboy ambled over to Smoke and Cal, munching on a biscuit stuffed with roast beef. His face was lined with wrinkles and tanned a dark brown from hours under the sun, but his eyes were sky-blue and twinkled with good-natured humor.

"Yessir, Boss," he mumbled around a mouthful of food.

Smoke put his hand on Pearlie's shoulder. "Cal, this here chowhound is Pearlie. He eats more'n any two hands, and he's never been known to do a lick of work he could get out of, but he knows beeves and horses as well as any puncher I have. I want you to follow him around and let him teach you what you need to know."

Cal nodded. "Yes, sir, Mr. Smoke."

"Now let me see that iron you have in your pants."

Cal pulled the ancient Navy Colt and handed it to

Smoke. When Smoke opened the loading gate, the rusted cylinder fell to the ground, causing Pearlie and Smoke to laugh and Cal's face to flame red. "This is the piece you pulled on Sally?" Smoke asked.

The boy nodded, looking at the ground.

Pearlie shook his head. "Cal, you're one lucky pup. Hell, if'n you'd tried to fire that thing it'd've blown your hand clean off."

Smoke inclined his head toward the bunkhouse. "Pearlie, take Cal over to the tack house and get him fixed up with what he needs, including a gun belt and a Colt that won't fall apart the first time he pulls it. You might also help pick him out a shavetail to ride. I'll expect him to start earning his keep tomorrow."

"Yes, sir, Smoke." Pearlie put his arm around Cal's shoulders and led him off toward the bunkhouse. "Now the first thing you gotta learn, Cal, is how to get on Cookie's good side. A puncher rides on his belly, and it 'pears to me that you need some fattin' up 'fore you can begin to punch cows."

Smoke and Sally grinned at each other, and Smoke glanced across the table at Pearlie, who was still stuffing food in his mouth as if he were in an eating contest at a state fair.

Pearlie had come to work for Smoke in as roundabout a way as Cal had. He was hiring his gun out to Tilden Franklin in Fontana when Franklin went crazy and tried to take over Sugarloaf, Smoke and Sally's spread. After Franklin's men raped and killed a young girl in the fracas, Pearlie sided with Smoke and the aging gunfighters he had called in to help put an end to Franklin's reign of terror.*

*Trail of the Mountain Man

Pearlie was now honorary foreman of Smoke's ranch, though he was only a shade over twenty-two years old. Boys grew to be men early in the mountains of Colorado.

Sally wiped her lips daintily with the edge of a linen napkin, her eyes on Smoke's. "What are your plans now, Smoke? Did the map that man Blackie made give you enough information to try and rescue Mary?"

Smoke shook his head. He held his coffee cup in both hands, his elbows on the table, and looked at Sally over the brim. "It shows how to get into the hole-in-the-wall, and the approximate location of the sentries, but we're going to need to know more than that to get in and back out alive, especially if we're bringing Mary out with us."

Pearlie looked up from his plate. "You know, we could get fifty men from Big Rock to ride with us if they knew we was goin' after Mary Carson. There ain't a man within fifty miles don't owe the Carsons more'n they can repay for favors the two of them have done."

Smoke shook his head. "It's not a question of numbers, Pearlie. If we go blasting our way into the hole-in-the-wall, Slaughter'll kill Mary before we can get within a mile of him."

"Well, what's the answer, then?" Cal asked.

"I'm going to have to find out more about the mountains around Jackson Hole, and the hole-in-the-wall," Smoke said.

"How're you gonna do that?" Pearlie asked.

Smoke grinned. "Why, from the men who know more about mountains than anyone else, of course."

Sally nodded. "You're going to go up into the high country and ask some of your mountain man friends about the area."

"Yes. Fall's coming on so they'll be down from the higher peaks, getting ready for the winter. It shouldn't be too hard to find a couple of old cougars up there who've been to Wyoming before." He took a final drink of his coffee and put the cup down. "And if they've been there, they'll know every path and pass and crevice in the area like the back of their hands."

Cal cleared his throat. "Uh, do you mind if Pearlie and I go with you up into the mountains, Smoke?"

Smoke grinned. "No, as a matter of fact, I'm looking forward to it, boys. Mountain lore is a part of your education that's been sorely missing until now. You might even learn a little about how to survive in the mountains from those old beavers."

Sally laughed. "And if you're not careful, the Last Mountain Man might also teach you a few things he's learned over the years," she said.

"Go get your gear packed, and put in some heavy clothes, 'cause it's going to be twenty degrees colder up in the high lonesome than it is down here," Smoke said, his eyes glittering at the prospect of once again traveling the peaks where he grew to manhood.

6

Sally stood on the porch and waved as the three men rode off toward the high lonesome. Smoke turned in his saddle and stared at her for a moment just before they got out of sight, and she knew it meant he'd be thinking of her on his journey.

Smoke, Pearlie, and Cal were all riding horses that were crosses from Smoke's Palouse mares and Joey Wells's big strawberry roan stud, Red. Joey and his wife had bought the old Rocking C Ranch in Pueblo, Colorado, after killing Murdock, the man who owned it. Sally, as a gift to Joey's wife, had given them some Palouse mares to breed with Red and start their remuda.*

The offspring Joey had sent to the Sugarloaf were all beautiful animals that had inherited their father's big size and strength and the Palouses' speed and endurance.

Smoke's stud was a blanket-hipped Palouse, red or roan-colored in front with hips of snow white, without the usual spots of a Palouse. He'd named him Joker because of his funny coloring.

Pearlie's descendant of Red was a gray-and-white Palouse

*Honor of the Mountain Man

he'd named Cold. When Smoke asked him why he'd named him that, Pearlie said it was because the sucker was cold-backed in the morning and bucked for the first ten minutes every day when Pearlie saddled him up.

Cal's mount was a quicksilver gray and was actually almost pure white, differing from a true albino by having blue eyes instead of pink. The bronc was a pale gray in front with snow-white hips without the usual Palouse spots. Cal had named him Silver and had formed a deep and immediate bond with the animal the first time he rode him.

As they approached the mountains, with the peaks hanging in the air and looking as if they were right overhead, Cal pulled out his makin's and began to build himself a cigarette.

"Miss Sally'd whup you if she saw you doin' that," Pearlie said.

Smoke glanced at Cal and smiled. "She would that, all right."

"But Smoke," Cal protested, "if I'm old enough to ride the herd and go after *bandidos,* I ought'a be old enough to smoke if 'n I want to."

"You get no argument from me, Cal. I agree with you. A man old enough to strap on a gun and saddle a horse is old enough to make his own decisions about how he lives his life. Like I always say, a man's got to saddle his own horse and kill his own snakes."

"But Miss Sally . . ."

Smoke nodded. "You're right, Sally don't agree with you starting to smoke, or drink, so young. It's that mothering instinct all women have, son, to try and tell a man what's best for him, even if he doesn't want to hear it. Don't pay it no mind, Cal. Just try not to light up in front of her and everything'll be all right."

As they rode up the slope, the sun hung over the distant peaks, gleaming a dull orange-red, like a frying pan left on the fire too long, surrounded by clouds a dull gray in color.

Smoke nodded toward the clouds. "Tell me what kind of weather we're going to be facing up there, boys."

Pearlie pursed his lips. "Well, clouds like that usually mean rain down in the valley, so I 'spect there'll be some snow off and on at the higher places and maybe some freezing rain down lower."

"Heavy or light?" Smoke asked.

"Heavy," Cal replied. "When the clouds are kind'a flat-like and fluffy, it means a light fall. When they're high and thick like that, it means it's gonna be a frog-drownin' son-of-a-buck of a storm."

Smoke grinned. "Looks like I don't have much to teach you boys about how to read the weather. We'll have to see what little bits of knowledge you can pick up from the mountain men we're going to meet."

"Who do you think'll be up here, Smoke?" Pearlie asked.

"Old Bear Tooth for one. He always makes his camp up in this area in the winter. And maybe Long John Dupree or Bull Durham will be somewheres nearby."

"Bull Durham, like the tobacco?" Cal asked.

Smoke laughed. "Yeah. His real name is Christopher Durham, but he's called Bull 'cause he's always got a chaw in his cheek, even when he drinks coffee or eats." He shook his head. "I don't know how he does it, but it doesn't seem to bother his appetite any. He eats about as much as Pearlie."

"Man knows what's good for him then," Pearlie said.

"Better shag those mounts, boys. We've got a long way to go and we're going to need to have time to make a good camp before nightfall or we're going to freeze our *cojones* off when the snow starts to fall."

It was mid-afternoon before they arrived at a place Smoke said would be suitable for a campsite.

"This place looks good enough for our first night," he said. "We've got that ledge over there to block the north wind, the ground is fairly level, there's a stream of water for drinking and washing, and there's plenty of wood-fall for our fires and good grass for the broncs nearby."

"Where do you want us to set up?" Cal asked.

Smoke stepped down off Joker and sat with his back against a tall fir tree. He built himself a cigarette and looked at them over the flame of a lucifer as he lit it. "I'll let you boys decide that. I'll just sit here and relax while you get the fire and coffee going."

Pearlie nodded. "You do that, Smoke. Makin' camp is young men's work, an' old codgers like you need your rest after bein' in the saddle all day."

Smoke leaned back against the tree, tipped his hat down over his eyes, and smoked. "Damn right, Pearlie, couldn't've said it better myself."

"Do you think we'll find any mountain men today, Smoke?" Cal asked.

"Ought to," Smoke replied from under his hat. "They've been watching us for the past three hours."

Pearlie glanced around over his shoulder. "I haven't seen anybody."

Smoke chuckled. "You weren't supposed to, Pearlie."

The smell of bacon and beans cooking on an open fire woke Smoke up.

"Coffee's ready," Cal called from where he and Pearlie sat next to a campfire.

Smoke got to his feet and stood and stretched for a moment, letting his eyes wander around the trees and bushes and boulders surrounding them.

As he walked to the fire, he called, "Might as well come on in and get warm, Bear Tooth. No need squatting out there in the cold."

A tall hulking man well over six feet tall and wearing a bearskin coat and moccasins stepped from behind a nearby fir tree. He was carrying a Sharps Big Fifty rifle that was almost as long as he was tall, and had a coonskin hat on. His face was covered with a dark, scraggly beard, and as he got closer he gave off an odor like he hadn't bothered to clean the bearskin particularly well before making it into a coat.

"How do, Smoke?" he growled, his voice husky and deep, as if he didn't get much practice speaking.

"Right well, Bear Tooth. Light and set and draw up a cup of *cafecito* with us."

"Don't mind if I do, young'un."

As he got closer, he could be seen to be older than he'd first looked. In spite of still-dark hair and beard, he had to be in his seventies, but he moved and acted like a man much younger.

He wrapped his hands around the coffee cup Pearlie handed him and took a deep swig. "Just right," he said, "strong enough to float a horseshoe."

Smoke nodded. "Remember old Puma Buck?"

"Shore," Bear Tooth replied with a grin.

"He used to say, the thing about makin' good coffee is it don't take near as much water as you think it do."

Bear Tooth laughed. "Old Puma had a way with words, all right." He hesitated a moment, then asked, "By the way, Smoke, whatever happened to ol' Puma? I heared some rumors he was kilt down Colorado way, but never met nobody who knew fer shore."

Smoke nodded. "You heard right, Bear Tooth. Puma was killed while trying to help some folks out that sorely needed helping." Smoke's eyes were unfocused as he thought back to that night, and in a low voice he told Bear Tooth the tale . . .

Puma Buck walked his horse slowly through underbrush and light forest timber in foothills surrounding Murdock's spread. His mount was one they'd hired in Pueblo on arriving, and it wasn't as surefooted on the steep slopes as his paint pony back home was, so he was taking it easy and getting the feel of his new ride.

He kept a sharp lookout toward Murdock's ranch house

almost a quarter of a mile below. He was going to make damned sure none of those *buscaderos* managed to get the drop on Smoke and his other new friends. He rode with his Sharps .52-caliber laid across his saddle horn, loaded and ready for immediate action.

Several times Puma had seen men ride up to the ranch house and enter, only to leave after a while, riding off toward herds of cattle that could be seen on the horizon. Puma figured they were most likely the legitimate punchers Murdock had working his cattle, and not gun hawks he'd hired to take down Smoke and Joey. A shootist would rather take lead poisoning than lower himself to herd beeves.

Off to the side, Puma could barely make out the riverbed, dry now, that ran through Murdock's place. He could see on the other side of Murdock's ranch house a row of freshly dug graves. He grinned to himself, appreciating the graves, some of them the result of his shooting, and appreciating the way Smoke had deprived the man of water for his cattle and horses.

Puma knew that alone would prompt Murdock to make his move soon; he couldn't afford to wait and let his stock die of thirst.

As Puma pulled his canteen out and uncorked the top, ready to take a swig, he saw a band of about fifteen or more riders burning dust toward the ranch house from the direction of Pueblo. Evidently they were additional men Murdock had hired to replace those he and Smoke and Joey had slain in their midnight raid.

"Uh-huh," he muttered. "I'll bet those *bandidos* are fixin' to put on the war paint and make a run over to Smoke's place."

He swung out of his saddle and crouched down behind a fallen tree, propping the big, heavy Sharps across the rough bark. He licked his finger and wiped the front sight with it, to make it stand out more when he needed it. He got himself into a comfortable position and laid out a box full of extra shells next to the gun on the tree within easy reach. He figured he might need to do some quick reloading when the time came.

After about ten minutes, the gang of men Puma was observing arrived at the front of the ranch house, and two figures Puma took to be Murdock and Vasquez came out of the door to address them. He couldn't make out their faces at this distance, but they had an unmistakable air of authority about them.

As the rancher began to talk, waving his hands toward Smoke's ranch, Puma took careful aim, remembering he was shooting downhill and needed to lower his sights a bit, the natural tendency being to overshoot a target lower than you are.

He took a deep breath and held it, slowly increasing pressure on the trigger so when the explosion came it would be a surprise and he wouldn't have time to flinch and throw his aim off.

The big gun boomed and shot a sheet of fire two feet out of the barrel, slamming back into Puma's shoulder and almost knocking his skinny frame over. Damn, he had almost forgotten how the big Sharps kicked when it delivered its deadly cargo.

The targets were a little over fifteen hundred yards from Puma, a long range even for the remarkable Sharps. It seemed a long time, but was only a little over five seconds, before one of the men on horseback was thrown from his mount to lie sprawled in the dirt. The sound was several seconds slower reaching the men, and by then Puma had jacked another round in the chamber and fired again. By the time the group knew they were being fired upon, two of their number were dead on the ground. Just as they ducked and whirled, looking for the location of their attacker, another was knocked off his bronc, his arm almost blown off by the big .52-caliber slug traveling at over two thousand feet per second.

The outlaws began to scatter, some jumping from their horses and running into the house while others just bent over their saddle horns and burned trail dust away from the area. A couple of brave souls aimed rifles up the hill and fired, but the range was so far for ordinary rifles that Puma never even saw where the bullets landed.

Another couple of rounds were fired into the house, and then Puma figured he had done enough for the time being. Now he had to get back to Smoke and tell him Murdock was ready to make his play, or would be as soon as he rounded up the men Puma had scattered all over the countryside.

Several of the riders had ridden toward Smoke's ranch and were now between Puma and home. "Well, shit, old beaver. Ya knew it was about time for ya ta taste some lead," he mumbled to himself. He packed his Sharps in his saddle boot and opened his saddlebags. He withdrew two Army Colt .44s to match the one in his holster and made sure they were all loaded up six and six, then stuffed the two extras in his belt. He tugged his hat down tight and eased up into the saddle, grunting with the pain it caused in his arthritic joints. He kept to heavy timber until he came to a group of six men standing next to a drying riverbed, watering their horses in one of the small pools remaining.

There was no way to avoid them so he put his reins in his teeth and filled both hands with iron. It was time to dance with the devil, and Puma was going to strike up the band. He kicked his mount's flanks and bent low over his saddle horn as he galloped out of the forest toward the gunnies below.

One of the men, wearing an eye patch, looked up in astonishment at the apparition wearing buckskins and war paint charging them, yelling and whooping and hollering as he rode like the wind.

"Goddamn, boys, it's that old mountain man!" One-Eye Jackson yelled as he drew his pistol.

All six men crouched and began firing wildly, frightened by the sheer gall of a lone horseman charging right at them.

Puma's pistols exploded, spitting fire, smoke, and death

ahead of him. Two of the gun slicks went down immediately, .44 slugs in their chests.

Another jumped into the saddle and turned tail and rode like hell to get away from this madman who was bent on killing all of them.

One-Eye took careful aim and fired, his bullet tearing through Puma's left shoulder muscle, twisting his body and almost unseating him.

Puma straightened, gritting his teeth on the leather reins while he continued firing with his right-hand gun, his left arm hanging useless at his side. His next two shots hit their targets, taking one gunny in the face and the other in the stomach, doubling him over to leak guts and shit and blood in the dirt as he fell.

One-Eye's sixth and final bullet in his pistol entered Puma's horse's forehead and exited out the back of its skull to plow into Puma's chest. The horse somersaulted as it died, throwing Puma spinning to the ground. He rolled three times, tried to push himself to his knees, then fell facedown in the dirt, his blood pooling around him.

One-Eye Jackson looked around at the three dead men lying next to him and muttered a curse under his breath. "Jesus, that old fool had a lot'a hair to charge us like that." He shook his head as he walked over to Puma's body and aimed his pistol at the back of the mountain man's head. He eared back the hammer and let it drop. His gun clicked . . . all chambers empty.

One-Eye leaned down and rolled Puma over to make sure he was dead. Puma's left shoulder was canted at an angle where the bullet had broken it, and on his right chest was a spreading scarlet stain.

Puma moaned and rolled to the side. One-Eye Jackson chuckled. "You're a tough old bird, but soon's I reload I'll put one in your eye."

Puma's eyes flicked open and he grinned, exposing bloodstained teeth. "Not in this lifetime, sonny," and he swung his right arm out from beneath his body. In it was his buffalo-skinning knife.

One-Eye grunted in shock and surprise as he looked down at the hilt of Puma's long knife sticking out of his chest. "Son of a . . ." he rasped, then he died.

Puma lay there for a moment. Then with great effort he pushed himself over so he faced his beloved mountains. "Boys," he whispered to all the mountain men who had gone before him, "git the *cafecito* hot, I'm comin' to meet 'cha."*

Bear Tooth, instead of looking sad, smiled as he nodded his head. "That's the way a mountain man ought'a go out, with his guns blazin' and spittin' death and destruction all round him."

Smoke smiled, too. "You're right, Bear Tooth. Old Puma wouldn't've wanted to die in bed, that's for sure."

Bear Tooth inclined his head at Cal and Pearlie. "You gonna introduce me to yore *compadres*, Smoke?"

Smoke introduced the boys, who both stood to shake hands with Bear Tooth.

"What you boys doin' up here on the slopes, Smoke? Teachin' the young beavers some'a the lessons 'bout mountain life ole Preacher taught you?"

Smoke hesitated a moment, then looked directly at the mountain man. "No, actually, we came up here to see you, Bear Tooth."

Bear Tooth pursed his lips, making his beard move as if it were home to tiny animals. "Ya came all the way up here to see me? Pardon me fer sayin' so, Smoke, but the idee of that kind'a makes the skin on my back crawl."

Smoke smiled. "Oh, there's nothing to worry about, Bear Tooth. I just need some information about a place you used to trap a few years back."

*Honor of the Mountain Man

Bear Tooth pulled a long rope of tobacco from his shirt pocket, bit off a sizable portion, and began to chew. "You talkin' 'bout Wyomin'?"

Smoke nodded. "A friend of mine's wife was taken by some hard cases and word is they're camping at the hole-in-the-wall near Jackson Hole."

Bear Tooth narrowed his eyes. "An' I reckon you want to know if'n there's some back way into the hole so's you can go in and get the woman out?"

Smoke nodded.

Bear Tooth scratched his beard, his eyes far off as he thought about it. "There's only one way in where they won't see ya comin'. On the back side of the second-highest peak there's a cave. It'll be kind'a hard to find this time of year 'cause of the snow, but the cave goes all the way through the mountain and comes out on the other side in a group of boulders. I'm bettin' those flatlanders won't know 'bout it."

"That's just what we're looking for. Can you tell me how to find it?"

Bear Tooth shook his head. "Nope, but an ole friend of mine, Muskrat Calhoon, can. I hear tell he's still trappin' up in those peaks round Jackson Hole."

"How can I find him?"

"He comes into town 'bout ever' two, three weeks to get his tobaccy and a little hair of the dog. Usually buys it at Schultz's General Store as I recall. You ask round town an' they'll let him know yo're lookin' fer him. Feel free to tell him yo're a friend of mine."

Cal cleared his throat. "Mr. Bear Tooth, how come they call him Muskrat? Is it because he traps 'em?"

Bear Tooth leaned his head back and laughed, showing a row of yellow-stained teeth ground down almost to the gums. "No, son, he don't trap 'em, he smells like 'em."

Smoke laughed along with Cal and Pearlie as he got up and walked to Joker. He pulled a paper bag out of his saddlebags and brought it over to the fire. "Bear Tooth, thanks for your help," he said, setting the bag in front of the mountain man. "My wife, Sally, made these bear sign before we left our ranch, and I'd be honored if you'd share them with us."

"Bear sign?" Bear Tooth asked, his eyes lighting up. He reached into the sack, pulled out a large, homemade doughnut, and stared at it for a moment before dunking it in his coffee, then popping the whole thing in his mouth.

Pearlie licked his lips and turned imploring eyes on Smoke. "Uh, Smoke, do you think there's enough bear sign there for all of us to share?"

Smoke nodded. "I guess so, Pearlie, long as you let Cal and me take one or two before you attack that bag."

"That's for danged sure," Cal said. "Otherwise won't none of us get a chance at any if'n Pearlie digs in first."

7

On the way back to Sugarloaf, Smoke decided to stop by Big Rock and see if the wounded man Monte had shot had any more information for them before heading up to Wyoming.

Pearlie slowed Cold as they pulled next to Longmont's Saloon. "You think we might have time to get a bite or two to eat at Longmont's 'fore we head back to the Sugarloaf?" he asked, a hopeful expression on his face.

"That hollow leg of your's beginning to feel empty, Pearlie?" Smoke asked, winking at Cal.

"Yes, sir. I'm so hungry my stomach thinks my throat's been cut."

Smoke glanced at the sun, nearing the middle of the sky but not giving off much heat as cold autumn air flowed down from the mountain passes and chilled the day.

"Well, it has been a few hours since you cleaned us out of fatback and sinkers, so I guess it won't hurt any if we stop and have a meal before bracing that gunny over at Doc's."

They tied their horses to the rail in front of Longmont's and got down out of the saddle. Smoke stood and looked at a trio of horses already tied there, noting the trail dust covering the animals and the strange brands on their flanks.

"Looks like we've got some strangers in town," he said, as they walked through the batwings.

By force of long habit, Smoke stepped to the side as he entered the saloon and diner and let his eyes adjust to the darkened room while he studied the men inside. When he'd lived by his guns, it'd been a trait that had saved his life on more than one occasion. Saloons were the most dangerous places in the West, accounting for more than three-quarters of the deaths in most towns.

Cal and Pearlie, trained by Smoke, stepped to the other side of the door and also waited, checking out the customers to see if any appeared dangerous. They both knew there were many men in the country who would like nothing better than to get a reputation for being the one who planted Smoke Jensen forked end up.

Smoke noticed his gambler friend of many years, Louis Longmont, sitting at his usual table in the saloon he owned, where he plied his trade, which he called teaching amateurs the laws of chance.

Louis was a lean, hawk-faced man, with strong, slender hands and long fingers, nails carefully manicured, hands clean. He had jet-black hair and a black pencil-thin mustache. He was, as usual, dressed in a black suit, with white shirt and dark ascot—something he'd picked up on a trip to England some years back. He wore low-heeled boots, and a pistol hung in tied-down leather on his right side. It was not for show, for Louis was snake-quick with a short gun and was a feared, deadly gun hand when pushed.

Louis was not an evil man. He had never hired his gun out for money. And while he could make a deck of cards do almost anything, he did not cheat at poker. He did not have to cheat. He was possessed of a phenomenal memory and could tell you the odds of filling any type of poker hand, and was one of the first to use the new method of card counting.

He was just past forty years of age. He had come to the West as a very small boy, with his parents, arriving from

Louisiana. His parents had died in a shantytown fire, leaving the boy to cope as best he could.

He had coped quite well, plying his innate intelligence and willingness to take a chance into a fortune. He owned a large ranch up in Wyoming Territory, several businesses in San Francisco, and a hefty chunk of a railroad.

Though it was a mystery to many why Longmont stayed with the hard life he had chosen, Smoke thought he understood. Once, Louis had said to him, "Smoke, I would miss my life every bit as much as you would miss the dry-mouthed moment before the draw, the challenge of facing and besting those miscreants who would kill you or others, and the so-called loneliness of the owl-hoot trail."

Sometimes Louis joked that he would like to draw against Smoke someday, just to see who was faster. Smoke always allowed as how it would be close, but that he would win. "You see, Louis, you're just too civilized," he had told him on many occasions. "Your mind is distracted by visions of operas, fine foods and wines, and the odds of your winning the match. Also, your fatal flaw is that you can almost always see the good in the lowest creatures God ever made, and you refuse to believe that anyone is pure evil and without hope of redemption."

When Louis laughed at this description of himself, Smoke would continue. "Me, on the other hand, when some snake-scum draws down on me and wants to dance, the only thing I have on my mind is teaching him that when you dance, someone has to pay the band. My mind is clear and focused on only one problem, how to put that stump-sucker across his horse toes-down."

Today, Louis was, as usual, sitting at his personal table, playing solitaire and drinking coffee, a long, black cheroot in the corner of his mouth. Louis looked up and saw Smoke, but he didn't smile as he usually did when Smoke paid him a visit. Instead, he cut his eyes toward the bar and gave his head a slight toss.

Smoke followed his gaze, letting his right hand unhook the hammer-thong on his Colt .44. There were three men standing at the bar, leaning on elbows and drinking whiskey with beer chasers. They looked like hard men, and all had their guns tied down low on their legs, showing they weren't typical cowboys.

Smoke spoke low, out of the side of his mouth. "Watch those three, boys, and keep your guns loose. Something tells me they ride for Slaughter."

Smoke and Cal and Pearlie joined Louis at his table, all three adjusting their chairs so they could watch the men at the bar.

"Howdy, Louis," Smoke said.

"Good afternoon, Smoke," Louis replied, his eyes too on the strangers.

"I notice you got some new customers. Anyone I might know?"

Louis tilted smoke out of his nostrils toward the ceiling and shook his head. "I don't believe so. But these men are very curious about the whereabouts of our sheriff, Monte Carson. They've asked just about everyone who's come in where he might be."

Smoke had filled Louis in on the happenings at Monte's, and had asked him to spread the word that Monte was away on a trip, letting his deputy Jimmy cover things for him in his absence. "Did they believe the story about Monte gone fishing?"

"Not for a moment."

Smoke leaned back in his chair and pushed his hat back on his head. "Do you think you could get Andre to fix us up some lunch? Pearlie's about to starve to death."

Louis grinned for the first time since they entered. "And when is he not?"

He motioned for the young black man who was the waiter to come to his table. "Bobby, would you ask Andre to fix three steaks, not too well done, and to fry some potatoes for Mr. Jensen and his friends?"

"Shore, Boss, and I'll bring some fresh coffee right over too."

While waiting for their food, Smoke got to his feet. "I

think I'll mosey on over to the bar and say hello to our friends there," he said.

Longmont sighed. "I'll tell Bobby to keep the mop handy. I have a feeling he'll be having a mess to clean up before long."

Smoke smiled, but there was no mirth in his eyes as he walked to the bar. He leaned on it next to the three men.

Smoke, who stood a few inches over six feet in height and had shoulders as wide as an ax handle, dwarfed the men next to him. The closest turned his head and looked up at Smoke's face.

"Howdy, boys," Smoke said, leaning his left elbow on the bar, keeping his right hand free hanging next to his pistol.

"You want somethin', mister?" a short, dark-haired man with a scraggly mustache growled out of the side of his mouth.

Smoke stared into the man's eyes, his gaze as hard as flint. "I hear you've been asking a lot of questions about our sheriff, Monte Carson."

"What's it to you, feller?" the man asked, a sneer turning up the corners of his lips.

Smoke hesitated for a moment, then backhanded the man across the mouth, slamming his face to the side and almost taking his head off. The man spun on his heels and fell facedown on the floor, his eyes crossed and vacant as blood spurted from his flattened nose and torn lips.

The gunny next to him reached for his gun, but before he could clear leather Smoke drew and slammed his .44 down on the man's head, driving him to his knees with blood spurting from his forehead.

Smoke turned the barrel of the Colt toward the third man, who was standing there with his eyes wide and his mouth hanging open. "I live in this town," Smoke said in a low voice ringed with steel, "and I don't like pond scum like you three smelling up the town."

Sweat appeared on the man's forehead as he slowly

moved his hand away from the butt of his pistol. "Uh . . . yes, sir," he mumbled.

"Now, I'm going to ask you once more, why are you fellows so interested in the whereabouts of Monte Carson?"

The man on his knees glanced up, wiping blood off his face, but didn't answer. The third man, who hadn't moved a muscle, looked at Smoke, his eyes switching from the hole in the Colt's barrel to Smoke's face. "We had a message from an old friend of his, that's all. We were just supposed to tell him hello." His face slowly drained of color as he spoke.

"And what was this friend's name?" Smoke asked, earing down the hammer on his .44 and putting it back in his holster.

The two men who were still conscious glanced at each other, sudden fear in their eyes. "I don't rightly remember," the man on his knees said as he grabbed the bar and pulled himself to his feet, swaying slightly. He had a slight quaver in his voice and his eyes fixed on Smoke's pistol.

The man on the floor moaned and rolled on his back, sleeving blood off his mouth with his arm. Smoke reached down, grabbed a handful of his hair, and hauled him to his feet, the man squealing in pain.

Smoke smiled and dusted the man's clothes off. "Well, like I said, this is a nice town, but as you can see, it's not too healthy to go around asking a lot of questions about things that don't concern you."

"Yes, sir, we can see that," the third man said, relieved that Smoke's gun was back in his holster.

"Now, why don't you fellows head on back to Wyoming and learn to mind your own business?"

"How'd you know we was from Wyomin'?" the second man said, before the third slapped him on the shoulder and said, "Shut up, Max."

Smoke leaned forward and whispered, "I know a whole lot more than you think I do, and I want you to take a message to your boss, Jim Slaughter."

"We don't . . ." the third man started to say until a look from Smoke silenced him in mid-sentence.

"Tell Slaughter that Smoke Jensen is coming to have a talk with him, and that if Mary Carson has even one hair out of place when I get there, they'll be finding pieces of his carcass all over the territory before I'm done with him."

"Smoke Jensen . . . THE Smoke Jensen?"

"There's only one I'm aware of," Smoke said.

"Gawd Almighty, Joe, you done drawed down on Smoke Jensen," the second man said to the one with blood all over his face.

Smoke looked at each man one at a time. "I'd suggest that after you give Slaughter my message, you boys look for a healthier climate, 'cause if I see you when I get there, I'll kill you deader'n a snake."

"All right, Mr. Jensen," Max said as he picked his hat up off the bar, ignoring the blood running down his face.

"Oh, and you can tell him Blackie Johnson and his friends send their regards from Hell."

The three men's eyes widened and their faces paled as they threw some coins down on the bar and walked rapidly out of the room without looking back.

"Smoke, your steak is getting cold," Louis called from his table.

Smoke glanced over and saw the gambler hooking his hammer-thong back on the pistol he wore on his right hip, and knew his friend had been backing his play.

Pearlie already had his head down and was stuffing his food into his mouth as if he hadn't eaten in days. Cal was smiling and watching the men leave the saloon.

"You shore know how to liven up a place, Smoke," he said.

As Smoke cut into his steak, Louis leaned forward. "Do you mind telling me why you did that?"

Smoke swallowed, took a drink of coffee, and looked up. "I wanted Slaughter to know that Monte got his message. I also wanted him to know what would happen if he hurt Mary."

"Do you think that's wise?"

Smoke shrugged. "Slaughter's not the kind of man to keep his word, so if he's planning to kill Monte when he gets his money, there wouldn't be any reason for him to keep Mary safe."

Smoke cut another piece of steak. "Now there is, and he'll be wondering why I'm dealing myself into this hand. I hope it'll make him nervous, not knowing just what's going on, and a nervous man sometimes makes mistakes."

8

Big Jim Slaughter sat at a table in the main room of a cabin and watched Mary Carson work in the kitchen. She was rolling dough into a long tube, fixing to bake a loaf of bread in the oven.

The cabin was one of five situated in a box canyon in the mountains just north of Jackson Hole, Wyoming. They were rough, had been made of weathered pine logs many years before, and had been used by hundreds of outlaws who'd holed up there while waiting for the law to tire of hunting for them.

There was only one road into the canyon, though there were several steep trails that could be used as exits in the event of a raid by lawmen or the Army. The trails were rough and winding and, though passable by men riding in single file, were too steep and narrow to be suitable for a force of men to use as an attack. Because of the remoteness of the area, and the many narrow passes that were heavily guarded, no one had ever attempted to roust the men hiding there, which made it an ideal place for what Slaughter had in mind.

Slaughter tipped his hat back on his head and leaned back in his chair, crossing his legs. He took a deep drink of the coffee Mary'd made and smacked his lips.

"I sure do appreciate you cooking for us, Mrs. Carson.

It's the first time we've had any food worth eating in over six months."

Mary spoke without turning around. "I don't mind. Keeping busy keeps my mind off . . . other things. I'd rather be doing this than sitting and worrying about Monte and what's going to happen when he finds you."

Slaughter smirked as he took a cloth bag out of his pocket and began to build himself a cigarette. "You worried that maybe he'll get himself killed?"

She turned and leaned back against the counter, dusting flour off her hands on the apron around her waist. She shook her head. "No, not really. Monte's been a sheriff for some time now, and I know that every day there is the chance some drunken cowboy or thief will shoot him." Her lips curled in a small smile. "It goes with being married to an officer of the law."

Slaughter's face puckered in puzzlement as he struck a lucifer on his pants leg. "Then what are you fretting about?"

Mary's eyes bored into his, making the back of his neck tingle, as if he were being watched by a rattlesnake. "I'm worried about how he's going to feel after he kills you and your men. Monte's never liked having to kill . . . it upsets him for weeks afterwards."

Slaughter choked on a lungful of smoke as he reared his head back and laughed and coughed. When he could get his breath, he asked, "You mean you're afraid he might lose some sleep if he manages to put some lead in me?"

"That's right," she answered. "He's not like you, Mr. Slaughter. Killing goes against his nature, though I'm told he's right good at it when he needs be."

Slaughter nodded his head. "Well, let me assure you, Mrs. Carson. If Monte does manage to plant me six feet under, he sure as hell won't lose any sleep over it. Matter of fact, he's liable to dance a jig on my grave."

He stabbed out his butt on the sole of his boot and dropped it in an empty can on the table that had once held tinned peaches. "But personally," he said, looking back up at her, "I don't think Monte is that good with a gun."

Mary stared at him with sad eyes, making him wonder just what was going through her mind. "Perhaps you've underestimated my husband, Mr. Slaughter. Have you heard back from the three men you sent to tell him what you wanted?"

The itch returned to the back of Slaughter's neck when she reminded him of the strange absence of Boots Malone, Blackie Johnson, and Slim Watkins. They'd had plenty of time to deliver his message to Monte Carson and make their way back to the hole-in-the-wall. If they didn't show up in the next couple of days, or if he didn't hear from Max or the other two he'd sent to find out what had happened to Blackie and the others, he'd have to ride into Jackson Hole and see if there was a telegraph message for him. Slaughter had been planning this operation for several years now, and he didn't much like being in the dark and not knowing how his plan was progressing.

"I'm sure they'll show up eventually, Mrs. Carson," he answered her, though his voice was less sure now.

She gave him a slight smile, her eyes still sad. "If those men told Monte that you'd taken me, then they're probably dead, or in jail." She turned and began kneading the bread dough. "And I wouldn't go making plans on how you're going to spend that money you want from Monte, because there's not a chance in Hell you're going to live to see a single dollar of it."

Slaughter gritted his teeth until his jaw ached and stood up from the table. He wasn't going to let this woman and her faith in her husband's ability get to him. He turned and walked out the door without another word.

Mary glanced at his back as he left, smiling to herself. She knew Monte was coming for her and that they would be together again soon.

Smoke refilled his coffee cup and sat back after telling Monte and Sally about what had happened at Longmont's.

Monte was healing fast and was already up and walking around the cabin, anxious to get moving toward Wyoming.

Sally glanced at him with worried eyes. "I really don't think you're ready to make that long a journey on horseback, Monte."

He took the bowl of beef soup she'd fixed him in both hands and drank the last of the juice. "There's no other way, Sally. Every day we wait puts Mary in that much more danger. There's no telling what those bast . . . uh, galoots are doing to her."

Smoke put his hand on Monte's shoulder. "Calm down, Monte. I don't think Slaughter will let any harm come to Mary until he's gotten his hands on the money. He's going to know you won't turn it over to him until you're sure Mary is still alive."

Sally nodded. "Smoke's right, Monte. From what you say, Slaughter is no fool, and he knows you're not the kind of man to give in unless he has Mary to hold over your head. I'm sure she is being treated well."

Monte stood up, grimacing at the pain the movement caused him. "Nevertheless, I can't just sit around here while she's in the hands of those outlaws." He looked at Smoke. "It's gonna take us more'n a week to get to Wyoming, longer if we have any early winter storms. By then, I'll be fit as a fiddle and ready to call the dance with Slaughter."

Smoke shrugged. "If that's the way you want it, Monte." He stood up. "I'll have Pearlie and Cal start packing our gear and getting some horses from the remuda for the trip. I figure we'll make better time if we each take a spare to ride when our mounts get tired."

Sally shook her head. "If you men insist on this foolishness, I'll pack enough food for the trip so you won't have to live on beans and fatback." She pointed her finger at Monte. "You're going to need steak if you want those wounds to heal without getting infected."

He grinned. "Yes, ma'am. I ain't never turned down none of your cooking, Sally, an' I ain't about to start now."

The sound of horses' hooves outside the cabin interrupted their talk. Smoke stepped to the window and pulled the curtains aside.

He looked back over his shoulder with a grin on his face. "Louis Longmont's riding up, and he's wearing his winter coat and pulling a packhorse. Looks like he wants to ante up in this game."

Monte smiled. "Good. Louis is the best man with a gun I know, next to you, Smoke, and if those bastards are holed up in the mountains, we're gonna need all the firepower we can muster to blast 'em out."

Tired of waiting for his men to return, Slaughter decided to ride into Jackson Hole to see if any telegrams had arrived for him. He left Mary in the care of Juanita Sanchez, common-law wife of one of the *bandidos* who lived full time in the hole-in-the-wall. He told her that if anything happened to Mary in his absence, he would personally slit her throat.

"You no need worry, Señor Slaughter," she told him, patting the Army Colt in a holster on her hip. "Any *bastardo* try to touch the *gringa* going to have a beeg hole in his gullet."

Slaughter took two of his top guns with him, Whitey Jones and Swede Johanson. Whitey, an albino with silver hair and snow-white skin and pink eyes, was a stone killer who favored a short-barreled ten-gauge Greener shotgun he wore in a cut-down holster on his right hip. Swede Johanson was a six-foot-six-inch giant of a man with blond hair, blue eyes, and a sweet-looking face that belied the fact that he had killed over twenty men, most of whom he'd beaten to death with his ham-sized fists. He wasn't quick on the draw, but he seldom missed once he cleared leather.

The three men tied their horses up outside the Cattleman's Bar, a misnomer since the only patrons were outlaws and footpads and other miscreants who rode the owl-hoot trail. There wasn't an honest rancher within twenty miles of Jackson Hole.

As they stepped to the bar, Slaughter stood next to an old man in buckskins and a beaver-skin cap who was leaning on his elbows watching the bartender fill a jug with whiskey.

Slaughter wrinkled his nose and glanced at the old mountain man. "Whew, what's that stink? Don't you ever bathe, old-timer?"

The man cut his eyes toward Slaughter and his companions and grinned. "Shore, sonny. I takes me a bathing ever' spring and ever' summer. I figger twice't a year is plenty. Any more'n that an' ya tend to git the fever."

"You want me to run this stink-pot outta here, Boss?" Whitey asked, his hand on the butt of his pistol.

Before Slaughter could answer, the mountain man jerked a twelve-inch Bowie knife from a scabbard on his belt and had the point of the blade under Whitey's chin, forcing his head up.

As a trickle of blood ran down the albino's neck, the mountain man said, "Now, fellers, I didn't come in here lookin' fer no trouble, but if'n trouble is what yo're hankerin' fer, then I'll be glad to oblige ya."

Slaughter laughed, liking the old man's guts. "No . . . no, old-timer," he said, holding his hands out. "We don't want any trouble. Go right ahead and finish getting your . . . supplies."

"Thank yee kindly, mister," the mountain man said with some irony, as if he didn't need Slaughter's permission to do anything he wanted to do.

He holstered his knife and winked at Whitey. "Sorry 'bout that nick, feller, but if'n you reach fer that six-killer again, I'll skin you like a beaver 'fore you can blink."

He took his jug from the bartender and picked up off the bar a Sharps .50-caliber rifle that was almost as long as he was tall.

He nodded at Slaughter and backed out the door, his finger on the trigger of the rifle. "See you gents later," he said, showing yellow stubs of teeth in a wide grin.

Whitey grimaced. "Why didn't you let me drill that sucker, Boss?"

Slaughter smiled, turning back to the bar. "You don't appreciate history, Whitey. That man there is one of the last of a dying breed. Another couple of years and there won't be any mountain men left."

Swede slapped his hand on the bar. "How about some whiskey, barkeep? My friend here needs something to calm his nerves."

Whitey took a step toward Swede, his eyes glittering hate, but Slaughter stopped him with a look. "Whitey, why don't you go on over to the telegraph office and see if there's any messages for me? I'll order us some food while you're gone."

"Yes, sir," Whitey said, glaring at Swede as if he could kill him.

By the time Whitey returned, Slaughter and Swede were digging into steaks that looked as if they'd been burned to a crisp. "Damn," Slaughter said as he tried to chew the tough meat, "this is making me appreciate Mrs. Carson's cooking more and more."

Swede nodded. "Yeah, maybe we shouldn't kill her after we get Carson's money. We can keep her around for the winter to keep us warm on cold nights."

Slaughter gave him a flat look. "Swede, Mrs. Carson is a lady and I don't want to hear any more talk like that. It's not her fault she married the wrong man."

"You're not gettin' soft on us, are you, Boss?" he asked, a funny look in his eyes.

Slaughter glared at him. "Anytime you think that, Swede, just give me a try and you'll find out how soft I'm gettin'."

Whitey sat at the table, glancing at the two men as if wondering what he'd interrupted. "Here's a telegram for you, Boss. It's from Max."

Slaughter took the paper and opened it up. As he read, his brow furrowed. "Well, I'll be damned."

"What's it say, Jim?" Swede asked, evidently willing to forget their words of a few moments before.

"Max says a man name of Smoke Jensen braced him in

Big Rock. Said to tell me if anything happened to Mary Carson he was going to cut me to pieces."

"Smoke Jensen?" Whitey asked. "The old gunfighter? I thought he was dead."

Slaughter looked at him. "So did I. Haven't heard anything 'bout him in years. Evidently he's joined forces with Monte Carson and wants to deal himself into this little fracas."

"What's he say about Blackie and Boots?" Swede asked.

"According to this, they won't be coming back. Jensen says they send their regards from Hell."

Swede leaned back in his chair, pushing his half-eaten steak away. "This is gettin' complicated, Boss. I thought you said Monte would bring us the money once he knew we had his wife."

Slaughter nodded, a thoughtful look on his face. "I must've figured him wrong. Now it looks like we may have a little more trouble getting our hands on our money than I thought."

"Is Max on his way back here?" Whitey asked.

Slaughter glanced at the telegram. "I don't think so. His last line says he wishes us luck, but he didn't figure on having to face Smoke Jensen for his share and he doesn't think it's worth it."

"That yellow-bellied bastard!" Swede said. "I told you he was the wrong man to send to Big Rock."

Slaughter looked over at him. "Like I said, Swede, any time you think you're good enough to take over leadership of this gang, you're welcome to give it a try."

Swede's eyes dropped. "It's not that. You're still the boss, Jim, but I don't like the idea of some gun-slick friend of Carson's joinin' up with him. It complicates matters."

"Don't worry. There ain't no way they can get into the hole-in-the-wall without us knowing about it first, and we've still got Mary Carson as our ace in the hole. Monte's got to come through with the money. He doesn't have any other choice in the matter, whether he's got some old geezer ex-gunman to ride with him or not."

Whitey caressed the butt of the Greener ten-gauge in his cut-down holster on his hip. "I wouldn't mind mixin' it up with this old Jensen feller. Might be fun to see what he's made of . . . see if all those stories 'bout him are true or not."

Swede cleared his throat. "Uh, he ain't all that old, Whitey."

The albino turned to look at his friend. "You know this galoot?"

Swede shook his head. "No, but when I was just a kid, my daddy and I were livin' in this old mining town just west of the Needle Mountains, place called Rico. It wasn't much more than a camp, and was filled with more gun-fighters than miners."

"What's that got to do with Smoke Jensen?" Whitey asked impatiently.

"I'm gettin' to it," Swede answered. "Anyway, I was in the tradin' post there one morning, gettin' supplies for my dad and me, and I saw these two men ride up from the window. One wasn't more'n a boy in his teens, an' the other was this old mountain man went by the name Preacher. Seems somebody had told Smoke Jensen the men who'd killed his father were in town . . ."

Smoke and Preacher dismounted in front of the combination trading post and saloon. As was his custom, Smoke slipped the thongs from the hammers of his Colts as soon as his boots hit dirt.

They bought their supplies, and had turned to leave when the hum of conversation suddenly died. Two rough-dressed and unshaven men, both wearing guns, blocked the door.

"Who owns that horse out there?" one demanded, a snarl in his voice, trouble in his manner. "The one with the SJ brand?"

Smoke laid his purchases on the counter. "I do," he said quietly.

"Which way'd you ride in from?"

Preacher had slipped to his right, his left hand covering the hammer of his Henry, concealing the click as he thumbed it back.

Smoke faced the men, his right hand hanging loose by his side. His left hand was just inches from his left-hand gun. "Who wants to know—and why?"

No one in the dusty building moved or spoke.

"Pike's my name," the bigger and uglier of the pair said. "And I say you came through my diggin's yesterday and stole my dust."

"And I say you're a liar," Smoke told him.

Pike grinned nastily, his right hand hovering near the butt of his pistol. "Why . . . you little pup. I think I'll shoot your ears off."

"Why don't you try? I'm tired of hearing you shoot your mouth off."

Pike looked puzzled for a few seconds; bewilderment crossed his features. No one had ever talked to him in this manner. Pike was big, strong, and a bully. "I think I'll just kill you for that."

Pike and his partner reached for their guns.

Four shots boomed in the low-ceilinged room, four shots so closely spaced they seemed as one thunderous roar. Dust and birds' droppings fell from the ceiling. Pike and his friend were slammed out the open doorway. One fell off the rough porch, dying in the dirt street. Pike, with two holes in his chest, died with his back against a support pole, his eyes still open, unbelieving. Neither had managed to pull a pistol more than halfway out of leather.

All eyes in the powder-filled and dusty, smoky room moved to the young man standing by the bar, a Colt in each hand. "Good God!" a man whispered in awe. "I never even seen him draw."

Preacher moved the muzzle of his Henry to cover the men at the tables. The bartender put his hands slowly on the bar, indicating he wanted no trouble.

"We'll be leaving now," Smoke said, holstering his Colts

and picking up his purchases from the counter. He walked out the door slowly.

Smoke stepped over the sprawled, dead legs of Pike and walked past his dead partner in the shooting.

"What are we 'posed to do with the bodies?" a man asked Preacher.

"Bury 'em."

"What's the kid's name?"

"Smoke."*

Whitey raised his eyebrows. "He was that fast, huh?"

Swede smiled. "Faster'n a rattlesnake strikin'. If you do go up against him, Whitey, you'd better get him with your first shot, 'cause you sure as hell won't get more'n one."

Tired of all this talk about Smoke Jensen, Big Jim Slaughter threw a handful of coins on the table and stood up. "Let's get back to the hole-in-the-wall, boys. If Carson's got some help, we need to make sure we're gonna be ready for 'em when they ride in."

"I'm ready for 'em right now," Whitey said, a sneer on his face.

Swede just smiled. "I'll remember you said that, Whitey."

*The Last Mountain Man

9

When Slaughter got back to his hideout in the hole-in-the-wall, he called all of his men together.

"Boys, we may be facing a little trouble. Seems Monte Carson has gotten some other men to ride with him and he's on his way out here."

Johnny Tupelow, who called himself the Durango Kid, leaned over and spat on the ground. He was a young man, barely out of his teens, and dressed in what he thought a soon-to-be-famous gun hawk should wear—black pants and shirt with a vest festooned with silver conchos and a hat slung low over his forehead. He wore a brace of pearl-handled Colt .45 Peacemakers on his hips and highly polished black boots that rose to his knees. "That mean he ain't gonna give us the money, Boss?"

Slaughter's lips curled in a nasty smile. "Oh, he'll give us the money, all right, or he'll be gettin' pieces of his wife in the mail for months to come." He hesitated. "I don't rightly know if he plans on puttin' up a fight or if he's just bringing some extra guns to make sure we keep our end of the bargain. In any case, until we find out just what his intentions are, I want two men at each sentry post around the clock. One to keep anybody who tries to get in here pinned down and the other to ride here to let us know we got company."

The Durango Kid looked around at the others, then asked, "Any idea who he's got ridin' with him?"

Slaughter hesitated. "Max said it was Smoke Jensen."

"Jensen?" the kid asked. "I thought he was dead."

"Evidently not, according to Max," Slaughter said.

"Any others?" the kid asked.

Slaughter shrugged. "Don't have any idea, but if the thought of goin' up against Jensen worries you, Kid, you're welcome to ride outta here anytime."

The kid leaned over and spat again, a smirk on his face. "Not likely, Mr. Slaughter. I reckon my share of fifty thousand is worth killing a couple of old men past their prime."

Slaughter didn't bother telling the Kid that if he went up against Monte Carson alone, Carson would in all probability plant him six feet under without getting his hair mussed. "Good. Whitey will make out a new schedule for standing watch. I figure it'll be a couple of weeks 'fore we see anybody, but it won't hurt to keep a sharp lookout just the same."

Smoke and his men were making good time toward Jackson Hole, Wyoming. The weather had been unusually mild for this time of year and they'd only had to contend with a few short-lived snowstorms. They made their final camp when Smoke figured they were less than a day's ride from Jackson Hole.

As they sat around the campfire, eating the last of the rations Sally had packed for the trip, Louis put down his empty plate. "I'll tell you something, Smoke. If Sally ever feels the need to leave you for someone who will really appreciate her, she's welcome to come to my place and cook for me anytime."

Smoke grinned. "I'll bet you won't say that in front of Andre," he said, referring to the French chef who'd been preparing meals for Louis for as long as Smoke could remember.

Louis shook his head. "Don't even think such a thing, my

friend. Andre would gut me like a fish if he even thought I was contemplating letting anyone else cook for me."

Pearlie grunted. "Hell, if Miss Sally ever left the Sugarloaf, Smoke wouldn't have any hands left to tend the stock. They'd all be off following her to wherever she was going. Most of 'em would travel ten mile just for one of her bear sign."

Cal laughed. "They'd have to leave awful early to beat you to 'em, or there wouldn't be any left for 'em to eat."

Smoke held up his hands to quiet the banter. "All right, men. We need to form a plan of action for when we get to Jackson Hole. Slaughter will have gotten my message by now, and if he's as smart as Monte says he is, then he's going to have men in town watching for us to arrive."

"You can bet on that, Smoke," Monte said. "Slaughter hasn't survived this long by not watching his back."

"I would suggest that we split up on the outskirts of town," Louis said as he pulled a long, black cheroot from his coat pocket and lit it off a burning twig from the fire. He tilted smoke from his nostrils and continued. "Slaughter will be waiting for Monte and an unknown number of men to arrive together. If we go in by ones and twos, his men won't know we're associated with Monte."

Smoke nodded. "Good idea, Louis. I propose that Monte camp just outside town, while Cal and Pearlie circle around and go in from the west, Louis from the north, and I'll enter from the south. With any luck, there won't be anyone there who will know who I am. That should give us time to locate this Muskrat Calhoon Bear Tooth told us about and see if he's going to be willing to help us find a back way into the hole-in-the-wall."

"Wait a minute, Smoke. I ain't gonna sit out here cooling my heels while you fellers do all the work," Monte said.

Louis pointed his cigar at Monte as if it were a gun. "You don't have any choice, Monte. Slaughter's sure to have given your description to his men. If they see you in town, they'll know Smoke and whoever else has offered to ride with you is there, too."

Smoke leaned toward Monte. "It's the only chance we have of getting close enough to free Mary without Slaughter getting wind of our presence, Monte."

"Hell, I know you're right, Smoke. It just sticks in my craw having you fellers take risks for Mary and me."

"That's what friends are for," Pearlie said from across the fire. "We all knew what we were gettin' into when we offered to help out, Monte. Hell, you'd've done the same for any one of us."

Monte nodded, accepting the wisdom of the plan Smoke laid out. "All right. I'll set up a camp and when you locate this Muskrat Calhoon you can bring him there."

Pearlie stood up and dusted off the seat of his pants.

"Where you goin', Pearlie?" Cal asked.

"To see if there's any of that apple pie left Miss Sally made," he said.

Louis stared at him in wonder. "Smoke, if you ever run short of money, you can hire Pearlie out to the circus. He could be billed as the man with the bottomless stomach."

Cal and Pearlie slowed their mounts to a walk as they entered the town of Jackson Hole. The light covering of snow on the ground from the last snowfall did little to make the town look any more inviting. The buildings were mostly made of the ponderosa pine logs that were so plentiful on the surrounding mountain slopes, and the streets were dirt and mud, with only a few boardwalks on the main street. Every other building seemed to be a saloon or gambling parlor, though there were several rather seedy boardinghouses and hotels for the mostly transient population.

"Jimminy," Cal said, his eyes wide as he glanced from side to side, noticing the hard-looking men who lounged along the streets, most with bottles of whiskey in their hands even though it was barely past breakfast time. "I can sure see why they call this area Robber's Roost."

Pearlie nodded as he let his hand drift to his hip to

loosen the hammer-thong on his Colt. "Yep. 'Bout the only citizens around here that don't make their livin' with a gun are the barkeeps and fallen doves in the whorehouses."

As he spoke, a girl who looked to be no more than fifteen stumbled out of a doorway and grabbed a cowboy leaning against the wall by the shoulder. She wore a tawdry dress made of red silk with green overlay that was cut almost down to her navel. After a few moments talking to the gent, he grinned and followed her back through the doorway.

Cal shook his head. "Not much like Big Rock, is it, Pearlie?"

"Not enough so's you can tell it, Cal." He swiveled his head, glancing to both sides of the street. "You figger there's any place we can rustle up some breakfast around here?"

Cal pursed his lips. After a moment, he pointed to the right side of the street. "There's a sign over that boardinghouse sayin' 'Good Eats.' I reckon that's as good a place as any to look. We gotta find us a place to bed down anyway."

They reined in before the building with the sign that read, "Aunt Bea's Boardinghouse, Clean Sheets and Good Eats."

When they entered they saw an entrance to the dining area off to the left. Pearlie removed his hat and made a beeline for the room, holding his nose in the air. "I smell bacon fryin' an' eggs cookin', Cal, boy. Looks like we struck pay dirt."

Cal just shook his head and followed his partner's nose. Pearlie was like a bloodhound when it came to food, and could smell out vittles as well as a hound could track a rabbit.

They sat at a table near the window, where they could watch the comings and goings along the main street, and put their hats on a chair.

After a moment, a rotund woman wearing a flour-stained apron approached the table.

"Howdy, boys. What can I git ya?" she asked.

She had gray hair done up in a bun and a face full of

wrinkles, showing she'd spent considerable time in the sun. Her eyes were sky-blue and seemed to twinkle with good nature.

Pearlie considered her question for a minute, then said, "I'd like four hens' eggs, scrambled, a pound of bacon, not too crisp, and some flapjacks with syrup. And about a gallon of coffee," he added.

"Are you Aunt Bea?" Cal asked.

"That's what most folks call me, sonny boy, leastways round here."

"I'll have a couple of eggs and some bacon and flap-jacks too," Cal said.

Aunt Bea's eyes narrowed as she studied Cal and Pearlie. "You boys don't exactly look like the usual sort we get around here. You just passin' through?"

Cal and Pearlie glanced at each other. They hadn't had a chance yet to get their story straight about why they were in Jackson Hole.

Finally, Pearlie answered her. "Yes, ma'am. We're just up from Texas way. Had a little trouble crost the border with the Mexican Federales and we figgered it'd be better for our health if'n we moseyed on up north for a spell."

The light seemed to go out of her eyes. "Oh, outlaws, huh?"

Cal, noticing her disappointment, quickly said, "Oh, no, ma'am. Leastways, not here in the States. It's just that the Rangers tend to take a dislike to anybody that causes trouble with the Mexican authorities, so we thought we'd leave Texas until they forgot about our . . . little problems."

Aunt Bea nodded. "Well, I hope you don't plan on stayin' here too long, boys. Jackson Hole ain't exactly a healthy place to hang around 'less you're tougher 'n boot leather. Some of the men round here like to eat young fellers like you for breakfast, if you know what I mean."

"Yes, ma'am," Cal said, putting on his most innocent expression.

Aunt Bea dusted her hands on her apron, causing a cloud

of flour dust to rise in the air. "Well, I'll be seein' to your food an' I'll have the boy bring you your coffee right out."

After she left, Cal leaned across the table. "Why'd you tell her we was runnin' from the law?"

Pearlie shrugged. "We got to fit in, Cal, boy. You can't just come to a place full of footpads, thieves, and rustlers and pretend to be choirboys. It wouldn't look right."

Cal leaned back. "I guess you're right, though I hate makin' her think we ride the owl-hoot trail."

Pearlie glanced at the kitchen door through which Bea had disappeared. "Unless I miss my guess, that lady likes to gossip, Cal, an' it won't hurt nothin' to have her spread the word we're on the run."

While Pearlie was talking, Cal looked out the window and saw Louis Longmont dismounting in front of the boardinghouse. Cal nudged Pearlie's shoulder and motioned at the window with his head.

Pearlie grinned and nodded, evidently glad to see a friendly face among the hard cases on the street.

Louis sauntered into the dining room, gave Cal and Pearlie a quick glance, but didn't acknowledge them in any other way. He sat at a table across the room and leaned back in his chair, pulling out his trademark long black cheroot and lighting it.

Aunt Bea brought them a large coffeepot and two mugs, said their food would be ready shortly, then walked over to Louis's table.

"Howdy, mister," they heard her say. "I'm Aunt Bea. You want breakfast or lunch?"

"I believe I'll have lunch, Aunt Bea. How about a steak, cooked just long enough to keep it on the plate, some fried potatoes, and some tinned peaches if you have any?"

Bea nodded. "Coffee?"

"Yes, please."

"Ah, a man with manners. Quite a rarity around here," she said, as she walked back toward the kitchen.

A few minutes later a boy that looked to be no more than twelve or fourteen came out of the back room with two large platters in his arms. He placed the plates in front of Cal and Pearlie and walked back to the kitchen.

Pearlie wasted no time. He put his head down and began to eat as if he were starving. Cal glanced over at Louis, smiled, and also began to eat.

Just as Louis was being served, several groups of men entered and the tables in the dining room began to fill up, it being close to the noon hour. Minutes later, Smoke walked in and took a table by himself, sitting as was his custom with his back to a wall where he could keep watch on the entrance to the room.

Soon all the tables in the room were filled. Pearlie, finally finished with his food, poured himself another cup of coffee and leaned back in his chair, building himself a cigarette. "Aunt Bea must do all right, from the looks of the crowd," he said, handing Cal his fixin's so he could make himself a cigarette also.

Just as Cal was lighting his cigarette, four men walked up to their table. The first one, a tall, skinny man with several days' growth of whiskers on his face, a tied-down Colt on one hip, and a large Bowie knife in a scabbard on the other, leaned over and put both his hands on their table.

"If you gents are through eatin', why don't you get your asses away from my table and let me an' my friends sit down?"

Pearlie glanced up at him through the smoke from the butt in the corner of his mouth, a mannerism he'd copied from his idol, Joey Wells. "Take it easy, pardner," he drawled, making no move to get up. "We'll leave when we're good and ready, an' not a minute sooner."

"You gonna let a pup like that sass you, Billy?" the man behind him said with a chuckle.

Billy backed away from the table and squared off, letting his hand dangle near the butt of his pistol. "Hell, no, I'm not," he growled. "Now, you young'uns can either get up of your own accord, or I'm gonna have to make you."

The three men with Billy spread out next to him, grim expressions on their faces.

"Hold on there, Billy Baxter!" Aunt Bea called from the kitchen door. She was holding a long-barreled Greener shotgun cradled in her arms. "I don't want no trouble in my place, you hear me, you hooligan?"

Before Billy could answer, Pearlie got to his feet. "Don't you worry none, Aunt Bea," he said, his eyes never leaving Baxter. "This *cabron* sounds like all talk to me, an' even if he does have the guts to go for that smoke wagon on his hip, he won't even clear leather 'fore I put his lights out."

Cal got to his feet and unhooked the leather hammer-thong on his Colt. "Four to two, Pearlie. Looks even enough for me," he whispered in a gravelly voice, his eyes on the men behind Baxter.

Louis, concerned about the turn of events, cut his eyes over to Smoke, who was sitting smiling and watching. Smoke winked at Louis, indicating he shouldn't worry.

Nevertheless, Louis leaned back and straightened out his right leg, resting his hand next to his pistol just in case.

Baxter's eyes shifted from Pearlie to Cal, seeing no back-up in either man. Sweat popped out on his forehead, though the room was cool. He licked suddenly dry lips, unsure of what his next move should be. The man next to him moved over a little, evidently trying to get out of the line of fire.

Suddenly, Baxter's hand grabbed for his gun butt. Before he could get his pistol halfway out of his holster, Pearlie had drawn and slammed the barrel of his Colt on top of Baxter's head, poleaxing him and dropping him to the floor. Only a shade slower, both Cal's pistols were out with hammers cocked and pointed at the remaining men, who were standing there with mouths open and eyes wide.

"Jesus God Awmighty," one of them croaked, holding his hands out away from his pistols, "that boy's faster'n a snake."

Pearlie slowly turned to the other men. "You gents better drag your friend outta here, 'fore he bleeds all over Aunt Bea's floor."

Aunt Bea rushed over to stare down at Baxter. She looked

up. "Damn right! Drag his sorry ass outta here and don't none of you bother to try an' eat here again, you hear me?"

Pearlie picked up his hat and gave a slight bow to Aunt Bea. "Sorry for the trouble, ma'am. I hope I didn't make too much of a mess."

She smiled and clapped him on the shoulder. "A little blood on the floor is better'n hair on the wall, sonny. It's not the first an' it won't be the last blood spilt in this town neither."

"Any chance of us gettin' a room for the night, ma'am?" Cal asked, holstering his pistol as Baxter's friends picked him up and carried him from the room.

"Sure, boys. Be a welcome change to have guests who don't shoot off their guns first chance they git. Come on over to the front and I'll give you a key."

10

Later that afternoon, after Smoke and Louis had also gotten rooms at Aunt Bea's Boardinghouse, the four men met in Smoke's room.

Louis looked at Pearlie. "Pearlie, you just about gave me a heart seizure when you braced that cowboy and his friends."

Pearlie grinned. "Oh, I wasn't worried, Louis. After all, Cal and me had you and Smoke to back our play."

Smoke chuckled. "Obviously, you didn't need us, Pearlie. You boys handled it just right. By now, everyone in town has heard about your little set-to with Baxter."

Cal frowned. "You don't think they'll be laying for us when we leave, do you, Smoke?"

Smoke shook his head. "I doubt it. Things like that must go on every day here in Jackson Hole. By tomorrow, it'll be old news."

Louis grinned. "Except I'll wager no one attempts to rush you from your table before you're ready again."

"Cal," Smoke said, "I'd like you and Pearlie to head on over to Schultz's General Store this afternoon and let it be known that you're looking for Muskrat Calhoon. Bear Tooth said that's where he usually gets his supplies for the winter and I need to know if he's still in town or has already headed up into the high lonesome."

"Yes, sir," Cal said.

"Louis and I will visit a few of the saloons and gambling houses to see what we can find out about Big Jim Slaughter. We'll see if we can get a handle on just how many men he has up at the hole-in-the-wall with him."

"Anything else you want us to do?" Pearlie asked.

"Yeah. Start buying up ammunition and gunpowder and dynamite while you're there. Not too much at one time, and try to spread out your purchases among several different places. We don't want anyone to think we're going to war."

Just after supper, Louis joined a table of men playing poker at a place called The Dog Hole Saloon and Gaming Room. He slipped his coat off and played wearing only his vest, with his sleeves rolled up. He'd found that when he won large sums of money, as he usually did, it eased competitors' minds to see that he had nothing up his sleeves. Of course, he had no need to cheat. Possessed of a remarkable memory and intelligence and a deep knowledge of the odds of drawing certain hands, he rarely lost, especially when playing cowboys who were usually both drunk and stupid.

After a couple of hours, one of the men at the table threw down his hand in disgust. "Boys, that about finishes me for the night. I'm busted."

"Perhaps you can get an advance from your boss and rejoin us later," Louis said as he raked in yet another pot.

The cowboy shook his head. "What boss? I ain't exactly workin' at the present time."

"Oh?" Louis said. He flipped a twenty-dollar gold piece across the table. "Then take this," he said. "I make it a practice never to take a man's food money from him."

The man picked up the gold piece. "Thanks, mister."

"Perhaps you could seek employment with Jim Slaughter." When the table got quiet, Louis looked around innocently. "Didn't I hear someone saying a gentleman named Slaughter was hiring men?"

The other men at the table seemed to relax slightly, as if the mention of Slaughter's name was risky, even in a town as hard as Jackson Hole.

"Just where'd you hear that, mister?" a man in a fur-lined deerskin coat across the table asked.

Louis shrugged. "Oh, I don't know. I believe a couple of gentlemen were discussing it at a roulette table earlier in the evening."

The man next to Louis leaned over and whispered, "It ain't exactly healthy to go around talkin' 'bout Slaughter's business hereabouts, Mr. Longmont. Word is he don't take kindly to anybody bein' too nosy 'bout his affairs, if you get my drift."

Louis smiled and put his finger to his lips. "Oh, of course. Then mum's the word regarding this Mr. Slaughter, whoever he might be."

"Besides," another man at the table, who was drunk, said, "I heard he's got all the men he needs. Must have over thirty men up there at . . ."

"Shut your mouth, Kyle!" the man in the deerskin coat shouted. "You talk too much an' you're liable to have somebody cut your tongue out for you."

Kyle looked at the man through bleary, bloodshot eyes. "Go to hell, Davis. Just 'cause you work for Big Jim don't give you the right to tell ever'body else in town what they can say."

"Ante up, gentlemen," Louis called, throwing a coin into the middle of the table to change the subject. "I believe it's my deal."

Davis looked pointedly at the stack of money in front of Louis. "And as for you, Mr. Fancy Tinhorn Gambler, make sure you deal off the top of the deck this time. I'm gettin' awfully tired of you winnin' all the pots."

Louis stared at Davis and put the cards down, pushing his chair back from the table. "Then perhaps you should make an effort to learn how to play poker, Mr. Davis, if you're tired of losing. Drawing to an inside straight like you did the last hand is a fool's play."

Davis jumped up from his seat. "A fool, am I?" he shouted, bringing a sudden hush to the room.

Louis looked at him without a trace of fear on his face. "You are either a fool or you are stupid, Mr. Davis. And I wouldn't care to wager which it is."

"Why you . . ." Davis shouted, and went for his gun.

Louis drew without standing up. His Colt exploded, spewing smoke and hot lead across the table before Davis could cock his pistol. The slug took him in the right shoulder, spinning him around and throwing him facedown on the floor.

Louis spun his Colt on his finger and deposited it in his holster without showing the slightest trace of emotion. "As I said, I believe it is my deal," he remarked to the men at the table.

"Uh . . . yes, sir, Mr. Longmont. I believe it is," said the man on his left.

As Louis dealt the cards, Davis groaned and writhed on the floor. "Perhaps someone should send for a doctor, before poor Mr. Davis bleeds to death," Louis said, as if it really didn't matter to him whether they did or didn't.

Smoke was standing at the bar in the Cattleman's Saloon. He was sipping a glass of whiskey and chasing it with beer, drinking slowly so as not to let the liquor cloud his judgment.

He'd spoken with several men, inquiring whether anyone in the area was hiring men who knew how to use a gun. The answer was always the same. The town was full of such men and, since there were no range wars going on at present, no one was actively hiring.

Evidently, word of his inquiries spread, and before long a tall man, broad through the shoulders, with a weathered face and tired eyes, stepped up next to him at the bar. The man wore a Colt low on his hip and a tin star on his vest.

He ordered a beer and after the barman brought it, leaned his elbow on the bar and looked at Smoke.

"Howdy, stranger. I don't believe I caught your name," he drawled in a nonchalant manner.

Smoke lit the cigarette he'd built and let smoke trail from his nostrils as he answered, "I don't believe I threw it."

The man chuckled. "A gunfighter with a sense of humor. That's a new one around here. My name's Pike. Walter Pike, but everyone around here just calls me Sheriff," Pike said, raising his eyebrows in silent interrogation of Smoke.

"Howdy, Sheriff Pike. I'm Johnny West," Smoke said, giving a name he'd once used while on the run years before.

"West, huh? Well, Johnny West, I don't recollect any wanted posters on you at my office, but I'll be sure and check again, first chance I get."

Smoke gave Pike a questioning look. "Sheriff, I understood this town was . . . rather open and understanding of men with a reputation. Are you telling me that's not the case?"

Pike took a deep swig of his beer, sleeving the suds off his mustache with the back of his arm. "No, you heard right, Mr. West. I don't ordinarily hassle men about what they did or didn't do 'fore they entered my town. I figure it's live and let live as long as they don't do anything to cause a ruckus here. However, I do like to let newcomers know that if they bust a cap in my town, they're gonna have me to answer to."

Smoke turned to look at the sheriff. "Are you that good?"

Pike grinned. "Oh, I'll be the first to admit I'm not the fastest gun in town, but I DO maintain an edge." He inclined his head at the door to the saloon.

Smoke turned and looked. Two men were standing just inside the batwings, both cradling short-barreled shotguns in their arms. Their eyes were fixed on Smoke and their fingers were on the triggers with hammers eared back.

Smoke grinned. "I see what you mean, Sheriff. A sensible precaution in a place known as Robber's Roost filled with more gunfighters than Dodge City at its prime."

Doubt showed in Pike's eyes for the first time since he spoke to Smoke. "You sure don't talk like your average gun slick, Mr. West. Just what are you doing here in Jackson Hole?"

Smoke shrugged. "Just a man passing through, Sheriff. Looking to pick up some spare change in the only way I know, by hiring my services out if anybody's interested."

Pike nodded. "Uh-huh. Well, there's nothing illegal about that, so far as it goes, Mr. West." He tipped his hat. "I just thought I'd amble on over and explain the rules of the town to you. You take it easy now, you hear?"

Smoke was about to reply when a man ran into the saloon. "Sheriff, Sheriff Pike. A gambler named Longmont just put some lead in Jack Davis over at the Dog Hole."

Pike loosened his Colt in its holster and smiled at Smoke. "See, Mr. West? Now I've got to go and make sure this Longmont was sufficiently provoked to justify shooting someone in my town."

"And if he wasn't?" Smoke asked.

"Then he'll either leave town of his own accord, or he'll stay forever in boot hill." Pike pulled his hat down tight over his forehead and walked out the batwings, his deputies close behind.

Smoke hesitated. He was tempted to follow and find out what had happened with Louis, but he didn't want to tip his hand by showing too much interest. Besides, he figured, Louis was perfectly capable of taking care of himself. He turned back to his whiskey and took a sip, wondering what Cal and Pearlie were doing.

Cal and Pearlie walked into Schultz's General Store and Emporium and were surprised to find a large, well-stocked establishment.

"Jimminy, Pearlie," Cal said, his eyes wide as he stared

around at the wealth of supplies in the store. "This place is bigger'n anything we got in Big Rock."

Pearlie nodded. "Yep, it sure is. I guess it's because this is the only place for hundreds of miles fer folks to buy supplies an' such to git through the winter."

The store was divided into several different parts. On one side was a wall covered with shelves stocked with all manner of foodstuffs—barrels of flour and beans and coffee, row upon row of tinned milk, meat, and fruits, and even cases stuffed with sides of beef and bacon and all manner of fowls.

Another section contained various and sundry mining and trapping equipment from shovels and picks to traps and axes and skinning knives.

The other side of the room was lined with rifles, pistols, cases of ammunition of all calibers alongside small wooden kegs of gunpowder, and cases containing sticks of dynamite and fuses.

A large man wearing an apron over a white shirt, with his sleeves rolled up, approached them with a grin. He was barrel-chested, with a large stomach, dirty blond hair, and ice-blue eyes over a handlebar mustache whose ends hung below ample jowls.

"Howdy, gents. What can I get for you?" he said in a thick German accent. "If I don't got it, they don't make it," he added with a grin.

Pearlie nodded at the section with ammunition and gunpowder. "We came to stock up on some cartridges and blastin' powder, an' maybe a few sticks of that dynamite," he said.

"You came to the right place," Schultz said. "I can fit you out with anything from musket balls to the latest rimfire cartridges from Colt or Smith and Wesson."

As the proprietor helped them load up what they needed, Cal cleared his throat. "By the way, Mr. Schultz, we heard tell an old friend of ours sometimes stopped by here 'fore headin' up into the mountains. His name is Muskrat Calhoon."

Schultz chuckled. "Well, as you can tell from the absence

of any stink, ole' Muskrat hasn't been in yet today, but I expect him 'fore too long. He'll likely be here in the next day or two if he wants to get through the mountain passes 'fore they get all snowed in."

Pearlie hefted the crate of ammunition onto his shoulder and handed Schultz a stack of bills. "Would you tell him a couple of old friends of his and Bear Tooth are in town? We're stayin' over at Aunt Bea's Boardin'house for the next couple of days."

"Gonna partake of a little night life 'fore you head on out, huh?"

Cal blushed and grinned as he picked up the kegs of gunpowder and crate of dynamite. "Yes, sir, we shore are."

"Well, if ole' Muskrat happens by, an' he ain't too drunk to listen, I'll tell him to look you up."

"Thank you kindly, Mr. Schultz," Pearlie said, and led Cal out the door.

On the way back to the boardinghouse, Pearlie said, "Jeez, Cal, I sure hope we find that old mountain man, or we ain't gonna have a prayer of gettin' to Miss Carson without those *bandidos* knowin' we're comin'."

Cal nodded. "Well, Mr. Schultz said he ain't been by yet, so there's still hope."

Pearlie raised his nose to the air as they neared Aunt Bea's. "Smells like Aunt Bea's cookin' fried chicken fer dinner."

Cal stared at Pearlie. "With a nose that good, maybe you could smell out this Muskrat feller."

Pearlie shook his head. "Only works fer food, Cal, boy, only fer food. If'n it worked fer fellers that needed a bath, it wouldn't get past you!"

11

After eating supper at different tables in Aunt Bea's dining room, Smoke and the others met in Smoke's room to compare notes on what they'd learned during the day.

"From what I can gather, Slaughter has all the men he needs," Smoke said. "At least he's not actively looking to hire any new gun hands."

Louis nodded. "That squares with what I could glean from my compatriots at the gaming tables. The best estimate I can come up with is he has between twenty and thirty hard cases up in the hole-in-the-wall with him. No one knows for sure since they never all come into town at the same time, but usually in groups of three or four, and then only when they need supplies or female companionship."

"How about you and Cal, Pearlie? What did you find out about Muskrat Calhoon?"

"Well," Pearlie drawled as he picked fried chicken from between his teeth with a toothpick, "Muskrat hasn't been in the store to buy his provisions yet, so the proprietor thought it'd be any day now since he's got to do it soon to beat the snows in the passes."

"Proprietor's gonna let him know some old friends of his and Bear Tooth are hankerin' to meet up with him.

We told him we was stayin' at Aunt Bea's Boardin'house," Cal added.

"Did you get the supplies we talked about?" Smoke asked.

"Yes, sir. We got four kegs of gunpowder, a case of dynamite sticks, and twenty boxes of ammunition."

"Did you remember to get some shells for my Sharps?" Smoke asked, referring to the Sharps Big Fifty long rifle he'd brought.

"Yes, sir," Pearlie answered, "two boxes of twenty shells each."

Louis raised his eyebrows. "You planning on doing some long-range shooting, Smoke?"

Smoke nodded. "Yeah. Depending on how close Muskrat can get us to the gang's camp, I figured a long gun might come in handy to spread a little fear and trepidation among the bandits."

"Smoke can hit a squirrel in the eye at fifteen hundred yards with that baby," Pearlie said, pride in his voice.

Just then, they heard a knocking at Pearlie and Cal's door, which was just down the hall from Smoke's.

Smoke stepped to the door, pulled his Colt from his holster, and peeked out into the hall. He could see an older man wearing buckskins waiting outside Pearlie's room.

Smoke holstered his gun and opened his door, stepping into the hallway. "Mr. Muskrat Calhoon?" he called.

The old mountain man whirled, a battered Colt Army revolver appearing in his hand in the wink of an eye.

"Yep, that be me, sonny boy. Who might ye be?"

Smoke held his hands out from his sides, showing he wasn't a threat. "My name's Smoke Jensen. Bear Tooth said we should look you up and see if you might be able to do us a favor."

Muskrat narrowed his eyes and studied Smoke for a moment. "Ye be the Smoke Jensen used to ride with Preacher?"

Smoke smiled. "Yes, sir. One and the same."

"Don't be callin' me sir, boy. Onliest ones ever did that was somebody tryin' to sell me somethin'."

"All right, Muskrat. Would you like to join us down here in my room?"

"That depends, young'un. If'n you got a wee mite of whiskey, I could be talked into it."

Smoke laughed out loud. "Well, then, come on in and we'll crack open a bottle of Old Kentucky bourbon, if that suits you."

"If'n it's got a bite, it'll suit me jest fine," the old man answered with a grin, exposing yellow stubs of teeth worn down almost to his gums.

As he passed by Smoke in the doorway, Smoke took a deep breath. Bear Tooth was right, this man was way beyond ripe.

Muskrat walked into the room and leaned his Sharps long rifle against the wall, then turned and looked at the others gathered there.

He pursed his lips. "You boys havin' a prayer meetin' or somethin'?"

Smoke introduced Muskrat to everyone in the room. Louis, having heard his request for whiskey, got up, poured a long draft into a water glass, and handed it to the mountain man. As he took a deep drink, Louis stepped over to the window and opened it, hoping it would let some of the odor out of the room lest they all suffocate.

Muskrat smacked his lips and held up the empty glass for a refill. "How's ol' Bear Tooth doin' these days?" he asked.

"Other than a little rheumatiz, he said he was doing all right," Smoke answered.

Muskrat nodded. "Rheumatiz goes with the territory if'n yo're gonna live up in the high lonesome durin' the winter."

He took another drink of his whiskey. "Course, Bear Tooth is gettin' on up in years, an' he ain't as spry as he used to be. Never could keep up with us younger fellers, even in his better days."

Muskrat leaned back in his chair and crossed his legs, looking from one man to another. "Now, I ain't no fool an' I know nobody looks me up jest to give me free whiskey, so jest what is it you young fellers want from ol' Muskrat?"

Smoke pulled up a chair and leaned forward, his elbows on his knees, and told Muskrat the whole story of the kidnapping and transportation of Mary Carson to the hole-in-the-wall.

"We aim to get her back, and put some lead in Big Jim Slaughter for what he did," Smoke said.

Muskrat nodded. "And you need ol' Muskrat to show you a back way into the hole-in-the-wall, eh?"

Smoke decided a little flattery was called for. "That's right. Bear Tooth said no man alive knows the mountains around Jackson Hole better'n you. He said if anyone could get us in there without being seen, it'd be you."

Muskrat grinned. "You don't have to shine me on, Smoke, boy. I never believed much in gettin' involved in other people's business nor feuds, but I surely don't like the idee of takin' a man's woman fer somethin' he did. It jest ain't right to git womenfolk involved in men's doin's. No, siree, Bob, it jest ain't right."

"Then you'll help us?" Pearlie asked.

"Damn straight, young man, damn straight."

Pearlie pulled a rolled-up piece of paper from a sack on the bed. "I got us a map of the surrounding mountains, an' it shows all the passes on it."

Muskrat looked at the paper and sneered. "Ain't never looked at no map in all my born days, young feller. Wouldn't know the first thing 'bout readin' one of those. Nope. I'm jest gonna have to take you up there personal-like and show you the way. Idn't no way I could 'splain to you how to git there."

"How soon do you think you can be ready to travel?" Smoke asked.

Muskrat cocked one eye at the whiskey bottle on the

dresser. "I reckon that there bottle'll last till dawn. Any time after that'll be jest fine with me."

Louis laughed, took the bottle from the dresser, and poured drinks all around, smiling when Cal noticed he'd only been given half as much in his glass as the other men.

Muskrat pulled a long twist of tobacco from his coat pocket, bit off a sizable chunk, and began to chew on it as he sipped his whiskey.

"Whilst we're waitin' fer this whiskey to run out, Smoke, ol' Preacher once told me you and he'd had a little set-to up near the Plaza of the Lions back when y'all first rode together. He said it had to do with some galoots that'd kilt your brother."

Smoke stared into the amber liquid in his glass, thinking back on his early days riding with Preacher . . .

"A group of men shot and killed my brother and stole some Confederate gold he was trying to return to its rightful owners. My father told me the story just before he died, and I promised him I would avenge his death. Preacher and I went after them after we'd buried my father up in the mountains.

"After I shot and killed Pike, his friend, and Haywood, and wounded Pike's brother, Thompson, Preacher and I took off after the other men who'd been involved in the theft. We rode on over to La Plaza de los Leones, the Plaza of the Lions. It was there we trapped a man named Casey in a line shack with some of his *compadres*. Preacher and I burnt 'em out and captured Casey, then I took him to the outskirts of the town and hung him."

Muskrat's eyebrows shot up. "Just hung 'em? No trial nor nuthin'?"

Smoke began to build himself a cigarette as he talked. "Yeah, Muskrat. I'm sure you remember that's the way it was done in those days. That town would never have hanged one of their own on the word of Smoke Jensen." He put a lucifer to his cigarette and took a deep puff. "Like as not they would've hanged me and Preacher instead. Anyway, after that, the sheriff there put out a flyer on me, accusing me of murder. Had a ten-thousand-dollar reward on it."

"Did you and Preacher go into hidin'?" asked Muskrat as he leaned over and spat brown tobacco juice into the room's trash can.

"No. Preacher advised it, but I told him I had one more call to make. We rode on over to Oreodelphia, looking for a man named Ackerman. We didn't go after him right at first. Preacher and I sat around doing a whole lot of nothing for two or three days."

"How come did you do that?" asked Muskrat.

"'Cause I wanted Ackerman to get plenty nervous. He did, and finally came gunning for us with a bunch of men who rode for his brand . . ."

At the edge of town, Ackerman, a bull of a man, with small, mean eyes and a cruel slit for a mouth, slowed his horse to a walk. Ackerman and his hands rode down the street six abreast.

Preacher and Smoke were on their feet. Preacher stuffed his mouth full of chewing tobacco. Both men had slipped the thongs from the hammers of their Colts. Preacher wore two Colts, .44s. One in a holster, the other stuck behind his belt. Mountain man and young gunfighter stood six feet apart on the boardwalk.

The sheriff closed his office door and walked into the empty cell area. He sat down and began a game of checkers with his deputy.

Ackerman and his men wheeled their horses to face the men on the boardwalk. "I hear tell you boys is lookin' for me. If so, here I am."

"News to me," Smoke said. "What's your name?"

"You know who I am, kid. Ackerman."

"Oh, yeah!" Smoke grinned. "You're the man who helped kill my brother by shooting him in the back. Then you stole the gold he was guarding."

Inside the hotel, pressed against the wall, the desk clerk listened intently, his mouth open in anticipation of gunfire.

"You're a liar. I didn't shoot your brother; that was Potter and his bunch."

"You stood and watched it. Then you stole the gold."

"It was war, kid."

"But you were on the same side," Smoke said. "So that not only makes you a killer, it makes you a traitor and a coward."

"I'll kill you for sayin' that!"

"You'll burn in Hell a long time before I'm dead," Smoke told him.

Ackerman grabbed for his pistol. The street exploded in gunfire and black powder fumes. Horses screamed and bucked in fear. One rider was thrown to the dust by his lunging mustang. Smoke took the men on the left, Preacher the men on the right side. The battle lasted no more than ten to twelve seconds. When the noise and the gunsmoke cleared, five men lay in the street, two of them dead. Two more would die from their wounds. One was shot in the side—he would live. Ackerman had been shot three times: once in the belly, once in the chest, and one ball had taken him in the side of the face as the muzzle of the .36 had lifted with each blast. Still, Ackerman sat in his saddle, dead. The big man finally leaned to one side and toppled from his horse, one boot hung in the stirrup. The horse shied, then began walking down the dusty street, dragging Ackerman, leaving a bloody trail.

Preacher spat into the street. "Damn near swallowed my chaw."

"I never seen a draw that fast," a man said from his storefront. "It was a blur."

The editor of the paper walked up to stand by the sheriff. He watched the old man and the young gunfighter walk down the street. He truly had seen it all. The old man had killed one man, wounded another. The young man had killed four men, as calmly as picking his teeth.

"What's that young man's name?" the editor asked the

sheriff, taking out a pad of paper and a pencil to record the day's events for his newspaper.

"Smoke Jensen. But he's a devil . . ."*

"What'd you fellers do next?" asked Muskrat.

"Well, we both had some minor wounds, and there was a price on my head, so we took off to the mountains to lay up for a while and lick our wounds and let the heat die down."

Smoke took a last puff on his cigarette and stubbed it out on the sole of his boot. "Except it didn't work out exactly that way. We chanced upon the remains of a wagon train that'd been burned out by Indians, and rescued a young woman. Nicole was her name. She was the lone survivor of the attack. There wasn't nothing else we could do, so we took her up into the mountains with us where we planned to winter."

"And whatever happened to that girl?" Muskrat asked, his eyes sparkling with interest.

"And," Smoke said, glancing at the almost-empty whiskey bottle, "that's a story for another night and another bottle of whiskey."

*The Last Mountain Man

12

Mary Carson was showing Juanita Sanchez how to make biscuits in the small cabin where she was being held prisoner.

"I pretty good with tortillas and tamales," Juanita said as she watched Mary roll dough into a flat sheet and then cut out circular pieces and place them on a sheet greased with lard, "but I never made biscuits."

Mary smiled as she reached up to wipe flour off her nose. "It really isn't all that difficult, Juanita. The main thing you have to remember is not to cook them too long, or they become as hard as rocks." She glanced sideways at the Mexican. "Perhaps that's why some cowboys call them sinkers."

Juanita giggled, just as Jim Slaughter and Whitey and Swede walked into the cabin.

"Well," Slaughter said with a frown, "I see you women are gettin' along all right."

Juanita blushed and stepped back away from Mary, as if she were afraid of seeming too friendly to the *gringa*.

Mary placed the metal sheet with the biscuit dough on it into the stove and closed the metal door. She turned and stared at the three men without a trace of fear on her face. "I was just showing Juanita how to make biscuits. I figured you men might like a change of pace from the Mexican food you seem to eat for every meal."

"I no do nothing wrong, Señor Slaughter," Juanita said, fear making her voice quaver.

Slaughter waved a dismissive hand. "I know you didn't, Juanita. Now, why don't you leave us so we can have a little talk with Mrs. Carson?"

"*Sí*, Señor."

After the woman left, Slaughter stepped to the stove, took a steaming coffeepot off the burner, and poured coffee for himself and his men.

They sat at the table, and he motioned for Mary to take a seat with them.

After she sat down, Slaughter wasted no time in preliminary conversation, but got right to the point of his visit.

"I hear from my men that a man named Smoke Jensen has joined your husband and they're on their way here."

He watched Mary's expression closely to see what effect his announcement would have on her.

She smiled and nodded. "I figured he would," she said.

"You knew this was gonna happen?" Swede asked, leaning forward and staring at her through narrowed eyes.

"Of course," she replied, looking from one to another of the men. "Big Rock is a small community, and we all tend to help one another out when needs be."

"Just what do you know about this Smoke Jensen?" Slaughter asked.

"He's the only man I know who's faster on the draw and more dangerous than my husband, Mr. Slaughter."

Slaughter's face showed his puzzlement. "But why would a man go so far as to travel several hundred miles and risk his life just to help a neighbor out in something that's none of his business?" he asked.

"Perhaps it's because you kidnapped me, Mr. Slaughter. You see, in the West, men value their womenfolk above all else. I've heard of men being hanged just for showing disrespect for a lady, and to go so far as to steal a man's wife to try and collect a debt . . . Well, it just isn't done where I come from."

"That don't exactly answer my question, Mrs. Carson.

This Smoke Jensen has quite a reputation as a gun hawk and a killer. He ain't no gentleman who's likely to go around avenging women who are disrespected, as you put it."

Mary leaned back in her chair and got a strange look on her face. "There's a lot you don't know about Smoke Jensen, Mr. Slaughter. It may well be that this situation has a . . . particular significance to Smoke."

"What do you mean?"

"I'm going to tell you men a story about Smoke that my husband once told me. It may explain why Smoke will never let you get away with what you've done."

Slaughter pulled a cigar out of his pocket, struck a lucifer on his boot, and lit it. As thick clouds of pungent, blue smoke trailed from his nostrils, he said, "Go ahead."

"When Smoke was just a young man, in his first years living in the mountains, he took a young woman as his wife. They lived up in the high lonesome for a couple of years. They had a baby, a son that Smoke loved very much." Mary's eyes misted as she recalled the details of the story.

"At the time, there was a price on Smoke's head and a band of bounty hunters tracked him up into the mountains. As luck would have it, when the men arrived at the small log cabin in the woods where Smoke and Nicole lived, Smoke wasn't there. One of their cows had wandered off and Nicole told him they needed milk for their son to drink, so Smoke went looking for the cow. While he was gone, the bounty hunters burst into the cabin, guns drawn. They were furious when they found Smoke wasn't there, and as men will, they began to do horrible things to his wife and son, trying to find out where Smoke had gone to . . ."

Some primitive sense of warning caused Smoke to pull up short of his home. He made a wide circle, staying in the timber back of the creek, and slipped up to the cabin.

By then Nicole was dead. The acts of the men had grown perverted and in their haste, her throat had been crushed.

Felter sat by the lean-to and watched the valley in front of him. He wondered where Smoke had hidden the gold.

Inside, Canning drew his skinning knife and scalped Nicole, tying her bloody hair to his belt. He then skinned a part of her, thinking he would tan the hide and make himself a nice tobacco pouch.

Kid Austin got sick to his stomach watching Canning's callousness, and went out the back door to puke on the ground. That moment of sickness saved his life—for the time being.

Grissom walked out the front door of the cabin. Smoke's tracks had indicated he had ridden off south, so he would probably return from that direction. But Grissom felt something was wrong. He sensed something, his years on the owl-hoot back trails surfacing.

"Felter?" he called.

"Yeah?" Felter stepped from the lean-to.

"Something's wrong."

"I feel it. But what?"

"I don't know." Grissom spun as he sensed movement behind him. His right hand dipped for his pistol. Felter had stepped back into the lean-to. Grissom's palm touched the smooth wooden butt of his gun as his eyes saw the tall young man standing by the corner of the cabin, a Colt .36 in each hand. Lead from the .36s hit him in the center of the chest with numbing force. Just before his heart exploded, the outlaw said, "Smoke!" Then he fell to the ground.

Smoke jerked the gun belt and pistols from the dead man. Remington Army .44s.

A bounty hunter ran from the cabin, firing at the corner of the building. But Smoke was gone.

"Behind the house!" Felter yelled, running from the lean-to, his fists full of Colts. He slid to a halt and raced back to the water trough, diving behind its protection.

A bounty hunter who had been dumping his bowels in the outhouse struggled to pull up his pants, at the same time pushing open the door with his shoulder. Smoke shot him twice in the belly and left him to scream on the outhouse floor.

Kid Austin, caught in the open behind the cabin, ran for the banks of the creek, panic driving his legs. He leaped for the protection of a sandy embankment, twisting in the air, just as Smoke took aim and fired. The ball hit Austin's right buttock and traveled through the left cheek of his butt, tearing out a sizable hunk of flesh. Kid Austin, the would-be gun hand, screamed and fainted from the pain in his ass.

Smoke ran for the protection of the woodpile and crouched there, recharging his Colts and checking the .44s. He listened to the sounds of men in panic, firing in all directions and hitting nothing.

Moments ticked past, the sound of silence finally overpowering the gunfire. Smoke flicked away sweat from his face. He waited.

Something came sailing out the back door to bounce on the grass. Smoke felt hot bile build in his stomach. Someone had thrown his dead son outside. The boy had been dead for some time. Smoke fought back sickness.

"You wanna see what's left of your woman?" a taunting voice called from near the back door. "I got her hair on my belt and a piece of her hide to tan. We all took a time or two with her. I think she liked it."

Smoke felt rage charge through him, but he remained still, crouched behind the thick pile of wood until his anger cooled to controlled venom-filled fury. He unslung the big Sharps buffalo rifle Preacher had carried for years. The rifle could drop a two-thousand-pound buffalo at six hundred yards. It could also punch through a small log.

The voice from the cabin continued to mock and taunt Smoke. But Preacher's training kept him cautious. To his rear lay a meadow, void of cover. To his left was a shed, but he knew that it was empty, for it was still barred from the outside. The man he'd plugged in the butt was to his right, but several fallen logs would protect Smoke from that direction. The man in the outhouse was either dead or passed out; his screaming had ceased.

Through a chink in the logs, Smoke shoved the muzzle of the Sharps and lined up where he thought he had seen a man move, just to the left of the rear window, to where Smoke had framed it out with rough pine planking. He gently squeezed the trigger, taking up slack. The weapon boomed, the planking shattered, and a man began screaming in pain.

Canning ran out the front of the cabin, to the lean-to, sliding down hard beside Felter behind the water trough. "This ain't workin' out," he panted. "Grissom, Austin, Poker, and now Evans is either dead or dying. The slug from that buffalo gun blowed his arm off. Let's get the hell outta here!"

Felter had been thinking the same thing. "What about Clark and Sam?"

"They growed men. They can join us or they can go to hell."

"Let's ride. They's always another day. We'll hide up in them mountains, see which way he rides out, then bushwhack him. Let's go." They raced for their horses, hidden in a bend of the creek, behind the bank. They kept the cabin between themselves and Smoke as much as possible, then bellied down in the meadow the rest of the way.

In the creek, in water red from the wounds in his butt, Kid Austin crawled upstream, crying in pain and humiliation. His Colts were forgotten—useless anyway; the powder was wet—all he wanted was to get away.

The bounty hunters left in the house, Clark and Sam, looked at each other. "I'm gettin' out!" Sam said. "That ain't no pilgrim out there."

"The hell with that," Clark said. "I humped his woman, I'll kill him and take the ten thousand."

"Your option." Sam slipped out the front and caught up with the others.

Kid Austin reached his horse first. Yelping as he hit the saddle, he galloped off toward the timber in the foothills.

"You wife don't look so good now," Clark called out to Smoke. "Not since she got a haircut and one titty skinned."

Deep silence had replaced the gunfire. The air stank of black powder, blood, and relaxed bladders and bowels, death-induced. Smoke had seen the men ride off into the foothills. He wondered how many were left in the cabin.

Smoke remained still, his eyes burning with fury. Smoke's eyes touched the stiffening form of his son. If Clark could have read the man's thoughts, he would have stuck the muzzle of his .44 into his mouth and pulled the trigger, insuring himself a quick death, instead of what waited for him later on.

"Yes, sir," Clark taunted him. He went into profane detail about the rape of Nicole and the perverted acts that followed.

Smoke eased slowly backward, keeping the woodpile in front of him. He slipped down the side of the knoll and ran around to one wall of the cabin. He grinned. The bounty hunter was still talking to the woodpile, to the muzzle of the Sharps stuck through the logs.

Smoke eased around to the front of the cabin and looked in. He saw Nicole, saw the torture marks on her, saw the hideousness of the scalping and the skinning knife. He lifted his eyes to the back door, where Clark was crouching just to the right of the closed door.

Smoke raised his .36 and shot the pistol out of Clark's hand. The outlaw howled and grabbed his numbed and bloodied hand.

Smoke stepped over Grissom's body, then glanced at the body of the armless bounty hunter who had bled to death.

Clark looked up at the tall young man with the burning eyes. Cold slimy fear put a bony hand on his shoulder. For the first time in his evil life, Clark knew what death looked like.

"You gonna make it quick, ain't you?"

"Not likely," Smoke said, then kicked him on the side of the head, dropping Clark unconscious to the floor.

When Clark came to his senses, he began screaming. He was naked, staked out a mile from the cabin, on the plain. Rawhide held his wrists and ankles to thick stakes driven into the ground. A huge ant mound was just inches from him. And Smoke poured honey all over him.

"I'm a white man," Clark screamed. "You can't do this to me." Slobber sprayed from his mouth. "What are you, half Apache?"

Smoke looked at him, contempt in his eyes. "You will not die well, I believe."

He didn't.*

"Jesus," Swede whispered, sweat appearing on his forehead.

Slaughter shook his head to clear it of the images Mary had implanted in his mind. "What happened to the rest of the men who rode off?" Whitey asked, though he thought he knew the answer.

Mary shook her head. "You don't want to know. Suffice it to say, they all died in horrible ways at Smoke's hand."

Slaughter stared at her through narrowed eyes. "So, you think our taking you has made this a personal matter with Jensen, huh?"

A small, sad smile tugged at the corners of Mary's mouth. "Yes, I do. And if I know my neighbors, Smoke Jensen won't be the only man to ride with Monte. I'm very afraid you've bitten off more than you can chew, Mr. Slaughter," she added with a slight nod of her head.

"This is all bullshit, Boss," Whitey growled as he stood up and drank the rest of his coffee. "Ain't no man gonna ride over three hundred miles just 'cause some old bounty hunters once kilt his wife and son."

Slaughter turned to look at the albino, a resigned look on his face. "I'm afraid you're wrong, Whitey. I would, and evidently so would this gunfighter named Smoke Jensen."

Swede sleeved sweat off his forehead, his eyes troubled. "I think we made a big mistake bringin' this woman here, Boss."

*The Last Mountain Man

Slaughter nodded. "Maybe so, but it can't be helped now. Remember, we're holed up in the best place on earth to defend against any attempt by Monte and his friends to rescue Mrs. Carson. There simply ain't no way they can get in here without us knowin' about it beforehand."

"So what are we gonna do about it?" Swede asked, his face knotted with worry.

Slaughter shrugged. "Nothing, for the moment. I'm sure that if we do no harm to Mrs. Carson, Monte will be more than glad to hand over the money he owes us and take his wife on home. If she tells him we've treated her all right, he won't have no kick comin'. After all, it IS our money he stole."

When Mary smiled, Slaughter whirled on her. "What are you grinnin' about?" he almost screamed.

"I'm afraid you've forgotten what kind of man my husband is, Mr. Slaughter. It doesn't matter whose money it is. Now that you've involved me in this matter, he will never rest until he sees you dead and buried. Even if you get the money in a trade for me, you will have to spend the rest of your lives looking back over your shoulders for Monte Carson. And someday, somehow, when you least expect it, he will be there and you will cease to exist."

13

Monte Carson was delighted to see Smoke and the others when they arrived at his camp with Muskrat Calhoon. He stepped from behind a tree and let the hammer down on his rifle when he saw them approaching the camp.

"Man, am I glad to see you," he said, leading them to his campfire where he had a pot of coffee brewing.

As the men stood next to the fire warming their hands, he filled coffee mugs from the pot and passed them out. The fall air was just above freezing, and in spite of their heavy coats the men were chilled to the bone from their long ride on horseback.

Muskrat lifted his nose to the air and took a deep whiff. "Smells like snow," he said.

Pearlie glanced at the cloudless sky, then back at the mountain man. "I don't see no clouds," he said. "How do you know it's gonna snow?"

Muskrat sipped at his coffee, making a loud slurping sound. "More'n fifty years in the high lonesome, pup," he answered with a stub-toothed grin. "After a while, ya git to know these things, or ya don't survive yer first blizzard."

Monte was impatient with the small talk. "Smoke, just what did you find out in Jackson Hole? Anything on Mary?"

"No, Monte, no one there mentioned seeing Slaughter or any of his men with a woman," Smoke said. "But that doesn't mean anything. Slaughter would hardly bring her to town where she might yell for help or attract attention he didn't want."

Louis lit a long cigar and between puffs added, "We did ascertain that he has between twenty and thirty men in the hole-in-the-wall with him, however."

Monte's face sobered. "Them's pretty long odds," he said.

"Is it yer woman he's taken, young man?" Muskrat asked, staring at Monte through narrowed eyes as if taking the lawman's measure.

Monte nodded. "Yes."

"Then, don't go gittin' discouraged 'bout odds nor nothin'. We got right on our side, an' ol' Muskrat gonna show you how to sneak up on the bastards and hit 'em 'fore they know what's happenin'."

Monte's expression lightened. "When can we get movin'?"

Muskrat glanced at the mountain peaks surrounding Monte's camp. "I'd say this here storm gonna blow for a day or two. Won't do no good to take off now an' git caught in it."

Smoke nodded his agreement. "Muskrat's right, Monte. It'll be better to use the time to plan just what we're going to do when we get in position around the hole-in-the-wall, after we see how the place is laid out and how many men he's got on sentry duty."

"Do you think we might fix some supper first?" Pearlie asked, a pained expression on his face. "I think a lot better when my belly's full."

Louis glanced at the cowboy. "I wasn't aware your belly ever got full, Pearlie, since I've never known you not to be hungry."

Cal walked to one of the packhorses and pulled a burlap bag off its back. He carried it to the fire and set it down. "Before we left, I had Aunt Bea fix us up a mess of fried chicken and biscuits and some tinned peaches an' stuff. It ought'a do to put the fire in Pearlie's innards out for a while."

After they'd eaten, they scattered their ground blankets near the fire and sat in a group, discussing how best to attack Slaughter's men without causing Mary to be harmed.

"Muskrat, have you ever been to the hole-in-the-wall?" Monte asked.

Muskrat pulled a pint bottle of whiskey from his coat and pulled the cork before replying. After fortifying himself with a drink that emptied half the bottle, he sleeved off his mouth with his arm.

"Yep. Passed through there on a couple'a occasions a few years back. Place is a deep valley betwixt several peaks. Got its own little stream runnin' through it, so it won't be possible to starve 'em out. They prob'ly got enough provisions to last 'em for weeks."

"If we positioned ourselves on the surrounding mountainsides, what kind of range are we talking about for shooting down into the camp?" Louis asked.

"Dependin' on jest where ya are, anywhere from a couple of hundred yards to a quarter mile or more," the mountain man answered.

Louis pulled a rifle from his pack. "I brought a new Remington Rolling Block rifle with me," he said, wiping the polished walnut stock with a rag. "It's a single-shot, but it's built strong and takes a .44-caliber rifle slug. I figure it's good for up to three hundred yards, shooting downhill."

Smoke nodded. "I have a Sharps .52-caliber, like yours, Muskrat. If I have to, I'm pretty accurate up to fifteen hundred yards."

Muskrat grinned. "Well, since my eyes've gotten a little dim with the passin' years, I can't hit nothin' past a thousand yards with my ol' Fifty," he said, referring to the Sharps Big Fifty.

Pearlie shook his head. "Our Winchesters aren't much good over two hundred yards, Smoke, so I guess Cal and me better be on the short side of the mountain."

Monte looked from one to the other of the men, a worried expression on his face. "Wait just a damned minute here. If we go firin' into those bastards, they're liable to shoot Mary."

Smoke held up his hand. "Hold on, Monte. We're not going to start anything until we know Mary's safe."

"And just how do you plan to do that, young feller?" Muskrat asked, tipping his bottle for another long drink.

Smoke glanced at him. "Why, I plan to go down into the robbers' camp and get her out before we let them know we're there."

Muskrat laughed. "You mean yo're gonna just traipse on down there an' tell this Slaughter feller, 'Excuse me, but I'm gonna take yer hostage on outta here'?"

The other men nodded. It was a fair question, and they all wanted to know how Smoke would be able to do it.

"Muskrat, you've been in this country for a lot of years. Do you remember how the Indians used to hunt buffalo, back when all they had were bows and arrows?"

The old man thought for a moment, then grinned. "Shore. They didn't have much range with those old bows, so they'd cover themselves up with an ol' buff'lo skin, smear some buff'lo crap on they skin, and creep right into the middle of the herd."

Smoke nodded. "That's how I plan to do it."

Pearlie looked over at Smoke, his face puzzled. "How's dressin' up like a buffalo gonna fool those men, Smoke?"

All the men around the campfire laughed, and Cal slapped Pearlie on the shoulder. "Sometimes, Pearlie, you're dummer'n dog shit."

Snow began to fall, just as Muskrat had said it would, so the men built up the fire and wrapped themselves in thick, woolen blankets, trying to get some sleep before tackling the long journey up into the mountain passes toward hole-in-the-wall.

"How long do you figger this snow's gonna last?" Pearlie asked Muskrat.

Muskrat held his hand out and looked at the size of the snowflakes, sniffed the air, and glanced up at the sky. "Oh, prob'ly till tomorrow afternoon. We should be able to be on our way by jest past our noonin'."

Just as Muskrat said it would, the snowfall began to lighten around noon the next day. The men finished off the last of Aunt Bea's fried chicken and packed the horses for their journey up into the mountains.

Muskrat stepped up on a paint pony such as Indians rode and said, "C'mon, horse, git movin'."

Cal spurred Silver up next to the mountain man. "How come you don't give your horse a name, Muskrat?"

Muskrat cut a piece of tobacco off a twist he pulled from his coat and stuck it in his mouth. As he began to chew, he glanced over at Cal. "Ya don't never want to give nuthin' a name ya might have to eat someday, young'un."

Cal's face showed his distaste. "You mean you'd eat your horse?"

Muskrat chuckled, "Hell, pup, I've seen times so bad up here in the winter I'd eat my partner, if'n I ever had one."

"I could never do that," Cal said with some feeling.

Smoke trotted Joker up next to the boy. "Don't never say never, Cal," he advised, a small smile curling his lips.

"That's right, boy," Muskrat added. "After twenty or thirty days of snow up to yer neck and nothin' to eat 'cept bark off'n trees, when yer stomach is pressin' agin yore backbone, you'd eat yer shoes if'n ya didn't need 'em to keep yer feet from freezin' an' fallin' off."

Cal finally smiled. He knew when he was being teased. "Now, I know Pearlie'd eat anything that didn't eat him first, but I just don't know as I could do it."

"Hell, I jest hope ya don't never need to find out jest what you'd do, pup," Muskrat said, and kicked his pony into a trot up the trail.

Smoke rode next to the mountain man, making sure he learned the way up the mountain, just in case he needed to lead the way back down.

He glanced around at the brilliant colors of fall foliage

on the mountain slopes. The sugar maples were in full bloom, their leaves bright yellow and red and orange, intermixed with aspen and birch whose leaves were a golden yellow and seemed to glow with an almost iridescent flame in the bright sunlight. The peaks in the background were already covered with a layer of snow, looking like pieces of chocolate cake covered with marshmallow icing.

"You ever get tired of the colors of fall, Muskrat?" Smoke asked.

The mountain man glanced around and smiled, his eyes twinkling in the sunlight. "Nope, cain't say as I do, Smoke. Some say it's what keeps mountain men so young inside, the glories we see ever'day up here in the high lonesome."

He shook his head and leaned to the side to spit a brown stream of tobacco juice at a lizard on the side of the trail, making it scamper to hide in a pile of fallen maple leaves.

"I cain't fer the life of me figger why anybody in they right mind would elect to live in a city or town when they got this beautiful country so close at hand."

Smoke grinned. He knew Muskrat was a kindred spirit. "Nor can I, Muskrat, nor can I."

As they followed the twisting, turning trail, which at times became no more than a path between copses of trees and outcroppings of granite boulders, Muskrat would point out to Smoke features to remember along the way . . . a boulder whose cracks and crevices looked like the face of a bear, a particularly old and weathered oak tree that looked to be over a hundred years old, a bubbling mountain stream they passed near a group of rocks that looked like a child's building blocks piled on top of one another.

The higher they climbed, the more the vegetation changed. Maple and birch trees became more and more scarce, and the evergreens such as fir and ponderosa pine began to become more prevalent.

"Are we going to have to climb above the tree line?" Smoke asked.

The old man shook his head. "Nope, but we're gonna come awfully close to it. Air's already gittin' so thin we gonna have to let the horses rest ever' little way or they'll founder."

"This is as good a time as any," Smoke said as they came again to a small mountain stream. "We can fill our canteens and make some coffee while the mounts rest up."

After they'd dismounted, Pearlie began to pile some rocks in a circle in the clearing to make a fire.

Muskrat walked over and shook his head. "Not out here in the open, little beaver. They'll be able to see the smoke."

He picked up the rocks and piled them at the base of a large fir tree, whose limbs stretched sixty feet in the air.

"Gather me up some deadfall, the drier the better," he said to Cal and Pearlie.

After they'd piled old branches and twigs under the tree, Muskrat used a small gathering of dead leaves and his flint to start a fire.

As the smoke curled upward, the branches of the tree dispersed and scattered it so it wasn't visible from more than a couple of hundred feet.

"This way won't nobody know we're here," Muskrat said as he watched Pearlie begin brewing a pot of coffee.

Then Muskrat pulled a package of jerked beef from his saddlebags and handed pieces out to the others. "Better git used to this," he said, "'cause it's gonna be a while 'fore we have a hot meal again."

"Are we gettin' close?" Monte asked, a hopeful expression on his face.

Muskrat pointed to a ridge about two hundred yards up the slope. "Jest over that ridge an' round a bend in the trail an' we'll be lookin' right down on the hole-in-the-wall."

"What about sentries?" Smoke asked.

Muskrat shook his head. "They all on the other side of the hole, on the downslope side. Nobody'll figger we gonna come at 'em from up the mountain."

* * *

It took them until just before dusk to make their way along the narrow mountain trails until they were in a position where they could look down into the hole-in-the-wall without being observed.

The place was laid out just as Muskrat had remembered. There were five crude log cabins arranged along the walls of the canyon, with a small mountain stream running through the center of the area. In addition, there were ten lean-to-type structures where most of the gunmen bedded down at night. The horses were kept in a large corral at the far end of the canyon, with saddles and blankets arrayed along the wooden fence surrounding the corral.

There was a large fire that seemed to be kept going day and night in the center of the cleared area between the cabins, where most of the men ate and gathered to drink and smoke and socialize during the evening hours.

The main trail into and out of the canyon could be seen winding down the mountainside, with several places where men in groups of two were stationed as sentries.

Muskrat pointed out vantage points around the canyon where Smoke and the others could place themselves so as to get clean shots down into the compound.

"All right, Smoke, I done my part, I got ya here. Now it's yore show from here on out," Muskrat said.

Smoke nodded. "The first thing we have to do is find out which cabin Slaughter has Mary in."

"Then what?" Louis asked as he knelt next to Smoke, cradling his Remington Rolling Block rifle in his arms.

"Then, we watch the sentries to find out what kind of schedule they're on. I'm going to need to intercept one after the sentries change, before he gets back to the camp, and take his place."

"You mean you're going down there amongst them *bandidos*?" Cal asked, his eyes wide.

"I don't see any other way to get Mary to safety before we attack," Smoke answered.

"Wait a minute, Smoke," Monte interjected. "Mary is my responsibility, so it should be me takes the chance on goin' down there."

Smoke shook his head. "You can't do it, Monte. Your wounds aren't healed enough to get the job done. I may have to carry Mary up part of the way on the steeper slopes. Your shoulder would never stand the strain."

"What can we do to help?" Pearlie asked.

"Keep your eyes peeled on those cabins. Mary will probably be in the one that Slaughter goes in and out of. He'll want her close by him in case of trouble."

In less than an hour, Louis saw two women make their way from the largest cabin toward the outhouse behind the building. One of the women was wide and short, the other tall and thin. They were accompanied by a cowboy, evidently along as a guard to make sure Mary didn't make a run for it.

Louis scrambled over to where Smoke was squatting, watching the sentries. "She's in the big cabin, Smoke, the one closest to the trail out of the canyon, on the north side."

Smoke raised his head up over the bushes he was behind and fixed the location in his mind. He gave a low whistle and the others came to squat next to him.

"All right men, get to your positions. As soon as I'm out of there and Mary is out of the line of fire, I'll give you a signal. When you hear it, let loose with everything you have to cover us until we get up here."

"What if they raise the alarm before your signal?" Monte asked.

Smoke smiled grimly. "Then don't wait. Pour as much lead and dynamite into the camp as fast as you can."

"How are you going to get her out of that cabin?" Louis asked. "Slaughter probably has his best men in there with him."

Smoke's teeth gleamed in the moonlight as he grinned. "Just keep a close eye on the cabin and you'll see," he said. Then he was up in a crouch and moving fast down the trail toward the nearest group of sentries.

14

It was almost dusk as Smoke made his way down a foot-path toward the sentries' post below. When he got close to the two men, he exited the trail and circled around until he was below the men, between their post and the camp in the canyon.

He stationed himself behind an outcropping of boulders and hunkered down to wait for the change of sentries, cupping his hands around his mouth and blowing on them, trying to keep them from stiffening up as the temperature dropped to near freezing.

He figured he wouldn't have long to wait. Most times sentries were changed about the time of the evening meal, so the men coming on duty could eat before taking up their post, and the men relieved of duty could have a hot meal waiting for them on their return.

Smoke climbed up on one of the boulders and peered over the cliff edge at the canyon below. He could see food being prepared at the large campfire in the center of the canyon. He was surprised at the number of women he saw working around the fire, but then realized these weren't the kind of men to deprive themselves of female company for any length of time. He supposed most of the women were prostitutes, as men like these weren't likely to be the marrying kind.

Before long his patience was rewarded with the sound of two men making their way up the trail toward the sentries on duty.

"Yo, Curly and Mike," one of the newcomers yelled. "Don't go shootin' us. It's just Joe and Charley comin' to relieve you."

"It's 'bout time," the larger of the two sentries called back. "Mike and me are 'bout to freeze our balls off up here."

The man who spoke, evidently named Curly, was just about Smoke's size. He was tall and broad through the shoulders, had a heavy whisker growth that made his jaws look blue in the fading light, and wore a bright red flannel shirt under a thick, black woolen coat and a dark hat pulled low over his forehead.

"He'll do," Smoke thought as he watched the four men talk for a moment before changing places.

"What's fer supper tonight?" Curly asked, rubbing his hands together and hunching his shoulders against the cold.

"What do ya think?" Joe answered. "Elk meat and beans and tortillas."

"Goddammit," Curly growled. "Don't those whores know how to cook anythin' else?"

Joe laughed. "They wasn't brought up here 'cause of their skills with a skillet, Curly."

"Yeah," Mike said. "Leastways they know how to keep a body warm at night."

"Yeah, but I'll bet that little lady the boss has in his cabin is a sight better at it than those whores," Curly said, his teeth showing in a wide grin.

Joe nodded. "Yeah, it's a shame the boss don't share her around some."

Smoke felt his mouth go dry and his heart hammer at the way the men were talking about Mary Carson. His hands clenched as his fury mounted. There would be no mercy shown this night for these bastards, he thought.

"Well, you boys keep your powder dry and try to keep

your fingers from freezin' off tonight," Mike said as he and Curly started down the trail, their hands in their coat pockets as they leaned into the frigid wind blowing down the mountain slopes.

Knowing he dared not make a sound, Smoke pulled his Bowie knife from its scabbard on the back of his belt and stood up, moving slowly so his knees wouldn't creak and give his position away.

He pulled his left-hand Colt and held it in one hand and the knife in the other. As the two men passed him, he stepped out and brought the Colt down hard on the back of Curly's head. When he collapsed with a grunt and Mike turned around, his eyes wide, Smoke swung the knife in an upward motion, letting the point of the blade enter his chest just below the left rib cage, the blade continuing up to pierce Mike's heart. He was dead before he hit the ground.

Smoke pulled both bodies off the trail and into the thick brush up the slope a ways. Working fast, he stripped Curly's coat, hat, and shirt off and laid them on the ground. After a moment, Curly began to groan and move his arms and legs.

"Sorry about this, Curly," Smoke said, "but you shouldn't talk in such a manner about a lady like Mrs. Carson."

In a quick movement, Smoke drew the knife across Curly's throat and rolled him over, so the spurting blood wouldn't get his clothes dirty.

As fast as he could, Smoke put on Curly's shirt, coat, and hat, then bent and took a handful of dirt and smeared it on his cheeks and jaws, hoping in the darkness it would look like the man's heavy whisker growth.

Satisfied the bodies couldn't be seen from the trail, Smoke walked down the side of the mountain toward the canyon below, whistling a low tune through lips growing stiff with the cold.

When he reached the canyon floor, he stayed in shadows away from the campfire until most of the other bandits had finished their meal, grabbed their women, and retired to the other cabins or their sleeping bags. He eased up to the pot of meat and beans and piled some on a tin plate, poured himself a cup of coffee, and walked off to the side, as near to Slaughter's cabin as he could get and still not arouse suspicion.

He sat on the ground with his back to a fir tree and ate and drank his coffee, trying to keep his muscles from stiffening up while he waited for his chance to make a move.

A drunken cowboy with one arm around a thickset woman, and a whiskey bottle in the other hand, walked by.

"Howdy, Curly," the man mumbled, glancing at Smoke, who sat with his head lowered as if he were concentrating on his food.

"Ummm," Smoke mumbled back as if his mouth were full of food.

"Cold enough for ya?" the man asked, squeezing his woman closer as he ambled by.

"Uh-huh," Smoke answered without looking up, hoping the man was too drunk to notice it wasn't Curly he was talking to.

After the pair passed, Smoke glanced up and saw the door to Slaughter's cabin open. A tall woman walked out and, followed by a man, proceeded toward the outhouse behind the cabin.

Smoke set his plate and cup on the ground and got to his feet, making his way around behind the outhouse.

The man was leaning away from the wind, trying to light a cigarette, when Smoke approached him.

"Got a light?" Smoke asked, making his voice low and guttural.

"Shore, Curly," the man answered, and held out the match.

When the light hit Smoke's face, the man's eyes widened. "Say, you ain't Curly . . ."

Before he could sound an alarm, Smoke's Bowie knife flashed, impaling the man's chest on the twelve-inch blade.

Smoke threw his arms around him and held him up as he died, then eased the body to the ground and pulled it behind the outhouse where it wouldn't easily be seen.

After a moment, the door opened and Mary stepped out, arranging her long dress.

Smoke stepped up to her. "Mary," he whispered, "it's Smoke."

"Oh!" she said, her hand flying to her mouth.

"Come on, we've got to make tracks before they miss you," he said, his voice harsh with urgency.

She nodded and followed him as he moved back into deep shadows near the wall of the canyon. He took her arm and walked as rapidly as he could toward a small footpath he'd seen near the outhouse. It wasn't much more than a clear area running up the slope between fir and pine trees, and was so steep at times that he had to almost carry her up the wall.

They had made it almost a hundred yards up the canyon wall before the door to the cabin opened and a large, broad-shouldered man appeared. He had a cigar in his mouth and stood on the small porch of the cabin for a moment, looking back toward the outhouse.

He must have sensed something was wrong when he didn't see the guard he'd sent with Mary, for he suddenly drew his pistol and ran toward the privy.

"Jack, where are you, Jack?" he hollered.

Smoke and Mary stopped and watched as he suddenly stiffened when he found Jack's body crumpled on the dirt behind the small structure.

He jerked the outhouse door open, then turned around and held his pistol in the air.

Before he could fire, Smoke cupped his hands around his mouth and screamed like a mountain lion, a harsh and guttural sound that would make the hairs on the back of a man's neck stand up.

Suddenly the night lit up with explosions of gunfire from all sides of the canyon walls. The first to fall were the sentries guarding the mountain passes into and out of the canyon.

Without waiting to see what happened next, Smoke

took Mary's arm and propelled her up the slope as fast as they could go.

Behind and below them, the outlaws' camp erupted in a nightmare of dynamite explosions, gunshots, and screams of men hit and dying.

Bandits rushed out of cabins and sleeping bags like ants from a disturbed mound. They ran into the center of the camp, pointed their pistols and rifles at the walls surrounding them, and fired blindly, shooting at the night as if they could somehow stop the death raining down on them.

A stick of dynamite landed square in the center of the main campfire, exploding and blowing burning logs and branches in all directions. Two of the smaller cabins caught fire, sending men and women screaming out into the darkness, their hair and clothes in flames.

Slaughter did his best to rally his men, shouting orders at them, trying to be heard over the explosions of gunfire and dynamite.

"Goddammit, get under cover," he screamed, crouching and firing upward at the barrel-flashes above with his pistol.

Finally, evidently figuring his pistol hadn't the range to reach their attackers, he ducked back into his cabin and reappeared moments later with a rifle, accompanied by Whitey and Swede, who also had long guns in their arms.

Meanwhile, men outlined by the light of the burning cabins and other fires started by dynamite were being cut down where they stood. Bodies littered the canyon floor, screams of pain and fear echoed through the night, punctuated by the booming explosions of high-powered rifles from above.

Before long, the outlaws learned to stay hidden, crawling behind fir and pine trees on their bellies, crouching next to dead bodies, and some even made their way to the corral trying to hide among their mounts to escape the withering fire from above.

The shooting slowed as targets became scarce.

Smoke and Mary eventually made it to the cliff tops

overlooking the valley below. She stepped up behind Monte, who was crouched behind a boulder pouring shot after shot into the men below.

"Monte," she said quietly.

He dropped his rifle and rose to throw his arms around her, his eyes finding Smoke and glistening in gratitude.

"We don't have a lot of time for a reunion," Smoke said, his voice urgent.

"We won't be able to keep them pinned down for long, so I want you and Mary to get on your horses and get the hell away from here," he added. "Find Muskrat and have him lead you down the mountain the fastest way. Get to Jackson Hole and take the first train out of town."

"What if it's not heading for Colorado?" Monte asked.

Smoke shook his head. "I don't care where it's going, just get her out of here."

As he led Mary toward the horses, Monte said, "What about you and the others?"

"Slaughter doesn't know who attacked him and his gang," Smoke said. "We'll give it another hour or two, then head back to Jackson Hole. We'll get back in the rooming house and act as if we don't know anything about the attack. After a few days, we'll make our way back to Big Rock."

"What do you think Slaughter's gonna do?" Monte asked as he saddled one of the packhorses for Mary.

Smoke shrugged. "If he's smart, he'll cut his losses and figure this was a bad idea."

"And if he's not?"

"Then he'll come looking for us at Big Rock, and we'll be ready for him."

Monte helped Mary up into the saddle, then swung up on his mount.

Smoke pointed off to the left. "Muskrat's over there. Find him and get moving."

Monte leaned down and stuck out his hand. As Smoke took it, he said, "Thanks, Smoke."

Smoke glanced at Mary, whose eyes were moist with gratitude.

"Don't mention it, partner. Just get Mary back to Big Rock. My advice is to take her to Sugarloaf and tell Sally we'll be back in a week or two."

Monte nodded and spurred his horse toward where Muskrat's big Sharps could be heard sending .50-caliber slugs toward the outlaws' camp.

Smoke picked up his Sharps, eared back the hammer, and leaned over a boulder, searching for someone to kill.

15

Close to midnight, Smoke and his friends fired their final shots at the outlaw camp and jumped on their horses to ride back to Jackson Hole. They left behind them a camp in ruins, with most of the cabins destroyed or severely damaged, the corral torn asunder and the horses scattered and running wild. At least ten men lay dead and many more were wounded.

As they rode back down the mountain, Smoke watching carefully for the landmarks Muskrat had pointed out to him, Louis pulled his bronc up next to Joker.

"You think there's any chance we killed Slaughter and put an end to this entire sorry episode?"

Smoke shook his head. "In all my years out here, Louis, I've trailed lots of men and had some on my trail, and I've never had a problem solved that easily. I think we'd better figure on Slaughter surviving our assault."

"What do you think he's going to do?"

"Well, first off it's going to take him a while to sort out the mess we left back there, at least a day or so. Then, he's going to get to thinking that the only place an attack like that could have come from would be Jackson Hole. I think he's going to come to town loaded for bear, looking for anyone who's new to town or doesn't fit in. He'll want revenge, and I don't think he'll be particularly selective on who he takes his anger out on."

"Perhaps we should pack our gear and get on the trail toward home before he comes looking."

"We can't. We've got to stay here long enough to give Monte and Mary time to get away clean. If we can stall him for a few days, there won't be any way he can catch up to them before they manage to get back to Big Rock."

"And if he and his gang comes to Big Rock looking to get even?"

"I'm going to send Sally a wire tomorrow morning. Monte and Mary have lots of friends back home. I'll tell her to organize the town and to be ready. We may be in for a monumental fight once he rebuilds his gang."

"Do you really think he'll go to all that trouble for a mere fifty thousand dollars?"

Smoke shook his head. "It's gone way beyond the money now, Louis. Slaughter's been dealt a severe defeat, and in his own backyard. It's his reputation he's going to be concerned with now. If word gets around that some country sheriff took Big Jim Slaughter on and kicked his ass, Slaughter won't be able to move without looking back over his shoulder all the time to see if someone else thinks they can do the same thing."

Just as they came down off the mountain slope and pulled onto the main trail headed toward Jackson Hole, a light snowfall began. Smoke and the others pulled their coats tight around them, settled hats low to keep the snow out of their eyes, and spurred their mounts toward town.

For the next two days, Smoke and Louis and Cal and Pearlie were careful to take their meals apart and not to be seen talking to each other. Louis continued to frequent the gaming halls, giving expensive lessons to the cowboys about the dangers of playing poker with an expert. Smoke spent most of his time in various saloons, hanging around and listening to idle talk. Cal and Pearlie made it a point to let everyone think they were miners, working a claim in the nearby mountains, so if Mr. Schultz told anyone they'd bought some dynamite and gunpowder, there wouldn't be any suspicions raised.

Sheriff Walter Pike walked up and stood next to Smoke at the Cattleman's Saloon bar. "Howdy, Mr. West."

Smoke took a drink of his beer before replying. "Hello, Sheriff Pike."

"Well, I've gone through all of my circulars and can't seem to find any recent paper on you, Johnny."

Smoke shrugged, as if it were no concern to him. "I told you, Sheriff. I'm just a law-abiding citizen hanging around until I can find some work."

Pike nodded, his experienced eyes taking in the way Smoke moved and handled himself. "Uh-huh, sure you are."

"What's that supposed to mean, Sheriff?"

"I've seen a lot of men come through here, West, and I've gotten to be a pretty good judge of character. You don't fit in with the rest of the pond scum in this town."

Smoke raised his eyebrows. "Oh?"

"No. Oh, I can see you're handy with a gun, that's evident. But you don't go around trying to impress everyone with how mean and tough you are, even though it's plain you could take just about anyone else in town with those six-killers on your hips."

"Sheriff, I make my living with these pistols. I'm not one to use them unless there's a profit in it for me. That's all."

Pike smiled. "I'm not so sure that's all, Johnny. You don't fit in, so I'm gonna be watchin' you to see just what your game is. All right?"

Smoke shrugged. "Sure, Sheriff. It's your town, you can do anything you want."

Pike tipped his hat. "See you around, Johnny."

"Be seeing you, Sheriff."

The next day, Smoke was having lunch in Aunt Bea's dining room when he glanced out of the window and saw a group of four men talking to Sheriff Pike on the board-walk in front of the Cattleman's Saloon. After a moment of conversation, the sheriff inclined his head toward Aunt Bea's Boardinghouse and said a few words. The four men looked over, nodded, and began to cross the street toward Bea's place.

Smoke took a deep breath. Unless he missed his guess, it was starting. Across the room Louis was at a table by himself, and Cal and Pearlie were sharing another table. Smoke caught their eyes and nodded slightly, cutting his eyes toward the dining room door. His friends nodded back, and he could see each of them reach down and take the hammer-thongs off their pistols. Louis leaned back and straightened his right leg, allowing him easy access to his pistol.

Smoke pushed his plate away, built himself a cigarette, and concentrated on his coffee cup when the four men entered the room.

A large, broad-shouldered man was the leader, and behind him was a tall, heavyset blond man, a thin, wiry albino, and a young kid in his teens wearing a black vest and twin pearl-handled Colts on his hips.

After standing in the doorway for a moment, surveying the customers, the tall man noticed Smoke and began to walk toward him, his friends fanning out behind him.

He stopped at Smoke's table. "Howdy, mister. Would you be Johnny West?"

Smoke slowly looked up. He took a deep drag of his cigarette and let smoke trail from his nostrils as he replied. "Maybe. Who wants to know?"

"I'm Big Jim Slaughter."

"So?"

The young kid's hand moved next to the butt of his pistol and his face clouded with anger. "So, watch your mouth, cowboy!" he snarled.

Smoke let his unconcerned gaze drift over to the young man. "I ain't no cowboy, sonny boy an' if your hand twitches again, I'll kill you where you stand," he said in a low, dangerous voice.

Slaughter put his hand on the Durango Kid's arm. "Hold on, Mr. West, there isn't any need for hostilities. May we join you?"

Smoke shrugged. "It's a free country."

After getting extra chairs from a nearby table, the four men sat down across from Smoke.

Slaughter got right to the point. "I heard you were asking around about me last week," he said, staring at Smoke to see his reaction.

"That's right. I was asking about a lot of people, trying to see if anyone was hiring guns."

"And were they?"

"Nope. For a supposedly wide-open town, it's been quiet as a church around here."

Slaughter leaned back in his chair. "I thought maybe someone had hired you to do a little job out at the hole-in-the-wall the other night."

"Oh?"

"Yeah. My men and I were attacked out there night before last."

Smoke let his lips curl in a nasty smile. "Well, then, it couldn't have been me done the job."

"Why not?" the albino interjected.

"'Cause if I'd hired out to attack you, Slaughter, you'd all be dead now, not sittin' here askin' me fool questions."

The Durango Kid's face flushed with anger and he dropped his hand to his side, saying, "Why, you . . ."

In the wink of an eye, Smoke's pistol was in his hand and he slapped the barrel backhanded across the kid's face, knocking him backward out of his chair. He landed spread-eagled on his back with his nose bent to the side and a deep gash running across his cheek, leaking blood.

"Goddamn!" Swede said. "I never even saw him draw!"

As the kid shook his head and started to get up, Smoke eared back the hammer and pointed the barrel at the kid's face. "You sure you want some more of this, sonny boy?" he growled.

The kid's eyes widened and his face paled, fear-sweat breaking out on his forehead. "Uh . . . no . . ."

Before he could answer, Aunt Bea appeared at the table, a long-barreled shotgun cradled in her arms. "We aren't gonna have any trouble in here, are we, boys?" she asked.

"No, ma'am," Slaughter replied, though his eyes remained fixed on Smoke. "Kid, get up and wait for us over at the Cattleman's," he said.

"But . . . but Mr. Slaughter," the kid whined.

Slaughter turned to stare at him, his face showing he would brook no argument. "I said go!"

"Yes, sir," the kid replied, his face flaming as blood spilled down onto his fancy black vest and shirt.

He got to his feet and walked rapidly out of the room without looking back.

Aunt Bea grunted. "If you men are going to stay here, you're gonna eat, not fight."

Slaughter smiled up at her. "Would you bring us three of the house specials, please, and some coffee?"

After she left, Slaughter addressed Smoke. "I thought the Durango Kid was supposed to be fast."

Smoke smiled. "Evidently not fast enough. The Kid ought'a change professions, 'fore he gets killed tryin' to be something he's not."

"You interest me, Mr. West. I might have a place for you in my organization."

"I don't come cheap," Smoke replied, as if he might be interested.

"I'll bet you don't," Slaughter said. "Would you be willing to travel?"

"Depends," Smoke said. "How far, an' what's the pay?"

"Me and my men are going to take a little trip over to Colorado in a few days. The pay's a hundred a month against a cut of what we make when we get there."

Smoke grinned. "A hundred a month, huh? That what you're paying these men?"

Slaughter nodded. "Yeah."

"Then I'm gonna cost you a hundred and a half," Smoke said.

"What?" Slaughter asked.

"And you're lucky I don't ask for two hundred, since I'm at least twice as good as what you got working for you now."

Slaughter laughed, while Swede and Whitey scowled. "All right, Mr. West. If we decide to use you, you'll get a hundred and fifty a month."

Smoke nodded. "Sounds fair."

"Good. I'll let you know in a day or so."

Smoke dropped his cigarette butt in his coffee and stood up. "You know where to find me."

Slaughter nodded. "That I do, Mr. West, that I do."

16

After Smoke left the room, Whitey glanced at the door to make sure he was gone, then turned back to Slaughter. "What'a you think, Boss?"

Slaughter rubbed the beard stubble on his face, his eyes contemplative. "I don't know yet. Mr. West could'a been one. He's certainly good enough with a six-shooter."

"Why didn't you let the Kid take him on, Jim?" Swede asked.

"We lost over half our men the other night, Swede, an' another third're so scared they ain't gonna be worth spit. West would've killed the Kid as easily as swattin' a fly."

"You think he's that good?"

Slaughter looked at him. "Did you see him draw? He has the fastest hands I've ever seen. He could snatch a double eagle off a snake's head and give him change 'fore he could strike."

"He don't look all that bad to me," Whitey said, his lips curled in a sneer.

Slaughter laughed. "Then you weren't lookin' at the same man I was."

As they ate, the three men looked around at the other customers in the dining room.

"See any other likely suspects?" Swede asked.

Slaughter nodded. "Those two over there in the corner impress me as being right sure of themselves."

Swede glanced over his shoulder at the table containing Cal and Pearlie. "You mean those two boys?"

"They're not exactly boys, Swede," Slaughter said. "Oh, I'll grant you they're young, but look at their eyes. They've seen plenty of action, an' the way they wear their guns shows they ain't no pilgrims."

"You want I should go brace 'em?" Whitey asked.

Slaughter thought for a moment, then shook his head. "No. Let's finish our food, then we'll see what happens."

Cal could see Slaughter and his men watching them out of the corner of his eyes.

"Pearlie," he said, "I think they're talkin' 'bout us."

Pearlie paused a moment from shoveling pancakes into his mouth to glance up at Cal. "I don't doubt it, Cal. I figger they gonna be lookin' at most ever'body in town for the next day or so, just like Smoke said. They got to know the men who blasted 'em came from here, so it's only natural to try an' figger out who it was."

"What're we gonna do if'n they come over here askin' a lot of questions?"

Pearlie gave a small shrug. "Just act like Smoke tole us. We're miners, pure an' simple. Don't wanna have no truck with gunfighters an' such."

Sure enough, when Slaughter and his men finished their breakfast, they got up from their table and ambled over to stand in front of Cal and Pearlie.

Slaughter stood there, looking down until the two men glanced up at him.

"Howdy, boys," he said.

Pearlie nodded, his mouth bulging with eggs and pancakes.

Cal just looked and didn't answer.

"I was wondering if you men were interested in hiring on with me and my men," Slaughter said.

"Doin' what?" Pearlie asked after he washed his food down with a slug of coffee.

Slaughter pointed to the pistol on Pearlie's hip. "Usin' those six-killers on your hip."

Pearlie looked at Cal and grinned. "See, Cal? The man thinks we're gun hawks."

He glanced back up at Slaughter and the two hard-looking men standing with him. "Thanks for the offer, mister, but my brother an' me is miners. We don't hire our guns out."

"Miners, huh?" Slaughter asked. "Doin' any good?"

Pearlie let his face get a suspicious look on it. "Some days're better'n others. Why?"

"Oh, no reason. Just wonderin'."

"Well, we're makin' enough to keep us in beans an' bacon, an' that's all anybody needs to know."

"You two must be the pair that bought some dynamite from Schultz's store the other day."

Pearlie leaned back and wiped his mouth with his napkin. "You been askin' round 'bout us?"

"Well, let's just say we're interested in anybody who bought dynamite."

"Yeah, we bought some. You ever tried to dig through twenty feet of granite, mister?"

"Schultz said these two men also bought a lot of cartridges at the same time."

Pearlie nodded. "Lot of men try to take other people's gold, 'stead of diggin' it out themselves. You got any more fool questions?"

Whitey stepped forward, his hand near his pistol. "I'd watch your mouth, miner man, 'fore somebody shuts it for you."

Pearlie scooted his chair back and let his hand rest on his thigh next to his holster. "You're welcome to try, mister, any time you think you're ready."

Slaughter raised his eyebrows. Not many men stood up to someone as mean-looking as Whitey.

"You're pretty tough for a miner," Slaughter said.

"I've mined in Tombstone, Deadwood, an' lots of other places filled with men who thought they were fast with a gun," Pearlie answered. "I ain't particularly fast, but I generally hit what I aim at an' I'm still alive, so call your dog off, mister, or somebody's gonna get a gut full of lead."

Slaughter grinned, shaking his head at Whitey. "You sure you don't want a job? I could use some men who ain't afraid to use their guns."

Pearlie shook his head. "No, I told you, we're minin' right now." He hesitated a moment. "But you might ask again after the snow fills the passes. If we don't dig out enough to get us through the winter, we might just take you up on your offer."

Slaughter smiled. "I'm afraid that'll be too late." He tipped his hat. "Good luck to you in your hunt for gold," he said, and turned to walk out the door.

"Jimminy," Cal said after they'd left. "I thought for a minute there that albino was gonna draw on you, Pearlie."

Pearlie nodded. "So did I. He's lucky he didn't, or he'd be headed for boot hill by now."

Pearlie rotated his head to loosen neck muscles made tight by the confrontation. Then he looked around the room. "Now where is Aunt Bea? I'm ready for some more pancakes an' coffee."

Louis, who'd been watching the scene with Slaughter and Pearlie, relaxed as the men left. He reached down and eased the hammer-thong back on his Colt, grinning when he saw Pearlie order more food. *Unbelievable how much chow that cowboy can consume,* he thought. *I do believe someday when the Grim Reaper comes for Pearlie, he's going to ask the man with the sickle what kind of food they serve up in heaven, and if he doesn't like the answer, he'll probably ask to be taken to the other place.*

17

After Smoke left Aunt Bea's dining room, he ambled over to the Cattleman's Saloon. He figured Slaughter and his men would show up there sooner or later, and he wanted to know what they had planned. He knew Slaughter was short of men and the Cattleman's was the logical place for him to go and try to hire new men for his mission of revenge.

When he entered the batwings, he stood for a moment to let his eyes adjust to the gloom. He let his gaze roam the room, and it didn't take him long to see the Durango Kid sitting at a table with some other men, probably also on the payroll of Big Jim Slaughter. The Kid'd evidently stopped off at the doc's office, since he had a piece of white plaster stuck to his cheek where Smoke'd slashed it with his pistol. Most of the blood had been cleaned off his vest and shirt, too.

When Smoke walked to the bar, the Kid stopped whatever he was saying and stared at Smoke with hard eyes, as if he might scare him with the ferocity of his look.

Smoke grinned and nonchalantly tipped his hat at the Kid as he sidled up to the bar. He stood so he could see the men in the room, not wanting to present his back to anyone who might want to put a bullet in it.

"What'll ya have?" the barkeep asked as he wiped down the bar with a dirty rag.

"Shot of whiskey with a beer chaser," Smoke said. He rarely drank whiskey and never this early in the day, but he had an image to project and had to stay in character.

As Smoke downed the whiskey and followed it with a drink of beer, the Kid leaned over and said something in a low voice to the men at the table with him, causing them to stare at Smoke with hate-filled eyes.

He could see the Kid's face getting redder by the minute, and knew it wouldn't be long before the young man who fancied himself a gun hawk would try his hand. There was just no way he could allow Smoke to pistol-whip him and keep his self-image as a gun slick intact.

Jim Slaughter and the albino and Swede walked through the batwings, striding to the center of the room as if they owned the place.

Slaughter nodded at Smoke, then turned to face the many tables where men were sitting and drinking their breakfast. He held up his hands for attention.

"Gentlemen, my name is Jim Slaughter an' I'm hirin' men who aren't afraid of usin' their guns. If anybody's interested, see me at my table and I'll tell you what the job is and what it pays."

When he was finished speaking, he walked over to a table in the corner where two men were sitting. He stood there, looking down at them for a moment until they hurriedly got to their feet and went to another table across the room. Slaughter and Whitey and Swede took their seats, and Slaughter motioned for the bartender to bring him a bottle of whiskey and some glasses.

While he was filling the glasses, the Kid got to his feet and hurried over to his boss's table. He stood there, talking animatedly for a moment, looking over his shoulder at Smoke as he spoke.

Slaughter got a pained look on his face and shook his head. The Kid kept talking, gesturing wildly with his arms. Finally, Slaughter lost his patience and pointed toward the table where the Kid had been sitting, as if he were sending an unruly child to bed without his supper.

The Kid hung his head and slouched back to his table, glaring at Smoke from under the brim of his hat.

In the next fifteen minutes, over twenty cowboys approached Slaughter's table to ask about the job he was offering. Smoke had no way of knowing how many took the outlaw up on his offer, but he supposed with the wages Slaughter was willing to pay, quite a few of them did. He briefly wondered where Slaughter was getting that kind of money, because the fifty thousand he expected to get from Monte wouldn't go far if split among twenty or thirty men.

After the last of the men in the saloon had finished talking with Slaughter, he got to his feet and began to walk toward Smoke, a half grin on his face.

Over his shoulder, Smoke saw the Durango Kid get to his feet, his face a mask of hate and humiliation. When Slaughter was no more than ten feet from Smoke, the Kid made his move, crouching and going for his pistol. As he aimed it at the back of Slaughter's head, Smoke drew in one lightning-fast motion and fired, his bullet passing only inches from Slaughter's ear.

Slaughter whirled and ducked, reaching for his own pistol just as Smoke's slug hit the Kid at the base of his throat, blowing out the back of his neck and almost severing his head from his body. The Kid was catapulted back onto his table, and one of the men there also grabbed iron.

Smoke's second shot took the Kid's friend in the forehead, blowing brains and blood and hair all across the room.

Slaughter came out of his crouch pointing his gun toward Smoke, until Whitey yelled, "Boss, no! He wasn't shootin' at you!"

Slaughter and Smoke stood there for a moment, pistols pointed at each other, until Smoke's lips curled in a grin. "You want to make it three, Slaughter?" he growled.

Slaughter glanced back over his shoulder at the bodies

sprawled spread-eagled on the table and floor. "What happened?" he asked, still holding his gun at waist level.

Smoke shrugged. "Evidently the Kid didn't take kindly to you dressing him down in front of the other men. Looked to me like he was going to plug you in the back."

Whitey and Swede rushed up to stand next to Slaughter. "He's right, Boss," Swede said. "The Kid already had his pistol out and was aimin' at the back of your head."

Slaughter relaxed and holstered his Colt. "And why didn't you do something about it?" he asked his two henchmen, scorn on his face. "Isn't coverin' my back what I pay you for?"

Whitey ducked his head, his eyes unable to meet Slaughter's. "It all happened so fast, Jim. How'd we know the Kid was gonna do somethin' crazy like that?"

Slaughter gave Smoke an appraising glance. "You mean the Kid had his gun out and pointed at me and West was able to draw and fire before he could pull the trigger?"

Swede nodded, his eyes on Smoke. "That's right, Boss. I ain't never seen nothin' like it. One second the Kid was set to shoot you in the back, and the next West's gun was in his hand blowin' the Kid to hell and back."

As they talked, Smoke broke open the loading gate on his Colt and punched out his empties, letting them fall on the floor. He reloaded his pistol and stuck it in his holster.

Slaughter walked up and stuck out his hand. "I guess I owe you my thanks, West," he said with a smile.

Smoke took his hand. "Don't take it personal, Slaughter. I couldn't care less if one of your men shoots you. It's just that I can't abide a back shooter."

Slaughter's eyes narrowed, then he smiled again. "Well, that's still one I owe you."

Smoke shrugged and turned back to his drink on the bar.

Slaughter leaned on the bar next to him and ordered a whiskey. When he picked up his glass, Smoke noticed his hand had a fine tremor. Evidently, the outlaw didn't like having someone try to gun him down.

After he finished his drink, Slaughter said, "I've decided to hire you on, West. I have need of someone who's as good with a gun as you are."

Smoke leaned back, sipping his beer, and stared at Slaughter. "Just where are you planning on going in Colorado?" he asked.

"A little town named Big Rock. There's a man there owes me fifty thousand dollars an' I aim to collect every dollar of it."

Smoke raised his eyebrows. "Big Rock, Colorado?"

"Yeah."

Smoke pursed his lips. "The gent owes you this money wouldn't happen to be Smoke Jensen, would it?"

Slaughter shook his head. "No, but I hear Jensen has thrown in with the man that I'm goin' after."

Smoke shook his head. "Then I'm not interested."

Whitey, who was standing next to his boss, leaned toward Smoke. "You mean you're afraid of that old gunman?"

Smoke smiled. "You might say that. I had a run-in with Jensen a few years back. I made the mistake of drawing down on him."

Slaughter smiled. "Well, what of it? I see you're still alive."

"Only 'cause Jensen was so fast he had the drop on me 'fore I cleared leather. He didn't need to shoot me 'cause I never got my gun out of my holster."

Swede looked as if he couldn't believe it. "That can't be! I ain't never seen nobody as fast as you are, West."

Smoke shrugged. "Jensen is. And you don't have enough money to cause me to go up against him a second time."

Whitey's face burned red. "Then you're tellin' us you're yellow?"

Smoke glanced at the albino, making his face suddenly pale. "There's a difference between being yellow and knowing when someone's faster'n you are. I feel a man ought'a know his limitations if he's gonna make his living with a gun."

Whitey opened his mouth to speak, but Smoke interrupted him. "Just like you should know yours, sonny. You say one more word, an' Slaughter here's gonna have to hire someone to replace you, 'cause you're gonna have an extra hole in your head."

Whitey's mouth clamped shut with an audible snap.

Slaughter nodded. "All right, West. But what you say don't change my mind. I still aim to get my money."

Smoke shrugged. "Well, good luck to you, Mr. Slaughter. But I'd advise you to take plenty of shovels with you to Colorado, 'cause if you go up against Smoke Jensen you're gonna have a lot of graves to dig."

Slaughter grinned. "I guess that won't be all bad. It just means there'll be fewer men to split the money with after I've put Jensen and his friends in the ground."

18

After supper that night, Smoke met with his friends in his room to plan their next move. They'd just settled down when a knock came at the door.

Four pistols were drawn and aimed as Smoke stepped to the door. "Who is it?" he called, standing to the side so a bullet fired through the wood wouldn't hit him.

"It's me, Muskrat Calhoon."

Smoke pulled the door open and stepped back to let the mountain man enter. Muskrat took off his coonskin hat and grinned. "Howdy, boys."

Smoke peered out in the corridor to make sure no one had followed the old man up the stairs, then closed and locked the door.

After everyone told Muskrat hello, he glanced around the room. "What kind'a meetin' is this? I don't see no nectar around."

Louis smiled, pulled a bottle of whiskey from the bureau drawer, and flipped it to the mountaineer.

Muskrat pulled the cork and took a deep swig. "Ah, that'll git the chill of winter outta my bones," he groaned with pleasure.

Smoke sat on the bed and leaned back against the headboard, motioning for Muskrat to take his chair.

"What can we do for you, Muskrat? I thought you were headed up into the high lonesome for your wintering."

As the old man took his seat, Pearlie moved quietly to the window and opened it a crack, hoping the night breeze would remove some of the smell.

"Well," Muskrat said, taking another sip of whiskey and smacking his lips, "I was on my way up the mountain when I got to thinkin' 'bout our little fracas the other night." He glanced around at the men watching him. "I ain't had so much fun since back in '42 when Preacher and Bear Tooth an' me blowed hell outta some Injuns down in Arizona."

His eyes opened wide. "I plumb forgot how good it feels to put some lead in folks that sorely need it. Hell," he continued, "it made me feel like I'se a young buck again 'stead of an old fart waitin' round to die."

Smoke nodded. "I know the feeling, Muskrat. Combat surely does get the juices flowing."

Muskrat shook his head. "No, Smoke, 'twas more'n that. It was that I'se doin' somethin' useful agin."

Louis spoke up. "Well, we certainly couldn't've done it without your help, Muskrat. We never could have found our way up to the hole-in-the-wall without your showing us the way."

Muskrat nodded. "That's why I decided to circle around and take me 'nother look at the hole-in-the-wall."

Smoke leaned forward, suddenly interested in what the mountain man had seen. After the battle the other night, they'd left so quickly they hadn't had time to fully assess the damage they'd done.

"What'd you see, Muskrat?"

"The place was a mess. All of the cabins was pret' near destroyed. A couple'a walls was still standin', but they ain't in no shape to keep nobody warm in the winter."

"What about the outlaws?" Pearlie asked.

"They had a pile of bodies all stacked up over near one corner of the valley, an' some of the men were diggin' a big hole." He shrugged. "I guess they gonna pile 'em all in there together 'fore they start to stink."

"How many men were left?" Smoke asked.

"I counted ten or twelve that was motivatin' on they own, an' four or five that was laid out on the ground blankets with bandages an' such like they was wounded pretty bad."

Smoke looked at the others. "Slaughter had four men with him in town today, and it looked like he managed to hire another fifteen or twenty."

"That gives him close to thirty hard cases to take with him to Colorado when he goes after Monte," Louis said, a worried look on his face.

"I noticed he had one of his men hangin' around the telegraph office," Cal said. "I guess he don't want nobody to send a wire warnin' Monte he's comin'."

"He knows at least some of the men who attacked his camp are still around," Smoke said, a thoughtful look on his face.

"How are we gonna get word to Miss Sally about his plans?" Pearlie asked.

Smoke shook his head. "I don't think we need to worry about that. Monte knows what kind of man we're up against. He'll be ready for whatever Slaughter decides to do."

"Do you think we ought to hightail it to Colorado and be waiting there for him when he shows up?" Louis asked Smoke.

Smoke shook his head. "No. I think a much better plan will be to see if we can slow him down along the way."

Muskrat smiled. "You mean you want to do like the Comanches did when they was fightin' the cavalry?"

Smoke gave a slow smile. "Exactly."

Cal gave Smoke a puzzled look. "What do you mean?"

"The Comanches were badly outnumbered by the Army, but they were much better horsemen and fighters. So, they'd hit and run, attacking at night and other times when the Army was least expecting it. They never stood their ground, but would ride in, kill a few men, and ride out again . . . over and over. Soon, the cavalry men couldn't get any sleep for worrying about when the next attack was coming."

Pearlie grinned. "We gonna wear war paint an' such too?"

"No," Smoke said, "but we're going to hit them fast and hard and ride away to fight another day. That'll serve two purposes. It'll slow them down and give Monte more time to get ready for them, and if we're lucky, we'll be able to cut their numbers down a mite before the final battle in Colorado."

Louis grinned. "Not to mention what it will do to their morale."

Smoke nodded. "Exactly."

Muskrat took a deep drink from his bottle and sleeved his lips off with the back of his arm. "You fellers want some company on this little jaunt?"

"You think you're up to it, Muskrat? We're going to be riding fast and hard."

Muskrat sat up straight in his chair and puffed out his chest. "Hell, sonny," he said to Smoke, "I been sittin' a saddle for more years than you been walkin'. The day I can't outride some mangy ol' gun hawks is the day I lay down and die."

"All right, here's what we're going to do," Smoke said, sitting forward, his elbows on his knees. "Louis and Muskrat and I will take our pack animals and equipment out of town and camp a half day's ride toward Colorado. Cal, you and Pearlie will hang around and keep an eye on Slaughter and his men. As soon as they mass up for the ride, you'll hightail it on down the road and we'll be waiting for them when they make their first camp."

"How'll we find your campsite?" Pearlie asked.

Muskrat laughed. "Don't you worry none, little beaver. You boys jest head on out the eastern trail toward Colorad'a, an' we'll see ya comin'."

In Big Rock, Monte and Sally Jensen were getting the town ready for whatever Slaughter had in mind. Mary had suffered no lasting ill effects from her abduction.

Monte called a town meeting, and he and Sally explained that Big Jim Slaughter was most probably on the way to seek vengeance for what Monte and Smoke and the others had done to him.

The townfolks, after hearing the story of the stolen Army payroll and how Monte had returned the money, were standing behind their popular sheriff and his wife. Not a single person in the entire town voted against helping the couple out.

Monte supervised getting the town fortified and ready for the anticipated onslaught. Barricades were erected at each end of the town, rifles were handed out, and men assigned to rooftops and high points as both lookouts and assault teams. Men were sent to station themselves miles from the town on the trails leading toward Wyoming, so they could return and give ample warning of Slaughter's approach, when and if it happened.

Sally took charge of the women in town, helping them cook large amounts of food to have ready in case there was an extended siege. The children were put to work helping build the barricades and fences at the entrances to the town. Everyone pitched in and worked as fast as they could to make Big Rock ready for the attack.

19

Big Jim Slaughter stood in the center of the valley at the hole-in-the-wall with his hands on his hips and surveyed the damage.

Several men were rolling bodies into a large, common grave and shoveling dirt and rocks over them. Another group of men, the outlaws who planned to stay in the hole-in-the-wall through the winter, were cutting logs and sawing limbs, working feverishly to repair the cabins destroyed in the fight.

Slaughter shook his head. "Damn! I'd give a hundred dollars to find out who Carson found up here to help him do this," he said.

Whitey, standing next to him, scowled. "My money's still on that gunny Johnny West."

Slaughter cut his eyes to his second in command. "I don't know, Whitey. It'd take a man with powerful *cojones* to come up here, kill half my men, and then stay in town when he'd have to know we'd come lookin' for whoever did this."

"Man'd have to be a damn fool to hang around after that," Swede said, "an' West don't look like no fool to me."

"Sheriff Pike didn't have no ideas?" Whitey asked.

Slaughter snorted through his nose. "Sheriff Pike ain't exactly on our side in this matter, boys. While he don't bother us none as long as we stay out of his hair, that don't mean he's all that anxious to help us. He did tell me Carson and his wife got on the first train out of Jackson Hole the morning after the attack, headed east. I'm sure they're headed back to that jerkwater town where he's sheriff."

Swede glanced at the group of men standing near a fire in the center of the compound, drinking coffee and warming their hands on the flames. The weather was turning steadily colder and snow flurries were becoming more and more common as the days passed. "You figure these extra men you hired are gonna do us any good?" Swede asked.

Slaughter followed his gaze. "Some of 'em are all right; some of the others are just gonna be cannon fodder."

"How many men we got total now?" Whitey asked.

"Close to thirty, thirty-five," Slaughter answered. "A few will probably drop out along the way to Colorado. It figures to be a hard trip, what with the weather turning so fast."

Swede nodded. "Yeah. It won't be so bad on the flatlands, but gettin' through the passes might be tough if we get a blizzard or two."

"How about supplies?" Slaughter asked Whitey. "You manage to get what we need in town?"

Whitey nodded. "Yes, sir. Every man has a rifle and at least one pistol. We got two wagons of foodstuffs and extra ammunition, along with some dynamite and gunpowder in case we need to blast our way into that town Monte Carson lives in."

Swede's brow furrowed. "You really think we're gonna have to tree Big Rock, Boss? Far as I know, ain't no western town ever been taken from the outside before."

Slaughter's face got a stubborn look on it. "We'll do whatever it takes to get Carson and get our money, Swede. If it means burning Big Rock to the ground, then we'll put fire to the town an' flush the bastard out."

"You think it'll come to that, Jim?" Whitey asked.

The outlaw shook his head. "No, I doubt it. I don't figure any town's gonna let itself get burned to the ground to protect an ex-outlaw an' his money. Once we let 'em know what's gonna happen if they don't give him up, they'll give us Monte faster'n you can spit."

Swede nodded. "I sure hope so. I don't hanker to kill a bunch of innocent women and children just to get Carson's hide hung on a barn door."

Slaughter turned hard eyes on Swede. "I really don't give a damn what you 'hanker' to do, Swede. When the time comes, you'll do what I tell you to do, is that clear?"

"Sure, Boss," Swede said, his eyes dropping. "I didn't mean nothin' by what I said."

Slaughter shook his head and walked away, toward the men by the fire. "Come on, boys, let's go start gettin' the men ready to ride. We got a long way to go and we need to stay ahead of the weather."

On the ridge overlooking the hole-in-the-wall, Pearlie lay on his stomach behind a large blueberry bush and peered at the activity through binoculars. Cal lay next to him, watching over his shoulder.

"What're they doin', Pearlie?" Cal asked.

"Just standin' there jawin', it looks like."

"I see a couple'a wagons over to the side."

Pearlie shifted his binoculars to take a look. "Uh-huh. It appears they're full of guns an' food an' stuff like that."

"So they are gettin' ready to head to Colorado, just like Smoke said."

"Yeah, looks like Smoke had Slaughter figgered right. He's plannin' on goin' after Monte an' his money, all right."

"You reckon we should head back to Jackson Hole, or stay out here and see what they do?"

Pearlie paused a moment, thinking. "It don't look to me like they gonna be goin' back to Jackson at all. They already got all their supplies, so I guess we ought'a plan on campin' up here in the woods so's we'll know when they take off."

Cal stepped back from the ledge to where he couldn't be seen from below and glanced at the sky. "Looks like snow in them clouds. It's gonna get mighty chilly up here come nightfall, Pearlie."

Pearlie nodded. "Yeah, an' we won't be able to make no fire neither, or else they'll see it."

Cal gave a halfhearted smile. "I guess that means you're gonna miss a meal, Pearlie. You think yer stomach can take goin' twenty-four hours without being stuffed plumb full?"

Pearlie glanced over his shoulder at his friend. "What makes you say that? 'Fore we left Jackson Hole, I had Aunt Bea fix us up a mess of fried chicken, some sinkers, an' I bought a couple'a cans of sliced peaches. We may freeze our butts off, Cal, boy, but we shore as hell ain't gonna go hungry."

Cal grinned. "I should'a know'd you had some food stashed somewheres or else you'd never've left Jackson Hole."

"Like Smoke always says, Cal, you gotta learn to plan ahead or else you'll git caught with your pants down."

A loud snapping sound from the forest nearby brought both men to their feet.

"What was that?" Cal asked.

Pearlie put a finger to his lips and whispered, "Sounds like we got company comin'."

Just as he finished talking, four men walked out of the brush, axes and saws over their shoulders. Evidently they were part of the crew of men cutting timber to repair the cabins down below.

"What the hell?" the man in the lead said, pulling up short with a surprised look on his face.

The man following him bumped into him, stumbling and dropping his ax.

The six men stared at each other for a moment, all of them too surprised to move at first.

"Take it easy, boys," Pearlie said. "We're just a couple of miners up here looking for gold."

"Bullshit!" the first man said, his hand dropping toward his pistol. "You're the men who shot us up the other night."

Pearlie crouched and filled his hands with iron, while

Cal took one step to the side to give the men less of a target to shoot at and drew his Colt Navy .36-caliber pistol.

Pearlie and Cal got off the first shots, taking two of the men in the chest and blowing them backward into the other two, knocking them all to the ground.

Pearlie thumbed off another shot, hitting one of the men on the ground in the forehead, exploding his head in a red mist of brains and blood and bone.

Cal's second shot took the fourth man in the shoulder just as he fired. The force of the blow threw the outlaw's aim off and his bullet tore into Cal's left thigh with a loud smack, spinning the young man around and throwing him to the ground.

As the man eared back his hammer for another shot, Pearlie put lead between his eyes, putting his lights out forever.

Pearlie rushed to Cal's side and leaned over him. "Cal, you all right, boy?"

Cal rolled over and sat up, his face covered with sweat from the shock of being shot. He pulled his leg up and looked at where the bullet had torn a hole in his pants and burned a shallow groove along the outside of his thigh.

His face paled and he looked as if he was about to faint. "Yeah, I guess so. He just winged me."

Pearlie shook his head. "I should'a know'd it. It's been over a month since you got shot the last time. You were past due, boy," he said, grinning with relief and teasing Cal about the number of times he'd been wounded in the past.

Cal's eyes fluttered and he took deep breaths to keep from passing out. "It was just a lucky shot," he moaned.

Pearlie stepped behind him and put his hands under his arms, lifting him to his feet. "Nevertheless, we got to git goin'. Them gunshots is gonna bring Slaughter an' his men up here like bees buzzin' round a nest with a stick poked in it."

Cal gingerly put his weight on his injured leg, grimacing with pain as he took off his bandanna and tied it in a knot to slow the bleeding. "You go get our horses an' I'll be there in a minute."

When Pearlie brought their mounts, Cal walked around and got on from the right side, his left leg unable to pull him into the saddle.

"Come on, Cal," Pearlie said. "We got to make tracks around the mountain to the other side where we can find some cover. They gonna be searchin' for us 'fore long."

Cal nodded, leaning over his saddle horn and holding on for dear life, trying his best to stay in the saddle. He knew if he passed out he was as good as dead.

In the valley below, Slaughter jerked around at the sound of gunshots on the ridge above them, his hand automatically going for his pistol.

When he realized they were not under attack again, he began to shout orders. "Whitey! Get some horses saddled and get some men up on that ridge and find out what the hell's goin' on!"

"Yes, sir!" Whitey shouted back, motioning to several men by the fire to follow him as he ran toward the corral.

"Goddamn!" Slaughter growled, putting his pistol back in its holster. "It's probably the same men who were here the other night."

"Maybe we should'a kept the sentries doubled up, Boss, 'stead of cuttin' 'em back to one man at each station," Swede said, his eyes scanning the mountainside, looking for any movement.

Slaughter glared at him, knowing Swede was right but resenting the implication that he himself had made a mistake. "You know we were short of men after the attack, Swede," he snarled.

Swede, realizing his mistake in questioning his boss's orders, nodded quickly. "That's right, Boss, an' who would'a figgered they'd hit again so soon?"

Mollified a bit by Swede's statement, Slaughter turned

and watched as Whitey and five men rode up the narrow trail leading to the ridge where the shots were heard.

In less than thirty minutes, Whitey came back down the trail alone.

He rode over to Slaughter and got down off his horse.

"What happened up there?" Slaughter asked.

"Four of the men cutting timber for the cabins were shot and killed," Whitey said. "From the tracks, it looks like two men were lying up there watching us and were surprised by the other four."

"Four to two and all four of our men were killed?" Slaughter asked, his face doubtful.

"Yes, sir. But it looks like they managed to put lead in one of 'em, 'cause there's blood on the ground where their tracks were."

"Blood but no body?"

Whitey nodded. "I've got the boys tryin' to track 'em down now. With any luck, they'll find 'em and kill 'em."

Slaughter snorted. "Huh, if I had any luck they'd already be dead." He pointed his finger in Whitey's face. "I don't want those men back in camp until they find and kill these bastards. It's probably part of the same bunch who attacked us the other night."

Whitey looked upward at the ridge. "Yeah, it's the same place they fired from before." He looked back at Slaughter. "What I'm wonderin' is, how'd they get up there without our sentries knowing about it?"

Slaughter's eyes narrowed. "There must be a back way up there that don't go by our sentry posts. That's the only way I can figure it."

"What are we gonna do about it?" Whitey asked.

Slaughter shrugged. "Nothing. It won't matter after tomorrow, 'cause we'll be on our way to Colorado."

20

Halfway down the back side of the mountain, on the opposite side from the hole-in-the-wall, Pearlie found a cave hidden among a group of granite boulders.

He dismounted and pulled his pistol, warily walking into the cave entrance. "Phew," he called to Cal, "smells like a bear crawled in here and died."

From his saddle, Cal said, "Be careful, Pearlie. Now's the time of year fer bears an' such to hibernate. Liable to be a big ol' grizzly in there just settlin' down fer winter."

"If'n there is," Pearlie replied, "it's gonna git awful crowded in here, 'cause we got to find a hole to crawl in 'fore those *bandidos* come after us."

When he disappeared into the black hole of the entrance, Cal shucked his Winchester rifle from its saddle boot and cradled it in his arms, ready to fire if Pearlie came running out of the cave with a bear on his trail.

After a few moments, Pearlie reemerged, taking a deep breath of fresh air. "Nothin' in there but some old bones. Looks like a bear had his dinner in there an' decided it weren't time for the long sleep just yet."

Cal rebooted his rifle and climbed painfully down from his saddle. His leg felt like it was on fire, but at least the bleeding had stopped.

"Come on," Pearlie said as he grabbed the reins to the

horses. "Let's see if we can get these mounts to go in there."

When they smelled the acrid bear-scent, both horses reared back and fought their reins, wanting no part of a dark place that smelled of a carnivore as large as a grizzly.

After some coaching and lots of heavy pulling, the boys finally managed to get the horses into the cave and back to where it opened up at the rear. There was a hat-sized opening in the rocks above that let a little sunlight and some welcome fresh air into the cavern, so the horses calmed down a little, helped some by handfuls of grain handed out by Cal.

"You try to get the broncs settled down and I'll go sweep our tracks and put some deadfall around the entrance," Pearlie said. "With any luck, the outlaws won't find us."

"And if our luck don't hold an' they do?" Cal asked.

"Then we'll blast hell out of 'em an' take as many with us as we can."

While Cal was trying to get the horses completely calmed down, Pearlie took a pine limb and used it like a broom to sweep away all tracks leading to their hiding place. After he was finished, he moved piles of fallen branches and limbs to the front of the cave, hiding the entrance from sight.

In less than an hour, the two men could hear sounds of horses and men outside the cave. Cal stayed in the rear, his hands on the noses of their mounts to try and keep them from whinnying or making any other sounds, while Pearlie took his rifle and lay on his belly just inside the entrance, peering through branches at the outside.

Five outlaws rode down the narrow trail through the piney woods, rifles and shotguns cradled in their arms. Pearlie could hear them joking about what they were going to do to the men who'd killed their friends.

"I jest hope we can catch 'em alive, so's we can string 'em up over a fire and roast their asses off," one of the men growled.

"I don't care if'n we git 'em alive, just so's we git 'em.

Slaughter'll have our butts if'n we come back without them bastards," another replied.

"Well," yet another added, "I ain't seen no sign of tracks nor nothin' fer the last hour, an' it shore looks like we gonna git a blizzard 'fore long." He shook his head, glancing at the sky, which was overhung with dark, roiling clouds blocking the sun and causing the temperature to drop rapidly.

"I vote we head on back 'fore we git trapped up here an' freeze our balls off."

The first man nodded. "Yeah. If those men are up here, they gonna die in the blizzard without no cover to git to. We can tell Slaughter there just ain't no way they could survive out here when the snows come."

There was a general mumbling of agreement, and the group of searchers jerked their mounts' heads around and headed back the way they'd come.

Only when they were out of sight and Pearlie couldn't hear them any longer did he let himself breathe a sigh of relief.

He walked back to the rear of the cave, and heard Cal talking in a low voice to Cold and Silver. Pearlie smiled. The boy did have a way with horses, he thought.

"Good work keepin' them animals quiet, Cal," he said. "I think they've given up on findin' us."

"Then we can get out of here an' head on back to town?" Cal asked, a hopeful gleam in his eye.

Pearlie shook his head. "Nope. Looks like there's a hel-luva storm brewin' out there. It wouldn't do fer us to get caught in it halfway to town, an' we still got to keep an eye on these bastards till they leave so's we can warn Smoke."

Cal wrinkled his nose. "I don't know if'n I can stand to spend the night in here, Pearlie. I cain't hardly breathe with the bear-stink so strong."

Pearlie shrugged as he walked to his saddlebags and took out a bag of fried chicken and biscuits and canned peaches. "Suit yoreself, Cal, but if'n you go out there tonight, I'm gonna have to build a big fire in the mornin' to thaw yore frozen butt out. It's gettin' mighty cold an' it ain't even dark yet."

Pearlie opened the bag of chicken and pitched a leg to Cal. "Here. I know you likes the legs the best."

Cal took a bite and as he chewed, he asked, "You got enough sinkers fer both of us?"

Pearlie pursed his lips. "I dunno. There might be one or two I can spare."

Slaughter was furious when the search party returned and reported they'd caught no sight of whoever killed the four men on the ridge.

"Goddammit!" he screamed, fire in his eyes. "There ain't no place to hide up there on the mountain. How could you not find any sign of them?"

Billy Bob Justice, the man in charge of the search, hung his head, not wanting to look at Slaughter. "I don't know, Boss. They just seemed to disappear. One minute they's tracks as plain as day leading around the mountain, an' the next they was gone with no trace."

"And you say it looked like there was only two of 'em?"

"We only found tracks of two hosses."

"What about the blood trail?" Slaughter asked.

"It went for about a hundred yards, then it petered out too," Justice said. "We figgered they's gonna freeze to death if they stay up there on the mountain with this blizzard that's comin'."

"Damn! I'm surrounded by fools," Slaughter yelled as he turned and walked toward the fire. He stood there a moment, warming his hands and thinking.

After a moment, he looked up at the sky as large, wet snowflakes began to fall. "All right, I guess it can't be helped." He turned to Whitey, who was standing next to him.

"Whitey, get the men ready and pack up our gear. I want to leave at first light, if this damned storm is over by then."

"Yes, sir."

"We need to get movin' before those men have a chance to get back to Jackson Hole and get reinforcements to come attack us again." He glanced around at the valley of the hole-in-the-wall. "Right now, we're easy targets down here since our sentries don't seem to be able to stop 'em."

"Yes, sir, I'll get the men ready," Whitey said.

"I just wish I knew who it is that's doggin' us," Slaughter said.

"Once we get on the trail, I'll have men watching our back trail to make sure they don't follow us an' surprise us along the way," Whitey said.

Slaughter nodded. "That's a good idea, Whitey. At least someone around here is thinking besides me."

He turned to Swede. "It might even be a good idea to leave a few men behind to set up an ambush, catch those bastards with their pants down if they try to trail us."

Swede nodded, his face grim.

"Swede, pick five men you think are pretty good with their guns. After we get five or six miles down the trail toward Colorado, you look for a likely spot for an ambush and get those men set up. We'll teach those sons of bitches not to mess with Big Jim Slaughter."

21

Unable to start a fire, Pearlie and Cal spent the night in the cave bundled in their ground blankets, and even covered themselves with brush and pine needles to try to keep from freezing. Luckily, the space was small enough that the warmth given off by the two horses helped keep the temperature bearable.

When he awoke, just after dawn, Cal felt as if his leg was on fire. He pulled the blanket off, and was alarmed to find his thigh swollen to almost twice its normal size.

Pearlie rolled over and glanced at Cal, sitting upright, staring at his leg.

"What's goin' on, pardner?" he asked, yawning widely.

Cal quickly covered his limb and said, "Nothin', just tryin' to wake up."

Pearlie climbed stiffly out of his blankets and walked to the cave entrance. Snow had drifted to a depth of three feet, and had almost covered the hole in the rocks.

Pearlie kicked and dug his way out into bright sunshine, grateful for the warmth of the sun, though the temperature was still below freezing.

He clambered back into the cave. "Damn," he said, "the weather is clearin'. I'd kind'a hoped the storm would stay around for a while to give us some cover."

He fished around in his saddlebags and pulled out a

couple of biscuits and one piece of fried chicken left from the night before.

Turning to Cal, he held them up. "Looks like we got to share one lonely piece of chicken an' two sinkers."

Cal tried to get to his feet, but his leg collapsed beneath him and he fell to the ground, his face furrowed with pain.

Pearlie rushed to his side. "What's the matter, Cal?"

"It's my leg, Pearlie. It hurts somethin' fierce an' it's kind'a swollen."

Pearlie, noticing the flushed appearance of Cal's face, put his hand on his friend's cheek. "Damn, boy! Yo're burnin' up with fever."

He pulled the blanket down and winced when he saw Cal's swollen thigh.

"Git those pants down an' let me take a look at that wound, Cal."

Cal unbuckled his belt and struggled to get his trousers down over the swollen leg. When it came into view, Pearlie gasped. The thigh was bright red, swollen, and there was pus flowing from the furrow the bullet had dug in Cal's flesh.

"Shit, boy. You done got suppuration in that bullet wound."

Cal laid his head back, breathing through his mouth. "It'll be all right, Pearlie. Just help me get up on my horse so's we can see what the outlaws are doin'."

"I'll get you up on your hoss, Cal, but we ain't gonna bother with no outlaws this mornin'. We gotta git you back to Jackson Hole so the doc can fix that leg."

Cal shook his head. "We cain't, Pearlie. We gotta keep an eye on them so we can warn Smoke when they leave."

"Bullshit, Cal," Pearlie said as he helped pull Cal's pants up. "If'n we don't git you some doctorin', yo're gonna end up losing that leg."

Cal's head lolled back, and he almost fainted from the pain when his trousers moved against his swollen flesh.

Pearlie quickly moved to their horses and began to

lead them from the cave. "I'll git the hosses saddled an' then I'll come back for you. You stay still now, you hear?"

It took the boys until almost noon to make their way down the mountain through the heavy drifts of snow. Several times Pearlie had to grab Cal's shoulder to keep him from passing out and falling off his horse.

By the time they reached Jackson Hole, Cal was almost unconscious from the pain in his leg and Pearlie was having to support his full weight to keep him in the saddle. He reined the horses in when they got to the doctor's office, and let Cal fall off Silver into his arms. He had to carry him into the doctor's waiting room.

Doctor Josiah Curry glanced up from his position in front of a cowboy with a swollen red jaw. The doc had a pair of dental pliers in his hand, and was fixing to pull an infected tooth.

"Doc," Pearlie said as he stood there with Cal cradled in his arms, "my friend's got a bullet wound that needs takin' care of."

"Take him in the other room and I'll be there directly," Dr. Curry said. He turned back to the cowboy, stuck the pliers in his mouth, and yanked a bloody tooth out of his gums.

"Yeow-w-w," the cowboy wailed, grabbing his jaw with both hands.

The doc stood up, threw the tooth into a wastebasket, and said, "That'll be twenty-five cents, Joey."

Joey released his jaw long enough to fish in his pocket and hand the doctor some change, then bolted from the room.

"You might want to wash that mouth out with some good whiskey," Dr. Curry called to his retreating back.

A muffled retort came from the cowboy. "Goddamned right!" he said, heading straight for the Cattleman's Saloon down the street.

Curry wiped his bloody hands on his coat and strolled over to look down at Cal on the table.

"When did this happen?" he asked as he pulled Cal's trousers down over the swollen thigh.

"Yesterday afternoon," Pearlie answered. "It 'tweren't much more'n a scratch so we didn't think nothin' of it till it started to swell up."

"How did it happen?" Curry asked, probing the area around the bullet wound gently with his fingers.

Pearlie scowled, wondering what the hell that had to do with fixing the leg. "He was shot," he answered in a tone of voice that indicated to the doctor that foolish questions weren't going to be tolerated.

The doctor raised his eyebrows, looked at the expression on Pearlie's face, and decided not to ask anything else.

He placed the back of his hand on Cal's forehead and whistled softly under his breath. "This boy's burning up with fever. The wound is seriously infected."

Pearlie nodded. Even he knew that much. "Is there anything you can do fer him, Doc?"

Curry probed the area of the wound again, shaking his head. "Well, I can drain some of the suppuration from the muscle. The latest medical books say that helps some, an' there's a new medicine out called aspirin that's supposed to be good for fever and such. That and some laudanum for the pain should do the trick."

"You think he'll get better?" Pearlie asked, not liking the paleness of Cal's skin.

The doctor shrugged. "If he doesn't respond within twenty-four hours, I may have to take the leg off."

Pearlie gritted his teeth. "He's young and he's strong, Doc, an' he's been shot plenty of times before. He'll do just fine."

Curry pursed his lips. "I hope so, 'cause if I have to take his leg off that high, he probably won't survive the surgery."

He turned to a metal tray of instruments and pulled out a long shining scalpel. "Now, why don't you go get some breakfast while I do my work? This is not something you want to watch."

Pearlie put his hand on Cal's shoulder, squeezed it, then picked up his hat and walked out of the room. He headed toward Aunt Bea's Boardinghouse, uttering a silent prayer that Cal would be all right.

Pearlie was on his second helping of flapjacks, eggs, and sausage when Sheriff Walter Pike sat down at his table.

"Howdy, son," Pike said, motioning to Aunt Bea to bring him some coffee.

He built himself a cigarette while he waited, not saying anything, but staring at Pearlie as if he might frighten him into confessing to some crime.

Pearlie ignored the sheriff, concentrating on finishing his food so he could get back to the doctor's office to see how Cal was doing.

After Pike got his cigarette going and sampled his coffee, he leaned back in his chair and crossed his legs, still staring at Pearlie.

"A cowboy over at the Cattleman's said you brought in your friend with a gunshot wound."

Pearlie took the last bite from his plate, put his fork down, and picked up his coffee cup. He glanced at the sheriff over the rim.

"That's right," he said, offering no more information.

"How did that happen to occur?" the sheriff asked.

"It didn't happen in town, Sheriff, so I can't see as it's any of yore business how it happened," Pearlie answered, staring back at Pike.

Pike nodded. "You sure you want to play it that way, son?"

Pearlie shrugged.

Pike took a deep drag of his cigarette and let the smoke trail from his nostrils as he talked. "A man came into town yesterday evening from the hole-in-the-wall. He said a couple of men had attacked some cowboys up there and killed four men. He also said one of the killers had been wounded."

"That so?" Pearlie said.

"You boys wouldn't happen to have been up near the hole-in-the-wall yesterday, would you?"

"Like I said, Sheriff, this didn't happen in town. Are you sheriff of the hole-in-the-wall, too?" Pearlie asked. "From what I hear, there ain't nothin' but outlaws and men ridin' the owl-hoot trail up that way. Are you paid to watch out for them galoots?"

"No, son, I'm not paid to bother with the hole-in-the-wall. But Big Jim Slaughter has offered a five-hundred-dollar reward for any information on the men who've been attacking him up there."

Pearlie nodded. "Five hundred dollars, huh? That's a right sizable chunk of change."

"More'n I make here in a year," Pike answered.

Pearlie stood up and threw some money on the table. "Maybe you ought to think about changing jobs then, Sheriff, if money means that much to you."

"Goddammit, son, I don't give a shit about the money!" Pike answered, standing up also. "But Slaughter has a couple of hard cases here in town who are gonna be awfully interested in anybody with a bullet wound."

Pearlie shrugged. "Let 'em come, Sheriff. I can take care of myself."

Pike stuck his finger in Pearlie's face. "I told you, I'm paid to keep the peace here in Jackson. I don't want any gunplay where innocent citizens might get hurt."

Pearlie gave a slow grin. "Don't worry none, Sheriff. If 'n I'm forced to draw iron, won't no innocent people get kilt."

"Your name's Pearlie, isn't it?"

Pearlie nodded.

"I want you to get your friend and get the hell out of my town as soon as he's able to travel."

"You got my word on that, Sheriff," Pearlie said as he

walked out of the boardinghouse dining room without looking back.

When he got to the doctor's office, he found the doctor washing off his instruments.

"How's Cal, Doc?" he asked.

"I got about two cups of pus out of that leg," the doctor answered, "and the swelling's gone down quite a bit. I've given him some laudanum, so he's resting quietly for now."

Pearlie stepped over to stand next to the table on which Cal lay. The boy's face was covered with sweat and he was mumbling in his sleep, turning his head from side to side.

"I've got a room in the back where you can keep him," the doctor said. "You need to keep feeding him beef broth and soup and keep his strength up if he's going to fight off the infection."

Pearlie nodded. "I can do that," he said.

"The next twenty-four hours should tell us if he's going to make it or not."

The doctor and Pearlie picked Cal up and carried him into the back room, placing him on a bed.

After the doctor left, Cal's eyes flicked open and he stared at Pearlie, his pupils pinpoints from the laudanum. "Howdy, Pearlie," he mumbled through dry, cracked lips.

"Hello, Cal. How're you feelin'?" Pearlie asked, sitting on the edge of the bed.

Cal's lips curled in a half grin. "I been shot, you fool," he answered. "How do you think I feel?"

Pearlie forced himself to grin back, though he felt more like crying seeing his friend so sick. "Well, hell, Cal. You been shot so many times before, I'd've thought you'd gotten used to it by now."

He reached down and wiped sweat off Cal's forehead. "I guess we gonna have to paint a big ol' bull's-eye on your carcass, make it easier for the outlaws to hit next time."

"Hell, pardner," Cal answered, "they don't seem to have no trouble hittin' me as it is."

"I done tole you, boy, you a magnet fer lead," Pearlie said.

"Pearlie, I want you to leave me here an' go warn Smoke about Slaughter. He needs to know what's goin' on."

"Don't you worry none 'bout Smoke, Cal. He's got Louis an' Muskrat with him. They can take care of theyselves."

"But . . ."

"No buts, Cal. You rest now while I go over to Aunt Bea's an' git you some grub. The doc says you got to eat so's you can git over this wound."

"All right, Pearlie," Cal said, letting his eyes close. "I am a mite tired . . ."

When he lapsed into unconsciousness, Pearlie stood up and walked out to the doctor's front room.

"You take care of my friend, Doc, money's no object," Pearlie said.

Dr. Curry smiled. "It's not a question of money, mister. It's in God's hands now. All we can do is wait to see what He's decided to do with your friend."

"Well, while God makes up His mind, I'm gonna go over to Aunt Bea's an' git him some grub so's he can get better," Pearlie said, his face grim.

22

Smoke stood on a promontory overlooking the trail leading from the hole-in-the-wall toward Colorado, his binoculars to his eyes.

Muskrat Calhoon stirred the small fire they'd built under the overhang of a group of boulders. The temperature was rising after the freezing chill of the snowstorm last night, but the air was still cold enough to freeze water in a canteen. "You see anythin', Smoke?" he asked.

Smoke shook his head. "No, but I figure Slaughter will be getting his men moving before too long, else he's going to have some heavy winter storms to deal with on his way to Colorado."

Louis poured himself another cup of coffee and leaned back on his ground blanket, lighting a long, black cheroot off a burning twig from the campfire. "I'm a little concerned that we haven't heard from Cal and Pearlie, Smoke."

Smoke nodded. They'd all heard what they took to be distant gunfire from the direction of the hole-in-the-wall the night before, and were worried that perhaps Cal and Pearlie had been discovered watching the outlaws' hideout. "Me too, Louis. If anything's happened to those boys, I don't know what I'd do."

Muskrat cut a piece of tobacco off a twist he pulled from his coat pocket. "Don't you worry none 'bout those two young'uns, Smoke. 'Pears to me they got enough hair to look out for theyselves."

"That's the trouble, Muskrat," Smoke answered, stepping down from his perch on a boulder. "They're too brave for their own good. I just don't want them to get hurt because of their loyalty to me."

Louis drained his cup. "This isn't just about you, Smoke," he said. "Both Cal and Pearlie are doing this for Monte and Mary. They hate an injustice as much as we do, and taking a man's wife to settle an old score just isn't done."

"I understand that, Louis, but would you want to try and explain it to Sally if either one of them is shot? She thinks of them as our sons."

Muskrat grinned. "It ain't never easy to 'splain nothin' to a woman, Smoke, 'specially if'n it concerns one of her pups."

Smoke smiled. Mountain men had a way of getting right to the heart of the matter, he thought. They were men of little or no formal education, but their years in the high lonesome seemed to endow them with knowledge of life and death that far outstripped men with college degrees.

"Sally's as tough as any man I know, Smoke," Louis said. "If worse comes to worst, she'll understand."

Smoke took a biscuit out of the frying pan sitting on red-hot embers and popped it into his mouth. "Well, let's hope it doesn't come to that. Cal and Pearlie are both too brave for their own good sometimes, but they're also smart and crafty. I believe it'll take someone smarter than Jim Slaughter to get the drop on them."

Back in Jackson Hole, Pearlie was staying out of sight as much as he could to keep from running into the men Slaughter had sent to look for them. Other than his frequent trips to Aunt Bea's for food for himself and Cal, he spent all his time sitting by Cal's bed, talking to him and forcing him to eat the beef soup and broth so he could heal properly.

Doctor Curry was encouraged that the swelling in Cal's

leg had gone down and not returned. The redness of the surrounding tissues was getting better hour by hour and his temperature had returned to normal, both good signs according to the doctor.

By the morning after his surgery, Cal was feeling fit enough to try to walk around the room on his injured leg, though the doctor forbade any longer journeys.

"Walking short distances will help get rid of the stiffness," he'd said, "but don't overdo it and undo what healing is going on."

As Pearlie watched Cal's appetite return, he began to have hope there would be no long-lasting effects from the wound and infection in his leg.

On the morning of the second day, Doctor Curry said it would be all right for Cal to mount a horse and ride, as long as he took frequent breaks and stopped if the swelling or redness returned.

"I've done all I can, boys," Doc Curry said. "Now it's just gonna take some time for the final healing to occur. You take it easy on that leg for the next couple of weeks, young man," he said to Cal.

"Yes, sir," Cal answered, glad to finally be given permission to ride out of town. Like Pearlie, he was concerned that Slaughter and his men would be on the move before they both could leave the area.

"C'mon, Cal. Let's go git a final breakfast at Aunt Bea's, then we can hit the trail," Pearlie said.

Cal nodded. "Good, I'm 'bout ready for some eggs and flapjacks 'stead of that damned beef soup you been forcin' down my gullet."

Pearlie grinned. "Forcin', hell! You sucked that stuff down like it was honey."

Pearlie forced a handful of greenbacks into the doctor's hand, thanked him again, and they set out for Aunt Bea's place.

An hour and a half later, they were just finishing their final cups of coffee when Sheriff Walter Pike stepped through the rear door of the dining room.

He made his way toward their table, a worried look on his face.

"Uh-oh," Pearlie said. "I don't like the way Sheriff Pike's lookin' at us, Cal."

"Me neither," Cal said, unconsciously unhooking the hammer-thong on his Colt Navy.

Pike stopped in front of their table. "Boys, I got some bad news for you."

"I kind'a figgered that from the sour look on yore face," Pearlie drawled, taking a drink of his coffee.

"Slaughter's men talked to Doc Curry. They found out about your bullet wound and they're waiting in front of the Cattleman's Saloon for you to try and leave town."

"How many of them are they?" Cal asked.

"Four."

Pearlie grinned. "Sounds like fair odds to me."

Pike shook his head. "You don't understand. These are hard men, hired killers every one." He hesitated, looking over his shoulder out the window. "Why don't you let me sneak you out of town the back way?"

Pearlie pursed his lips. "I don't know. What do you think, Cal?"

Cal shrugged, pulling his Navy out and flipping open the loading gate to check his loads. "Seems to me if we take care of 'em now, it'll be four less men Smoke will have to worry about later."

Pearlie nodded and stood up from the table. He put his hat on, pulling it down tight on his head. "Thanks for the offer, Sheriff, but I think we'll go out the front door after all."

"You boys are crazy!"

Cal grinned. "We've been told that before, Sheriff."

They walked out the front door. A slight limp in Cal's gait was the only sign of his injury.

As they stood next to their horses, four men stepped off the boardwalk in front of the Cattleman's Saloon and spread out in the street.

"Hey, you there," one of the men called, his hand hanging next to his pistol. "We want a word with you."

Cal and Pearlie squared around, facing the men. "I got the two on the left," Pearlie said under his breath.

Cal nodded, not speaking, his eyes watching the eyes of the men in the street. Smoke had taught him not to look at the hands, for the eyes would give the first signal a man was about to draw.

Sheriff Pike stepped out of the dining room door. "I don't want no trouble in town, boys," he called to the men.

"It's too late for that, Sheriff," one of the men said. "Slaughter offered to pay you for your help, an' you should'a taken him up on it. Now it's our play."

As the outlaw's eyes narrowed, Cal and Pearlie crouched and stepped apart, to give less of a target, then filled their hands with iron.

Pearlie fired a fraction of a second faster than Cal, but the two shots were so close together they sounded as one.

Two of the men across the street grabbed their chests as they were blown backward, one landing in a water trough, staining the water red with the blood that spurted from a fist-sized hole in his chest. Neither had managed to clear leather before they were dead.

"Goddamn!" one of the remaining bandits yelled as he clawed at his pistol.

Pearlie's second shot took him in the throat, blowing out the back of his spine and almost taking his head off as he spun and flopped on the ground like a chicken with its neck wrung.

The fourth man was a mite faster on the draw, managing to get off a shot that missed Cal's head by inches and splintered the wooden post next to him.

Cal thumbed back the hammer on the Navy and without consciously aiming put a bullet between the man's eyes, snapping his head back and dropping him like he'd been poleaxed.

Sheriff Pike had his gun only half out of his holster when it was all over.

"Jesus, Mary, Mother of God," he exclaimed at the sight of four men blown to hell in less than three seconds.

Pearlie and Cal looked around, still holding their pistols out in front of them, making sure there were no more outlaws who wanted to ante up in this hand.

Bystanders on the street, who'd ducked for cover at the sound of gunfire, returned from their hiding places to gather around the outlaws' bodies, staring over at Cal and Pearlie as if they'd never seen anything like them.

Pearlie holstered his pistol and turned to the sheriff. "Sheriff Pike, if you have no further need of us, we'll git on our way," he drawled, as if shooting down four men was an everyday occurrence in his life.

Pike removed his hat and sleeved sweat off his forehead with the back of his arm. "Uh . . . no, I don't think you need to stay around."

He glanced at the bodies lying sprawled on the dusty street. "In fact, I'd be obliged if you'd get out of my town and not return," he said with a sickly grin. "You're givin' boot hill too much business to hang around."

Pearlie swung into the saddle. He tipped his hat at Pike. "From what you say, Slaughter pays pretty good. There ought to be enough money in their pants to pay for their burials."

Pike nodded.

Cal inclined his head toward Aunt Bea's dining room as he stepped into his stirrups. "Give what's left over to Aunt Bea an' tell her we 'preciate the good grub."

As they rode slowly out of town, the mayor of Jackson Hole walked up to Sheriff Pike.

"Who the hell were those men, Sheriff?" he asked.

Pike shook his head. "I don't rightly know, an' I didn't ask. But I'm sure glad I'm not the one they're after."

"You mean Jim Slaughter?"

Pike nodded. "Yeah, an' I'd be willin' to bet we won't be seein' Big Jim Slaughter and his Marauders back here next year, not if those two are any indication of what he's gonna be facin' in Colorado."

23

Jim Slaughter rode at the head of a procession of thirty-four of the hardest men he could find. There wasn't one of them who wasn't wanted by the law in one place or another, most for murder, armed robbery, or rape.

He glanced at the man riding next to him. "Whitey, you got those men watching our back trail like I told you?"

"Yes, sir," the albino answered, looking back over his shoulder. "I've got two groups of four men each. One group is about five miles back and the other is two miles back. That way, if the first group gets into trouble, the second group can ride up here and warn us."

Slaughter nodded. "That's good. I don't know who the hell is bent on causin' me trouble up here, but whoever they are, they're sure persistent about it."

Swede, riding on the other side of Slaughter, glanced at him. "Yeah, two attacks in a couple of weeks that cost us fifteen men dead and another six wounded so bad they cain't fight no more."

"You don't think Monte Carson could have spent some of that fifty thousand to hire gunnies to come after us, do you?" Whitey asked.

Slaughter shook his head. "Naw, Monte's not that smart, an' besides, he knew if I suspected he had anything to do with this I'd've killed his wife pronto."

Swede agreed. "He's right, Whitey. I asked all around an' nobody'd been approached for a job like that."

"Maybe he hired them someplace else," the albino continued, still not convinced. "Hell, maybe it was that Smoke Jensen everybody's jawin' about."

Slaughter jerked his head toward Whitey. "You know, that's not too unlikely. Maybe Monte brought the old gunman up here with him an' a few of his friends. That might explain why nobody in Jackson knew anything about it."

"But if Jensen was involved, why didn't he finish the job?" Whitey asked. "From what I hear about the old man, it ain't like him to leave a job half done."

"What do you mean, half done?" Swede asked, leaning over in his saddle to glare at Whitey. "He got Monte's wife back and Monte an' the rest of whoever helped him out free an' clear. What more did he need to do?"

Whitey shook his head. "It still don't sound like Smoke Jensen to me. I think he would'a come into the hole-in-the-wall with his guns blazin' till he was sure Jim was dead."

Slaughter shook his head. "No, I don't agree, Whitey. With odds of twenty to one, he'd have to be a fool to press his attack any more than he did." Slaughter hesitated. "And from what I hear, Smoke Jensen ain't no fool, else he wouldn't have survived as long as he has. He got what he came for an' he left a winner, like Swede says."

Whitey gritted his teeth until his jaw muscles bulged. "Well, he sure as hell ain't gonna stay no winner. When we git to Colorado, I'm gonna blow his damned head off."

Slaughter smiled, shaking his head. "You think you're that good, Whitey?"

Whitey glared at him, his eyes narrowed. "Don't you?"

Slaughter shrugged. "Well, I know I'd hate to go up against you." After a moment he added, "Course, if I did, I'd kill you, but that don't mean this old gunny Jensen can."

"What'a you think, Swede?" Whitey asked, his tone indicating he was itching for a fight.

Swede laughed. "I don't know, Whitey. You and Big Jim

are the fast draws around here. I know I could beat the bastard to death with my fists if it came to that, but I wouldn't want to go up against no quick-draw artist with a handgun."

One of the men from the rear of the column came galloping up to them. "Hey, Boss, we been ridin' without stoppin' since dawn. You think we might stop fer a noonin' soon?"

Slaughter grinned. "Yeah, there's no big hurry. Let's stop and build a fire, cook some vittles, and rest our backsides. It's been a long time since I spent all day in a saddle and my bacon is achin'."

From a ridge halfway up the slope of a nearby mountain, Smoke, Louis, and Muskrat Calhoon watched the procession as it stopped and men began to build a fire and cook their food.

Smoke glanced back over his shoulder. "I'm getting a mite worried, Louis. We've been tracking those bastards since ten o'clock this morning and we still haven't heard from Cal or Pearlie."

Louis's face showed his concern. "Me too, Smoke. Those boys would have been here by now if they were able to travel."

Smoke's hands unconsciously formed into fists at his side. "I just hope Slaughter and his men haven't managed to put lead into the boys," he growled. "'Cause if they have . . ." He let the sentence hang in the air unfinished, but Louis shivered at the tone of his friend's voice. *God help them if they've killed Cal or Pearlie,* he thought, *because there's no telling what Smoke would do.*

Louis had heard the story of Smoke scalping and skinning men who'd harmed his family in the past, and he knew Slaughter could expect nothing less if he'd hurt Cal or Pearlie.

Smoke turned to the mountain man. "Muskrat, will you backtrack for a few miles and see if you can find any trace of Cal or Pearlie? I need to know they're safe before we start our attacks on Slaughter."

Muskrat nodded. "Sure thang, Smoke. You an' Louis fix you somethin' to eat an' I'll head on back down the trail a piece an' see what's goin' on back there."

Smoke and Louis stepped out of their saddles and pulled the horses back into the brush so there was no chance of them being seen if Slaughter posted lookouts.

"I guess we'll have to have a cold nooning," Smoke said. "No way to build a fire with the outlaws so close."

"That's true, but all is not lost," Louis said with a grin. "I took the trouble to acquire some provisions before we left Jackson Hole for just such an eventuality."

He pulled two cans of potted meat, a can of sliced peaches, and a can of sliced pears from his saddlebags. "We may have to eat it cold, but that doesn't mean it has to taste bad."

"Louis," Smoke said, licking his lips, "I always knew there was something about you I liked."

Barely an hour had passed before Muskrat returned. He jumped out of the saddle and squatted next to Louis and Smoke, smiling as they handed him his share of the food. He didn't bother with knives or forks, just shoveled the food into his mouth with his fingers, hardly bothering to chew before he swallowed.

"What'd you find out?" Smoke asked.

The mountain man glanced up from his plate with a sly look on his face. "Slaughter ain't as dumb as I thought he was," he began. "He's left two parties of men behind to guard his back trail. One is hunkered down four or five mile back, an' the other two mile back."

Smoke thought about it for a moment, then looked over at Louis. "That means if Cal and Pearlie were delayed for some reason and try to catch up with us, they're liable to be ambushed by those bastards."

Muskrat nodded, as did Louis.

"So, we've got to take out the rear guard first, before we do anything else," Smoke finished.

"An' we got to do it quietlike, so's the others don't know nothin' 'bout it," Muskrat added.

After Slaughter's main body of men finished lunch and packed up their gear and moved on, Smoke crossed to the other side of the trail, leaving Muskrat and Louis where they were. They set up an ambush not far from the edge of the road, and waited for the two groups of rear guards to come.

It took the first party of four men an hour and a half to appear. They were moving slowly down the trail, keeping their eyes to the rear.

As they came abreast of the ambush site, Smoke stood up, signaled to Muskrat and Louis, and broke from cover.

He had the tomahawk he always carried in his right hand and his Bowie knife in his left. As the first man turned and caught sight of Smoke, he let fly with the tomahawk. It turned over in the air three times and embedded itself in the cowboy's chest, knocking him backward off his horse with a harsh grunt.

The second man turned just in time to see Smoke fling himself through the air. Then the man was knocked off his horse. Seconds after they landed with Smoke on top, Smoke buried his knife to the hilt in the outlaw's abdomen and jerked upward as hard as he could, filleting the man like a fish where he lay.

Smoke rolled off the body in time to see Louis and Muskrat take out the other two. Louis with a long, wicked-looking stiletto, Muskrat by the simple expedient of swinging his long-barreled Sharp's Big Fifty like a baseball bat and caving in the side of his opponent's head, which made a sound like a pumpkin being dropped from a second-story window onto hardpan.

"Let's get these bodies out of sight and wait for the others," Smoke said.

* * *

Cal and Pearlie were riding along, keeping their mounts at an easy, ground-eating lope.

"We gotta be careful, Pearlie," Cal said. "We don't want'a ride up Slaughter's rear 'fore we see 'em."

"Don't you worry none, pup," Pearlie said, using the same term for Cal that Muskrat had, knowing it irritated his young friend. "I got my eyes an' ears open. We'll see them 'fore they see us, I guarantee it."

The words were barely out of his mouth when four men stepped from the bushes next to the trail.

"Hands up, gents," the lead man called, a shotgun cradled in his arms, its barrel pointed at Cal's chest.

"Shit, Pearlie," Cal mumbled under his breath, "I thought you was watchin'."

"I was watchin' the trail, Cal, not the bushes alongside it," Pearlie answered, his face flaming red at being caught with his pants down.

As they raised their hands and climbed down from their horses, the head man pointed his shotgun at Pearlie. "What the hell are you two galoots doin' followin' us?" he asked.

Pearlie raised his eyebrows in puzzlement. "Followin' you? We weren't followin' nobody."

"Oh, yeah?" the man asked, his suspicion evident. "Then what were you doin' on this trail today?"

Pearlie decided to take a chance. "They tole us in Jackson Hole Big Jim Slaughter an' his men were headed out this way."

"So you two decided to ride up behind us an' bushwhack us, huh?"

Pearlie shook his head. "No, you got it all wrong, pardner. Mr. Slaughter asked us to join his gang last week an' we decided to take him up on his offer."

"Why'd you change yore minds?"

Cal grinned. "That blizzard changed our minds, that's what. We 'bout near froze our butts off up in the mountains lookin' fer gold."

Pearlie nodded. "Yeah, an' diggin' in that frozen

ground in the winter's like tryin' to dig granite." He gave an elaborate shrug. "So, we decided to take a job with Mr. Slaughter until next spring when the weather's a bit more to our likin'."

The man didn't look convinced. "Still sounds suspicious to me," he said. "I'll tell you what. You hand down those pistols an' we'll take you on up to see Big Jim." He nodded. "We'll let the boss decide what to do with you."

Cal and Pearlie handed the man their pistols and the four men followed them down the trail.

After a couple of miles, Cal noticed a series of dark stains ahead of them in the dirt of the road. He nudged Pearlie with his arm and inclined his head toward the bloodstains.

Pearlie grinned and gave his head a slight nod. When they pulled abreast of the stains, Pearlie and Cal reined in their horses, jerking their heads around toward the men behind them.

The leader raised his shotgun. "Hey, what the hell's the matter with you two?" he yelled.

"We got to pee," Pearlie said, making sure all the men's eyes were on him and Cal.

Seconds later, Louis, Muskrat, and Smoke stepped from the bushes. "Drop your guns or we'll kill you where you sit," Smoke called in a loud voice.

The four men raised their hands, eyes wide at the sight of men stepping from the bushes to capture them.

After Cal and Pearlie retrieved their pistols, they made the men get down off their horses. "Now," Smoke asked, "how can we make sure these men don't join up with Slaughter later?"

Muskrat grinned and drew his finger across his throat, his tongue sticking out. "I say kill 'em an' scalp 'em as a warnin' to that bastard Slaughter."

One of the outlaws gave a nervous laugh, until he looked into Muskrat's eyes and knew he was seconds away from death. The laughter died in his throat.

Smoke nodded, his face serious. "That's one way. Any other suggestions?"

Louis walked over to the men and held out his hands. "Give me your boots," he said.

"Are you crazy?" the leader of the bandits asked. "Our feet'll freeze out here. We'll lose all our toes."

Louis shrugged. "I'll give each of you a couple of shirts from your saddlebags to wrap around your feet. That should protect your toes long enough to get back to Jackson."

The man looked at his partners and shook his head. "No way, mister."

Louis shrugged and pulled out his Arkansas Toothpick. "All right, it's your choice. I guess I'm going to have to cut your Achilles tendons," he said, motioning to the back of his ankles with the knife, "and let you crawl all the way back to Jackson."

"Hold on, stranger," the man said, hurriedly pulling off his boots and handing them to Louis, as did his companions.

Cal and Pearlie rounded up the men's horses and the group rode away, while the outlaws began the long walk back toward Jackson Hole.

"Why didn't ya let me scalp 'em?" Muskrat asked Louis.

"This way's better. By the time those men get to Jackson, their feet will be in such bad shape they won't be able to walk for weeks, and by then this will all be over."

Muskrat shook his head and spat a brown stream of tobacco juice onto the ground. "Damn it all, man, I hadn't scalped anybody in a couple of years. I'm gonna git outta practice."

24

Slaughter sat by the campfire as dusk closed in on his group of hired killers. He'd sent Whitey back along their back trail to tell the men he'd posted there to come in for supper and to get some sleep.

As he scraped the last of his beans and fried fatback off his plate, Whitey rode up in a cloud of dust, his face carrying a worried look on it.

Damn, looks like more bad news, Slaughter thought as he built himself a cigarette and lit it off an ember from the fire.

"Boss," Whitey said, squatting next to Slaughter, looking over his shoulder as if he was afraid someone was behind him.

"Yeah?"

"I rode at least six miles back, an' I searched both sides of the trail goin' an' comin'."

"And?" Slaughter said, letting smoke trickle from his nostrils in his impatience.

"There was no sight of any of our men . . . not a trace."

"You see any blood on the trail?"

Whitey shook his head. "Nothin'—no tracks, no blood, just an empty trail."

"Damn!" Slaughter said, slamming his hand on his thigh. "I told you someone was out to get me, make me look bad."

Whitey stared at his boss, an unbelieving expression on his face. "Takin' out eight men without leaving a trace or firin' a shot goes way beyond tryin' to make you look bad, Jim."

Slaughter dipped his head, wiped his face with both hands, and took a deep breath. "Yeah, I guess you're right."

"What are we gonna do about it, Boss?" Swede, who was sitting next to Slaughter, asked.

"You don't dare post any more men away from the main group," Whitey said. "We can't afford to lose any more guns."

Slaughter waved a dismissive hand. "I can always hire more guns, that's not the problem. I just don't want the men to get the idea we're fighting a losing battle here."

Swede cleared his throat. "Uh, you ever think that maybe we'd be better off just forgittin' 'bout that money Monte Carson owes us an' goin' on down the trail, Boss?"

Without warning, Slaughter backhanded the big man across the face, knocking him backward onto his back, his head stirring up coals and embers in the fire.

Swede jumped to his feet, frantically brushing small fires out of his hair, his face a mask of hate and fury as he glared at Slaughter.

Slaughter's lips curled in a slow grin, his fingers wrapped around the butt of a Colt Peacemaker. "Go on, keep talking like that, Swede, and I'll put one in your gizzard."

Swede's face slowly relaxed and his fists unclenched. "I didn't mean nothin' by it, Boss. It was just a suggestion."

Slaughter pointed his finger at Swede. "Just be sure you don't ever say anything like that in front of the men."

Swede hung his head. "I won't."

"Good, now you and Whitey go get some shut-eye. We're gonna need to keep a sharp lookout tomorrow."

The outlaws' campfire had almost died out when Smoke waved his hand at Muskrat, pointing to the men sitting guard at regular intervals around the camp.

Muskrat nodded, the stubs of his teeth glowing in re-flected moonlight as he grinned. Seconds later, he was gone from sight, moving as silently as a cloud.

Smoke hunkered down, moving on his toes and plac-ing his feet carefully so as not to make a sound. He moved from shadow to shadow, never letting the guard he was stalking get a glimpse of his movement.

It took Smoke twenty minutes to cover the thirty yards to the guard. He came up behind him, put his hand over his mouth, and slit his throat with one quick slash of his Bowie knife.

He eased the man back and laid him flat on the ground, then he moved the knife blade in a semi-circle around the man's head. He hooked his fingers in the slit and gripped and pulled, yanking a bloody scalp off in one piece.

Smoke got no enjoyment from desecrating the dead man's body, but he wanted to sow seeds of doubt and fear into the men riding with him, and nothing did that quite like a bloody corpse, killed with no sounds.

Muskrat, at the same time, was doing exactly the same to the other guard at the opposite end of the camp, but he was enjoying it considerably more.

Louis, Cal, and Pearlie had been waiting for almost an hour by the time Smoke and Muskrat returned, hands bloody from their grisly task. Smoke was carrying a pot in one hand.

Cal took one look at their hands and made a face. "Did you have to do that, Smoke?" he asked.

Smoke gave him a serious look. "Cal, once you kill a man, it doesn't make any difference to him what you do to his body, it's just a piece of meat. If scalping those men makes a few of the outlaws think better of this journey and they take off, then we've saved some lives by what we did."

Cal shook his head. "No matter what you call it, I don't think I could do it."

Smoke put his hand on the young man's shoulder. "That's why I didn't ask you to do it, Cal."

"Did you scalp your man too?" Pearlie asked Muskrat.

The old mountain man nodded, grinning. "Yeah, but that's not all I did."

Smoke cut his eyes at the old man. "What else did you do?"

"I cut some chunks outta his arm an' leg, and made a couple of slashes over his liver, like I was takin' some home to eat."

"Oh, no . . ." Cal said, covering his mouth.

"Aw, come on, pup. I ain't gonna eat it. I jest wanted some of the men back there to git the idea that some-body was."

Smoke grinned. "Good move, Muskrat. Wish I'd thought to do the same."

Louis shook his head with a low laugh. "I don't know about those fellows over there, Smoke, but you and Muskrat are sure scaring the hell out of me!"

Pearlie sniffed the air, looking pointedly at the pot Smoke was carrying. "Uh, do I smell grub?"

Smoke nodded. "Yeah. Since we can't build a fire, I stole some of their beans and fatback. It's still warm, so help yourselves."

As Pearlie grabbed for the pot, Cal knocked his hand away. "Uh-uh, Pearlie. You go last. That way there's a chance the rest of us will get something to eat too."

Slaughter rolled over, brushing a light coating of snow off his ground blanket and sleeping bag. Covering a wide yawn with his hand, he grabbed the coffee cup lying next to his saddle and began to move toward what was left of the campfire.

That's strange, he thought, eyeing the mound of coals and embers that were almost died out. *The guards are supposed to keep the fire going through the night.*

Sensing something was not right, he glanced at the sky. There was as yet no sign of dawn, so it was still very early. He bent over and felt the coffeepot sitting on the edge of the fire. It was barely warm. Now he knew something was seriously out of kilter. The one thing men on guard duty made sure of was hot coffee to keep them awake during the long, quiet nights.

Slaughter went back to his sleeping bag and pulled his Colt pistol from his holster. He eared back the hammer and moved quickly over to Whitey and Swede, who were sleeping next to each other.

He shook Whitey's shoulder. "Whitey, wake up," he whispered. "Something's goin' on."

Whitey came awake with a start, his hand automatically grabbing for his gun. "What . . . ?" he said sleepily.

"Get up, and wake Swede up too. I'm going to check on the guards," Slaughter said as he moved away into the darkness.

Whitey and Swede got out of their blankets and followed Slaughter toward the guard posts.

Just as they caught up to him, they heard Slaughter gasp. "Jesus!" he said, stepping back, a match flaring in his hand.

By the light of the match, Swede and Whitey could see what was left of the guard. Bare white skull gleamed, reflecting the light, and chunks of both arms were missing and deep cuts had been made over the man's liver.

Swede bent to the side and vomited in the grass, his gasping heaves loud in the stillness of the pre-dawn hours.

"Shut up, you fool," Slaughter whispered urgently.

"But . . . but that's Joe Lacy," Swede said. "Him an' me used to be saddle partners."

"He's just dead meat now," Slaughter said. "You and Whitey drag him off into the bushes over there. I don't want any of the other men to see this."

"But, Boss, it looks like somebody ate on him," Swede said, dry heaving again.

Slaughter slapped him across the face, gently so as not to make too much noise. "Shut the hell up, I said. You got to get a hold on yourself, Swede, or you ain't gonna be any use to me."

Swede sleeved off his face and nodded. "All right, Jim, I'll try."

"Now, do like I said and get Joe's body out of sight. I'm gonna go take a look at the other guard. I have a feeling he's gonna be in a similar shape or we'd've heard something from him by now."

"But, Boss, who could've done this?" Whitey asked, looking around at the darkness surrounding them, a worried expression on his face.

"The same ones who attacked us at the hole-in-the-wall an' the same ones who killed or ran off our guards yesterday," Slaughter said. "Now get movin', we ain't got all night."

As dawn began to lighten the sky, the men in the gang began to move out of their sleeping blankets and stand and stretch and make their way to the campfire. Slaughter had gotten it going again and had several large pots of coffee brewing and beans and bacon cooking in large cast-iron skillets.

"Gather around here, men," he called. "I got some bad news for you."

As the outlaws crowded near the fire, warming their hands and getting mugs of coffee, Slaughter stood in front of them. "It seems some of the men I hired to go to Colorado with us have turned yellow and deserted us during the night."

The men began to mumble and talk to one another, but no one questioned Big Jim Slaughter to his face.

He held up both hands. "No need to worry, though. We pass through several towns on the way to our destination, and I'm sure I can hire suitable replacements for the yellow-bellies that took off."

Whitey, at a nod from Slaughter, joined in. "Yeah, an' I'll bet they'll be better to have by our sides in a fight than the cowardly dogs that left."

"How many of us are there left now?" Billy Bob Justice called from the rear of the crowd.

"We still have over twenty-five hands, all good men with a gun," Slaughter answered. "And with the extras I'm gonna pick up along the way, we'll have plenty of men to do the job I have planned."

"By the way, Mr. Slaughter," called out Jimmy Silber, "just what is the job we're headed for?"

Slaughter smiled and shook his head. "You'll find out when we get there, Jimmy. Until then, you're all being paid damn good wages to go for a ride in the country, so enjoy it."

"Damn good wages don't do much good if'n we don't live to spend 'em," Jimmy muttered, turning his back and walking toward his horse.

Sensing he was losing some of the men, Slaughter held up his hands. "And just to make things interesting, there's gonna be a thousand-dollar bonus in it for every man who stays the course until we're done. That's in addition to the hundred-dollars-a-month wages," he added.

Jimmy Silber slowed, thought about it for a minute, then walked back to the fire, holding out his cup for more coffee. "I can always use an extra thousand or so dollars," he said with a grin.

Swede and Whitey accompanied Slaughter back to his sleeping blankets.

"How the hell are we gonna give ever'body an extra thousand, Boss?" Whitey asked. "That won't leave diddly for us."

Slaughter grinned. "Just how many men do you think are gonna survive this little expedition, Whitey? You know with Monte waitin' for us, he's gonna be loaded for bear."

He struck a lucifer on his pants and lit a cigarette. "I figure we're gonna lose two out of three of these men just getting our hands on the payroll, and as for the rest"—he shrugged—"they may not survive to get their share either."

Whitey grinned. "I getcha, Boss."

Slaughter nodded. "Yeah, once we get our hands on that money, I may just retire and settle down someplace. I may even give up the owl-hoot trail."

Swede grinned. "That'll be the day."

25

Smoke eased back on his hands and knees from the bushes he was lying behind, until he could get to his feet and return to his friends without being seen by Slaughter's men. He'd been watching the efficient way Slaughter dealt with the dead men he and Muskrat had left for him to find.

"What'd you hear, Smoke?" Pearlie asked.

Smoke shook his head, reluctant admiration on his face. "Slaughter is a smooth operator. He hid the guards' bodies, and told his men they deserted the gang. He didn't say anything about them being killed."

"So all that was for nothin'?" Cal asked, remembering the sight of Smoke's and Muskrat's bloody hands.

Smoke shook his head. "Not for nothing, Cal. We cut the number of outlaws down by ten men, over a third of their strength. And more importantly, we showed Slaughter we can get to him any time we want to, which has got to be eating on him inside." Smoke took a long drink from his canteen, wishing they were far enough away to build a fire so he could have some hot coffee.

Louis stepped over to Cal. "You don't realize how important that is, Cal. Once you break a man's confidence, make him know in his heart he is vulnerable, you are only a step away from breaking his spirit. And when a man's spirit is broken, it shows to those around him, making it tougher for him to be an effective leader."

Muskrat nodded from where he sat on his haunches, and bit off a chaw of tobacco from the twist he always carried. "That's right, young'un. Men won't hardly foller nobody they don't have confidence in, 'specially if'n it means puttin' their butts in a wringer like a gunfight."

Cal held up his hands. "All right, I understand," he said with a grin.

Pearlie laughed. "Smoke, you know ol' Cal's like that mule we got back at Sugarloaf, the one we call Jezebel. Sometimes you have to hit her in the head with a two-by-four to git her attention, then she MIGHT do what you want her to."

"Speakin' of gittin' somebody's attention, what do you plan to do now, Smoke?" Muskrat asked as he leaned over to spit a glob of brown juice at a ground squirrel nearby.

Smoke hesitated, looking back over his shoulder toward Slaughter's camp. "Well, I figure we're wasting our time here, and sooner or later we're going to make a mistake and I don't like the odds for a head-to-head fight with twenty hard cases."

"Does that mean we're going to return to Big Rock?" Louis asked with a hopeful expression. He was getting awfully tired of cold food and missed Andre's kitchen magic back at his saloon.

Smoke nodded. "Yeah. Eventually. We need to get home and make sure Monte has the town ready for Slaughter and his men's attack."

Louis looked at Smoke suspiciously. "I don't know as I particularly like that word 'eventually.'"

Smoke grinned. "Well, I don't think we should leave without a little good-bye party first, do you?"

Pearlie slapped his thigh. "Hot damn! Now yo're talkin', Smoke. I'm sure gittin' tired of all this pussyfootin' around."

Cal nodded his agreement. "Let's strike up the band and call the dance, Smoke. Those hombres'll never know what hit 'em."

Smoke gave Cal a hard look. "You sure you're up to this, Cal? Your leg is going to take quite a beating if we ride into that camp with our six-guns blazing."

Cal felt of his thigh. "It's a mite sore, I won't lie to you, Smoke. But it'll be all right, an' the wound's pretty near all healed up."

"I thought you didn't like the odds of a head-to-head fight," Louis said.

Smoke shook his head. "I don't plan on a siege, Louis. What I want to do is hit 'em hard, bust up and wound or kill as many as we can in one lightning strike, then hightail it toward Big Rock as fast as we can."

"They'll come after us," Louis cautioned.

"Sure, but it'll take them a while to get organized, and by then we'll be so far ahead of them they'll never catch us."

"What 'bout me?" Muskrat asked.

Smoke looked at the old man. "Are you willing to continue to help us for another week or so?"

"I ain't never quit no job a'fore, young'un, an' I don't intend to now."

Smoke grinned. "Then, what I need you to do is follow Slaughter's gang after our attack, but stay out of sight and don't do anything that might get you killed."

Muskrat arched an eyebrow, as if the very thought that Slaughter and his men were good enough to kill him was an insult. "And jest what do you want me to do, 'sides foller them?"

"If we do this right, we're gonna kill another ten or so of his men, so he's going to have to hire more gun hawks in the towns between here and Big Rock. I need you to let us know just how many men we're going to be facing when he gets to Big Rock. You'll have to stay back out of sight and every time he leaves a town send me a wire telling me if he's managed to get any more men."

"You think we'll have enough time to get ready, Smoke?" Pearlie asked.

"Sure. It's going to take Slaughter twice as long to make the trip with all those men, especially since they're going to want to spend a few nights in the towns along the way getting liquored up and whored up."

Muskrat got to his feet, brushed the seat of his pants off,

and stuck out his hand. "Then you best be on your way, little beaver," he said to Smoke.

Smoke took his hand and gripped it hard. "Thanks for all you've done, Muskrat. We couldn't have done this without you."

The mountain man nodded, a grin on his lips. "I know. But I been hankerin' to make a trip down Colorader way fer some years now. I figger it's 'bout time I looked ol' Bear Tooth up an' seen how he's doin'."

Smoke turned to the others. "Let's saddle up and shag our mounts, boys. We're burning daylight."

Louis, Cal, and Pearlie all pulled out their pistols and began to check their loads. Dawn was just breaking and they wanted to hit the outlaws' camp before the hard cases were up and functioning with clear heads.

As they got on their mounts, Muskrat said, "I'll give you boys a little coverin' fire from up here with my ol' Sharps. I ought'a be able to put lead in a couple of those bastards 'fore the fight's over."

Smoke grinned and pulled his hat down low as he put the spurs to Joker, the reins in his teeth and both hands filled with iron.

Sally Jensen and Mary Carson strolled down the board-walk of the main street of Big Rock, Colorado, watching the construction going on around town.

"I haven't seen this much activity since Smoke and I founded the town some years ago," Sally said.

"That was during the Tilden Franklin affair, wasn't it?" Mary asked.

"Yes, about six months before you and Monte became en-gaged. He'd taken control of the town called No-Name, and we wanted decent folks to have a place to live and raise their children without having gunmen running the town."*

*Trail of the Mountain Man

"Well, you've certainly succeeded."

Sally glanced at her companion. "In a large part, that's due to Monte's influence, Mary. He manages to keep the riffraff out of town while letting men be men and not overly regulating their natural horseplay."

Mary nodded. "Big Rock is a good town, Sally, and Monte is a good man. I'm so happy we have so many friends here that have pledged to help us in our fight with Jim Slaughter."

Judge Proctor passed by the ladies on the boardwalk, tipping his hat in greeting.

"Good morning, ladies."

"Good morning, Judge," they both replied.

The portly man looked around at the men on nearby roofs, nailing up railings and walls with gun ports in them. "Looks like a fine day for construction," he said.

Both ladies smiled. "Yes it does, Judge," Sally replied.

As they were talking, the town preacher, Ralph Morrow, and his wife, Bountiful, approached.

Morrow tipped his hat to Sally and Mary, and Bountiful walked over to take Mary's hand. "Oh, Mary, I'm so glad you are all right after your ordeal."

Mary smiled, winking at Sally. They both knew Bountiful. While she was a lovely young woman who cared deeply about her husband's congregation, she was inclined to be a bit theatrical at times.

"Oh, it wasn't so bad," Mary replied. "Actually, Mr. Slaughter treated me quite well and made sure the other men did the same."

Sally, while listening to Mary tell the men and Bountiful something of her journey with Jim Slaughter, noticed Ralph was wearing a gun tied down low on his hip. While he'd never actually been a gun hawk, Ralph was a tough man who knew his way around a six-killer and wasn't afraid to mix it up when duty or honor called for action.

"Ralph, I notice you're wearing a pistol," Sally said.

"Yes, I am. And Bountiful and I have set up the church at the end of the street with cots and bedding and huge pots of soup and other food we're going to keep ready in case of a long siege. We intend to do our part to help protect Monte and Big Rock from the depredations of men like Big Jim Slaughter and his henchmen."

Over Ralph's shoulder, Sally saw Johnny North and his wife, Belle, riding into town, a packhorse behind them with a suitcase strapped on it. North, an ex–gun slick, had married the Widow Colby after the Tilden Franklin affair, and lived about twenty miles outside of Big Rock on a ranch next to the Sugarloaf. Evidently a lot of people who liked and admired Monte Carson were coming into town to stay until the fight was over.

"Hello, Johnny, Belle," Sally called, waving to the Norths as they rode by.

"Mornin', Sally," Johnny replied, a grin on his face. "Good day for a gunfight, ain't it?"

Sally nodded, her right hand unconsciously falling to check the short-barreled .32-caliber pistol she was wearing in a holster on her right hip. The people of Big Rock were used to seeing Mrs. Jensen wearing men's trousers and a tucked-in shirt with a pistol on a belt around her waist. Sally was very practical in her dress and didn't give a hang what the conventions said about what young ladies of refinement should wear. If she was going to ride a horse or engage in gunplay, she believed in dressing accordingly, and to hell with what anyone thought about it.

Sally and Mary said good-bye to the judge and the Morrows and continued their walk. When they came to the general store they had to step out into the street to avoid the crowd of men and women going in and out.

Peg Jackson, the owner's wife, was behind the counter, a curl of hair down over her forehead as she worked to get people's orders ready. Ed, her husband, was busy nailing boards across the big front window of his store. He stopped to tip his hat to Sally and Mary.

"Hello, Ed," Sally said.

"Howdy, Sally, Mary," he replied, sleeving sweat off his face.

"Business looks like it's booming," Sally said.

He smiled. "Yes, it is. However, in view of the nature of this . . . emergency, I'm selling ammunition and building supplies at my cost." He shook his head. "I wouldn't want to profit off the Carsons' troubles."

"That's awfully nice of you, Ed," Mary said.

"Heck," he answered, blushing, "it ain't nothin'. Everybody's pitchin' in. That's what friends are for."

They were interrupted by the approach of Haywood Arden, the editor of the *Big Rock Guardian*, the town newspaper. He was gray-haired with ink stains on both hands, and wore a white shirt with the sleeves rolled up and a plaid vest.

"Mary, do you have time for a quick interview?" he asked.

"Why, what do you need to know, Haywood?" she asked.

He pulled out a pad and pencil. "I know the leader of the gang is Jim Slaughter, but I don't know the names of any of his cohorts."

Sally put her hand on Mary's shoulder. "I can see you're going to be busy for a while, so I'll just go on up to Monte's office and see how the preparations for the attack are going."

Mary nodded as she turned back to Haywood. "There was this albino named Whitey Jones, and this very tall man called Swede Johanson . . ."

Sally walked to the sheriff's office and knocked on the door.

"Come in," Monte called.

She entered to find him leaning over his desk, staring at a sketch of the town.

"Oh, hello, Sally."

"Hello, Monte. I just came by to see how you're doing with the fortification of the town."

"Here," he said, "let me show you."

She stepped to the desk and watched as he pointed out where the citizens of the town were building blockades and fortifications in preparation for Slaughter's attack.

When he finished, he stood back. "So you can see, Sally, once the outlaws come into town, the blockades will funnel them down to the center of Main Street."

She glanced again at the drawing. "Where you have both sides of the street covered by men on rooftops and in buildings along the way."

He nodded. "That's right. We'll have maximum firepower and minimum chance of any citizens getting shot."

Suddenly, his face fell and he leaned forward, both hands on his desk.

"What is it, Monte?" Sally asked, sensing his discomfort.

He shook his head. "I just don't feel right, letting the town get in the middle of my problems," he said. "There's bound to be someone that takes lead 'cause of me and what I did years ago. It just isn't right."

Sally smiled. "This is our town, Monte, and you are our sheriff and our friend. There is not one person in Big Rock who, even if they know they are going to be shot, will not stand next to you in your time of need. Like Ed Jackson said to Mary a while ago, that's what friends are for."

Monte looked up at her. "I know, I just don't want anyone hurt on account of me."

She nodded. "Then work as hard as you can to make our defenses as good as you can. That's all anyone here expects."

26

Jim Slaughter was in the process of folding up his ground blanket and sleeping bag when he heard what sounded like hoofbeats coming from the mountain slope on the east side of the camp.

He straightened up, his hand going to the butt of his pistol, and looked toward the sound. He could see nothing through the heavy morning mist, which hung close to the ground like dense fog. Though the sun was peeking over the horizon, it shed little warmth and even less light through the haze.

He glanced over his shoulder toward the campfire and saw that most of his men were still milling around, grabbing biscuits and beans and coffee, most of them still half asleep at this early hour.

Damn, he thought, *we're all targets out here with no sentries left to stand guard.* "Whitey," he called, pulling his pistol and grabbing his rifle from his saddle boot on the ground.

"Yeah, Boss?" Whitey answered from over near the fire.

Before he could reply, four shapes materialized out of the fog like crazed ghosts on a fierce rampage, orange blossoms of flame exploding from the guns they held in their hands.

Their faces were covered with bandannas and their hats were pulled low over their faces as they rode straight into the knot of men around the campfire, shooting as fast as they could pull the triggers.

David Payne, a gunny from Missouri who'd ridden with Quantrill's Raiders, drew his pistol and got off one shot before a bullet took him in the throat and flung him backward into the fire, scattering embers and ashes into the air.

Jim Harris, a tough from Texas who'd fought in the Lincoln County War, had his gun half out of his holster when two slugs tore through his chest, blowing blood and pieces of lung on the men next to him. He only had time for a surprised grunt before he hit the ground, dead.

Slaughter's men scattered as fast as their legs could carry them, some diving to the ground, others trying to hide behind trees or saddles on the ground as the marauders galloped through camp.

An ex-Indian scout called Joe Scarface managed to get his rifle cocked, and was aiming it at one of the riders, when an explosion from the direction of the mountainside was followed by a large-caliber bullet plowing into his back between his shoulder blades, which lifted him off the ground like a giant hand and threw him facedown in the dirt, a hole you could put your fist through in his chest.

"Goddamn!" Slaughter yelled, glancing over his shoulder. They were under attack from all sides, it seemed. He dove to the ground behind his saddle as one of the riders, a big man with broad shoulders on a big, roan-colored horse with snow-white hips, rode right at him.

He buried his face in the soft loam of the ground, and felt rather than saw the bullets from the big man's pistols tear into his saddle and the ground around him as the giant Palouse jumped over him. Miraculously, he was unhit.

"Shit!" he said, spitting dirt and leaves out of his mouth. He recognized that horse. It was the one Johnny West had been riding in Jackson Hole. So he was one of the bastards who'd been killing his men all along. The son of a bitch had played him for a fool.

Whitey Jones ran for his saddle, hunched over, expecting a bullet in his back the whole way. As he bent to grab his Greener shotgun, one of the raiders rode by, his pistol pointing at the albino.

Whitey whirled, pointing his express gun just as the rider fired. The bullet grazed Whitey's cheek and tore a chunk out of his left ear, spinning him around and snapping his head back, blood spurting into his eyes and blinding him momentarily.

Ike Mayhew, one of the men who'd joined Slaughter's gang in Jackson Hole, snapped off two quick shots and saw one of the riders flinch as one of his slugs hit home. He grinned, and had eared back the hammer for another shot when the man he'd hit leaned to the side and fired point-blank into his face. Mayhew's head exploded in a fine, red mist as the .44-caliber bullet blew his brains into his hat.

Two more explosions from the distant mountainside sent two more men to the ground, one dead and one with his left arm dangling from a shattered bone. Milt Burnett screamed in pain as he grabbed his flopping arm and went to his knees, just as a gray-and-white Palouse rode directly over him, its hooves pounding his chest to pulp. He died choking on bloody froth from a ruptured lung.

Whitey sleeved blood out of his eyes and rolled onto his stomach, pointing his ten-gauge at the back of a raider and letting go with both barrels. Just as he fired, Ben Brown, one of the men who'd been with Slaughter for several years, stepped between them, his arm outstretched as he aimed his pistol.

Whitey's double load of buckshot hit Brown square in the back, blowing him almost in half as he spun around, dead before he hit the ground.

Swede, too far from his saddle to get his gun, pulled his long knife out and stood there, waiting as a rider rode down on him. He bared his teeth and screamed a defiant yell, holding the knife out in front of him.

The rider's eyes grew wide as he saw the man had no gun and he held his fire, lashing out with his leg and catching Swede in the mouth with a pointed boot as he raced by, knocking out several of his teeth and putting out Swede's lights as his head snapped back and he somersaulted backward, unconscious.

Jimmy Silber, thoughts of his thousand-dollar bonus still in his mind, fired pistols with both hands, crouched near the fire. When his guns were empty, he bent over to punch out his empties. Then a sound made him turn his head.

He looked up just as a young man on a gray horse rode toward him. The last thing Jimmy saw was a tongue of orange from the man's pistol as the slug tore the left side of his face off and left him standing there, dead on his feet.

The entire firefight lasted only four or five minutes, but to the men of Slaughter's command it seemed like hours before the four riders rode off into the mist, disappearing as quickly and as silently as they'd arrived, leaving bodies lying all over the Wyoming countryside.

Slaughter got to his feet, brushing dirt and leaves and sweat off his face. Whitey was twenty feet away, squatting over the prone body of Swede, shaking his shoulder to see if he was alive.

Slaughter looked around him as he walked toward his two lieutenants. He counted five or six dead and several more so severely wounded he knew they'd either be dead soon or of no use to him in his quest for the fifty thousand dollars.

"Whitey, how's Swede?" he asked, standing over the two.

Whitey turned his head, and Slaughter saw a bleeding furrow along his left cheek and most of his ear missing. Blood was streaming down Whitey's face, but it wasn't spurting, so Slaughter figured he'd be all right, though quite a bit uglier than he was before.

"Looks like he's lost most of his front teeth and he may have a broken jaw," Whitey said, shaking Swede's shoulder.

The big man finally opened his eyes, wincing at the pain the movement caused him. He rolled to the side and spat out pieces of teeth along with blood and mucus.

"Goddamn," he mumbled, barely understandable, "what the hell hit me?"

"One of those bastards kicked you in the face," Whitey said. "I saw the whole thing. He had you dead in his sights and instead of blowing your head off, he tried to kick it off when he seen you didn't have no gun."

Swede mumbled something else, but Slaughter couldn't quite get it. "What'd he say?" he asked.

Whitey grinned. "He said the son of a bitch is gonna wish he'd shot him if he ever sees him again."

Slaughter walked to the campfire and poured himself a cup of coffee, looking around him at the mess the attackers had made of his command. "Well, from the looks of things, we'll probably be seein' more of 'em than we want to. It don't look like they have any intention of leaving us alone on our way to Colorado."

Whitey helped Swede to his feet and poured him some water from a canteen. As the big man washed blood and more bits of teeth from his mouth, groaning in pain as he did so, Whitey glanced at Slaughter.

"So, you haven't had enough yet, huh?"

Slaughter pulled his makin's out and began to build himself a cigarette. "Hell, no! This has gone too far for me to quit now. I'm gonna get that money, kill Carson and everybody helping him, and then I'm gonna kill his wife an' his friends an' his dog if he has one. I'm gonna make the sumbitch wish he'd never laid eyes on me."

Swede looked up, blood dripping from his ruined mouth. "You can count me in on that, Boss. Nobody gets away with doin' this to me, nobody!"

"How about you, Whitey? You in or out?" Slaughter asked.

Whitey shrugged. "Hell, Boss, you know I'm in. I been with you through good times and bad, an' damned if this ain't one of the worst so far . . . but I'm in."

"Good. Then let's check the men out and see how many we've got left who are able to go on."

"What are we gonna do about the wounded?" Whitey asked.

"Those that can ride we'll take with us to the next town. Those that can't . . ." He shrugged, as if their fate held little interest for him.

"The other boys may not like that much," Swede mumbled through swollen lips.

Slaughter whirled on him. "I don't give a good goddamn what the boys like or don't like," he growled. "They'd better learn to like what I tell them to like or they'll end up just like those other suckers out there, facedown in the dirt as dinner for the worms."

Swede glanced at Whitey, as if wondering whether Slaughter would show as little concern for *him* if he were seriously wounded.

Whitey gave his head a little shake, letting him know not to pursue the matter any further, and began to wander among the men lying on the ground, looking to see if any were capable of riding.

He rolled Jimmy Silber over, wincing when he saw what was left of his face and head. "Jesus, I guess he won't be seein' any of that thousand-dollar bonus," Whitey murmured to himself, letting the body fall back to the ground.

After he'd made the rounds and salvaged what wounded men he thought might be able to make the trip, Whitey approached Slaughter, who was still standing by the campfire, drinking coffee, lost in his own thoughts.

"You want me to have the men make up a burial party?" he asked.

Slaughter looked at him like he thought he was crazy. "Hell, no. We're gonna mount up and head on down the trail. Stayin' here is just inviting another attack by West and his cohorts."

Swede looked up, his eyebrows raised. "West? You mean that big fellow was Johnny West?"

Slaughter nodded. "Yeah. I recognized that big roan Palouse he was ridin'. It was the same one he had in Jackson Hole."

"I never trusted that son of a bitch," Whitey said. "I knew he was a ringer from the get-go."

"Well, he fooled me," Slaughter said, a wry expression on his face. "Hell, I even tried to hire him."

"You were right as rain about one thing," Swede said.

"What's that?"

"He was damn sure a killer. He went through us like grain through a goose an' never got a scratch on him."

Whitey slapped his pistol in its holster. "He won't be that lucky the next time I see him."

"If you don't get these men mounted up, we might not live long enough to see that," Slaughter said, throwing the remainder of his coffee on the fire and turning to saddle up his horse.

27

Two days later, Slaughter and his men rode toward the outskirts of Pueblo, Colorado. They'd lost two of the wounded on the trail already when Roscoe Archer, known throughout Arkansas as "The Butcher," fell sideways off his horse. He'd taken a bullet in the left arm, which Whitey had bandaged with the outlaw's own bandanna. The arm had since swollen to three times its normal size and was almost black.

Archer screamed when he hit the ground and sat hunched over, holding his injured arm tight against his body. Tears streamed down his face.

Blackjack Tony McCurdy, his partner for the past three years, jumped off his horse and squatted next to his friend.

"Hey, Roscoe," he said, watching as the other men continued to ride on by. "You got to git up, or they're gonna leave your sorry butt here for sure."

Roscoe shook his head, rocking back and forth, cradling his arm as if it were a newborn baby he had to protect. "I don't care," he said, looking at his riding partner through eyes reddened and bloodshot from fever. "I can't stand this pain no longer, Blackjack. You got to help me."

"Help you? I ain't no doctor, Roscoe. Maybe they got one in that town up yonder that'll fix you up."

Roscoe shook his head. "Uh-uh, I ain't fixin' to let no

sawbones cut my arm off. I can't face going the rest of my life with only one arm." He hesitated. "You got to put one in me, Blackjack . . . put me outta my misery."

"I can't do that."

Roscoe grabbed Blackjack's arm. "I'd do it for you, pal."

Blackjack gritted his teeth, then suddenly drew his pistol and shot Roscoe in the heart, knocking the big man flat on his back, ending his pain forever.

After a moment of quiet consideration, Blackjack removed Roscoe's boots and tooled leather gun belt, and took all the money he had in his pockets. He took off his own boots and slipped on Roscoe's. "I always did like these handmade boots you got in Del Rio, partner," he said to the dead man as he hurried to get back on his horse and join the others.

Slaughter glanced back over his shoulder at the men riding behind him. "Damn, we're down to fifteen men. We need to see if we can pick up a few here," he said, tilting his head at the sign that read, "Pueblo, Colorado."

Whitey looked around at the town as they entered the city limits. "It looks pretty promising," he said. "Most mining towns like this have their fair share of hard cases and men who fancy themselves gun hawks."

"Take the men to the biggest saloon in town. I'm going to have a word with the sheriff."

"The sheriff?" Swede asked, able to talk a little better now that the swelling had gone down in his face and jaw. He still couldn't eat anything solid and was living on mashed-up beans and biscuits soaked in coffee.

"Yeah. I'm gonna make him an offer that he'll have a hard time turning down."

While the men proceeded to the nearest saloon, Slaughter reined in before a wooden building with a hand-lettered sign on it reading "JAIL."

He walked through the door and found a tall, heavyset man with a huge potbelly leaning back in a chair with his feet up on two planks, which were stretched across a couple of beer barrels and evidently served as his desk.

The man spoke around a toothpick in the corner of his mouth. "Yeah? What can I do for you, mister?"

"You the sheriff?" Slaughter asked.

The man looked pointedly at a tin star on his shirt. "You think I'm wearin' this for decoration?" he asked sarcastically.

Slaughter grinned, then slapped the man's feet off the desk and when he started to get to his feet, backhanded him, knocking him spinning back into his chair. As the sheriff grabbed for his gun, Slaughter drew his pistol and stuck the barrel against the sheriff's nose.

"I doubt if they pay you enough to try what you're thinkin' of tryin'," Slaughter growled.

"What . . . what do you want?" the sheriff said, his eyes crossed, fixed on the hole in the end of Slaughter's gun against his face.

"What's your name?"

"Will, Will Durant."

"Well, Will, I'm here to help you out."

Durant took his eyes off Slaughter's pistol long enough to give him a disbelieving stare.

"I'm gonna start by putting this back in my holster, but don't even think about tryin' to outdraw me, Will. Men a lot better an' faster'n you have tried an' they're all forked end up now."

"Who ARE you, mister?"

"My name is Jim Slaughter."

"Big Jim Slaughter?" the sheriff asked, sweat breaking out on his forehead.

"There's some that calls me that," Slaughter answered.

"What can I do for ya, Mr. Slaughter?" Durant asked, his face regaining some of its color as Slaughter holstered his Colt.

"It's what we can do for each other, Will. I'm going to give you a hundred dollars, an' you're gonna point out the baddest men in town to me. The ones who give you bad dreams at night. The kind you don't want to run into on a dark night."

"Why would you want . . ."

Slaughter held up his hand. "Will, don't ask foolish questions. All you have to know is you're gonna be a hundred dollars richer, an' you're gonna have a lot less men you have to worry about in a couple of days."

Durant grinned weakly. "All right, Mr. Slaughter. Let's take a walk around town an' I'll show you the badasses, an' this stinkin' town's got plenty of 'em."

By just after dusk, Slaughter and Sheriff Durant had picked out twenty men who were known to make their living using their guns instead of their wits. As the men were pointed out to him on his rounds with Durant, Slaughter approached each of them and told them to meet him after dark at the Lucky Lady Saloon on the edge of town.

As he walked through the batwings, followed by Whitey and Swede, Slaughter looked around at the saloon, which was little more than a large tent with planks for a bar and whiskey bottles with no labels on them lining the shelves. He shook his head. "What a name for this place." He laughed. "There isn't a lady in sight, and if there was, no one in their right mind would call her lucky."

"You got that right, Boss," Swede said, looking around at the motley crew of men assembled. "I've seen better places than this in ghost towns."

Slaughter walked to the bar and motioned for the barman to give him a bottle. He took it and banged it on the wood to get the attention of the men sitting around the room so they'd quiet down enough for him to be heard.

"My name's Jim Slaughter," he said, smiling at the murmur of voices as the men recognized the name. "I've got a little job planned a few miles from here, an' I need to hire some men who know their way around a six-gun, and ain't afraid of usin' it."

"What kind'a job?" asked a portly man with a full beard.

"The kind where you do what you're told an' you make a lot of money," Slaughter replied.

"That ain't good enough for me," the man said belligerently.

Slaughter shook his head, an almost sad look in his eyes. "What's your name, mister?" he asked in a pleasant tone of voice.

"Augustus Skinner. Why do you want to know?"

"So they'll know what to put on the cross over your grave on boot hill," Slaughter replied, drawing his pistol and pulling the trigger.

The gun exploded, sending an ounce of molten lead hurtling into Augustus Skinner's chest, knocking him backward off his chair to land in the lap of a man sitting behind him.

The men in the room all jumped at the sound of the gunshot, some reaching for pistols, until they saw Whitey ear back the hammers on his ten-gauge Greener and grin at them over the sights.

"Somebody drag that carcass out of here so we can get down to business without it stinkin' up the place," Slaughter said, holstering his pistol and pulling the cork from his whiskey bottle.

As he took a deep drink, two men grabbed what was left of Augustus Skinner by the heels of his boots and dragged him through the batwings, leaving a trail of blood on the floor. The barman scurried from behind the bar and quickly covered the mess with sawdust.

"Now, are there any other questions?" Slaughter asked.

A man in the back of the room stood up, holding his hands out from his sides so Whitey wouldn't mistake his intentions. "If it wouldn't piss you off too bad, I'd kind'a like to know what the job pays 'fore I sign on," he said.

Slaughter laughed, as did most of the men in the room. "No, that's perfectly all right. I'm payin' a hundred a month or any part thereof, and there's a bonus of a thousand dollars a man when the job's over."

"I got one more question," the man added.

Slaughter frowned impatiently. "Yeah?"

The man grinned. "Where do I sign up?"

As the others in the room laughed, Slaughter held up

his hands. "Let me warn you before you all rush up here to join our little group. This is no cakewalk. The men we're goin' up against are tough and are also good with their guns. A lot of you won't be coming back OR collecting the money. It's a dangerous job and that's why the pay is so high."

"Mr. Slaughter," another man across the room said, "livin' in this town is dangerous, an' we ain't exactly gettin' paid for it. I'm ready for damn near anything that'll get me a stake so I can get outta here 'fore winter sets in."

"All right, those of you who are interested, the drinks are on me. The rest of you can leave with no hard feelings."

Not one of the men left the room. The pay Slaughter was offering was three times what they could earn doing anything else other than mining, and these were not the sort of men to break their backs digging in the mountains around Pueblo hoping to find enough gold or silver for beans and bacon.

Slaughter turned to the bartender. "Set 'em up an' keep 'em comin' till I say enough."

"Yes, sir!" the barman answered, taking several bottles of amber-colored liquid off the shelves behind him.

None of the men noticed the rather seedy-looking man dressed in buckskins standing outside the batwings, leaning back against the wall and whittling on a stick as if he had nothing better to do with his time.

As Smoke led his friends toward Big Rock, Louis twisted in his saddle and spoke to Pearlie, riding behind him. "How are you doing with that wound? Is it showing any signs or symptoms of suppuration?"

Pearlie stretched his neck and moved his left arm around in a circle to see if there was any pain or soreness. He'd taken a bullet that skimmed along the skin over his left shoulder blade, burning a furrow half an inch deep but not penetrating any deeper. Though the wound wasn't serious, Smoke and the others were worried about infection.

"No, Louis, it seems to be healin' up right nice. A tad stiff, but no more'n you'd expect."

As he spoke, Pearlie noticed Cal had a wide grin on his face.

"What'a you find so funny, Cal?" he asked suspiciously.

"Oh, a thought just sort'a occurred to me," the boy answered.

"Since when did you start thinkin', Cal?" Pearlie asked. "You ain't got a brain in that empty head of your'n."

"Well, it just seemed kind'a funny to me," he answered. "The four of us rode through them outlaws, guns blazin' and goin' off all around us, an' you the onliest one got shot."

"So?"

"So . . . maybe I ain't the only lead magnet around now. It might just be that you're gonna take my place as the one always seems to take a bullet ever' time we git in a fight."

Smoke and Louis looked at each other, smiling. It was good to see the boys back to normal, bitching and arguing with each other as only the best of friends could.

"I don't see it that way, Cal," Pearlie said.

"Why not?"

"Way I see it, this here bullet I took was probably headed for you, sure as hell, an' I just sort'a got in the way."

"You sayin' you took lead that was meant for me?"

Pearlie nodded. "Yeah, so that means you owe me for savin' you the misery of gittin' shot again."

Cal stared at Pearlie through narrowed eyes. "If'n that's so, an' I ain't sayin' it is, mind you, I bet I know what you think I ought'a give you for savin' me."

"What's that, Cal?"

"I bet lettin' you have my share of the first batch of bear sign Miss Sally makes when we git home would square things."

Pearlie pursed his lips as he considered this. "Well, now, that just might make things right between us."

Cal shook his head, grinning. "Forgit it, Pearlie. I been thinkin' on those bear sign for the past hundred miles. The worst thing 'bout bein' away from home all these weeks has been missin' Miss Sally's cookin', so you ain't gittin' none of MY bear sign, no, sirree!"

As he listened to the boys banter back and forth, Smoke thought, *I miss you too, Sally, but it's not your cooking I miss the most!*

28

Jim Slaughter lay in bed next to the whore he'd bought for the night and listened to her snore softly. Finally, unable to sleep, he sat up in bed, poured himself a glass of whiskey, and lit a cigarette.

He leaned back against the headboard, smoking and drinking and thinking about Monte Carson. He realized he should have known there was something not quite right about the man the day they'd robbed the Army payroll, years ago . . .

Jim Slaughter sat on his dun stud in the early morning hour, hoping the fog that was just lessening with the coming of dawn wouldn't mess up his plans.

He had ten men with him, some still wearing remnants of the gray uniforms of the Confederacy and some wearing the blue of the Union. His gang wasn't made up of men who had any political ideals. Most were men who had been on the owl-hoot trail long before the North and South decided to settle their differences on the battlefield.

He pulled out a battered gold pocket watch and checked the time. The special train carrying the Army payroll was scheduled to be in Fort Smith, Arkansas, at ten in the morning. It was now half past eight, so it should be along any minute now. He didn't like planning the robbery so close to the fort, but it was the only suitable location for miles, so he'd have to chance having the fort send out a posse after them. Of course, if there were no guards from the train left to spread an alarm, he didn't have much to fear from any pursuit.

He grabbed his binoculars and looked down the sloping hillside at the twisted, blackened metal of the tracks where they'd dynamited them just before dawn. The section was at the end of a sharp curve in the tracks, and should be invisible to the engineer of the train until it was too late to stop the speeding locomotive.

His informant at Fort Smith had said this payroll, meant for the troops stationed at nearby forts guarding the Indian Nations, should total forty or fifty thousand dollars. The information had cost Slaughter fifty dollars, but was well worth it if true. The informant, a sergeant in the supply division, had also said there would be no more than eight guards on the train.

Slaughter glanced over his shoulder at the men sitting in their saddles, waiting his command. They were all experienced gunmen, some who hired out to various ranches involved in range wars, some stagecoach robbers, and a couple who'd had experience robbing trains in the past. It was a mixed bunch, men he'd hired with the promise of a big score and lots of money to split up afterward.

He looked to the east and could just make out through the morning mist what looked like smoke from an engine over the horizon.

"Get ready, men," he called. "Load 'em up six and six an' don't worry none if some blue-belly gets in front of one of your bullets. We're gonna get that payroll no matter how many guards they have guarding it. In fact, I wouldn't be too concerned if none of the guards live through the robbery."

One of his men eased a flea-bitten gray horse up next to Slaughter. "You didn't say nothin' about killing a bunch of guards when you talked about this," the man said.

"What's your name again?" Slaughter asked.

"Monte. Monte Carson," the man replied, his eyes meeting Slaughter's directly. The outlaw sensed there was no backing down in this man.

"What did you expect, Carson? You think we were gonna ride down there to that train and hold out our hands and them guards were gonna just hand over the Army's money without a fight?"

Carson hesitated. "No, but I figured if we got the drop on 'em there wouldn't be no need of killin' 'em."

Slaughter turned back to his binoculars. "You let me worry about leadin' this here gang, Carson. You just fill your hands with iron and follow me, all right?"

Carson nodded and reined his horse back to the rear of the group of men, a worried look on his face.

Minutes later, a steam locomotive pulling a passenger car, boxcar, and caboose pulled into view. Slaughter pulled his bandanna up over his nose and motioned for his men to get ready. The dance was about to begin.

The train raced around the curve in the tracks, steam and smoke pouring from its smokestack as if the engineer was intent on making up lost time. *Hell*, Slaughter thought, *he must be doing twenty-five miles an hour!*

Suddenly the engineer must have seen the ruptured tracks, for the screech of metal on metal as he applied full brakes could be heard even from where Slaughter and his men sat.

"Shag your mounts, boys," Slaughter cried, holding his reins in his left hand and a Colt Army .44 in his right as he put the spurs to his horse and galloped toward the slowing train.

The engine was still speeding when it hit the torn tracks, veered sharply to the left, and tipped over. It plowed up thirty feet of Arkansas soil before it finally stopped with the engineer's and fireman's bodies hanging unconscious in the broken and twisted engine compartment.

The passenger car just behind the engine was also on its side with several bodies strewn along the furrow in the dirt where it'd been dragged. Four or five men dressed in

Army blue were staggering from the wreckage, wobbly on their legs as they tried to figure out what had happened.

Slaughter's men rode down on them, guns blazing. The soldiers quickly scattered and took cover behind the wrecked car. A man in the boxcar eased open the door, poked the barrel of a rifle out, and began to return the outlaws' fire.

One of Slaughter's men went down hard, a bullet having torn his throat out. His name was Johnny Rodriguez and he was from somewhere in Mexico. He'd been real proud of the long handlebar mustache that was now soaked in blood.

As bullets from Slaughter's men peppered the wall of the boxcar, the man inside pulled the door shut with a clang. Two of the soldiers behind the passenger car fell backward, wounded by gunfire, while another of Slaughter's men tumbled from his horse to be trampled by the men racing behind him. His broken, twisted body was thrown around like a child's rag doll before it came to rest in the dirt.

As the gang separated and rode around the train, circling behind the defending soldiers, the men realized their position was hopeless and they threw down their guns, raising their hands in the air.

Slaughter reined in his horse in front of them. "Keep them hands reachin' for the sky, boys," he called, motioning for one of his men to keep the soldiers covered.

He took his remaining eight men and stood in front of the boxcar containing the payroll.

"Open up that door and come out with your hands up an' you won't be hurt," he yelled.

"You go to hell!" a muffled voice from inside the car yelled back.

Slaughter went to his saddlebags and took out four sticks of dynamite tied together with string. He walked to the boxcar and placed the dynamite on the ground underneath the door. Pulling out a long black cigar, he struck a lucifer on his pants leg, lit the stogie, then lit the fuse to the dynamite.

"Get back, boys," he called, running from the car.

Seconds later, the boxcar, which had remained upright after the wreck, was lifted off its wheels as the dynamite exploded and blew wooden boards and framework all to hell.

After the smoke cleared, Slaughter could see the car lying on its side, a strongbox among the wreckage lying next to the wounded guard, who was covered with soot and grime. He was holding his shattered right arm and glaring at the outlaws. His rifle lay nearby but was out of his reach.

Slaughter grinned at his men, pulled his Colt from its holster, and climbed up into what was left of the boxcar.

"I told you to come out," he said.

"You'll pay for this," the man said. "The Army will track you down and you'll spend the rest of your lives in the Yuma prison."

"I don't think so," Slaughter said calmly, and pointed his pistol at the man and shot him between the eyes, blowing the back of his head off and sending blood and brains all over the strongbox lying next to him.

"Goddammit! You didn't have to do that!" yelled the man who'd called himself Monte Carson.

Slaughter looked over his shoulder, smiled, and said, "I know I didn't HAVE to. I wanted to."

He bent, picked up the box, and heaved it off the car to the ground in front of his men. "Get that lock off and let's see what we have, boys," he called.

Carson, who was nearest to the box, jumped down off his horse and grabbed the box. He pulled out his pistol and shot the lock off, opening the top of the box.

He pulled several canvas bags out and laid them on the ground. Using a knife, he slit the top of one of the sacks and held it up to view. It was filled to the brim with fresh, new greenbacks.

The men nearby all cheered and shot their guns in the air when they saw how much money was in the bags.

"Gather up those bags," Slaughter said as he climbed down from the car. "We still got some work to do."

He walked around the passenger car toward the soldiers who were still standing with their hands in the air.

"All right, boys, get on your knees and face the car," he said, drawing his pistol.

The soldiers looked at him with fear-widened eyes as they kneeled and faced away from him.

He stepped behind the men, eared back the hammer of his pistol, and pointed it at the back of their heads.

"Hold on," called Monte Carson. "There ain't no need of that."

Slaughter glanced over his shoulder. "I told you once, we ain't gonna leave no witnesses."

Carson drew his pistol in a lightning-quick move and pointed it at Slaughter. "And I told you, we ain't gonna kill no defenseless men."

Slaughter's face paled as he looked down the barrel of Carson's gun. "Listen, Carson. If we leave these men behind, they'll warn the Army post at Fort Smith an' we'll have a platoon of soldiers on our trail 'fore we can git away."

"How they gonna warn 'em? Fly?" Carson asked, still holding his pistol pointed at Slaughter. "It's more'n fifteen miles to the fort. By the time these soldiers walk that far, we'll be in the next county, an' they ain't none of 'em seen our faces."

Slaughter hesitated, then shrugged. "What the hell? I guess you're right." He holstered his sidearm and walked to his horse. "Stick that money in your saddlebags and let's burn dust an' get outta here," he said, relieved when Carson put his gun away and began to stuff the canvas sacks in his saddlebags.

They'd been riding hard for twelve hours when one of the men shouted, "Hey, look behind us!"

As the gang reined to a halt, they could see trail dust

rising from a patrol of Army men less than five miles behind them.

"How the hell did they get on our trail so fast?" one of the gang asked.

"One of them soldiers must've rounded up Rodriguez's or Benning's hoss," another of the bandits replied, referring to the men who'd been killed in the battle. "He must've near rode him to death to get to the fort that fast."

"Now look what you've done," Slaughter growled at Carson. "You might've killed us all by lettin' those men go. I ought'a shoot you down right here."

Carson turned his eyes on Slaughter and let his hand fall to hang next to his pistol. "You're welcome to try, Slaughter. Any time."

Slaughter got a cold feeling in the pit of his stomach when he looked into Carson's eyes, and he remembered how quick he'd been on the draw back at the train tracks.

"Well, it can't be helped now," Slaughter said sullenly. "We gotta split up. Ever'body scatter, an' we'll meet in two weeks down in Del Rio."

"What about the money?" an albino named Whitey asked.

Slaughter thought a moment, then said, "There's no time to split it up now. That posse's gonna be on us like ticks on a dog 'fore long. Carson, you keep the money with you an' we'll divide it up in Del Rio, then head down into Mexico."

As a couple of men started to protest, distant gunshots could be heard as the Army patrol got closer, ending the argument and causing the men to spur their horses in different directions to get away from the patrol.

Slaughter took a final drag on his cigarette and stubbed the butt out angrily. *Yeah,* he thought, *I should'a known a do-gooder like Carson wasn't to be trusted with the money.*

He drained his whiskey, turned to the whore, and slapped her on the butt. "Wake up," he snarled, "I ain't payin' you to sleep."

29

Smoke glanced around at the changes to Big Rock since his last visit there as the group rode into town. They'd been greeted several miles from town by the sentry team stationed there, and he was glad the citizens of Big Rock were taking the threat posed by Slaughter seriously.

As they traveled down Main Street, he could see new construction on many of the rooftops, small wooden walls with gun ports built in, behind which men could kneel and have a clear field of fire to the street below. When he looked down the side streets they passed, he could see barricades at the end of the streets, constructed so men on horses couldn't pass. Windows of many of the storefronts were boarded up to protect the expensive glass panes that had had to be brought in from Denver by wagon.

"Wonder where ever'body is," Cal said, looking around at the almost deserted streets.

"Inside, I suspect," Louis said, "watching us pass by. It seems the town is exceptionally well prepared for the upcoming onslaught by Slaughter and his minions."

Pearlie glanced at Louis. "I wish you'd speak English, Louis. That way a body could understand what you're sayin'."

Louis's suspicions were confirmed when several men, some holding Winchesters and others shotguns, stepped from doorways to wave and shout hello to the returning heroes.

"Golly, they're treatin' us like we did somethin' special," Cal observed.

"You did, Cal," Smoke said, smiling and nodding at the townspeople. "You went out of your way and put yourself at some risk to help out a friend, all with no expectation of reward." He glanced back over his shoulder at his young friend. "There aren't many people who'd do something like that, and that's why the citizens are treating you special."

"Hell, it weren't all that much," Pearlie said.

Louis looked at Smoke and grinned. Both knew it was indeed a brave and noble thing to do and that not many men had such friends as Monte Carson and his wife, Mary, had.

As they drew abreast of the sheriff's office, Monte walked out the door, a wide grin on his face and a long-barreled shotgun cradled in his arms.

"Damn, but it's good to see you made it back safe and sound," he said. "Come on over to Louis's place an' I'll treat you all to some lunch."

"Yes, sir," Pearlie said before anyone else could speak, and he spurred his horse into a canter toward Louis's saloon and restaurant down the street, leaving the others to eat his dust.

Smoke laughed. "Monte, you should know how dangerous it is to mention food to Pearlie when he's astride a horse. You're liable to get run over in the rush to the table."

They all gathered around a table in Louis's place and watched as Louis had an emotional greeting from his employees, especially his chef Andre, who actually wept with joy at seeing his old friend and boss back safely.

"Andre, cook us up some steaks, fried potatoes, sliced tomatoes and peaches, and some of your special coffee," Louis requested. "It's been so long since we had a hot meal I can hardly remember what good food tastes like."

"Uh, Andre," Pearlie said, "could I have some sarsaparilla

instead of coffee? My mouth's been waterin' all mornin' just thinkin' 'bout gittin' some more of that stuff."

Andre nodded. "For you, Monsieur Pearlie, anything you want for bringing my friend back alive."

Once they had coffee in front of them, Smoke asked Monte about the preparations he'd made for Slaughter's raid.

The sheriff put a match to his pipe, took a sip of coffee, and began to talk. "We've fortified most of the buildings, both on the roofs and the doors. Double-backed the doors with two inches of wood to stop any bullets from penetratin' and covered most of the windows where people are gonna be stationed."

"I noticed you've barricaded some of the side streets but not Main Street," Louis said.

Monte nodded, smiling. "That was Sally's idea. The entire town is now a giant trap. The outlaws can get in on the main street, but once they're in town they're gonna play hell gettin' out again."

"But," Cal said with a puzzled look on his face, "what's to keep 'em from jest turnin' around and headin' back the way they came?"

Monte grinned. "We've got a couple of wagons loaded high with hay and boards in a circle in their beds. Once those bastards get past the city limits, I have some men ready to station the wagons blocking the street, and then they're gonna crawl up into the hay and defend the entrance just in case Slaughter's men try to get back out that way."

"So, the entire town will be like a giant mousetrap," Pearlie said. "The rats can get in, but they cain't get out again."

"You got it, Pearlie," Monte said, grinning around the stem of his pipe, sending blue clouds of foul-smelling smoke toward the ceiling.

"How about the citizens?" Smoke asked. "Are they all behind us?"

Monte nodded. "To a man. And that really surprised me. Even some of the men I've had to arrest on more than one occasion are standing firm with us."

Louis smiled and shook his head. "It does not surprise me, my friend. The people of this town know you're the best sheriff we could ever hope to have, and the men you've incarcerated know it as well. I don't believe you realized just how many friends you have in Big Rock, Monte."

Monte nodded. "You're certainly right there, Louis. Mary and I both thank our lucky stars we decided to settle here."

Just then, Andre appeared with two kitchen helpers following behind him bearing platters heaped high with delicious-smelling food for the hungry men.

Pearlie reached down and fiddled with his belt.

"What are you doin', Pearlie?" Cal asked.

Pearlie looked up, his eyebrows raised. "Why, I'm loosenin' my belt to make room for all that food. If the sheriff is buyin', then I plan to eat my fill."

Smoke laughed. "That I've got to see. I've never known you to quit eating because you're full, Pearlie. It's always been because you ran out of food."

Louis glanced at Monte. "If the look on Pearlie's face is any indication, Monte, you may have to get an advance on your paycheck to pay for his meal."

After they'd finished eating, Smoke and Cal and Pearlie headed out toward the Sugarloaf. As he passed the general store, Smoke saw Preacher Morrow and his wife, Bountiful, talking to Haywood and Dana Arden. Just as Smoke drew abreast of the foursome, they were joined by Ed and Peg Jackson, the proprietors of the store. When they saw him, the group all waved and shouted hello.

Seeing them together reminded Smoke of the time they'd all arrived from back East, hoping to make a life out West. They were the greenest pilgrims he'd ever seen, and before the day was out, he'd had to save their bacon . . .

Ever since gold had been discovered in the area, wagons had rolled and rumbled, bringing their human cargo toward No-Name Town. The line of wagons and buggies and riders and walkers was now several miles long. Gamblers and would-be shopkeepers and whores and gunfighters and snake-oil salesmen and pimps and troublemakers and murderers and good solid family people . . . all of them heading for No-Name with but one thought in their minds. Gold.

At the end of the line of gold-seekers, not a part of them but yet with the same destination if not sharing the same motives, came the pilgrims on a half-dozen wagons. Ed Jackson was new to the raw West—a shopkeeper from Illinois with his wife, Peg. They were both young and very idealistic, and had no working knowledge of the real West. They were looking for a place to settle. This No-Name Town sounded good to them. Ed's brother Paul drove the heavily laden supply wagon, containing part of what they just knew would make them respected and secure citizens. Paul was as naive as his brother and sister-in-law concerning the West.

In the third wagon came Ralph Morrow and his wife, Bountiful. They were missionaries, sent into the godless West by their church, to save souls and soothe the sinful spirits of those who had not yet accepted Christ into their lives. They had been looking for a place to settle when they hooked up with Ed and Peg and Paul. This was the first time Ralph and Bountiful had been west of eastern Ohio. It was exciting. A challenge.

They thought.

In the fourth wagon rode another young couple, married only a few years. Hunt and Willow Brook. Hunt was a lawyer, looking for a place to practice all he'd just been taught back East. This new gold rush town seemed just the place to start.

In the fifth wagon rode Cotton and Mona Spalding. A doctor and nurse, respectively. They had both graduated only last year, mulled matters over, and decided to head West. They were young and handsome and pretty. And like the others in their little caravan, they had absolutely no idea what they were riding into.

In the last wagon, a huge, solidly built vehicle with six mules pulling it, came Haywood and Dana Arden. Like the others, they were young and full of grand ideas. Haywood had inherited a failing newspaper from his father back in Pennsylvania and decided to pull out and head West to seek their fortune.

"Oh, Haywood!" Dana said, her eyes shining with excitement. "It's all so wonderful."

"Yes," Haywood agreed, just as the right rear wheel of their wagon fell off.

Smoke was up long before dawn spread her shimmering rays of light over the land. He slipped out of his blankets and put his hat on, then pulled on his boots and strapped on his guns. He checked to see how Horse was doing, then washed his face with water from his canteen. He built a small, hand-sized fire and boiled coffee. He munched on a thick piece of bread and sipped his coffee, sitting with his back to a tree, his eyes taking in the first silver streaks of a new day in the high-up country of Colorado.

He had spotted a fire down below him, near the winding road. A very large fire. Much too large unless those who built it were roasting an entire deer—head, horns, and all. He finished the small, blackened pot of coffee, carefully doused his fire, and saddled Horse, stowing his gear in the saddlebags.

He swung into the saddle, and made his way slowly and quietly down from the high terrain toward the road miles away using the twisting, winding trails. Smoke uncased his U.S. Army binoculars and studied the situation.

Five, no—six wagons. One of them down with a busted back wheel. Six men, five women. All young, in their early twenties, Smoke guessed. The women were all very pretty, the men all handsome and apparently—at least to Smoke—helpless.

He used his knees to signal Horse, and the animal moved out, taking its head, picking the route. Stopping after a few hundred twisting yards, Smoke once more surveyed the situation. His binoculars picked up movement coming from the direction of No-Name. Four riders. He studied the men, watching them approach the wagons. Drifters, from the look of them. Probably spent the night in No-Name gambling and whoring and were heading out to stake a gold claim. They looked like trouble.

Staying in the deep and lush timber, Smoke edged closer still. Several hundred yards from the wagon, Smoke halted and held back, wanting to see how these pilgrims would handle the approach of the riders.

He could not hear all that was said, but he could get most of it from his hidden location.

He had pegged the riders accurately. They were trouble. They reined up and sat their horses, grinning at the men and women. Especially the women.

"You folks look like you got a mite of trouble," one rider said.

"A bit," a friendly-looking man responded. "We're just getting ready to fulcrum the wagon."

"You're gonna do *what* to it?" another rider blurted.

"Raise it up," a pilgrim said.

"Oh. You folks headin' to Fontana?"

The wagon people looked at each other.

Fontana! Smoke thought. *Where in the hell is Fontana?*

"I'm sorry," one of the women said. "We're not familiar with that place."

"That's what they just named the town up yonder," a rider said, jerking his thumb in the direction of No-Name. "Stuck up a big sign last night."

So No-Name has a name, Smoke thought. *Wonder whose idea that was.*

But he thought he knew. Tilden Franklin.

Smoke looked at the women of the wagons. They were, to a woman, all very pretty and built up nice. Very shapely. The men with them didn't look like much to Smoke; but then, he thought, they were easterners. Probably good men back there. But out here, they were out of their element.

And Smoke didn't much like the look in the eyes of the riders. One kept glancing up and down the road. As yet, no traffic had appeared. But Smoke knew the stream of gold-hunters would soon appear. If the drifters were going to start something—the women being what they wanted, he was sure—they would make their move pretty quick.

At some unspoken signal, the riders dismounted.

"Oh, say!" the weakest-jawed pilgrim said. "It's good of you men to help."

"Huh?" a rider said, then grinned. "Oh, yeah. We're regular do-gooders. You folks nesters?"

"I beg your pardon, sir?"

"Farmers." He ended that, and summed up his feelings concerning farmers by spitting a stream of brown tobacco juice onto the ground, just missing the pilgrim's feet.

The pilgrim laughed and said, "Oh, no. My name is Ed Jackson, this is my wife, Peg. We plan to open a store in the gold town."

"Ain't that nice?" the rider mumbled.

Smoke kneed Horse a bit closer.

"My name is Ralph Morrow," another pilgrim said. "I'm a minister. This is my wife, Bountiful. We plan to start a church in the gold town."

The rider looked at Bountiful and licked his lips.

Ralph said, "And this is Paul Jackson. Ed's brother. Over there is Hunt and Willow Brook. Hunt is a lawyer. That's Cotton and Mona Spalding. Cotton is a physician. And last, but certainly not least, is Haywood and Dana Arden. Haywood is planning to start a newspaper in town. Now you know us."

"Not as much as I'd like to," a rider said, speaking for the first time. He was looking at Bountiful.

To complicate matters, Bountiful was looking square at the rider.

The woman is flirting with him, Smoke noticed. He silently cursed. This Bountiful might be a preacher's wife, but what she really was was a hot handful of trouble. The preacher was not taking care of business at home.

Bountiful was blond with hot blue eyes. She was staring at the rider.

All the newcomers to the West began to sense something was not as it should be. But none knew what, and if they did, Smoke thought, they wouldn't know how to handle it. For none of the men were armed.

One of the drifters, the one who had been staring at Bountiful, brushed past the preacher. He walked by Bountiful, his right arm brushing the woman's jutting breasts. She did not back up. The rider stopped and grinned at her.

The newspaperman's wife stepped in just in time, stepping between the rider and the woman. She glared at Bountiful. "Let's you and I start breakfast, Bountiful," she suggested. "While the men fix the wheel."

"What you got in your wagon, shopkeeper?" a drifter asked. "Anything in there we might like?"

Ed narrowed his eyes. "I'll set up shop very soon. Feel free to browse when we're open for business."

The rider laughed. "Talks real nice, don't he, boys?"

His friends laughed.

The riders were big men, tough-looking and seemingly very capable. Smoke had no doubt but what they were all that and more. The more being troublemakers.

Always something, Smoke thought with a silent sigh. People wander into an unknown territory without first checking out all the ramifications. He edged Horse forward.

A rider jerked at a tie-rope over the bed of one wagon. "I don't wanna browse none. I wanna see what you got now."

"Now see here!" Ed protested, stepping toward the man.

Ed's head exploded in pain as the rider's big fist hit the shopkeeper's jaw. Ed's butt hit the ground. Still, Smoke waited.

None of the drifters had drawn a gun. No law, written or otherwise, had as yet been broken. These pilgrims were in the process of learning a hard lesson of the West: You broke your own horses and killed your own snakes. And Smoke recalled a sentiment from some book he had slowly and laboriously studied. When you are in Rome, live in the Roman style; when you are elsewhere, live as they live elsewhere.

He couldn't remember who wrote it, but it was pretty fair advice.

The riders laughed at the ineptness of the newcomers to the West. One jerked Bountiful to him and began fondling her breasts.

Bountiful finally got it through her head that this was deadly serious, not a mild flirtation.

She began struggling just as the other pilgrims surged forward. Their butts hit the ground as quickly and as hard as Ed's had.

Smoke put the spurs to Horse and the big horse broke out of the timber. Smoke was out of the saddle before Horse was still. He dropped the reins to the ground and faced the group.

"That's it!" Smoke said quietly. He slipped the thongs from the hammers of his .44s.

Smoke glanced at Bountiful. Her bodice was torn, exposing the creamy skin of her breasts. "Cover yourself," Smoke told her.

She pulled away from the rider and ran, sobbing, to Dana.

A rider said, "I don't know who you are, boy. But I'm gonna teach you a hard lesson."

"Oh? And what might that be?"

"To keep your goddamned nose out of other folks' business."

"If the woman had been willing," Smoke said, "I would not have interfered. Even though it takes a low-life bastard to steal another man's woman."

"Why, you . . . pup!" the rider shouted. "You callin' me a bastard?"

"Are you deaf?"

"I'll kill you!"

"I doubt it."

Bountiful was crying. Her husband was holding a hand-kerchief to a bloody nose, his eyes staring in disbelief at what was taking place.

Hunt Brook was sitting on the ground, his mouth bloody. Cotton's head was ringing and his ear hurt where he'd been struck. Haywood was wondering if his eye was going to turn black. Paul was holding a hurting stomach, the hurt caused by a hard fist. The preacher looked as if he wished his wife would cover herself.

One drifter shoved Dana and Bountiful out of the way, stepping over to join his friend, facing Smoke. The other two drifters hung back, being careful to keep their hands away from their guns. The two who hung back were older and wiser to the ways of gun slicks. And they did not like the looks of this young man with the twin Colts. There was something very familiar about him. Something calm and cold and very deadly.

"Back off, Ford," one finally said. "Let's ride."

"Hell with you!" the rider named Ford said, not taking his eyes from Smoke. "I'm gonna kill this punk!"

"Something tells me you ain't neither," the other drifter who was hanging back said.

"Better listen to him," Smoke advised Ford.

"Now see here, gentlemen!" Hunt said.

"Shut your gawddamned mouth!" he was told by Ford.

Hunt closed his mouth. *Heavens!* he thought. *This just simply was not done back in Boston.*

"You gonna draw, punk?" Ford asked.

"After you," Smoke said quietly.

"Jesus, Ford!" one of the riders who'd hung back said. "I know who that is."

"He's dead, that's who he is," Ford said, and reached for his gun.

His friend drew at the same time.

Smoke let them clear leather before he began his light-ning draw. His Colts belched fire and smoke, the slugs taking them in the chest, flinging them backward. They had not gotten off a shot.

"Smoke Jensen!" one of the other drifters said.

"Right," Smoke said. "Now, ride!"*

Smoke grinned at the memory of just how green the now upright and solid citizens of Big Rock had been when they first arrived out West. Even so, he'd recognized their inner strength and worth, and they'd been among the first people he invited to live in Big Rock when he and Sally founded it later that year.

"What're you grinnin' at, Smoke?" Cal asked.

"Oh, nothing, Cal. Just thinking back on old times."

Pearlie laughed. "You mean back in the old days before we became civilized?"

Smoke threw back his head and laughed with the boys. It was true. The more things changed, the more they remained the same.

*Trail of the Mountain Man

30

Smoke felt his heart swell inside his chest at the sight of his cabin on the Sugarloaf. He looked at Cal and Pearlie. "Why don't you boys clean some of the trail dust off in the bunkhouse while I tell Sally hello?"

Cal and Pearlie glanced at each other and grinned. "You mean you don't want us to stick around awhile and tell Miss Sally hello, too?" Pearlie asked, an innocent look on his face.

"I've been gone from home for more'n a month. What do you think?"

"Yes, sir, we understand," Cal said, elbowing Pearlie in the side to make him shut his mouth.

The boys peeled off at the bunkhouse, while Smoke rode on up to the main cabin.

By the time he got down off Joker, Sally was running from the porch toward him. She threw her arms around his neck and gave him a very solid, very long kiss.

Smoke leaned back and stared at her, his love evident in his eyes. "What? Don't a man get some breakfast when he comes home from work?"

Sally took him by the hand and marched toward the cabin. "How about we have some dessert first?"

"But you always say that'll ruin my appetite," he teased.

She looked back over her shoulder at him, her eyes

twinkling. "That's not all I'm going to ruin if you don't hurry up."

"But don't you want to hear about my trip?"

"Later!" she growled.

"Yes, ma'am," he said, quickening his steps.

A while later, Sally fixed breakfast and Smoke invited Cal and Pearlie to join them. Pearlie went straight for the bear sign cooling on a windowsill.

Sally slapped his hand when he reached for one. "Not now, Pearlie. AFTER breakfast."

She cut her eyes at Smoke and winked. "You'll ruin your appetite."

"Aw, Miss Sally," Pearlie protested, "I've never known anything to ruin my appetite."

"Nevertheless, sit down and eat," she commanded, her hands on her hips.

"Boy, I ain't never heard nobody have to tell Pearlie that," Cal observed, digging into thick slices of fried ham, scrambled hens' eggs, and flapjacks so light he thought they were going to float off the plate.

While they ate, the men took turns filling Sally in on the happenings on their journey to and from Jackson Hole, Wyoming.

Her eyes widened on hearing of Cal's and Pearlie's wounds. "We need to have Dr. Spalding take a look at those, Smoke."

He held up his hands. "Already done, dear. He gave them both a clean bill of health, though he did say Cal didn't have too much room left on his body without bullet scars on it."

"I tole the doc I guess he'd have to start over again on the same ol' scars," Pearlie said around a mouthful of ham, "'Cause he dang sure ain't gonna quit gittin' shot."

Smoke cocked his head. "I hear hoofbeats," he said, rising from his chair, his Colt appearing in his hand as if by magic.

He opened the door and looked out, then holstered his pistol.

"Better set another place, dear," he said. "We've got company."

After a few moments, Muskrat Calhoon stepped through the door. "Howdy, young'uns," he said. When he caught sight of Sally, he removed his coonskin cap and gave a slight bow. "Mornin', ma'am."

"Good morning, Mr. Calhoon," Sally replied. "My husband has told me how much you helped him and I want to thank you."

Muskrat cut his eyes to the bear sign on the windowsill. "A couple of those'd do jest fine as thanks, ma'am."

Sally shook her head. "No, you have to join us for breakfast first. Then we'll have the bear sign."

Muskrat glanced at Smoke. "That's why I never married. Dang women are always denyin' a man his pleasures."

"She's a hardheaded woman all right," Smoke said with a smile, "but she's the only one I have."

Muskrat sat at the table and piled his plate so high with food he could barely be seen behind it. "I will say one thing, ma'am, this is the best food I've had in many a year," he declared, as he stuffed ham and eggs and pancake in his mouth all at one time.

Sally caught Smoke's eye and wrinkled her nose. "I'll go prepare a bath for Mr. Calhoon. I'm sure he'd like to . . . freshen up after he eats."

Muskrat turned fear-widened eyes on Sally. "I got to bathe too 'fore I git any bear sign?"

She smiled. "No, you can have the bear sign first, but the bath comes second."

He glared at Smoke. "You're right, son, she is a hard woman!"

After Muskrat had his bath and Sally had thrown his clothes in a tub of hot water with lye soap in it, Smoke gave him some of his older buckskins to wear while the mountain man's dried.

"What news do you have of Slaughter, Muskrat?" Smoke asked while they were having smokes and coffee on the porch.

"He managed to hire hisself another twenty or twenty-five gunnies," Muskrat replied. "Some of the worst pond scum in Pueblo from what I could gather."

"That figures," Pearlie said, still chewing on a bear sign doughnut in his hand.

"That means he must have more'n thirty men with him, Smoke," Cal said.

Smoke nodded. "Yes. We're certainly going to have our work cut out for us in Big Rock."

"I figger with the way they're travelin', they'll be here in two or three days at the outside," Muskrat said, taking a deep puff off a stogie Smoke had given him.

"Sally, we'd better get moved into town. Have all the surrounding ranchers been warned?"

"Yes, dear," she said from the kitchen where she was washing dishes. "The Norths are already there, and the others in the area have been put on guard."

"You got room in that there town fer an ol' beaver like me?" Muskrat asked.

Smoke grinned. "Hell, yes. We can sure use that Sharps Big Fifty of yours."

Muskrat nodded. "Good, 'cause I ain't had so much fun since Bear Tooth and me went to war agin the Pawnee."

"You went to war against the Pawnee tribes?" Cal asked, his eyes wide.

"Shore did, boy. It happened like this, me an' Bear Tooth was trappin' beaver up in the high lonesome near the Pawnee's main camp, an' a couple'a right pretty young squaws happened by one mornin'." The old mountain man waggled his eyebrows. "Well, we was jest young bucks ourselves at the time, an' one thing led to another an' 'fore we knew it, we got to showin' them pretty young thangs the difference 'tween a white man an' an Injun when it came to . . ."

Smoke groaned. There was no stopping a mountain man once he'd started on one of his tall tales.

31

Slaughter held up his hand to halt the column of men riding behind him when he came to the sign saying "Big Rock, Colorado."

He twisted in the saddle. "Men, load 'em up six and six, and watch your butts. I don't know if Monte Carson is in this town or not, but if he isn't, we're gonna raise hell until they tell us where he's hiding."

Behind him, men pulled Winchesters and shotguns out of saddle boots and cradled them in their arms. They were ready to go to war, and each one felt there wasn't a town in the West that could stand up to a group such as theirs. Shopkeepers and pilgrims and cowboys were simply no match for men trained to use their guns to make war, and the sooner these citizens realized that, the sooner Slaughter would pay them their money.

"What do you think, boys?" Slaughter said to Whitey and Swede as they rode into town.

Swede shook his head. "I just hope it's gonna be as easy as you think it is, Boss. Treein' a western town ain't never been done before."

"There is a first time for everything, Swede," Slaughter said. "This is the roughest bunch of men I've ever had the pleasure to ride with. There ain't a one of them that hadn't killed more men than they can count. Hell, with this band of desperadoes, I could take Dodge City itself."

Whitey pulled his Greener express gun from his saddle boot and broke it open, checking his loads. "I just want a chance at that Johnny West, or whatever he's callin' himself today." He snapped the gun closed with a savage grin. "I'm gonna spread his guts all over Main Street if he's in town."

Slaughter glanced at the albino. "A piece of advice, Whitey. I've seen West draw, so don't give him a chance to go for his gun. He's snake-quick and that shotgun won't do you no good if he feeds you a lead pill first."

"He won't even have time to blink before I blow him all to hell," Whitey growled, his eyes fierce.

"Hey, Boss," Swede said, his head swiveling back and forth as he looked at buildings on either side of the street.

"What is it now, Swede?" Slaughter said, impatient with Swede's constant whining.

"There's something wrong here."

"What'a you mean?"

"There ain't nobody on the street. It looks like the town's deserted."

Slaughter looked around. For once, Swede was making some sense. Something was out of kilter here, all right. There wasn't a citizen in sight, not even a dog or a chicken. Something was going on, and Slaughter began to worry that perhaps he'd underestimated the ease with which they would take the town.

"Uh-oh," Whitey mumbled.

"What is it?" Slaughter asked.

"Look over yonder," Whitey said, pointing ahead down Main Street.

There was a large sign stuck on a post in the center of the street. Painted on it in large red letters was "Slaughter's Marauders . . . Welcome to HELL!"

"Shit!" Slaughter exclaimed, pulling his Colt, the hairs on the back of his neck stirring with the warning. Now he knew they were in deep trouble.

He jerked the reins of his horse's head around, getting

ready to make a quick exit of the town. Then he saw three wagons blocking the street out of town.

"Damn! They've got us blocked in," he said. He noticed his men were looking around, suddenly worried expressions on their faces, though most were too stupid to realize the trap they were in.

"Jim Slaughter," a voice called from the roof of the Big Rock Hotel just up the street.

Slaughter turned to look up, putting a hand up to shield his eyes from the sun.

The man he knew as Johnny West was standing there, next to Monte Carson. Carson had a long-barreled shotgun in his arms, while West had his hands empty.

"Yeah, what do you want?" Slaughter called back.

Monte Carson said in a loud voice, "If you and your men drop your weapons, your men can leave peacefully. You, however, will be arrested, and in all probability, hanged."

"My men and I haven't broken any laws," Slaughter called back. "We just came into town to have a drink and be on our way."

"I AM the law here, Slaughter," Monte said, earing back the hammers on his shotgun. "You got one last chance to come out of this alive. Drop your guns, NOW!"

"That one's mine!" Whitey growled, swinging his Greener toward Smoke.

Almost quicker than the eye could follow, Smoke drew and fired, his Colt exploding and belching fire and gun smoke toward the albino.

Whitey twisted in the saddle, a hole in his right chest pumping scarlet blood onto the back of his horse's head. "Uh!" he groaned with the impact, looking down at the wound in his chest in disbelief.

His lips pulled back over his teeth in a snarl and with a mighty effort, he tried to raise the barrel of his shotgun toward Smoke, until a second shot punched a neat hole in the center of his forehead, exiting out the back of his skull and striking a man behind him in the chest. Both men toppled off their horses as Slaughter's men all aimed and opened fire.

Jensen and Carson dove behind a wooden wall that'd been erected on the rooftop just as bullets began to pockmark the boards.

Without warning, gun barrels appeared in many of the windows of the buildings along Main Street, and all began to fire into the heaving mass of men and horses that was Slaughter's gang. The horses reared and stampeded and crow-hopped, throwing some men to the ground, while others hung on for dear life as they galloped down streets and alleys trying to find a way out of the hell that Big Rock had suddenly become.

Slaughter leaned over his horse's neck, saving his life as a slug meant for him took the animal in the throat and threw them both to the ground.

The outlaw scrabbled on his hands and knees through clouds of cordite and gun smoke toward the entrance to the hotel. Maybe he could survive long enough to kill Monte Carson, whose treachery had caused this whole mess.

Swede leaned down in the saddle, spurring his horse forward and firing blindly at windows and doors as he rode down the middle of Main Street, desperately looking for a hole to crawl into.

Juan Garcia and Chuck Clute, two outlaws from Texas who'd come to Wyoming to escape the Texas Rangers, wheeled their mounts around and raced back down Main Street, trying to get out of town the way they'd come in. *To hell with Slaughter and his thousand dollars,* Garcia thought as he emptied his gun at fleeting shadows in windows.

They were twenty yards from the wagons blocking the entrance to town when four men stood up from behind haystacks in the wagons, all leveling shotguns at the bandits.

"Oh, shit!" Chuck Clute yelled when he saw the shotguns explode in his direction. Those were to be his last words on earth, as several hundred molten slugs of 00-buckshot shredded his chest and blew out his spine.

Garcia was stopped as suddenly as if he'd run into a

brick wall by the express-gun loads, which catapulted him backward out of the saddle to land on his back in the dirt. His last view was of white clouds in a blue sky overhead before he began his journey to Hell.

Boone Marlow, who'd raped and killed more women than he had fingers, jumped off his horse and jerked open the door under the sign saying "General Store."

He stopped short at the sight of a man with a Winchester in his arms. "Welcome to Big Rock," Ed Jackson said as he pulled the trigger.

His slug hit Marlow in the upper stomach, doubling him over just as Peg Jackson pulled the trigger on the small .32-caliber pistol she held in her hand. The bullet, though small, made quite a mess of the top of Marlow's head when it blew out his brains.

Dusty Rhodes, a footpad and burglar from Memphis, Tennessee, who'd left that state after killing an entire family when caught robbing their house, made it to the end of Main without being shot. He jumped off his horse, gun in hand, and burst through the doors of the church, his eyes wide and sweat dripping from his face.

A man wearing a minister's collar was stirring some soup at a table loaded with food and blankets.

Rhodes aimed his pistol, a grin appearing on his face. "Hands up, preacher man. You're gonna be my ticket outta here."

Pain exploded in Dusty Rhodes's head as Bountiful Morrow swung a two-by-four piece of wood into the back of his skull, crushing the bone and scrambling his brains. As he fell forward, blood spurting from his eyes and ears, she said, "Welcome to our church. Would you like to kneel and pray?"

Sam Fleetfoot, on the run from the Indian Nations for murdering three Indian marshals, tried to jump his pony through a window in a boardinghouse to escape the murderous fire from the buildings all around him.

He made it through the window, shattering the glass, but was knocked off his horse to land on his back on the wooden floor. A large piece of glass fell straight down. Sam Fleetfoot held up his hands, getting his fingers sliced off as the sheet of windowpane neatly severed his neck. His eyes were still open as his head rolled away from his body, but it was doubtful they could see the blood spurting from his neck.

Muskrat Calhoon calmly took a twist of tobacco out of his shirt pocket as bullets thunked into the wooden wall he was standing behind on the roof of the *Big Rock Guardian*. He bit off a sizable chunk of tobacco, then rose up and leaned his Sharps over the wall. It took but a second for him to spot and aim at a man riding down the street over three hundred yards away. He put the sight six inches over the man's head and slowly caressed the trigger. He was spun half around by the recoil as the big rifle belched two ounces of lead toward the outlaw.

Ernest Melton, noted murderer from Montgomery, Alabama, who'd killed two deputies and a family he took hostage in an escape before heading to Wyoming, never felt the slug that penetrated his spine between his shoulder blades and blew him over his horse's head, broken almost in half by the power of the Sharps cartridge.

Muskrat jacked another shell into the chamber and fired again, this time at a man running toward a dressmaker's shop. As the slug hit Happy Jack Morco in the shoulder and blew his right arm clean off, Muskrat mumbled, "Ya don't need no dresses nohow where yo're goin', sonny." Evidently Happy Jack didn't think so either, for he fell squirming to the ground, where his screams of pain could be heard even over the noise of the gunfight, until he bled to death.

Haywood Arden stood in the doorway of his newspaper office, a shotgun in his arms, shouting, "Extra, extra, read all about it! Murderers killed in fatal attempt to take over town!" He punctuated his shouts by firing both barrels of the American Arms twelve-gauge and blowing Frank Broadwell and Chester Hughes out of their saddles as they rode hell-bent down the street.

Dana Arden calmly handed him another shotgun and began to reload his, saying, "Nice shot, Haywood."

Marty Prembook, a stone killer who hired his gun out to anyone with the money to pay for it, decided he wasn't being offered enough for this job and jerked his horse's head around and galloped toward an alleyway. James Hunt, rapist, mugger, and pederast, saw Prembook making a getaway and followed as fast as his horse would run.

As they entered the alley, two figures stepped from the darkness of shadows along the buildings on either side.

Pearlie and Cal raised their Colts and fired as one. Two outlaws twisted and bent and fell out of their saddles to the ground. Hunt was killed instantly. Prembook, severely wounded, held up his hand. "Mercy . . . mercy," he cried.

Pearlie hesitated, then jumped as Cal fired from behind him and punched a hole just above Prembook's nose.

Pearlie looked at Cal, his eyebrows raised, until Cal pointed and he could see the gun in Prembook's other hand, hammer still cocked. Pearlie grinned and held up a finger, showing he owed Cal one.

From his vantage point on the roof of the hotel, Smoke saw Swede riding down the street toward the livery. He took two quick steps, jumped to the roof next door, and hurriedly climbed down the stairs on the side wall. Weaving through the alley, he entered the livery stable through the rear door.

Swede was trying to burrow under some hay in the corner when Smoke stepped out into the light.

"You got two choices, outlaw," Smoke growled, his hands hanging at his sides, relaxed.

Swede jerked around at the sound of Smoke's voice, a pistol in his right hand, barrel pointed down at the ground.

"What're those?"

"You can drop that gun and give yourself up and hang."

Swede smiled sadly. "Not acceptable. What's the other choice?"

"I can kill you right here."

"I got a pistol in my hand. Not even you are that fast."

Smoke gave a small shrug. "I have a feeling we're fixing to find out. Right?"

"Goddamned right!" Swede said, and jerked the barrel of his Colt upward.

In one lightning-fast movement, Smoke drew and fired from the hip without aiming. His gun exploded a split second before Swede's did, his slug hitting the big man in the chest.

Swede's bullet grazed Smoke's throat, drawing a fine line across his neck that began to slowly ooze blood.

Swede stood there, a surprised look on his face. Then he looked down at the hole in his chest and the spreading red stain on his shirt.

"You've killed me."

Smoke nodded. "It appears that way."

Swede grinned, then coughed, blood trickling down the corners of his mouth. "Then I'll see you in Hell."

Smoke nodded. "Maybe, but not today."

Swede's grin faded and he fell forward onto his face.

Monte Carson stood up from behind the wooden barrier on the roof and aimed his shotgun down. Ike Black and James Blaine, both men who'd ridden with Quantrill's Raiders and were used to firefights, had dismounted and were standing behind their horses, firing over the saddles at the window to the general store.

Monte pulled the triggers on his shotgun and reeled back as both barrels exploded buckshot at the men. Both men and both horses were knocked off their feet by the force of the blast. When Ike Black struggled to his feet, Monte dropped the shotgun and drew his pistol, shooting the man in the top of his head and driving him to his knees, where he stayed, as if in supplication, though he was dead as a stone.

Otis Andarko, Charley Adams, and Joe Belcham ran their horses up on the boardwalk and made it as far as Longmont's Saloon. They dove off their mounts and scrambled through the batwings, huffing and out of breath from the exertion.

The three men had been *comancheros* in the past, making their living selling whiskey to the Indians, and guns that were then used to kill innocent settlers.

As they straightened up, they saw two men standing at the bar. One was dressed in a black coat, with starched white shirt and knee-high, highly polished black boots. The other wore a red checked shirt and Levi's jeans and looked like a cowboy.

"Well, looky what we got here, boys," Otis said as he dusted off his pants. "A tinhorn cardsharp and a sodbuster."

Louis Longmont picked up a shot glass and drained the whiskey in one draft. "Johnny," he said to Johnny North, standing next to him.

"Yeah, Louis?"

"Should we kill them now, or have another drink first?"

Johnny pursed his lips. "Gosh, I don't know, Louis. What do you boys think?" he asked the three men standing in the doorway.

Joe Belcham couldn't believe his ears. He looked at his two friends, then back at the two men at the bar. "But we got you outnumbered three to two," he said, his hand moving toward his gun.

Louis shrugged. "I know the odds aren't fair, but we don't have time for you to go get more men."

"What?" Otis asked.

It was to be his last question as Louis and Johnny filled their hands with iron and blew the three men back out through the batwings. None of the three managed to clear leather, much less get off a shot, before they were dead.

"Louis, let me buy you a drink this time," Johnny said.

"Don't mind if I do," Louis said as Johnny poured.

Blackjack Tony McCurdy managed to get through Dr. Spalding's office door with only two minor flesh wounds. As he burst into the room, the doctor looked up and said, "I'll be with you in a minute, sir, as soon as I finish removing a bullet from this arm."

Haywood Arden lay on the table with his wife, Dana,

holding his hand. "I told you not to stand in the doorway like that," she said. "I told you you'd get shot."

Haywood nodded, his face covered with sweat. "I know, dear, but what can I say? It was my first shootout."

Blackjack, who'd shot his first man when he was thirteen years old, and hadn't minded that it was his father he'd killed, stepped over to grab Dr. Spalding by the arm.

"Shut the hell up. What's wrong with you people? Can't you see I have a gun?" he said, sticking out his hand with the Colt in it toward Dana.

"Oh, that," Spalding said casually. Then in one quick motion and with a flick of his wrist, he slashed the extensor tendons of Blackjack's right hand with the scalpel he was holding.

The pistol dropped to the floor as Blackjack screamed and grabbed his bleeding right hand with his left. He looked down and saw scarlet stains covering the boots he'd taken from Roscoe Archer's body. His face paled and he fainted, falling to the floor.

"That's right, have a seat and I'll see to that nasty wound as soon as I'm finished here," Spalding said, turning back to Haywood.

Monte Carson climbed through the rooftop door and let himself down to the top floor of the hotel. He'd just finished punching out his empties and reloading his Colt when he heard a sound behind him.

He turned and found Big Jim Slaughter pointing a pistol at him.

"You're the cause of all this," Slaughter said, a crazed look in his eye.

Monte smiled. "No, I'm not, Jim. It's your greed and your stupidity that's brought you here."

"I'm gonna kill you, Carson."

"I don't think so, Jim. Not now, not ever."

As Slaughter eared back the hammer on his Colt, Monte dropped to one knee and raised his pistol, firing twice in rapid succession.

The first bullet hit Slaughter in the right chest and spun

him around, while the second entered the back of his head and knocked him to the floor, where he landed face-down in a pool of his own blood.

Monte got up, walked over to him, and rolled him over. Slaughter's face was gone, blown away by the exiting slug from Monte's .44.

Big Jim, you don't look so big now, Monte thought.

Monte stepped to the window and looked at the carnage below. All of the outlaws were either dead or wounded and out of action.

Slaughter's Marauders were as dead as their founder, and dead too was the past of Monte Carson, respected sheriff in Big Rock, Colorado.

EPILOGUE

Smoke and the acrid smell of cordite hung like an early morning fog over Big Rock, Colorado. The odors and sounds of men wounded and dying and dead assailed the townspeople, who were going about the grisly task of piling corpses in the back of buckboards for the short trip to boot hill, separating out the wounded, who would be first cared for by Doc Spalding, then jailed by Monte Carson, the man they'd come to kill.

Smoke Jensen walked from the livery stable, blood oozing from a close call on his neck. He looked up and down the street, his ears still ringing from the sound of his Colts when he blew Swede to Hell and gone, his pistol hanging at his side.

He took a deep breath, and realized with a start how much he loved the smell and feel and gut-wrenching excitement of a fight. It was not something he was proud of, but he was a pragmatic man, and he knew that one's basic nature could be suppressed, but never changed. He guessed it was something he was going to have to work on.

"Hey, Smoke," Louis called from over by his saloon. "You all right?"

Smoke came out of his reverie and fingered the wound on his neck. "Yeah, Louis, I'm all right," he answered, and moved to join his friend.

Louis and Johnny North picked up the three dead men in front of the saloon and heaved them in the back of the buckboard Ralph Morrow was driving down the middle of Main Street.

"Looks like you boys had your share of action," Smoke observed.

Louis shrugged. "These men had the gall to interrupt our conversation over two glasses of Napoleon brandy. What else could we do but shoot them for their impertinence?"

Cal and Pearlie sauntered up to join them, Pearlie still reloading his pistol.

"You boys all right?" Smoke asked, relieved to see them walking and know they had no serious wounds. Sally would have his skin if anything ever happened to either one of them.

Pearlie was about to reply when a door slammed from across the street and a man staggered onto the boardwalk, his right hand bleeding and his left filled with iron. As he raised his pistol and fired, Pearlie shoved Cal to the side and stepped in front of him.

Blackjack Tony McCurdy's bullet hit Pearlie in the side, punching through the thin layer of fat on his flank half an inch under the skin and exiting out the back.

As Pearlie doubled over, four pistols were drawn and fired almost simultaneously by Smoke, Cal, Louis, and Johnny. The bullets all hit Blackjack, lifting him off his feet and flinging him back against the wall next to Doc Spalding's office just as the doc came bursting out of the door.

Spalding held out his hands, "I'm sorry, Smoke," he said as he ran to take a look at Pearlie. "He was unconscious and I was removing a bullet from Haywood. He must've woken up and sneaked out the door."

"That's all right, Cotton," Smoke said from where he was squatted next to Pearlie, who was moaning and groaning and holding his side.

The doctor kneeled down and moved Pearlie's hand, checking his wound. Then he looked up and smiled. "I think all this cowboy needs is a small bandage and something to eat."

"Did somebody mention food?" Pearlie said, sitting up and grinning.

"Why'd you do that, Pearlie?" Cal said. "Why'd you take that bullet for me?"

"Hell, boy," Pearlie said as he struggled to his feet. "We done got a record goin' here. You been through two gunfights without gittin' wounded." He shook his head. "I jest didn't want'a spoil your streak."

"Go on in, Pearlie, and have Andre fire up the stove. Tell him I said to fix you anything you want," Louis offered.

Pearlie put his arm over Cal's shoulder and began to hobble into the saloon.

Cal looked at him. "Now, I done thanked you fer takin' that bullet. Don't go tryin' to make it more'n it is."

Pearlie straightened up and quit limping. "Can't blame a feller for tryin', can you?"

Monte Carson stepped through the door to the hotel and made his way across the street. His shoulders were slumped with fatigue and he looked dead tired, but he had a smile on his face.

"Well," he said, "it's finally over."

Smoke nodded. "Yes, I believe it is. Did you finish Slaughter?"

Monte nodded. "His raiding days are over."

Smoke looked up and glanced around the town, watching his friends and neighbors emerge from their stores and offices and homes to begin cleaning up the town. "Then it was worth all this."

Two weeks later, Smoke and Sally stood in front of boot hill. A light snow was falling and the white blanket over the graves and markers almost made the place look pretty.

Smoke nodded at the marker in front of them that said simply "Jim Slaughter."

He put his arm around Sally. "You know, sweetheart, if it wasn't for you, I could've ended up like that."

She stared at him. "What do you mean, Smoke?"

"I realized during the fight in town that I love the feeling of putting everything you are and everything you own on the line in a fight to the death."

She shook her head. "I know you do, dear, and that is why I've never tried to change you, or to keep you from doing what you know you have to do. But you are as far different from the man lying there as day is from night. You may enjoy the contest of a fight, but you never start a fight or pick on someone who is weaker than you are."

She put her hand on his cheek. "You have a wonderful soul, Smoke, and in the final analysis, that is what separates you from men like Jim Slaughter."

They walked up the street away from the cemetery, arm in arm.

"What are your plans now, Smoke?" Sally asked.

He thought for a moment, then smiled. "After the snow season's over, I thought I might take Cal and Pearlie on a little trip down Texas way."

She looked at him. "You're going to the King Ranch and get some Santa Gertrudis cattle like I wanted to, aren't you?"

He nodded. "That idea of yours to cross them with our shorthorns is a good one. Besides, there's nothing much going on down Texas way right now, no range wars or Indians left to fight, so it'll be a nice quiet trip and I need the rest."

JUSTICE OF THE
MOUNTAIN MAN

1

Smoke Jensen buttoned up his buckskin shirt and walked into the kitchen where his wife, Sally, was bent over putting biscuits in the oven. He stepped up behind her and hugged her.

"You shouldn't do that to a man fixing to leave town for a few weeks," he said, his voice husky with desire.

Sally grinned as she leaned back against him. "Why, do what, Mr. Jensen, sir?"

He gave her an extra squeeze. "You know what, you tease."

She turned, placing her arms around his neck. "Do you really have to go, Smoke? Our herd is doing fine without those bulls you want to get."

He poured himself a cup of coffee and sat at the kitchen table, eyeing her with one eyebrow raised. "Sweetheart, it was your idea in the first place to cross our shorthorns with the Santa Gertrudis from Texas. You having second thoughts now?"

She shook her head as she poured herself a cup and sat across the table from him. "Yes, it was my idea, but I just hate the idea of you traveling all that way right now, just after that mess with Jim Slaughter was cleared up."*

*Heart of the Mountain Man

He grinned. "You think the old man's too old for the trip?"

She shook her head, eyeing the scar on his neck from the bullet wound he'd received in the shoot-out in Big Rock. "No, but you're just now getting over being shot, and knowing you, it might just happen again on your trip."

"Now what makes you say that? After all, I'll have Cal and Pearlie with me to keep me out of trouble."

"A lot of good that'll do. When the three of you go off on a trip together, it always seems to lead to gunplay."

"But, Sally, we really need those bulls. I know the herd is all right as it is, but if we get some of those Santa Gertrudis bulls from Richard King on the King Ranch down in Texas, it'll almost double the amount of meat on our shorthorn crosses, and make them more resistant to both drought and cold weather."

Sally finished her coffee, got up from the table, and broke three eggs into a cast-iron skillet and began to scramble them, looking over her shoulder at Smoke as she worked. "I know it'll be better, but I hate to see you go that far to get them."

"It won't be so bad. Cal and Pearlie and I'll take the train to Fort Worth and buy some horses there to ride the rest of the way. Heck, most of the trip'll be fun."

She smirked. "Yeah, I know your idea of fun. You and the boys will play poker all the way down there and you'll win their wages for the next year, and then turn around and give them back."

Smoke grinned. "You're probably right, but it will be a lesson they need to learn. Don't play cards with money you can't afford to lose."

She laughed and handed him his plate of scrambled eggs and bacon. "Here, tinhorn," she said, "start on these while I get your biscuits out of the oven."

Smoke noticed a plate of dough on the counter formed into the shape of bear sign, Sally's famous doughnuts. "What's that I see on the counter?" he asked.

Sally laughed. "You don't think you're going to get Pearlie and Cal out of town without an ample supply of bear sign to take along, do you?"

"Hell, to take enough to last Pearlie until he gets back, we'll have to pack a steamer trunk full!"

A knock came at the door and Cal and Pearlie walked in. Pearlie, a tall, lanky, cowboy with mustache and sun-wrinkled face and sparkling sky-blue eyes, tipped his hat back. "Did I hear something about bear sign?"

Sally held her hand up. "Uh-uh, Pearlie. You stay away from that dough at least until it's baked!"

Pearlie nodded and sat next to Smoke, leaning over as he smelled Smoke's breakfast. "Hmmm, that sure smells good, Miss Sally."

She shook her head. "You and Cal get yourselves some coffee while I scramble up another batch of hens' eggs and bacon."

Almost before the words were out of her mouth, Pearlie, a noted food-hound, had his hat off and was strad-dling a chair at the table. Cal, younger and a tad more polite, said, "Thank you, Miss Sally," before he removed his hat and took a seat.

As the boys dug into the food, Smoke leaned back and thought about how they'd both come to work for him and Sally, and how they'd since become almost part of the family . . .

Calvin Woods, going on nineteen years old now, had been just fourteen when Smoke and Sally took him in as a hired hand. It was during the spring branding, and Sally was on her way back from Big Rock to the Sugarloaf. The buckboard was piled high with supplies because branding hundreds of calves makes for hungry punchers.

As Sally slowed the team to make a bend in the trail, a rail-thin young man stepped from the bushes at the side of the road with a pistol in his hand.

"Hold it right there, miss."

Applying the brake with her right foot, Sally slipped her hand under a pile of gingham cloth on the seat. She grasped the handle of her short-barreled Colt .44 and eared back the hammer, letting the sound of the horses' hooves and the squealing of the brake pad on the wheel mask the sound. "What can I do for you, young man?" she asked, her voice firm and without fear. She knew she could draw and drill the young highwayman before he could raise his pistol to fire.

"Well, uh, you can throw some of those beans and a cut of that fatback over here, and maybe a portion of that Arbuckle's coffee too."

Sally's eyebrows rose. "Don't you want my money?"

The boy frowned and shook his head. "Why, no, ma'am. I ain't no thief, I'm just hungry."

"And if I don't give you my food, are you going to shoot me with that big Navy Colt?"

He hesitated a moment, then grinned ruefully. "No, ma'am, I guess not." He twirled the pistol around his finger and slipped it into his belt, turned, and began to walk down the road toward Big Rock.

Sally watched the youngster amble off, noting his tattered shirt, dirty pants with holes in the knees and torn pockets, and boots that looked as if they had been salvaged from a garbage dump. "Young man," she called, "come back here, please."

He turned, a smirk on his face, spreading his hands. "Look, lady, you don't have to worry. I don't even have any bullets." With a lightning-fast move he drew the gun from his pants, aimed away from Sally, and pulled the trigger. There was a click but no explosion as the hammer fell on an empty cylinder.

Sally smiled. "Oh, I'm not worried." In a movement every bit as fast as his, she whipped her .44 out and fired, clipping a pine cone from a branch, causing it to fall and bounce off his head.

The boy's knees buckled and he ducked, saying, "Jimminy Christmas!"

Mimicking him, Sally twirled her Colt and stuck it in the waistband of her britches. "What's your name, boy?"

The boy blushed and looked down at his feet. "Calvin, ma'am, Calvin Woods."

She leaned forward, elbows on knees, and stared into the boy's eyes. "Calvin, no one has to go hungry in this country, not if they're willing to work."

He looked up at her through narrowed eyes, as if he found life a little different than she'd described it.

"If you're willing to put in an honest day's work, I'll see that you get an honest day's pay, and all the food you can eat."

Calvin stood a little straighter, shoulders back and head held high. "Ma'am, I've got to be straight with you. I ain't no experienced cowhand. I come from a hardscrabble farm and we only had us one milk cow and a couple of goats and chickens, and lots of dirt that weren't worth nothing for growin' things. My ma and pa and me never had nothin', but we never begged and we never stooped to takin' handouts."

Sally thought, *I like this boy. Proud, and not willing to take charity if he can help it.* "Calvin, if you're willing to work, and don't mind getting your hands dirty and your muscles sore, I've got some hands that'll have you punching beeves like you were born to it in no time at all."

A smile lit up his face, making him seem even younger than his years. "Even if I don't have no saddle, nor a horse to put it on?"

She laughed out loud. "Yes. We've got plenty of ponies and saddles." She glanced down at his raggedy boots. "We can probably even round up some boots and spurs that'll fit you."

He walked over and jumped in the back of the buckboard. "Ma'am, I don't know who you are, but you just hired you the hardest workin' hand you've ever seen."

Back at the Sugarloaf, she sent him in to Cookie and told him to eat his fill. When Smoke and the other punchers rode into the cabin yard at the end of the day, she introduced Calvin around. As Cal was shaking hands with the men, Smoke looked over at her and winked. He knew she could never resist a stray dog or cat, and her heart was as large as the Big Lonesome itself.

Smoke walked up to Cal and cleared his throat. "Son, I hear you drew down on my wife."

Cal gulped. "Yessir, Mr. Jensen. I did." He squared his shoulders and looked Smoke in the eye, not flinching, though he was obviously frightened of the tall man with the incredibly wide shoulders standing before him.

Smoke smiled and clapped the boy on the back. "Just wanted you to know you stared death in the eye, boy. Not many galoots are still walking upright who ever pulled a gun on Sally. She's a better shot than any man I've ever seen except me, and sometimes I wonder about me."

The boy laughed with relief as Smoke turned and called out, "Pearlie, get your lazy butt over here."

A tall, lanky cowboy ambled over to Smoke and Cal, munching on a biscuit stuffed with roast beef. His face was lined with wrinkles and tanned a dark brown from hours under the sun, but his eyes were sky-blue and twinkled with good-natured humor.

"Yessir, Boss," he mumbled around a mouthful of food.

Smoke put his hand on Pearlie's shoulder. "Cal, this here chow-hound is Pearlie. He eats more'n any two hands, and he's never been known to do a lick of work he could get out of, but he knows beeves and horses as well as any puncher I have. I want you to follow him around and let him teach you what you need to know."

Cal nodded. "Yes, sir, Mr. Smoke."

"Now let me see that iron you have in your pants."

Cal pulled the ancient Navy Colt and handed it to Smoke. When Smoke opened the loading gate, the rusted cylinder fell to the ground, causing Pearlie and Smoke to laugh and Cal's face to flame red. "This is the piece you pulled on Sally?" Smoke asked.

The boy nodded, looking at the ground.

Pearlie shook his head. "Cal, you're one lucky pup. Hell, if'n you'd tried to fire that thing, it'd've blown your hand clean off."

Smoke inclined his head toward the bunkhouse. "Pearlie, take Cal over to the tack house and get him fixed up with what he needs, including a gun belt and a Colt that won't fall apart the first time he pulls it. You might also help pick him out a shavetail to ride. I'll expect him to start earning his keep tomorrow."

"Yes, sir, Smoke." Pearlie put his arm around Cal's shoulders and led him off toward the bunkhouse. "Now the first thing you gotta learn, Cal, is how to get on Cookie's good side. A puncher rides on his belly, and it 'pears to me that you need some fattin' up 'fore you can begin to punch cows."

Pearlie had come to work for Smoke in as roundabout a way as Cal had. He was hiring his gun out to Tilden Franklin in Fontana when Franklin went crazy and tried to take over Sugarloaf, Smoke and Sally's spread. After Franklin's men raped and killed a young girl in the fracas, Pearlie sided with Smoke and the aging gunfighters he had called in to help put an end to Franklin's reign of terror.*

Pearlie was now honorary foreman of Smoke's ranch though he was only a shade over twenty years old himself. Boys grew to be men early in the mountains of Colorado.

Smoke's thoughts were interrupted when Pearlie stuffed the last of his bacon and eggs into his mouth and washed it down with a giant drink of coffee. "Ah, that's 'bout the best food I ever ate, Miss Sally."

He paused and glanced at the dough sitting on the counter. "Uh, any idea when those bear sign gonna be ready?"

Sally laughed and pointed at the front door. "You men go on out on the porch and have your cigarettes and I'll let you know."

*Trail of the Mountain Man

The three men settled on wooden chairs on the porch and all rolled cigarettes to have with their final cups of coffee.

"When you figgerin' on headin' down Texas way, Smoke?" Pearlie asked.

Smoke glanced at the sky, which was the clear, bright blue of a spring morning. The temperature was still in the low fifties, but it promised to be a beautiful day. "I suspect most of the snow'll be out of the passes by now, so the train shouldn't have any problem making it to Texas. How about we get packed and try to get off tomorrow on the afternoon train?"

"Sounds good to me," Cal said, his face brightening at the prospect of travel to far-off places.

Pearlie nodded. "That'll do."

"You got the boys ready for the spring calving and branding?" Smoke asked.

"Yep. An' the foreman over at Johnny North's has said he'll keep a close watch on the place while we're gone and be sure and help if Miss Sally needs anything."

Smoke flipped his butt over the railing into the dirt. "Good, then it's settled. We'll take the buckboard into town in the morning so Sally can get some last-minute shopping done, and then we'll take off."

Pearlie's nose twitched. "You boys smell anything?" he asked.

Smoke sniffed the air and grinned. "Why I do believe that first batch of bear sign smells like it's about ready."

Cal jumped to his feet and started toward the kitchen, but Pearlie grabbed the back of his belt and jerked him back down. "Don't you know better'n to try an' eat 'fore your betters, boy?" he asked as he sprinted toward the cabin door.

"Take it easy, Cal," Smoke said as he got slowly to his feet. "There'll be plenty to go around."

Cal's face fell. "Not if'n Pearlie gets there first. That boy can eat his weight in bear sign!"

2

The next morning Smoke, along with Sally and Cal and Pearlie, loaded up the buckboard and headed for Big Rock. Smoke and Sally rode up top, with Cal and Pearlie and their luggage in the back of the wagon.

As they entered the town, Sheriff Monte Carson was standing in the door to his office, drinking coffee from a tin cup and puffing on his battered corncob pipe.

Smoke slowed the buckboard and pulled it to the side of the street in front of Monte's office. After he helped Sally down, she said she would be in Ed and Peg Jackson's general store, picking out the provisions she would need while the men were away on their trip to Texas. She gave a small smile. "Why don't you boys go on over to Longmont's and tell your friends good-bye while I'm shopping, Smoke?"

After she left, Monte gave her an approving look. "You got a good woman there, Smoke. One who knows when to step back an' let her man be with his friends."

Smoke nodded. "I know it, Monte. And I'd appreciate it if you and Mary could drop in on her every once in a while when I'm out of town."

"No problem, Smoke," the sheriff answered.

Pearlie shuffled his feet impatiently. "We gonna go on over to Longmont's, Smoke?" he asked.

Monte cocked an eye at Smoke's foreman. "You must be 'bout starved, Pearlie, since you probably ain't had nothin' to eat since you left the Sugarloaf this mornin'."

Pearlie rubbed his stomach. "Well, now that you mention it, Monte, I could use a bite or two."

"Damn, Pearlie, it ain't been more'n two hours since you ate last," Cal said as the men walked toward Longmont's Saloon down the street.

Pearlie put his arm over Cal's shoulder, speaking in a fatherly tone even though he wasn't more than a couple of years older than the boy. "Cal, like I done tole you, ya' gotta eat ever' chance ya get, 'cause you never know when the next opportunity for grub is gonna present itself."

Smoke led the way through the batwings of Louis Longmont's saloon and, as was his habit from years of having men on his trail, immediately stepped to the side of the door and waited for his eyes to adjust to the gloom of the room before he walked further.

Louis Longmont was, as usual, sitting at his private table in a corner of the saloon, drinking coffee laced with chicory and smoking a long, black cigar.

When he saw Smoke and the others, he grinned and waved them over, calling out to a young, black waiter to come to the table.

After the men sat down, Louis glanced at the waiter. "Johnny, I'm sure these men have all had breakfast already, but that lanky one there on the end has never been known to take a seat in this establishment without ordering some nourishment."

Smoke grinned. "You're right, Louis. We'll all have some of Andre's wonderful coffee, but I'm sure Pearlie will want something extra."

"Just a light snack, to get me through till the train leaves, Louis. How about some flapjacks with blueberry syrup and half a pound of bacon on the side?"

"I see that you're moving very well, Pearlie," Louis said. "I guess that wound you suffered during our excitement last month has healed properly."

Pearlie fingered his flank, where a bullet meant for Cal had punched through his side just under the skin when he'd pushed Cal out of the way.*

He made a face, as though in pain. "Well, it still smarts a mite if'n I move wrong, but I guess the discomfort was worth it to save Cal's hide."

"I swear to God," Cal said, an aggrieved expression on his face. "It wern't more'n a scratch, Pearlie. Hell, Doc Spalding didn't even put a bandage on it!"

The men at the table all laughed as Pearlie assumed an aggrieved expression. "I guess that's the thanks I get for savin' the boy's life," he moaned.

The waiter appeared and began unloading coffee for everyone and a plate piled high with pancakes and bacon, and Pearlie's face lightened as he grabbed a fork and dug in with apparent gusto.

Monte fired up his pipe and leaned back in his chair, looking at Smoke. "I see you got your bags packed in the back of the buckboard, Smoke. You boys plannin' on takin' a trip?"

Smoke explained to him how they were going to go down to Texas and talk to Richard King about buying some of his prize Santa Gertrudis bulls to cross with his shorthorn herd.

"Well," Monte said, glancing out the window, "spring's a good time to travel to Texas, 'fore the sun gets hot enough to melt your pistols."

Louis arched an eyebrow. "Richard King? Seems I've heard the name before."

Smoke laughed. "You should have, Louis. King was a steamboat operator who became a serious breeder of cattle. He took the native longhorn cows and bred them with expensive blooded bulls to form a breed called the Santa Gertrudis. He bought seventy-five thousand acres down in Nueces County in Texas, just up from the Rio

*Heart of the Mountain Man

Bravo. He calls his place the King Ranch, and word is it now covers almost a million acres scattered over four counties."

"Whew," Monte said, tipping his hat back, "and I thought we had some large spreads here in Colorado."

"He ships most of his beef and hides out of Galveston on steamboats and sailing ships, but he's agreed to sell me some of his bulls so his stock won't get too inbred," Smoke said.

As Pearlie finished his meal, the men settled into a comfortable discussion of cattle, ranching, and local gossip. As they talked, Smoke thought how lucky he was to have friends like Monte and Louis . . .

He and Monte Carson had become very good friends over the past few years. Carson had once been a well-known gunfighter, though he had never ridden the owl-hoot trail.

A local rancher, with plans to take over the county, had hired Carson to be the sheriff of Fontana, a town just down the road from Smoke's Sugarloaf spread. Carson went along with the man's plans for a while, till he couldn't stomach the rapings and killings any longer. He put his foot down and let it be known that Fontana was going to be run in a law-abiding manner from then on.

The rancher, Tilden Franklin, sent a bunch of riders in to teach the upstart sheriff a lesson. The men killed Carson's two deputies and seriously wounded him, taking over the town. In retaliation, Smoke founded the town of Big Rock, and he and his band of aging gunfighters cleaned house in Fontana.

When the fracas was over, Smoke offered the job of sheriff of Big Rock to Monte Carson. He married a grass widow and settled into the job like he was born to it. Neither Smoke nor the citizens of Big Rock ever had cause to regret his taking the job.

Louis Longmont, on the other hand, owned the saloon

in Big Rock called simply Longmont's, and was Smoke's friend of many years. Longmont's was where he plied his trade, which he called teaching amateurs the laws of chance.

Louis was a lean, hawk-faced man, with strong, slender hands and long fingers, nails carefully manicured, hands clean. He had jet-black hair and a black pencil-thin mustache. He was, as usual, dressed in a black suit, with white shirt and dark ascot—something he'd picked up on a trip to England some years back. He wore low-heeled boots, and a pistol hung in tied-down leather on his right side. It was not for show, for Louis was snake-quick with a short gun and was a feared, deadly gun hand when pushed.

Louis was not an evil man. He had never hired his gun out for money. And while he could make a deck of cards do almost anything, he did not cheat at poker. He did not have to cheat. He was possessed of a phenomenal memory and could tell you the odds of filling any type of poker hand, and was one of the first to use the new method of card counting.

He was just past forty years of age. He had come to the West as a very small boy, with his parents, arriving from Louisiana. His parents had died in a shantytown fire, leaving the boy to cope as best he could.

He had coped quite well, plying his innate intelligence and willingness to take a chance into a fortune. He owned a large ranch up in Wyoming Territory, several businesses in San Francisco, and a hefty chunk of a railroad.

Though it was a mystery to many why Longmont stayed with the hard life he had chosen, Smoke thought he understood. Once, Louis had said to him, "Smoke, I would miss my life every bit as much as you would miss the dry-mouthed moment before the draw, the challenge of facing and besting those miscreants who would kill you or others, and the so-called loneliness of the owl-hoot trail."

Sometimes Louis joked that he would like to draw against Smoke someday, just to see who was faster. Smoke allowed as how it would be close, but that he would win.

"You see, Louis, you're just too civilized," he had told him on many occasions. "Your mind is distracted by visions of operas, fine foods and wines, and the odds of your winning the match. Also, your fatal flaw is that you can almost always see the good in the lowest creatures God ever made, and you refuse to believe that anyone is pure evil and without hope of redemption."

When Louis laughed at this description of himself, Smoke would continue. "Me, on the other hand, when some snake-scum draws down on me and wants to dance, the only thing I have on my mind is teaching him that when you dance, someone has to pay the band. My mind is clear and focused on only one problem, how to put that stump-sucker across his horse toes-down."

While the other men talked, Smoke smiled at his recollections of Louis and Monte, knowing he was going to miss them on his upcoming trip.

3

Smoke stood on the train platform, his arms around Sally's neck. "Good-bye, Sally. I'll be back before you know it," he said, staring into her eyes and almost wishing he weren't going.

"Smoke," she began, a serious look on her face.

"I know," he interrupted with a grin. "Ride with my guns loose and loaded up six and six."

She nodded, not smiling. "I'm serious, Smoke. There's liable to still be some of those old wanted posters out on you down in Texas. You know how backward those Texicans are."

"Yes, dear, I'll be extra careful, and I'll make sure Cal and Pearlie watch my back at all times."

She glanced over his shoulder to stare fixedly at Cal and Pearlie. "I'm counting on you boys to keep the big man out of trouble, you hear?"

Pearlie nodded, while Cal looked anxious to get on the train so the adventure could begin.

"I mean it, Pearlie. There'll be no more bear sign if anything happens to Smoke!" she warned.

A look of horror came over his face at the thought. "Don't you worry none, Miss Sally. He'll be safe as if he were in church."

"That'll be the day," she replied with a smile as she

hugged Smoke's neck and brushed his cheek with her lips. "There'll be more of that waiting for you when you get back," she whispered in his ear, a mischievous look in her eyes.

As the train pulled through the mountain passes, most still with quite a bit of snow on the ground from the winter snows, Smoke and the boys moved into the smoking car. They sat at a table and Pearlie pulled out a weathered packet of cards.

"You ready to lose the Sugarloaf, Smoke?" he asked, grinning around a cigarette stuck in the corner of his mouth as he shuffled the cards in the manner of an experienced poker player as Louis Longmont had shown him.

Smoke leaned back and pulled a long black cigar from his shirt pocket. "You boys don't have a chance," he growled. "Louis loaned me a couple of his poker-playing cigars. No way I can be beat long as I smoke these."

Cal's forehead furrowed. "That ain't fair, Smoke! You already beat the tar outta us every time we play. You don't need no special ceegars to hep you do it."

Pearlie began to deal the cards. "Shut up, Cal. Cain't you see he's just funnin' with us?"

They began to play stud poker, using some chips kept on hand in the smoking car for the passengers to use. As the day wore on, the miles passed, and the pile of chips in front of Smoke grew steadily larger, while Cal's and Pearlie's shrank slowly.

A few other men in the car began to gather around, drawn by the lure of a poker game and the evident fun Smoke and the boys were having playing.

Finally, a man wearing a bowler derby and boiled white shirt stepped over, a thin, short cigarillo hanging from his mouth.

"Mind if I sit in?" he asked, pulling up a chair without waiting for an answer.

Smoke pursed his lips. He'd seen men like this hundreds of times in his years on the trail. Tinhorns, they traveled from town to town making a living off suckers who didn't know the difference between a shaved card and one marked with the sharp edge of a signet ring.

Pearlie and Cal looked to Smoke to see what he was going to do. He gave them a sly wink and grinned at the stranger. "Sure, have a seat. This is just a friendly game, however. Might not be up to your standards."

The tinhorn waved a hand. "Oh, I'm not really much of a poker player, so I'll fit right in. My name's Maxwell Gibbons."

"I'm Smoke, and this is Cal and Pearlie," Smoke said, omitting his last name.

Max pulled a small wad of greenbacks from his coat pocket and put them on the table in front of him. "What's the game?"

"Stud poker," Smoke answered as he shuffled and dealt the cards.

Without being obvious, Smoke kept his eye on Max as the game progressed, and the stack of chips in front of the newcomer steadily grew.

He could see Cal and Pearlie becoming more and more frustrated as their money seemed to disappear before their very eyes.

Soon, Smoke had had enough of Max's trickery, and he picked up the deck of cards and stared at the gambler. "I want to show you something, tinhorn," he growled, menace in his voice. Smoke placed the cards on the table and proceeded to cut four aces in a row. Then he picked the cards up, shuffled them, and dealt four hands faceup, giving himself four aces and Pearlie four kings and Cal four queens.

Max's eyes widened, then narrowed as his face flushed bright red. "I . . . I don't understand," he murmured, his eyes shifting around the car to see if anyone was watching.

"Oh, I think you do," Smoke said. He pointed at the signet ring on Max's hand. "You've been shaving the face cards ever since you sat down so they'd be easy to pick out of the deck."

Max pushed his chair back, his hand drifting toward his coat. "You calling me a card cheat, mister?" he said, his voice suddenly harsh.

Smoke leaned back in his chair. "I'll be calling you dead if that hand moves another inch," he said, his voice calm and deliberate.

Max looked in Smoke's eyes, and his face paled at what he saw there. "Uh . . . just who are you, mister?" he asked, letting his hand drop to his side.

"My name's Smoke Jensen."

Max gulped. "*The* Smoke Jensen?"

"There ain't but the one, tinhorn," Pearlie piped up from across the table.

"Uh . . . gosh, Mr. Jensen. I'm sorry 'bout all this. I'll just take my stake and go on about my business," Max said, reaching for his money.

Smoke shook his head. "I don't think so, Max. Just leave it and don't let me see your face again until we get to Texas." He leaned forward toward the gambler. "If I do, I'll be forced to kill you."

"But . . . but where'll I go? The train isn't all that big," Max protested.

Smoke shrugged. "That's up to you, Max. You could always get off at the next station."

"But that's in the middle of nowhere."

"Your choice, tinhorn. Get off and wait for the next train, or take a bullet. Makes no difference to me either way," Smoke said as he gathered up the pile of money and chips and handed them to Cal and Pearlie.

"Damn!" Max muttered as he grabbed his hat and stalked out of the car toward the front of the train. He stopped in the doorway and looked back at the table. "I'll get you for this, Jensen, just you wait."

Smoke didn't answer, but let his hand fall to the butt of his pistol, and Max hastily departed from sight.

"Golly, Smoke," Cal said as he counted the money in front of him. "How'd you know he was cheatin'?"

Smoke grinned. "I've played poker in too many saloons

and with too many really good card sharks over the years not to recognize the type, Cal."

"Then, why'd you let him sit in with us?" Pearlie asked as he built himself a cigarette.

"I figured you boys needed a lesson in the realities of life on the trail. Louis Longmont once told me, Smoke, someday a man's going to come up to you and tell you he can make a jack jump up out of a deck of cards and spit in your eye, and you're going to be tempted to bet against him. Don't, he said, because sure as I'm sitting here, you are going to wind up with spit in your eye and an empty bankroll."

Cal and Pearlie laughed out loud. "That sounds like Louis," Cal said. "He has a way with words."

"And it's the truth," Smoke said. "Remember, a man's not going to ask you to take a bet he can't win, so the best thing to do is not bet with strangers."

"What do you want us to do with this money Max left?" Pearlie asked.

"Keep it. You can use it for spending money on the trip."

The train slowed as it pulled into a small town that wasn't much more than a water stop, and Smoke and the boys saw Max step out of the car ahead, carrying his carpetbag in his hand. As the train pulled out, they waved through the window at him, but he didn't wave back.

4

James Slade, who called himself the Durango Kid, stood in his stirrups and shaded his eyes against the sun as he surveyed the small herd of cattle in the valley below him.

"Looks like 'bout a hundred head," he said.

Curly Bob Gatling, who was bald as a billiard ball, grunted in reply. He was a man of few words, preferring to let the sawed-off twelve-gauge shotgun he wore in a modified holster on his belt speak for him.

Rawhide Jack Cummings, the third member of the gang, which also included Three-Fingers Juan Gomez, pulled out a Henry repeating rifle and jacked a shell into the chamber.

"Can you see how many men they got ridin' the herd?"

"Appears there's only three or maybe four," the Kid answered.

"Then let's do it," Gomez growled, pulling a Colt Navy revolver from his holster.

Down below, Jimmy Little Deer, an Osage Indian living in the Indian Territories, sleeved sweat off his face. He glanced around at the herd he was watching, glad they seemed to be calm. In this heat, he didn't feel up to chasing a bunch of dogies into the brush of the Oklahoma Territory countryside.

"Hey, Carlos," he yelled, looked across the backs of a

group of beeves toward his riding companion, Carlos Bear Claw. "How about we take our noon now?" he hollered.

Carlos nodded and cupped his hands around his lips to call to the third member of their group, Hank Stalking Horse. The three men were little more than teenagers, but could ride as well as men much older since they'd been raised in a saddle since they were pups.

The three Indian boys walked their mounts to a camp-fire they had going over on the edge of the herd, and stepped out of their saddles.

"Damn, but I'll be glad when this day's over," Jimmy said as he bent to pour himself a cup of coffee from the pot on the edge of the fire.

Hank paused in the making of a cigarette to look at the horizon. "Do you hear hoofbeats?" he asked.

Jimmy cocked his head, then nodded. "Yeah, maybe the foreman's sendin' somebody to relieve us."

Hank started to laugh at the notion when a loud thump was heard as a bullet smacked him dead center in the chest, knocking him backward and sending him flying spread-eagled onto the hot coals of the fire. Then a distant explosion of gunfire sounded.

"What the . . . ?" Jimmy said, grabbing for the ancient Colt Navy in a worn holster on his belt.

"Rustlers!" Carlos shouted, running for his horse to try to get his Winchester from the saddle boot.

As he leaned over the horse, a bullet shattered his skull, sending brains and blood spraying in the air in a fine, red mist.

Jimmy managed to get his pistol out and get off two wild shots at the four men riding down on him, but they missed their mark.

Curly Bob's shotgun didn't. The twin loads of buckshot took Jimmy square in the chest and blew a hole in his back as big as a bucket, killing him instantly.

The Durango Kid reined in, smoke still pouring from the barrel of his Colt. "Good work, boys," he said. "Now see if these galoots have anything worth takin', then put their hosses on a dally rope and we'll get to roundin' these beeves up."

"How much you think we'll get for 'em in Fort Worth, Kid?"

The Kid pursed his lips, thinking. "They ought'a bring about ten bucks a head, so figger 'bout a thousand dollars, give or take."

Three-Fingers Juan Gomez grinned, exposing a gold front tooth. "Not bad pay for a few days' work runnin' them down to Hell's Half Acre," he said.

"Don't forget," Kid said. "Soon's we get 'em outta the territories, we gotta put a runnin' iron over 'em an' change those brands."

Two days later, after crossing the border into Texas, the men stopped and applied a straight branding iron over the brand of the Osage tribe, changing the brand to one unrecognizable. Then they were back on the trail, headed for Fort Worth, Texas, where they hoped to sell the beeves to someone who cared more about the price of cattle than their origin.

Since the train carrying Smoke and Cal and Pearlie didn't have sleeping cars, it stopped on the way down to Texas for an overnight stay in Fort Smith, Arkansas, to give the passengers a chance for a bath and some good food.

Smoke and the boys got off the train and stretched, trying to get kinks out of their backs that were put there by jolting iron wheels traveling over uneven tracks for several hundred miles.

Pearlie rubbed his gut. "Damn, Smoke. You think we could get some food here? My stomach's so hungry it thinks my throat's been cut."

"Your stomach's always hungry, Pearlie," Cal observed as he put his hands in the small of his back and bent over backward, trying to loosen up. "I think you were born hungry."

"Hell, Cal. We ran outta Miss Sally's bear sign over

twenty-four hours ago an' I ain't et hardly nothin' since then."

Smoke grinned. "I guess those two steaks you put away this morning for breakfast don't count."

"That were more'n six hours ago, Smoke. A body cain't hardly go that long without somethin' to eat."

"All right. Let's go see if we can find a restaurant somewhere in this cow town," Smoke said.

As the boys and Smoke walked down the street toward the center of town, Pearlie glanced to the side and saw a large, wooden structure off in a field by itself, with a chest-high wooden fence around it.

"What do you think that is, Smoke?" he asked.

Smoke followed his gaze. "Unless I'm mistaken, that's the town gallows."

"Gallows?" Cal asked. "Hell, it's got six ropes hanging from it."

Smoke nodded. "Yeah. It's an idea of Hanging Judge Isaac Parker, the federal judge here in Fort Smith. Word is, he was hanging so many men, they had to increase the capacity of the gallows so as not to fall too far behind."

Pearlie's eyebrows shot up. "You mean they hang 'em six at a time down here?"

Smoke turned away. "Yes, that's what I hear, so you boys better be on your best behavior. It wouldn't do to get in trouble in this territory."

Pearlie's expression lightened up when he saw a combination saloon and dining hall down the street. "Now that's what I call hospitality," he said. "You can wet your whistle at the same time you fill your gullet."

Cal stepped to the side, pulling Smoke with him. "Look out, Smoke, it don't do to get between Pearlie and food. He's liable to run you plumb over."

They took seats at a table in the dining room close to the big double doors leading to the adjoining saloon. A large woman wearing a white apron with a hand towel thrown over her shoulder stepped to their table.

"Howdy, gents. My name's Mabel. What can I get for you today?"

Pearlie spread his hands out. "I want a steak this big, with fried taters, sliced onions, and a loaf of baked bread." He hesitated a moment, then added, "An' a jug of beer to go along with it."

Mabel threw back her head and laughed. "Now that's what I like. A man with an appetite. How about you boys?"

Smoke said, "We'll have the same, but bring us some coffee while we wait, please."

"Sure thing, mister," Mabel said, and waddled off toward the kitchen. She glanced back at Pearlie, and gave him a wink as she walked.

Smoke was about to tease Pearlie about his newfound friend when the braying of loud laughter came from the saloon. He glanced through the big door and saw three cowboys rousting a young black man who was trying to mop the floor.

The tallest, a man well over six feet in height, reached out with his boot and kicked the young man in the seat of his pants, sending him sprawling onto his bucket of water, spilling it on the wooden planks of the floor.

Smoke sighed and got to his feet. "I'll be right back," he said, his eyes on the men at the bar.

Pearlie reached out and touched his elbow. "Now, Smoke, you know Miss Sally said for you to stay out of trouble."

Smoke grinned a hard grin, his lips tight. "Oh, this won't be any trouble. This is gonna be fun."

Both Cal and Pearlie shook their heads and got to their feet, in order to cover Smoke's back in the fracas they knew was coming.

As Smoke walked toward the cowboys, he noticed two men sitting at a nearby table, watching the proceedings with interest. One of the men was dressed in high fashion, wearing knee-high black boots, corduroy trousers, and a bright red flannel shirt. He sported two ivory-handled six-guns on his hips. The other was dressed less flamboyantly, but was impressive nonetheless. Standing six feet tall, he was lean and wiry and had eyes that Smoke recognized as belonging to a man used to facing death and unbowed by the experience.

Smoke walked to the young man, now on his hands and knees trying to clean up his mess. Smoke reached down and pulled him to his feet.

"What's your name?" he asked.

"Billy Williams, sir," the boy replied.

"Don't you worry none about cleaning that up, Billy." Smoke cut his eyes to the men standing at the bar, watching him with amused expressions. "I'm sure these men will be glad to do it for you, since they caused it."

The smiles left the faces of the men and they looked at each other angrily.

Finally, the tall one stepped forward, hitching his pants up. "Just who the hell do you think you are, mister, mixin' up in our fun like this?" he asked.

Smoke shook his head. "I'm just a man who doesn't like to see three grown men pick on a young boy like this. What else do you boys do for fun? Pull the wings off of flies, kick dogs, slap women?"

The man looked astonished that anyone would speak to him in such a manner. He cast his eyes toward the men sitting at the table nearby, looking to see if they were going to interfere. The one in the knee-high boots just shrugged and took a leisurely drink of his beer.

The cowboy turned back to Smoke. "You apologize for that, or I'll kill ya!" he growled.

Smoke smiled back at him, unconcerned. "Apologize for calling you a low-life pond-scum who picks on children? Why? It's evidently the truth."

"You son of a bitch . . ." the man growled, and went for his gun.

Before his pistol was half out of leather, Smoke had drawn and slapped the barrel of his Colt down across the man's forehead, buffaloing him and knocking him to his knees, senseless.

"Goddamn!" one of the man's companions said, his voice awed. "I didn't even see his hand move."

"He's quicker'n greased lightning," the other man observed, holding his hands well out from his pistol.

Smoke holstered his gun and pointed at the man on his hands and knees in front of him. "You gents with this man?" he asked.

"Yes . . . yes, sir, but we didn't have nothin' to do with what he did."

"But you didn't do anything to stop him, did you?" Smoke asked.

"Uh . . . no, sir," the other man said, his eyes dropping to the floor.

"Then I'd suggest you two fellows clean this mess up, before you get the same thing your friend did."

The two looked at each other, then walked over to the young black boy and took the mop out of his hand. As they started to clean the floor, Smoke winked at the boy and walked back to his table in the dining room.

Just after the waitress brought them their food, the two men who'd been observing the action in the saloon sauntered into the dining area and stood next to Smoke's table.

He looked up from cutting his steak, leaned back in his chair, and gave them a look. "Can I help you gentlemen?" he asked.

He noticed for the first time the shorter of the two men was wearing a gold star on his chest. It appeared to be hammered out of two twenty-dollar gold pieces and said "U.S. Marshal" on it. The man was also carrying a shotgun cradled in his arms.

"Hello, mister," the man with the gold star said. "I'm Marshal Bill Tilghman, and this is my associate, Marshal Heck Thomas."

Smoke nodded; he'd heard of both men, who were famous throughout the West as marshals who always got their men.

"Uh-huh," Smoke said, and continued looking at the men, waiting for them to make their play, whatever it was.

Tilghman glanced at Thomas, who said, "Mind if we ask you what your name is?"

"I'm Smoke Jensen, and this is Cal and Pearlie, friends of mine," Smoke answered.

The two marshals glanced at each other again, clearly surprised a man of Smoke's reputation was in town.

"Do you have business in Fort Smith, Mr. Jensen?" Tilghman asked.

Smoke noticed his hands were tight on the shotgun, as if he expected Smoke to draw down on them.

Smoke shook his head. "No. As a matter of fact, we're on our way down to Texas to buy some bulls for my ranch in Colorado."

Thomas's eyes narrowed. "We've had some reports of stolen Indian Territory cattle being moved down Texas way for sale. You wouldn't know anything about that, would you, Mr. Jensen?"

Smoke smiled. "No. I've made a deal to buy some of Richard King's Santa Gertrudis bulls off the King Ranch. You don't suspect him of selling these stolen beeves, do you?"

Thomas smiled, apparently relieved at Smoke's news. "No, of course not. Mr. King is a highly respected rancher in Texas."

"We may see you later, Jensen," Tilghman said. "Heck and me are gonna be travelin' down to Texas ourselves. We aim to find those rustlers and bring 'em back up here for Judge Parker to deal with."

"Good for you," Smoke said. "Now, do you gentlemen mind? My steak's getting cold."

"Go on back to your meal, Mr. Jensen," Thomas said.

"Nice talkin' to you," Tilghman added as the two men walked off.

After the lawmen left, Pearlie leaned across the table. "I wonder what put a bee in their bonnet. They didn't have no cause to be roustin' you like that, Smoke."

Smoke swallowed the piece of steak he was chewing,

washed it down with a gulp of coffee, then answered. "Sure they did, Pearlie. Like it or not, I've still got quite a reputation as a gunfighter, and tracking and fighting gun-fighters is what those men do for a living." He shook his head as he cut another piece of meat. "No, I don't blame them for checking me out. In their place, I'd be doing the same thing."

Cal scratched under his arms and around his back. "You think we'll have time for a bath and maybe a couple of hours' sleep here in town 'fore the train leaves again?"

Smoke cut his eyes at Pearlie, who was watching the waitress hand out pieces of pie to a nearby table. "That all depends on if we can get Pearlie out of here before midnight."

Pearlie got a pained expression on his face. "Aw, Smoke. It won't take long to try just one piece of pie."

5

When they got back on the train, Smoke noticed Marshal Heck Thomas and Bill Tilghman also boarded, though they sat in a different car from the men from Big Rock.

"You think they're followin' us?" Pearlie asked as he shuffled a deck of cards prior to resuming their poker game.

"No," Smoke answered. "They're probably just doing what they said they were going to do, heading down south to try and locate the men who've been rustling cattle from the Indian Territories."

As the train pulled out of the station, Cal glanced out the window at the gallows sitting in an open field, surrounded by its wooden fence.

"I'm sure glad we didn't have no cause to meet that Hangin' Judge Parker," he said.

"I've always thought an innocent man has nothing to fear from the law," Smoke said, "but with Isaac Parker I'm not so sure. Word is his first inclination is to hang a man, whether he's proven guilty or not."

"But that ain't right," Pearlie said.

Smoke nodded. "It may not be right, but it seems to be what the folks out here want from their judge. I guess they feel if the man's not guilty of what he's been charged with, he's probably guilty of something else just as bad."

Cal shook his head. "Helluva way to run a court, if you ask me."

Evidently, Cal and Pearlie were getting to be better cardplayers under Smoke's tutelage, because it took him the entire two-day trip to Fort Worth to win all their money from them.

As they entered the famous cow town, Cal's and Pearlie's eyes were glued to the window, staring at the extensive stockyards with their many cattle pens and slaughter yards on the outskirts of town.

"I never seen so many beeves in my whole life," Cal whispered in awe.

Pearlie nodded. "Yep, quite a few steaks on the hoof out there, all right." He wrinkled his nose. "Guess the folks here in Texas get kind'a used to the smell," he opined.

"You boys think that's something, wait until you see downtown. On the one hand, it's the most opulent city in Texas, and on the other, it's got more whorehouses and gambling dens than any place this side of Dodge City," Smoke said.

"What's that they call the red-light district, Smoke?" Pearlie asked.

"Hell's Half Acre," Smoke answered, "though I've heard it covers a lot more area than that now."

When the train stopped, Smoke and the boys got off and took their gear to the Cattleman's Hotel on North Main Street, supposedly the best hotel in town.

Cal's eyes opened wide at the numerous saloons and gambling houses and places of prostitution that lined the street on either side of the famous hotel. "You wouldn't think such a nice hotel would be smack dab in the middle of all of this," Cal said.

Smoke laughed. "People out here on the frontier have a more pragmatic way of looking at things, Cal. I guess they figure this is where most of the cattlemen stay when they come to town, and gambling and women and whiskey is what they want most after some months on the trail pushing a bunch of stubborn beeves to the market."

They walked through huge double doors into a lobby that was two stories high, with marble floors and polished oak countertops, with heavy overstuffed chairs situated around the room for customers to lounge in as they read the *Fort Worth Star,* a local paper, and had their morning coffee.

"Jimminy," Cal said, staring around at the room. "I ain't never seen such in all my born days."

Though Pearlie tried to look bored with it all, it was plain that he too was impressed with the establishment.

Smoke walked up to the desk and stood there, waiting for a man in a black coat and starched white shirt to wait on him. The man, a snooty expression on his face, glanced at them and then turned around, fooling with some papers on a rear desk and ignoring them completely.

After a minute, Smoke cleared his throat. When the man turned, giving him a disdainful glance, Smoke smiled. "How about this, mister? I jump over this counter, grab you by the neck, and choke you until you learn some manners."

"Why . . . I never . . ." the man started to say, until Smoke made as if to climb up on the counter.

The man cleared his throat and warily approached the boys. "Yes, sir. May I help you?"

"Reservation for three in the name of Smoke Jensen," Smoke said mildly.

The attendant's eyes widened and he swallowed, his Adam's apple moving convulsively. "Did you say Smoke Jensen?" he asked.

"Your hearing is evidently as poor as your manners," Smoke answered, his eyes hardening.

"Uh . . . yes, sir, Mr. Jensen. I have a suite on the top floor. Three bedrooms around a large sitting area."

He pushed a notebook toward Smoke, who took a quill pen from the ink pot and signed his name.

"Where are the baths?" he asked. "My partners and I've been on a train for most of a week and we'd like to get cleaned up."

"The baths are right down the hall from your room. There is an attendant there to take care of any of your needs."

Smoke bent to pick up his valise and then stopped, staring in the man's eyes. "And just what is your name?" he asked.

"Why . . . uh . . . it's Jason, sir."

As Smoke started to leave, Jason asked, "Why would you want to know my name, Mr. Jensen?"

Smoke growled out of the side of his mouth without turning, "I always like to know the name of a man I may have to kill."

Walking up the stairs, Cal and Pearlie burst out laughing. "Why did you say that, Smoke?" Pearlie asked around a grin.

Smoke shook his head. "I never could stand pomposity in a man, or ill manners. Maybe it'll make him think twice before he looks down his nose at a customer just because they're dressed in buckskins."

Down the street, at another fine hotel in Fort Worth, the Durango Kid was registering at the front desk.

"And how many men will be staying?" the clerk asked.

Durango looked over his shoulder, eyeing Curly Bob Gatling, Rawhide Jack Cummings, and Three-Fingers Juan Gomez.

"There'll be three of us, since I suppose you don't allow Meskins to stay here," the Kid answered.

Gomez's eyes narrowed and his lips turned white. "What you mean by that, Kid?" he asked.

"No offense, Juan," the Kid said, "but you'll have to stay down the street over that cantina. This hotel is for whites only."

Gomez stared at the Durango Kid for a moment, then muttered, *"Bastardo"* under his breath as he bent and picked up his gear. "I not forget this, Kid," he called over his shoulder as he walked out the door.

The Kid spread his arms. "Hey, Three-Fingers, it's not *my* rule."

Curly Bob shook his head. "You shouldn't ought'a done that, Kid," he said.

"Hell, you want to stay in a place that'll take a Meskin?" he asked. "If you do, head on down to the cantina. I'm sure they'll let you share a room with Gomez."

"That ain't it, Kid," Curly Bob said. "You know Three-Fingers don't like to be called a Meskin. His momma was half-white."

The Durango Kid smiled. "So he says. Anyhow, if he don't like bein' called a Meskin, maybe he ought'a ride with somebody else stead'a me."

"All this jawin' is makin' me thirsty," Rawhide Jack Cummings said. "How's 'bout we head on over to a dog hole an' git some whiskey an' check out the women in this here town?"

"Sounds good to me," Kid said. "Let's dump our gear in our rooms an' see what the local nightlife is like."

On the way to a saloon, they stopped by the cantina at the end of Main Street and asked Gomez if he wanted to join them.

"You sure you want a Meskin to go with you?" he asked, a sarcastic tone to his voice.

"Aw, come on, Juan," Kid said, trying to make amends. "You know I didn't mean no disrespect. It's just I didn't want any trouble at the hotel."

"All right," Gomez said grudgingly, "let us go get drunk and forget about it."

"Now you're talkin', podna," Curly Bob said, throwing his arm around Gomez's shoulders and leading him down the street toward the array of saloons and whorehouses on the block.

6

Smoke and Cal and Pearlie finished dinner at the Cattleman's Hotel, Pearlie topping his meal of steak and potatoes and canned peaches with a thick slice of apple pie covered with a slab of cheese.

"You think you can still walk after all that food?" Smoke asked.

Pearlie smiled as he wiped a piece of cheese off his chin. "Sure. This little snack was probably enough to get me through the night too."

"Smoke," Cal said.

"Yeah?"

"How about you takin' us out to see the sights? I ain't never been in no big-city saloon or gamblin' halls before."

Smoke pursed his lips. "I don't know, Cal. Sally'd kill me if she thought I was leading you young'uns astray."

"Heck-fire, Smoke," Pearlie interrupted. "What Miss Sally don't know won't hurt her none."

Smoke laughed. "You mean, what she doesn't know won't hurt me none."

"Please, Smoke. I don't know when I'll ever get another chance like this," Cal pleaded.

Smoke held up his hands. "All right, but only on one condition."

"Anything!" Cal said, his eyes lighting up at his chance to see the town.

"You boys have got to promise me you won't do any gambling, no matter how much you want to."

"Why, that's easy, Smoke. You done won all our money on the train," Pearlie said, a mischievous look in his eyes.

Smoke took a wad of bills out of his pocket and doled it out to Cal and Pearlie. "You know I wasn't going to keep this, didn't you, Pearlie?"

Pearlie shrugged. "Well, let's just say I hoped you weren't."

Smoke threw some money down on the table and grabbed his hat. "Well, boys, I guess it's time to further your education, though not in a way Sally would approve of."

He stood up. "Let's go see what Hell's Half Acre has to offer."

The Durango Kid, Curly Bob Gatling, Rawhide Jack Cummings, and Three-Fingers Juan Gomez entered the Silver Dollar Saloon, pushing through the batwings and strutting into the place as if they owned it. They were more than a little drunk, this being the third bar they'd visited.

The Kid walked up to a table occupied by a couple of cowboys, who also were well into their cups and had two rather buxom ladies of the night sitting with them.

Kid stepped in front of the younger of the two and laid his hand on the butt of his pistol. "Excuse me, gentlemen, but I think you're sittin' at our table."

The young man glanced up at Kid with bleary eyes. "What the hell you talkin' 'bout, mister? We been here all night."

Gomez stepped around the table to stand behind the cowboy, slipping his Colt Navy out of his holster and holding it where no one could see, the barrel against the boy's backbone. "I don't think you heard my pardner. You at our table, gringo!" he growled in a low voice.

The other man at the table started to get up, until Rawhide Jack put his hand on his shoulder, pushing him back down in his chair. "I wouldn't do that if I were you, podna," he whispered in his whiskey-rough voice, his eyes glittering madly.

"Come on, Jake," the first man said, his face pale with fear. "I think we've had enough for one night."

Jake glanced at the four men standing over them. "Yeah, there's plenty of other places we can spend our money."

As the two men got up to leave, one of the girls whined, "Hey, fellahs, what about us?"

Kid bent down and stroked her cheek with his hand, a leer on his face. "Don't you worry none, pretty lady. We'll take good care of you."

Mollified somewhat, she glanced at her friend across the table and shrugged. "Hell, any port in a storm, I always say."

"What're you girls drinkin'?" asked Rawhide Jack.

"Whiskey. What else?" one answered.

Kid pulled out a wad of bills and handed it to her. "Then why don't you mosey on over to the bar an' get us a bottle or two an' some glasses, honey?"

After the women left, the men took seats around the table, sitting so they could see the rest of the room. Life on the owl-hoot trail had taught them to be cautious in new towns.

Curly Bob scratched his chin. "How much money you think we're gonna git for them beeves we got stashed in that corral 'cross town, Kid?"

Kid looked at the many cowmen in the room, all spending money as if it grew on trees. "I figure we'll get 'bout eleven thousand dollars, give or take."

"What's that apiece?" Rawhide Jack asked. "I never was too good at doing sums."

"That'll be three thousand for you and Curly Bob and me, an' two thousand for Three-Fingers," Kid answered as he pulled a small cloth sack out of his pocket and began to build himself a cigarette.

Juan Gomez's eyes widened. "Why for I only get two thousand, Kid?"

Kid cut his eyes at the Mexican. "'Cause you didn't help much with the brandin' on the way down here, Juanito."

Gomez's face flushed red. He held up his left hand with only three fingers on it. "You know I cannot use running iron with this hand," he snapped.

Kid shrugged. "That ain't my problem, Three-Fingers. I only know we three did most of the work on the trail down here, so it stands to reason we get most of the money."

Gomez started to stand up out of his chair, his hand falling toward his Navy pistol. "Why, you son of a . . ."

He stopped when Kid's Colt Army appeared from under the table, pointed at his gullet. "Now don't go gettin' that Meskin temper of yours all fired up, Juan. I'm still the ramrod of this outfit, an' if I say you get two thousand, you get two thousand. *Comprende, compadre?*"

Gomez stared at the pistol in Kid's hand for a moment, as if he were going to draw anyway, but the flat, hard look in Kid's eyes told him he wouldn't hesitate to shoot him dead if he tried.

Finally, he sat back down, his hands on the table, his eyes glittering hate. "We will see, Señor Kid, we will see," he whispered through a voice tight with anger.

Rawhide Jack slapped Gomez on the shoulder. "Come on, Juan. Lighten up an' enjoy the night. We don't get to a town like this very often."

"Yeah, podna, take it easy," Curly Bob said. "Hell, we may get more'n eleven thousand for them beeves anyway."

The conversation stopped as the two whores returned to the table, both carrying bottles of whiskey with no labels on them.

"You boys ready to party?" one asked.

Kid eased the hammer down on his Colt and slipped it in his holster. "Hell, yes!" he shouted, grabbing one of the girls and pulling her onto his lap.

None of the Kid's men noticed two men sitting across the room at a table by themselves, drinking beer and watching their every move.

Smoke and Cal and Pearlie ambled down Main Street, trying to make a choice of the many saloons they passed. As they came to the Silver Dollar, Cal, who was getting impatient to see the inside of a big city saloon, said, "How 'bout this one, Smoke?"

Smoke shrugged. "One's about as good as another," he answered, leading the way through the batwings.

Smoke stepped to the side as he entered, his back to the wall as he surveyed the room and let his eyes get accustomed to the smoky light after the darkness of the street. He'd been too many years looking over his shoulder for someone trying to make a name for himself by killing the famous Smoke Jensen not to be overly cautious when entering barrooms.

As his eyes roamed over the patrons, he noticed Heck Thomas and Bill Tilghman sitting at a corner table to his left. The two men didn't see him enter, their attention being on someone else at the other end of the room.

Pearlie noticed the two marshals also. "Hey, Smoke. There's them two lawmen who braced us in Fort Smith. Wonder what they're doin' here."

"Me too, Pearlie. It sure doesn't look like they're having much fun, does it?"

Cal brushed past Smoke and Pearlie. "There's a table over yonder, Smoke," he said, as two men at a table off to the right got up from their chairs and walked toward the stairs with a couple of women on their arms.

"Let's get it," Smoke said, glad the table was across the room from the lawmen. He didn't want to have to put up with any more questions from them tonight.

They took their seats at a table next to four men who were entertaining two women, and who evidently were feeling no pain, for there were two empty whiskey bottles on the table and they were starting on a third.

As they sat down, one of the men at the table next to them glanced over at Smoke and grinned drunkenly. Smoke smiled back and tipped his hat.

Pearlie got up and walked to the bar, returning after a few minutes with a small bottle of whiskey and a pitcher of beer.

"Who's the beer for, Pearlie?" Cal asked, reaching for the whiskey.

Pearlie slapped his hand. "It's for young pups who aren't old enough to be drinkin' whiskey, Cal."

"Hell. A man old enough to get shot ought'a be old enough to drink whiskey if'n he wants to," Cal protested.

"Speakin' of that," Pearlie said as he poured himself and Smoke a small drink, "you ain't been shot in over a month. That ought'a be a record for you."

Cal took a drink of his beer, sleeving the foam off his lips with the back of his arm. "I wouldn't want'a talk too much 'bout that, Pearlie. As I remember it, you were the last one in this group to take a bullet."

Pearlie rubbed his side, a rueful expression on his face. "Don't remind me. It still hurts when the weather changes."

Smoke leaned back in his chair, thinking about how Pearlie had gotten shot, and how close he'd come to losing his friend . . .

Jim Slaughter was in the process of folding up his ground blanket and sleeping bag when he heard what sounded like hoofbeats coming from the mountain slope on the east side of the camp.

He straightened up, his hand going to the butt of his pistol, and looked toward the sound. He could see nothing through the heavy morning mist, which hung close to the ground like dense fog. Though the sun was peeking over the horizon, it shed little warmth and even less light through the haze.

He glanced over his shoulder toward the campfire, and saw that most of his men were still milling around, grabbing biscuits and beans and coffee, most of them still half-asleep at this early hour.

Damn, he thought, *we're easy targets out here with no sentries left to stand guard.* "Whitey," he called, pulling his pistol and grabbing his rifle from his saddle boot on the ground.

"Yeah, Boss?" Whitey answered from over near the fire.

Before he could reply, four shapes materialized out of the fog like crazed ghosts on a fierce rampage, orange blossoms of flame exploding from the guns they held in their hands.

Their faces were covered with bandannas and their hats were pulled low over their faces as they rode straight into the knot of men around the campfire, shooting as fast as they could pull the triggers.

David Payne, a gunny from Missouri who'd ridden with Quantrill's Raiders, drew his pistol and got off one shot before a bullet took him in the throat and flung him backward into the fire, scattering embers and ashes into the air.

Jim Harris, a tough from Texas who'd fought in the Lincoln County War, had his gun half out of his holster when two slugs tore through his chest, blowing blood and pieces of lung on the men next to him. He only had time for a surprised grunt before he hit the ground, dead.

Slaughter's men scattered as fast as their legs could carry them, some diving to the ground, others trying to hide behind trees or saddles on the ground as the marauders galloped through camp.

An ex-Indian scout called Joe Scarface managed to get his rifle cocked, and was aiming it at one of the riders when an explosion from the direction of the mountainside was followed immediately by a large-caliber bullet plowing into his back between his shoulder blades, which lifted him off the ground like a giant hand and threw him face-down in the dirt, a hole you could put your fist through in his chest.

"Goddamn!" Slaughter yelled, glancing over his shoulder. They were under attack from all sides, it seemed. He dove to the ground behind his saddle as one of the riders, a big man with broad shoulders on a big, roan-colored horse with snow-white hips, rode right at him.

Slaughter buried his face in the soft loam of the ground, and felt rather than saw the bullets from the big man's pistols tear into his saddle and the ground around him as the giant Palouse jumped over him. Miraculously, he was not hit.

"Shit!" he said, spitting dirt and leaves out of his mouth. He recognized that horse. It was the one Johnny West had been riding in Jackson Hole. So he was one of the bastards who'd been killing his men all along, he realized. The son of a bitch had played him for a fool.

Whitey Jones ran for his saddle, hunched over, expecting a bullet in his back the whole way. As he bent to grab his Greener shotgun, one of the raiders rode by, his pistol pointing at the albino.

Whitey whirled, pointing his express gun just as the rider fired. The bullet grazed Whitey's cheek and tore a chunk out of his left ear, spinning him around and snapping his head back, blood spurting into his eyes and blinding him momentarily.

Zeke Mayhew, one of the men who'd joined Slaughter's gang in Jackson Hole, snapped off two quick shots, and saw one of the riders flinch as one of his slugs hit home. He grinned and eared back the hammers for another shot as the man he'd hit leaned to the side and fired point-blank into his face. Mayhew's head exploded in a fine, red mist as the .44-caliber bullet blew his brains into his hat.

Two more explosions from the distant mountainside sent two more men to the ground, one dead and one with his left arm left dangling from a shattered bone. Milt Burnett screamed in pain as he grabbed his flopping arm and went to his knees, just as a gray and white Palouse rode directly over him, its hooves pounding his chest to pulp. He died choking on bloody froth from a ruptured lung.

Whitey sleeved blood out of his eyes and rolled onto his stomach, pointing his ten-gauge at the back of a raider and letting go with both barrels. Just as he fired, Ben Brown, one of the men who'd been with Slaughter for several years, stepped between them, his arm outstretched as he aimed his pistol.

Whitey's double load of buckshot hit Brown square in the back, blowing him almost in half as he spun around, dead before he hit the ground.

Swede, too far from his saddle to get his gun, pulled his long knife out and stood there, waiting as a rider rode down on him. He bared his teeth and screamed a defiant yell, holding the knife out in front of him.

The rider's eyes grew wide as he saw the man had no gun, and he held his fire, lashing out with his leg and catching Swede in the mouth with a pointed boot as he raced by, knocking out several of his teeth and putting out the man's lights as his head snapped back and he somersaulted backward, unconscious.

Jimmy Silber, thoughts of his thousand-dollar bonus still in his mind, fired pistols with both hands, crouched near the fire. When his guns were empty, he bent over to punch out his empties, but a sound made him turn his head.

He looked up just as a young man on a gray horse rode toward him. The last thing Jimmy saw was a tongue of orange from the man's pistol as the slug tore the left side of his face off and left him standing there, dead on his feet.*

Smoke shook his head at the memories, grinning to himself when he thought of how the boys had teased each other about the incident, even though both had been as close to death as it is possible to be . . .

*Heart of the Mountain Man

* * *

As Smoke led his friends toward Big Rock, Louis twisted in his saddle and spoke to Pearlie, riding behind him. "How are you doing with that wound? Is it showing any signs or symptoms of suppuration?"

Pearlie stretched his neck and moved his left arm around in a circle to see if there was any pain or soreness. He'd taken a bullet that skimmed along the skin over his his left shoulder blade, burning a furrow half an inch deep but not penetrating any deeper. Though the wound wasn't serious, Smoke and the others were worried about infection.

"No, Louis, it seems to be healin' up right nice. A tad stiff, but no more'n you'd expect."

As he spoke, Pearlie noticed Cal had a wide grin on his face.

"What'a you find so funny, Cal?" he asked suspiciously.

"Oh, a thought just sort'a occurred to me," the boy answered.

"Since when did you start thinkin', Cal?" Pearlie asked. "You ain't got a brain in that empty head of your'n."

"Well, it just seemed kind'a funny to me," he answered. "The four of us rode through them outlaws, guns blazin' and goin' off all around us, an' you the onliest one got shot."

"So?"

"So . . . maybe I ain't the only lead magnet around now. It might just be that you're gonna take my place as the one always seems to take a bullet ever' time we git in a fight."

Smoke and Louis looked at each other, smiling. It was good to see the boys back to normal, bitching and arguing with each other as only the best of friends could.

"I don't see it that way, Cal," Pearlie said.

"Why not?"

"Way I see it, this here bullet I took was probably

headed for you, sure as hell, an' I just sort'a got in the way."

"You sayin' you took lead that was meant for me?"

Pearlie nodded. "Yeah, so that means you owe me for savin' you the misery of gittin' shot again."

Cal stared at Pearlie through narrowed eyes. "If'n that's so, an' I ain't sayin' it is, mind you, I bet I know what you think I ought'a give you for savin' me."

"What's that, Cal?"

"I bet lettin' you have my share of the first batch of bear sign Miss Sally makes when we git home would square things."

Pearlie pursed his lips as he considered this. "Well, now, that just might make things right between us."

Cal shook his head, grinning. "Forgit it, Pearlie. I been thinkin' on those bear sign for the past hundred miles. The worst thing 'bout bein' away from home all these weeks has been missin' Miss Sally's cookin', so you ain't gittin' none of my bear sign, no, sirree!"*

Cal looked up from making himself a cigarette and saw the distant look in Smoke's eyes and the slight grin on his face. "What you thinkin' 'bout so hard, Smoke?" he asked, licking the paper and trying to roll the cigarette as expertly as Pearlie did.

Smoke came out of his reverie and shook his head. "Just thinking on how glad I am to be here with you boys," he answered.

"Well, if you're so glad to be with us," Pearlie said, "how about takin' a drink or two of whiskey and joinin' in the fun?"

Smoke picked up his glass and held it up. "Don't mind if I do. Here's to us, boys, let's let her rip!"

*Heart of the Mountain Man

7

As the evening wore on, Cal and Pearlie became more and more excited by the activities of the saloon, especially the women who were constantly approaching the table and asking if the boys would like to buy them a drink.

Finally, Smoke realized his presence was inhibiting Cal and Pearlie from having a good time. "Boys," he said, "I think I'll just mosey on back to the hotel and give you some space to maybe do some entertaining on your own."

Cal and Pearlie glanced at one another. Then Pearlie grinned. "All right, Boss Man. We'll see ya bright an' early in the morning to see 'bout gettin' them beeves."

As Pearlie said this, the man at the next table cocked an ear. He leaned over the back of his chair and said, "Did I hear you men were interested in buying some livestock?"

Smoke glanced at him, immediately realizing this was no regular cowboy, and he very much doubted he was a rancher either. He wore clothes that were too fancy and had his pistol tied down low on his leg, more in the manner of a gunny than a cowman.

Smoke nodded, however, not wanting to be rude, especially to a man who looked half drunk. "Yes. We're in the market for some bulls. Why do you ask?"

"Well," the stranger said, rubbing his chin, "I got some prime beef on the hoof down at one of the corrals on the edge of town. Don't rightly know how many bulls there are in the bunch, but I'd be happy for you to take a look an' see if they interest you."

Smoke considered this for a moment, then said, "I assume you've got a bill of sale for the animals."

The man's face darkened and he got up from his chair. "Why'd you ask a damn-fool question like that, mister? You implyin' I'm a rustler?"

As he spoke, the man let his hand fall to his pistol butt.

Smoke gently unhooked the hammer-thong off his Colt and stood and faced the man. "I don't know what you are, mister. All I know is you asked me if I wanted to buy some cattle and I asked you if you had a bill of sale. If that bothers you, it's just too damned bad, 'cause it means you're either a poor businessman, or a thief, and in either event I don't think I'd care to do business with you."

"Do you know who you're talkin' like that to, mister?" the man asked.

"No, but I'm sure you're going to tell me," Smoke answered. "Loudmouths always seem to think they're more important than they are."

"I'm the Durango Kid," Kid said, his jaw thrust out belligerently, "an' I aim to kill you for talkin' to me like that."

"You make a move toward that smoke wagon, and you'll be dead before you clear leather," Smoke said calmly, his eyes flat and deadly.

The threat in them must have given Kid some warning, because he asked, "Just who are you, mister?"

"I'm Smoke Jensen."

"Holy shit," Rawhide Jack Cummings said from behind Kid. "You don't wanna mess with Smoke Jensen, Kid. I hear tell he's faster'n greased lightning."

"To hell with him," Kid growled, glancing over his shoulder at his friends, as if to make sure they were backing his play. "I'll kill him where he stands."

Smoke gave a lazy grin that didn't reach his eyes. "You want to tell me your real name, or do you want Durango Kid on your marker on boot hill?" he asked.

An uncertain look crossed Kid's face. He'd never met anyone he couldn't intimidate before, and he suddenly became concerned that just maybe he'd bitten off more than he could chew.

Cal and Pearlie, still sitting at the table, had their hands on their pistol butts, not to protect Smoke from Kid, because they knew he could handle the gun slick, but to guard against Smoke being shot in the back by one of Kid's friends.

Three-Fingers Gomez stepped up to whisper in Kid's ear, "Maybe you better take this outside, Kid. Fewer witnesses."

Kid thought for a moment, then turned and sat back down at his table, saying, "I'm not through with you yet, Jensen."

Smoke shook his head. He looked down at Cal and Pearlie. "You boys be careful, and I'll see you back at the hotel later."

"Yes, sir," Cal said, his face relaxing now that the threat of imminent violence had passed.

When they saw Smoke leaving the table, two girls in revealing dresses ambled over to the table and sat down across from Cal and Pearlie. "You boys lookin' for some company?" one of them asked, a coquettish look on her face.

"Well, I do believe we are," Pearlie answered, signaling the bartender for another couple of glasses.

Walking toward the batwings, Smoke accidently bumped a poker player's back as he brushed past his chair. Without looking back, Smoke mumbled an apology and continued on his way.

Max Gibbons, the gambler Smoke had braced and had thrown off the train, looked up, his face scowling as he recognized the mountain man.

He threw in his hand and gathered up his chips, raking them into his hat. "Excuse me, gentlemen," he said, "I'll be back shortly."

He slipped his bowler hat on his head and followed

Smoke from the building, not sure why, but hoping for some chance to avenge himself to occur.

As Smoke walked through the batwings, Kid watched him with eyes that glittered hate. "I'm gonna go outside an' take care of that hombre," he whispered to his friends. "Watch those men he was with and make sure they don't do nothin' to interfere."

He stood up and walked toward the bar. When he got there, he glanced back to make sure Cal and Pearlie weren't watching, then slipped out the back door, unnoticed in the crowded room.

Smoke walked a few feet down the boardwalk, pausing to stop and build himself a cigarette, smiling to himself at the way Cal's eyes had lit up when the "hostesses" of the saloon asked him to buy them a drink. "Well," he muttered to himself, "the kid's got to learn the facts of life sometime. Might as well be now."

He didn't notice Max Gibbons standing in the shadows just outside the doorway to the saloon, staring at him with undisguised hatred.

He ducked his head and applied a lucifer to his cigarette. As he blew out the match, a voice came from the darkened recesses of the alleyway next to him.

"Hey, Jensen! You ready to settle our differences now?"

Smoke whirled, crouching, his hand dropping toward the butt of his Colt as he tried to see into the blackness in front of him.

The Durango Kid stepped forward into the scant light from lanterns on the front wall of the Silver Dollar Saloon. He had his pistol in his hand, held at waist level, the hammer already cocked back. "I'm gonna kill you, Jensen, an' then ever'body will know who the fastest gun in the West is," Kid growled, his voice low and menacing.

Smoke's hand twitched. He knew he'd have to draw as fast as he ever had to stand a chance against a man with his gun already drawn and leveled.

Just as he started to make his play, twin gunshots sounded from deep darkness behind the Durango Kid, and the gunman's eyes opened wide and he uttered a sharp scream as the front of his chest exploded in an eruption of blood and bone caused by a bullet passing through his back and exiting out the front of his shirt.

The Kid's body was thrown forward to land sprawled face-downward in the dirt of the alleyway, dead before he hit the ground.

Smoke filled his hand with iron and stared into the alley, noticing a dark figure hightailing it out the rear of the passageway and around the corner of the saloon. Seconds later he heard the back door of the Silver Dollar open and close.

Suddenly, the street was filled with onlookers as men and prostitutes poured out the batwings of the saloon, to stand in a group looking down at the body of the Kid.

Marshals Bill Tilghman and Heck Thomas pushed their way through the crowd, guns drawn, and stepped to Smoke's side.

"I'll take that pistol, Jensen," Tilghman said, his Colt pointing at Smoke's belly.

Smoke let the pistol hang by his finger and handed it to the lawman. "Someone shot him from behind," Smoke said. "I saw him run up the alley and enter the saloon by the back door."

Thomas squatted and examined the two bullet holes in the Kid's back, then used the toe of his boot to flip the Durango Kid over onto his stomach, where a single exit hole of one of the bullets could be seen.

"Somebody drilled him in the back twice, that's for sure," the lawman said, glancing over his shoulder at Smoke.

Max Gibbons stepped to the front of the crowd, grabbing Tilghman by the shoulder. "Jensen did it, Marshal. I saw him," he said, his eyes fixed on Smoke with undisguised satisfaction.

"The tinhorn's lying, Marshal," Smoke said angrily, "and if you give me five minutes with him alone, I'll make him admit it."

Tilghman shook his head. "The only place you're goin' is

to the local lockup until I can get you to Fort Smith, Jensen, where Judge Parker will listen to all relevant testimony . . . an' then sentence you to hang by the neck until you're deader'n that fellow on the ground."

Smoke took a step toward Gibbons, who rapidly backed away, until Tilghman grabbed his arms and pulled them behind him.

"Marshal," Smoke protested, "check my pistol. It hasn't even been fired."

"He reloaded it, Marshal," Gibbons said hurriedly. "I saw him do it."

Pearlie elbowed his way through the crowd to stand before Tilghman and Thomas. "Marshal, Smoke Jensen didn't shoot nobody in the back. He don't have to, since he can outdraw anybody in the country."

"We got a witness, mister," Tilghman said, inclining his head toward Gibbons, who dropped his gaze when Pearlie and Cal turned to stare at him.

He put his hand on Smoke's shoulder and pulled him down the street toward the local jail. "You'll have a chance to say your piece at the trial," Thomas said to Pearlie as he followed Tilghman and Smoke down the street.

Smoke turned his head to Pearlie and cut his eyes toward Gibbons, indicating Pearlie should have a talk with him. Pearlie nodded, his eyes flat and angry. "I'll get to the bottom of this, Smoke," he called, then turned and followed Gibbons as he tried to disappear into the crowd.

8

The next morning, Pearlie showed up at the jail and asked to speak with Smoke.

Sheriff Billy Jackson pursed his lips, thinking on it for a moment. "I'll have to see that shootin' iron, boy," he drawled, holding out his hands.

Pearlie unstrapped his belt and holster and handed them over.

"I'll give ya' five minutes," the sheriff said, hanging Pearlie's gun on a hat rack. "If'n ya' want more'n that, you'll have to ask the marshal."

Pearlie nodded and followed the sheriff through an iron-clad door into a back room where Smoke lay on a cot, his hands behind his head, apparently asleep.

After the sheriff left, Pearlie walked to stand with his hands on the iron bars of the cell. "Smoke," he called softly, "wake up."

Smoke blinked his eyes open and sat up, yawning.

"How can you sleep at a time like this?" Pearlie asked.

Smoke shrugged. "There's not much else to do in here, Pearlie. What did you find out?"

"We followed Gibbons to his hotel room. Cal's sitting in the lobby now, makin' sure he don't leave town till we get a chance to talk to him."

"Why didn't you ask him about it last night?"

"That Marshal Thomas an' Tilghman were with him most of the night, takin' down his statement an' writin' it all up legal like."

Smoke made himself a cigarette and stared out the barred window of the cell thoughtfully for a while as he smoked. Finally, he whirled around. "You know, Pearlie, there was something not right about those gunshots last night, and I've been trying to put my finger on it."

"What do you mean, Smoke?"

He shook his head. "They didn't sound quite right, and I think I know why."

"Didn't sound right?" Pearlie asked.

"Yeah. I don't think the Kid was shot with a .44. The shots weren't loud enough, and if it'd been a .44 from that short a distance, both bullets would've gone clear through him."

"So . . . what do you think he was shot with?"

"I think it must've been a .36, probably a Colt Navy or possibly a Scofield."

"But, Smoke," Pearlie said, "you carry a Colt .44 New Model Army."

Smoke grinned. "Exactly my point, Pearlie."

"What do you want me to do about it?"

"Go to the doctor and see if you can get him to dig that bullet out of the Kid. If it's a .36 like I suspect, have him write a letter to that effect and bring it to Fort Smith."

"Why cain't I just have the doc tell the marshals?"

"Because we're leaving for Fort Smith in about an hour. Tilghman and Thomas have three or four other men they're taking back for trial and they seem to be anxious to get on the trail."

"I thought they was after some cattle rustlers."

Smoke shrugged. "Evidently, the man they were after was the Durango Kid, so they've kind'a lost interest in that case."

"But why don't they go after the men with him?"

"The man who did all the talking, the only one they had evidence against, was the Kid, according to Tilghman.

The marshal said they've given a list of the stolen cattle to the local sheriff, and if they surface, he can make the arrest."

"But," Pearlie protested, "what's their hurry to get back to Fort Smith?"

"It's my guess Judge Parker's running low on men to hang, and he wants to keep his reputation up."

"So, what else do you want me an' Cal to do besides talk to the doc?"

"See if you can get Gibbons to admit in front of witnesses that he lied about seeing me shoot the Kid."

"How can we do that?" Pearlie asked.

Smoke grinned. "It's been my experience that two things will loosen a man's tongue faster than anything else."

"What two things?"

"Whiskey, and a woman willing to listen to a man brag."

"The whiskey's no problem, but where are we gonna get a woman willin' to do that for us?"

Smoke's eyes narrowed. "You and Cal looked like you were getting pretty friendly with a couple of women from the Silver Dollar last night. Any chance of sweet-talking one of them into doing it for us?"

Pearlie thought for a moment, then smiled. "I guess so, though our night with them was interrupted by the gunfight."

Smoke reached through the bars and patted his shoulder. "Then you and Cal will just have to get reacquainted with them tonight. And, Pearlie," he added, "spare no expense."

"Where are we gonna git that kind'a money?" he asked.

Smoke handed him a piece of paper with a handwritten note on it. "Have the telegraph office send this to Sally at the Sugarloaf. She can have all the money you need wired to the bank here in Fort Worth."

Pearlie nodded and took the note. He reached in to shake Smoke's hand. "We won't let you down, Smoke. Me an' Cal'll git the job done."

Smoke smiled. "I know you will, Pearlie. Just make sure

you do it fast. From what I hear, Hangin' Judge Isaac Parker doesn't waste any time once he decides to stretch a man's neck."

"You can count on us, Smoke. We'll git what you need 'fore you even come to trial."

"I hope so, Pearlie. I don't like to think of not seeing Sally and the Sugarloaf again."

9

Tilghman walked into the back room of the jail and unlocked Smoke's cell. He held in his hands a pair of manacles. "Hold your hands out, Jensen," he said.

Smoke stuck his hands out. "Do I have to wear those, Marshal? I'll give you my word not to try and escape," he said.

Tilghman placed the cuffs on Smoke's wrists and snapped them shut. "It's not that I don't trust you, Jensen," he said, an apologetic look on his face. "It's just that it's the rules. All prisoners have to wear these while bein' transported."

Smoke shrugged. "Yeah, Marshal, we wouldn't want to go breaking any rules, would we?"

"Listen, Jensen," Tilghman replied, his face hard. "We've had over a hundred marshals killed in the line of duty in Judge Parker's jurisdiction, over a third of 'em while transportin' prisoners. So, even if I don't always agree with the rules, I *do* follow 'em."

He led Smoke out of the jail and helped him climb up into an enclosed wagon with bars on the sides instead of wood. Three other hard-looking men were already inside, manacled as Smoke was.

As Tilghman started toward the front of the wagon, Smoke asked, "Isn't Marshal Thomas coming along?"

Tilghman glanced at him, as though considering whether the question deserved an answer. Finally, he said, "No. We decided he should stay and try to get a line on those cattle stolen from the Indian Territories after all."

Smoke snorted. "You can start with the men riding with the Durango Kid. He tried to sell me some beeves without papers the night he was killed."

Tilghman stopped and turned to look at Smoke. "Why didn't you tell me this earlier?"

"You didn't ask, Marshal. You were too interested in trying to get me to admit to back-shooting the Kid."

"He tell you where they were keepin' those beeves?"

"He said something about a rented corral on the edge of town."

Tilghman nodded, scratching his beard. "That makes sense. They'd blend right in with all the other cattle waitin' for the slaughterin' yards to get to 'em."

"It shouldn't be too hard to find out which one he meant," Smoke said, "if you ask around in the right places."

Tilghman nodded. "Thanks for the tip, Jensen. I'll be sure an' tell Judge Parker how you helped out."

Smoke laughed. "Yeah, maybe I'll get a softer rope around my neck."

"Don't say that, Jensen. Judge Parker is a fair man."

"Uh-huh, and how many men out of the last hundred he's tried has he found not guilty?" Smoke asked.

Tilghman's face burned a fiery red. He mumbled something and turned to go.

"I didn't get that, Marshal," Smoke called.

"Three," Tilghman repeated. "He found three not guilty."

"Sounds like my chances aren't too good then," Smoke said.

"All I can promise you is you'll get a chance to tell your side of it, Jensen. It'll be up to you to convince Parker you're tellin' the truth."

"Fat chance," Smoke answered.

Tilghman shrugged. "Better than the chance you gave the Durango Kid."

"I told you it wasn't me killed the Kid."

"You know, Jensen, I've been doin' this job for a lot of years, an' outta all the men I've caught and transported, ain't none of 'em ever been guilty according to them. So you can keep on talkin', but ain't nobody gonna be listenin' to you."

He turned to walk toward the sheriff's office. "Now I gotta go tell Heck what you told me 'bout them beeves."

After he left, Pearlie and Cal walked up to the wagon. "Smoke, we got your message to Sally, an' she's gonna be wirin' us the money soon's the bank opens up in Big Rock," Pearlie said.

"She say anything else?" he asked.

"Yeah," Cal said, "she said to tell you her and Monte and Louis would be in Fort Smith by the time you got there an' not to worry. They weren't about to let no judge hang you for something you couldn't do."

Smoke smiled. It was just like Sally to take on the hanging judge, or anyone else who threatened her husband. It reminded him of the time the outlaw Lee Slater and his three hundred bounty hunters had him trapped up in the high lonesome and she came to the rescue, her guns blazing . . .

"Sally's gone!" Bountiful yelled, bringing her buggy to a dusty, sliding halt.

"What?" Sheriff Monte Carson jumped out of his chair. "What do the hands say?"

"I finally got one of them to talk. He said he took her down to the road day before yesterday, and she hailed the stage there. He said she had packed some riding britches in her trunk, along with a rifle and a pistol. She was riding the stage down to the railroad and taking a train from there. Train runs all the way through to the county seat.

Lord, Lord, Monte, she's just about there by now. What are we going to do?"

Monte led her into his office and sat her down. Bountiful fanned herself vigorously. He got her a drink of water and sat down at his desk. "Nothin' we can do, Miss Bountiful. Sally's gone to stand by her man. And them damn outlaws and manhunters down yonder think they got trouble with Smoke. I feel sorry for them if they tangle with Miss Sally. You know she can shoot just like a man and has done so plenty of times. She's a crack shot with rifle and pistol. Smoke seen to that."

Nearly everyone on Main Street had seen the elegantly dressed lady step off the train and stroll to the hotel, a porter carrying her trunk. As soon as the desk clerk saw her sign her name, he dispatched a boy to run fetch the sheriff.

Sheriff Silva was standing in the lobby, talking to several men, and he nearly swallowed his chewing tobacco when Sally walked down the stairs.

She was wearing cowboy boots and jeans—which she filled out to the point of causing the men's eyeballs to bug out—a denim shirt, which fitted her quite nicely too, and was carrying a leather jacket. She had a bandanna tied around her throat, and a low-crowned, flat-brimmed hat on her head. She also wore a .44 belted around her waist and carried a short-barreled .44 carbine, a bandolier of ammo slung around one shoulder.

"Jesus Christ, Missus Jensen!" Sheriff Silva hollered. "I mean, holy cow. What do you think you're gonna do?"

"Take a ride," Sally told him, and walked out of the door.

Silva ran to catch up with her. "Now you just wait a minute here, Missus Jensen. This ain't no fittin' country for a female to be a-traipsin' around in. Will you please slow down?"

Sally ignored that and kept right on walking at a rather brisk pace.

She turned into the general store, and was uncommonly blunt with the man who owned the store. "I want provisions for five days, including food, coffee, pots and pans and eating utensils, blankets, ground sheets, and tent. And five boxes of .44's too. Have them ready on a pack frame in fifteen minutes. Have them loaded out back, please."

"Now you just hold up on that order, Henry," Sheriff Silva said.

"You'd better not cross me, Henry," Sally warned him, a wicked glint in her eyes. "My name is Mrs. Smoke Jensen, and I can shoot damn near as well as my husband."

"Yes'um," Henry said. "I believe you, ma'am."

"And you"—Sally spun around to face the sheriff—"would be advised to keep your nose out of my business."

"Yes'um," Silva said glumly, and followed her to the livery.

Sally picked out a mean-eyed blue steel that bared its teeth when the man tried to put a rope around it. Sally walked out into the corral, talked to the big horse for a moment, and then led it back to the barn. She fed him a carrot and an apple she'd picked up at the store, and the horse was hers.

"That there's a stallion, ma'am!" Silva bellered. "He ain't been cut. You can't ride no stallion!"

"Get out of my way," she told him.

"It ain't decent, ma'am!"

"Shut up and take that pack animal around to the back of the store."

"Yes'um," Silva said. "Whatever you say, ma'am."

While Sally was saddling up, he turned to the hostler. "Send a boy with a fast horse to Rio. Tell them deputies of mine down there that Sally Jensen is pullin' out within the hour and looks like she's plannin' on joinin' up with her husband. Tell them to do something. Anything!"

"Sheriff," the hostler said, horror in his voice. "Don't look. She's a-fixin' to ride that hoss astride!"

"Lord, have mercy! What's this world comin' to?"

* * *

It was nearing dusk when Al Martine and his bunch spotted Smoke high up near the timberline in the Big Lonesome.

"We got him, boys!" Al yelled, and put the spurs to his tired horse.

A rifle bullet took Al's hat off and sent it spinning away. The mountain winds caught it, and it was gone forever.

"Goddamn!" Al yelled, just as another round kicked up dirt at his horse's hooves, and the animal started bucking. It was all Al could do to stay in the saddle.

A slug smacked Zack in the shoulder and nearly knocked him from the saddle. The second shot tore off the saddle horn and smashed into Zack's upper thigh, bringing a scream of pain from the outlaw.

"He's got help!" Pedro yelled. "Let's get gone from here."

The outlaws raced for cover, with Zack flopping around in the saddle.

Smoke looked down the mountain. "Now who in the devil is that?" he muttered.

Sally punched .44 rounds into her carbine and settled back into her well-hidden little camp in a narrow depression with the back and one side a solid rock wall.

"Who you reckon that was a-shootin' at us?" Tom Post yelled over the sounds of galloping horses.

"I don't know," Crown answered, yelling. "But he's hell with a rifle, whoever he is."

Using field glasses, Sally watched them beat a hasty retreat, and then laid out cloth and cup, plate and tableware, and napkin for her early supper. Just because one was in the wilderness, surrounded by godless heathens, was no reason to forgo small amenities.

She opened a can of beans, set aside a can of peaches for dessert, and spread butter on a thick slice of bread. Before eating, she said a prayer for the continuing safety of her man.

* * *

"He's up there," Ace Reilly said, his eyes looking at the timberline in the good light of morning. The air was almost cold this high up.

Big Bob Masters shifted his chew from one side of his mouth to the other and spat. "Solid rock to his back," he observed. "And two hundred yards of open country ever'where else. It'd be suicide gettin' up there."

Ace lifted his canteen to take a drink, and the canteen exploded in his hand, showering him with water, bits of metal, and numbing his hand. The second shot nicked Big Bob's horse on the rump, and the animal went pitching and snorting and screaming down the slope, Big Bob yelling and hanging on and flopping in the saddle. The third shot took off part of Causey's ear, and he left the saddle, crawling behind some rocks.

"Jesus Christ!" Ace hollered, leaving the saddle and taking cover. "Where the hell's that comin' from?"

Big Bob's horse had come to a very sudden and unexpected halt, and Big Bob went flying ass over elbows out of the saddle to land against a tree. He staggered to his feet, looking wildly around him, and took a .44 slug in the belly. He sank to his knees, both hands holding his punctured belly, bellowing in pain.

"He's right on top of us," Ace called to Nap. "Over there at the base of that rock face."

Smoke was hundreds of yards up the mountain, just at the timberline, looking and wondering who his new ally might be. He got his field glasses and began sweeping the area. A slow smile curved his lips.

"I married a Valkyrie, for sure," he muttered as the long lenses made out Sally's face.

He saw riders coming hard, a lot of riders. Smoke grabbed his .44-40 and began running down the mountain, keeping to the timber. The firing had increased as the riders dismounted and sought cover. Smoke stayed a good hundred yards above them, and so far he had not been spotted.

"Causey!" Woody yelled. "Over yonder!" He pointed. "Get on his right flank—that's exposed."

Causey jumped up, and Smoke drilled him through and through. Causey died sprawled on the rocks that were still damp from the misty morning in the ligh lonesome.

"He's up above us!" Ray yelled.

"Who the hell is that over yonder?" Noah hollered just as Sally fired. The slug sent bits of rock into Noah's face, and he screamed as he was momentarily blinded. He stood up, and Smoke nailed him through the neck. Smoke had been aiming for his chest, but shooting downhill is tricky, even for a marksman.

Big Bob Masters was hollering and screaming, afraid to move, afraid his guts would fall out.

Smoke began dusting the area where the outlaws and bounty hunters had left their horses. The whining slugs spooked them and off they ran, reins trailing, taking food, water, and extra ammo with them.

"Goddamnit!" Woody yelled, running after them. He suddenly stopped, right out in the open, realizing what a stupid move that had been.

Smoke and Sally fired at the same time. One slug struck Woody in the side; the .44-40 hit him in the chest. Woody had no further use for a horse.

Smoke plugged Yancey in the shoulder, knocking the man down and putting him out of the fight. Yancey began crawling downhill toward the horses, staying to cover. He had but two thoughts in mind: getting in the saddle, and getting the hell gone from this place.

"It's no good!" Ace yelled. "They'll pick us all off if we stay here. We got to get out of range. Start makin' your way down the slope."

The outlaws and bounty hunters began crawling back, staying to cover. Smoke and Sally held their fire, neither of them having a clear target and not wanting to waste ammo. They took their time to take a drink of water, eat a biscuit, and wait.

Haynes, Dale, and Yancey were the first to reach the horses, well out of range of the guns of Smoke and Sally.

Haynes looked up, horror in his eyes. A man dressed all in black was standing by a tree, his hands filled with iron.

"Hello, punk!" Louis Longmont said, and opened fire.*

Smoke's eyes cleared and he came back to the present, resolving to leave his memories of Sally until he could see her again in person. It was too painful to think of her while locked away from her touch.

He looked at Pearlie. "I just found out Marshal Thomas is going to stay in town. Once you get Gibbons to talk, make sure the marshal is there to hear it."

Pearlie nodded. "Will do. Anything else?"

"How about the doctor?"

"It took fifty dollars, but he's gonna dig the slug out soon as the viewin's over, 'fore the undertaker puts him in the ground."

"Have him talk to Thomas after he gets the bullet out. Thomas will be able to tell the difference if it's a .36 like I suspect."

Pearlie stepped close to the bars of the wagon and whispered, cutting his eyes at the men in the lockup with Smoke, "You gonna be all right, Boss?"

"Sure, Pearlie. These men have more on their minds than doing anything against me. Now, you go get to work, you're burning daylight."

Pearlie touched his hat. "Yes, sir!"

*Code of the Mountain Man

10

Smoke settled down in the wagon, his back against the front wall, figuring that way the ride would be marginally smoother over the rough terrain they were going to be traveling over.

The three men with him sat sullenly against other sides of the wagon, their heads down, looking dejected. Finally, one of them, who appeared to be about five feet tall, raised his face to look at Smoke.

"Howdy," he said. "My name's Shorty Robinson."

Smoke nodded. "I'm Smoke Jensen, Shorty. Glad to make your acquaintance."

At the mention of Smoke's name, the other two men glanced up, suddenly interested. "You *the* Smoke Jensen?" a man at the rear asked. He was broad-shouldered, with a thick beard so black it almost appeared blue in the sunlight filtering in through the bars.

Smoke gave a slight grin and nodded.

"My name's Dynamite Dick Bodine," the bearded man said. He cocked his thumb over his shoulder pointing at the other occupant of the wagon. "And this is Jonathan Mayhew."

Smoke nodded again at the other man, who asked, "What are you in here for, Mr. Jensen?"

"You can call me Smoke, since we all seem to be in rather the same predicament."

"All right, Smoke," Mayhew said.

"Tilghman thinks I back-shot an outlaw named the Durango Kid," Smoke said.

Bodine's eyes narrowed. "I never figured a man with your reputation with a six-killer would have to back-shoot anybody."

Smoke shrugged. "I didn't, as a matter of fact, but it doesn't look like Tilghman believes me."

He looked at the men one at a time. "What are you gentlemen charged with?"

Bodine smiled. "I robbed the Union Pacific Railroad. Used a mite too much dynamite tryin' to open the boxcar holding the safe. Blew it an' the man guarding it into 'bout a thousand pieces." He shrugged. "It were an accident, but that don't seem to cut no ice with the marshal there. I figure the Hangin' Judge gonna stretch my neck just as far as if I'd done it a-purpose."

Smoke kept his expression blank.

Bodine continued. "Mayhew there, he's a card shark who shot a man over a poker hand."

Mayhew got a pained expression on his face. "The scoundrel had the effrontery to accuse me of cheating, just because he didn't have the slightest idea of the odds of drawing to an inside straight."

Shorty Robinson smirked. "They got me for killin' two men in a fight. They made fun of my . . . stature, so naturally, I had to show 'em my knife made me just as tall as they was." He gave a short laugh. "An' a lot taller after they was spread out in the street tryin' to hold they guts in."

Smoke shook his head. For traveling companions, these men left a lot to be desired, he thought.

Tilghman came out of the sheriff's office and climbed up on the wagon after hitching his horse to the rear with a dally rope.

"Gentlemen, hold on to your hats, we're headin' out,"

he said, as he cracked his blacksnake whip over the team leading the wagon.

As they pulled out of town, Smoke saw Cal and Pearlie standing in the doorway of the bank, waiting for it to open. They smiled and waved at him as he passed, evidently trying to keep his spirits up. Well, he thought to himself, *I couldn't have better men—and women,* he added, thinking of Sally—*trying to get me out of trouble.* It was an uncomfortable thought that his safety depended on other people, since he'd always been a man who depended only on his own strength and intelligence to get him through trouble.

After the wagon passed, Cal turned to Pearlie. "We got to do something, podna. I hate seein' Smoke trussed up like an animal headin' to slaughter."

"Don't you worry none, Cal," Pearlie answered, his eyes hard. "Ain't nothin' gonna happen to Smoke if I have anything to say 'bout it."

A man in a black suit and boiled shirt and high collar unlocked the door and ushered them into the bank.

Twenty minutes later Pearlie and Cal exited with two thousand dollars in fresh greenbacks in their pockets, and a promise that there was more available if they needed it.

They walked down the street to the local doctor's office and knocked on the door.

A slight man with a badly pockmarked face opened the door. "We got your money," Pearlie said, holding up a handful of cash. "Now, let's get to work an' see just what kind'a bullet we find in that galoot on your table."

The doctor took the bills and counted them as he headed back into his surgery suite. Satisfied, he stuck them in his coat pocket and stepped up to a table upon which lay the dead man, who was dressed in a fine suit of clothes for the viewing.

"Here," the doc said, "help me get his coat and shirt off."

After they had the body uncovered, the doctor rolled it

onto its stomach. Taking a large scalpel, he enlarged the entrance wound of the bullet that remained in the body. Then he used a long probe to follow the track the slug had made as it coursed into the Kid's chest.

After a few minutes, the doc nodded to himself. "Yep, just as I thought. It's in his right lung."

He went to a side table and picked up an instrument that looked like two small rakes connected to a wheel with a handle on it. "Here, boys, hold these tines in between his ribs while I open the spreader."

He placed the small rakes in between two of Kid's ribs and looked at Cal for help.

Cal's face blanched white and he said, "Uh . . . I don't think . . ." Then he grabbed his mouth and ran from the room.

Pearlie shook his head and stepped up to the table. "Young'un just don't have the stomach for this kind'a work."

The doc smiled. "Not many people do when you get right down to it, son."

He turned the handle and the spreader opened Kid's ribs wide enough for him to get his hand in the chest. He looked at the ceiling while he felt around inside the body, searching with his fingers for the slug he couldn't see.

After a minute, he smiled. "Gotcha!"

He withdrew his hand, and between his fingers was a lead bullet. He handed it to Pearlie after wiping the blood off with a rag.

Pearlie pulled a .44 bullet from his belt and held it up next to the one from Kid's body. He smiled. Sure enough, the .44 was quite a bit larger. Smoke had been right. The Kid had been shot with a .36-caliber gun.

"I'm gonna need you to write a letter to Marshal Thomas tellin' him we took a .36-caliber bullet outta the Kid's body, Doc."

"I'd be glad to, Pearlie. I'd sure hate to see an innocent man hang for something he didn't do."

11

On the trip northward, the men in the wagon began to talk, there being nothing much else to occupy their minds since the scenery was uniformly bleak and unchanging for the most part.

Dynamite Dick Bodine said to Smoke, "I heard you killed over two hundred men. Is that about right, Smoke?"

Smoke tried to keep a pained expression off his face. He'd heard the same question in one form or another many times over the years. "I don't keep a tally of the men I've put in the ground, Dynamite. To me, that'd be too much like notching one's gun butt. To make a man's life, no matter how depraved or worthless, nothing more than a number to be bragged about over a glass of whiskey diminishes not only the man doing it, but the man he killed as well."

"That don't answer the question, Jensen," Dynamite said, his voice becoming harsh.

Smoke's voice became hard as steel as well. "I don't intend to answer, Dynamite. I will say this, though. I never killed a man who didn't draw on me first, or who didn't deserve to be buried forked end up." He hesitated. "And if that's not clear enough for you, I can come over there and try to make it plainer!"

Dynamite's face softened and he dropped his eyes. "I didn't mean nothin' by it, Smoke. Just a question, is all."

"Good," Smoke said, his voice returning to normal. "Then the matter is dropped."

Tilghman, who'd been listening to the conversation, smiled to himself. Maybe this Jensen fellow wasn't the cold-blooded killer he'd been led to believe he was. Tilghman liked a man who didn't brag about his accomplishments. It meant he was sure enough of himself that he didn't have to try to make others think he was bigger'n he was.

The conversation caused Tilghman to reflect for a moment on the men he'd killed in the line of duty over his years as both a local peace officer, and more recently as a federal marshal working under Judge Isaac Parker. Though he felt no guilt about the killings, reasoning as Judge Parker did that he hadn't killed the men, the law had, he still felt that he'd failed somehow every time he'd had to shoot someone rather than talking them into surrendering. Finally, he put his mind to other things. The day was far too pretty a one to spend it thinking morbid thoughts.

In Fort Worth, Pearlie and Cal found Marshal Heck Thomas having his breakfast at Aunt Ida's Boardinghouse. It wasn't as fancy as the high-priced hotels in town, but it was a lot cheaper, and the food was in fact better, being more like home cooking.

The boys approached Thomas's table. "Marshal," Pearlie began, "I hate to interrupt your meal, but we have some news about the killing of the Durango Kid you might be interested in."

Thomas stared at them as he chewed a bite of wheat cakes for a moment, then washed it down with a drink of coffee and pointed at the chairs across the table from him. "If you're gonna talk business during my breakfast, you might as well grab a seat and have some food while you do it."

Pearlie grinned, and Cal just shook his head. "You don't know what you're doin', Marshal," Cal said. "Pearlie's such a food hog, you're liable to be here all day if we have to wait for him to finish eatin' 'fore he tells you what we came for."

Thomas smiled. "Well, how about you give your order to Aunt Ida over there, an' whilst she's cookin' it, you can tell about your news?"

He signaled the heavyset woman wearing a flour-stained apron over to the table.

Pearlie ordered four hens' eggs, a half-pound of bacon, skillet-fried potatoes, and a pot of coffee. Cal just smiled and ordered a short stack of wheat cakes and two eggs.

Thomas smiled after the cook left the table. "I see what you mean about your friend."

Pearlie got right to the point. "Marshal, what caliber gun do you use?"

Thomas's eyes narrowed. "A Colt Army .44. Why?"

"Could I see one of your cartridges?"

Thomas stared at Pearlie as if he had lost his mind for a moment, then pulled a bullet out of his belt and handed it to Pearlie.

Pearlie pulled the bag containing the slug taken from the Kid's body and the note the doctor had written. He handed both to Thomas.

Thomas slowly sipped his coffee as he read the note, then held up the slug next to his .44-caliber cartridge and compared them. "I agree with the doc," he said, raising his eyes to Pearlie. "This does appear to be a .36, and not a .44."

"You know that Smoke Jensen carries only Colt .44's," Pearlie said, "and that's the guns you and Tilghman took away from him."

Thomas pursed his lips and thought for a moment. "You're right, it don't seem to make much sense, but we still got that witness who said he saw Jensen shoot the Kid."

Pearlie leaned back as Cal started to talk, telling the

marshal about their run-in with Max Gibbons on the train. "So you see, Marshal Thomas, he's just a tinhorn gambler tryin' to get even with Smoke for kickin' him off the train an' showin' he was a cheat."

"You might be right, son, but how are you gonna prove it?"

"If you'll help us, we plan to get him to admit he lied 'bout Smoke," Pearlie said, sticking a napkin in his shirt as he prepared to dig into the meal Aunt Ida was placing before him.

"And just how do you plan to do that?" Thomas asked.

Pearlie speared some eggs on his fork and glanced at Cal. "You tell him, Cal, an' I'll just get started on this food."

It was almost ten o'clock that evening when a buxom redhead sidled up to the table where Max Gibbons was playing poker. She stood next to him, her hand casually resting on his shoulders and playing with the back of his head as she watched the game.

After a few hands, she leaned down and whispered in his ear, "I just love a man with strong, quick hands. How about we go up to my room and you can practice some of those moves on me?"

Gibbons looked at her, then at the men he was playing with. He'd managed to take most of their money already, so leaving with the woman would be a good excuse to get out of the game with his winnings.

"Boys," he said, stuffing his money in his coat, "I've just had an offer I am loath to refuse. I shall return later, if I'm not too worn out."

"What's your name, little lady?" he asked as they walked up the stairs hand in hand.

"Ruby. Ruby Redlin," she answered, squeezing his hand and winking at him.

In her room, she slipped out of her dress while he began to disrobe. She lay back on the bed, dressed only in her corset, which emphasized her more-than-ample breasts.

"Say," she said, a thoughtful look on her face. "Aren't you the man who saw that gunman shoot down the Durango Kid the other night?"

Gibbons glanced at her as he pulled off his boots. "Yeah. Why?"

"Oh, I was just thinking it must take an awful lot of courage to stand up and point the finger at a man like that. Why, what if he'd gotten out of jail and come after you?"

Gibbons laughed and crossed the room to lie next to her on the bed. "Jensen ain't never gonna get out of jail, 'less it's to get his neck stretched."

Ruby leaned over and began to rub his chest and stomach, her hand drifting lower and lower. "Well, he really don't have no reason to be mad at you anyway. After all, all you did was tell what he done. I guess it don't take as much courage as I thought it did."

Gibbons bristled at her suggestion that his act didn't take bravery. "Hell, woman. It took a lot more guts than you think it did. Jensen's a well-known killer."

"Yeah, but how could he get angry with you for just telling what you saw?" she asked, her hand disappearing into his shorts.

Gibbons stiffened, laid his head back, and closed his eyes. "Like I said, you don't know all the details," he mumbled, reaching out to grab at the fastenings on her corset.

She leaned over and whispered in his ear, "Then, tell me, darling. I find it so exciting."

"That Jensen had the nerve to call me a card cheat," Gibbons said, his hands busy. "So, to get even with him, I lied about what happened out there. He didn't shoot the Kid. Someone else did, but because of me, Jensen's going to hang for it." He leaned back, a proud expression on his face. "That'll teach the son of a bitch to mess around with Max Gibbons."

"Did you see who did shoot the Kid?" Ruby asked, her eyes wide with admiration.

"Naw, it was too dark. But the Kid was facing Jensen when he got plugged in the back."

"Then that was awfully brave of you to lie about a famous gunfighter like that. Just think what he'd do if he ever got out of jail."

Gibbons's face paled for a second. Then he forced a laugh. "Hell, like I said, Jensen's going to be hung. I don't have nothing to worry about."

He buried his face between Ruby's breasts, not noticing the smile that curled her lips as she lay her head back on the pillow, already thinking on what she was going to buy with the money the tall, lean cowboy had given her to get Gibbons to talk.

In the room next to Ruby's, Marshal Heck Thomas sat back from the wall with the small hole drilled in it he'd had his ear against.

He looked at Cal and Pearlie and grinned. "You boys were right after all. The son of a bitch gave a false statement to federal marshals 'bout your friend."

Pearlie slapped his thigh and stood up. "You gonna arrest him now, Marshal?"

Thomas thought on it for a moment, then smiled wickedly. "No. Gibbons is gonna spend some time in Yuma Prison for his lies, so I think I'll just let him finish what he's doin'. It figures to be a very long time 'fore he gets to do it again, at least with a woman, so I'll just let him have his last fling."

"Are you gonna let Marshal Tilghman know he's transportin' an innocent man?" Cal asked, his face worried.

Thomas nodded. "Yeah. Trouble is, Bill's halfway to hell an' gone in some of the worst country there is between here and Fort Smith. I don't have no way to get in touch with him till he reaches Fort Smith. I'll just have to wire the judge with the details of what we've found out so he can let Jensen go when they get there."

"You think there'll be any problem with the judge?" Pearlie asked. "I've heard he sure likes to hang people."

Thomas's face sobered. "Judge Parker is a good man, a God-fearin' man who always tries to do what's right. I'm sure once he's heard the evidence, he'll decide Jensen is innocent."

"And if he don't?" Pearlie asked.

Thomas rubbed his chin. "Well, we could make sure by figuring out just who did shoot the Kid. Then there wouldn't be no doubt of Jensen's innocence."

"Would you mind if we . . . kind'a helped you nose around about that?" Cal asked.

Thomas smiled. "Son, one thing I've learned in all my years out here in the territories, don't never turn down help when it's offered."

12

Marshal Bill Tilghman slowed the team of horses driving the prison wagon near a grove of mesquite trees, pulling it to a stop where both the animals and the prisoners could enjoy some shade. Out on the edge of the Oklahoma Territory Indian Nations, the heat was almost unbearable, even though it was still a couple of months before summer would officially begin.

"Hey, Tilghman," Dynamite Dick Bodine said, his voice raspy and dry. "How 'bout some water back here, or are you tryin' to save the Hangin' Judge the expense of a rope by starvin' us to death?"

Tilghman climbed down from the hurricane deck of the wagon, grabbed a large canvas bag under the seat, and walked back to the rear of the wagon.

He thrust the bag through the bars. "There's some canteens, an' some jerky and biscuits an' a couple of apples apiece for you gents."

The three prisoners riding along with Smoke tore into the bag, grunting in their haste to get water and food. Smoke stayed in his position against the forward wall of the cage.

Tilghman raised his eyebrows. "Ain't you hungry an' thirsty, Jensen?"

Smoke nodded. "Yes, but I can wait until the others get

their fill. I'm more used to going without food and water from my days in the mountains."

Tilghman walked over to stand in the shade of the wagon next to where Smoke reclined. He made two cigarettes from a small cloth sack and passed one through the bars to Smoke. After they both had their cigarettes going, Tilghman said, "I've heard you used to be a mountain man. Is that true?"

Smoke nodded, his mind going back to his early days in the West, riding the slopes with his friend Preacher.

"Yeah. I came out here with my dad when I was just fifteen years old," Smoke said.

Tilghman nodded. "Those must've been some times, what with the Indians an' all."

Smoke laughed. "There were times we'd go a whole year and not see another white man."

"I've been told the Indians pretty much left the mountain men alone."

"Some did," Smoke said, his eyes becoming vague with memories that seemed as if they'd happened only yesterday. "Others came at us every chance they got . . ." *Like the ones attacked my father and me the day we met Preacher,* he thought to himself, his mind going back to the day he and his father first laid eyes on the man known as the first mountain man . . .

Preacher galloped up to the pair, his rifle in his hand. "Don't get nervous," he told them. "It ain't me you got to fear. We fixin' to get ambushed . . . shortly. This here country is famous for that."

"Ambushed by who?" Emmett asked, not trusting the old man.

"Kiowa, I think. But they could be Pawnee. My eyes ain't as sharp as they used to be. I seen one of 'em stick a head up out of a wash over yonder, while I was jawin' with you. He's young, or he wouldn't have done that. But that don't mean the others with him is young."

"How many?"

"Don't know. In this country, one's too many. Do know this: We better light a shuck out of here. If memory serves me correct, right over yonder, over that ridge, they's a little crick behind a stand of cottonwoods, old buffalo wallow in front of it." He looked up, stood up in his stirrups, and cocked his shaggy head. "Here they come, boys . . . rake them cayuses!"

Before Kirby could ask what a cayuse was, or what good a rake was in an Indian attack, the old man had slapped his bay on the rump and they were galloping off. With the mountain man taking the lead, the three of them rode for the crest of the ridge. The packhorses seemed to sense the urgency, for they followed with no pullback on the ropes. Cresting the ridge, the riders slid down the incline and galloped into the timber, down into the wallow. The whoops and cries of the Indians were close behind them.

The Preacher might well have been past his so-called good years, but the mountain man had leaped off his spotted pony, rifle in hand, and was in position and firing before Emmett or Kirby had dismounted. Preacher, like Emmett, carried a Sharps .52, firing a paper cartridge, deadly up to seven hundred yards or more.

Kirby looked up in time to see a brave fly off his pony, a crimson slash on his naked chest. The Indian hit the ground hard and did not move.

"Get me that Spencer out of the pack, boy," Kirby's father yelled.

"The what?" Kirby had no idea what a Spencer might be.

"The rifle. It's in the pack. A tin box wrapped up with it. Bring both of 'em. Cut the ropes, boy."

Slashing the ropes with his long-bladed knife, Kirby grabbed the long, canvas-wrapped rifle and the tin box. He ran to his father's side. He stood and watched as his father got a buck in the sights of his Sharps, led him on his fast-running pony, then fired. The buck slammed off his pony, bounced off the ground, then leaped to his feet, one arm hanging bloody and broken. The Indian dodged for cover. He didn't make it. Preacher shot him in the side and lifted him off his feet, dropping him dead.

Emmett laid the Sharps aside and hurriedly unwrapped the canvas, exposing an ugly weapon with a potbellied, slab-sided receiver. Emmett glanced up at Preacher, who was grinning at him.

"What the hell are you grinnin' about, man?"

"Just wanted to see what you had all wrapped up, partner. Figured I had you beat with what's in my pack."

"We'll see," Emmett muttered. He pulled out a thin tube from the tin box and inserted it in the butt plate, chambering a round. In the tin box were a dozen or more tubes, each containing seven rounds, .52-caliber. Emmett leveled the rifle, sighted it, and fired all seven rounds in a thunderous barrage of black smoke. The Indians whooped and yelled. Emmett's firing had not dropped a single brave, but the Indians scattered for cover, disappearing, horses and all, behind a ridge.

"Scared 'em," Preacher opined. "They ain't used to repeaters. All they know is single-shots. Let me get something outta my pack. I'll show you a thing or two."

Preacher went to one of his pack animals, untied one of the side packs, and let it fall to the ground. He pulled out the most beautiful rifle Kirby had ever seen.

"Damn!" Emmett softly swore. "The blue-bellies had some of those toward the end of the war. But I never could get my hands on one."

Preacher smiled and pulled another Henry repeating rifle from his pack. Unpredictable as mountain men were, he tossed the second Henry to Emmett, along with a sack of cartridges.

"Now we be friends," Preacher said. He laughed, exposing tobacco-stained stubs of teeth.

"I'll pay you for this," Emmett said, running his hands over the sleek barrel.

"Ain't necessary," Preacher replied. "I won both of 'em in a contest outside Westport Landing. Kansas City to you. 'Sides, somebody's got to look out for the two of you. Ya'll liable to wander round out here and get hurt. 'Pears to me don't neither of you know tit from tat 'bout stayin' alive in Injun country."

"You may be right," Emmett admitted. He loaded the Henry. "So, thank you kindly."

Preacher looked at Kirby. "Boy, you heeled—so you gonna get in this fight, or not?"

"Sir?"

"Heeled. Means you carryin' a gun, so that make you a man. Ain't you got no rifle 'cept that muzzle-loader?"

"No, sir."

"Take your daddy's Sharps then. You seen him load it, so you know how. Take that tin box of tubes too. You watch out for our backs. Them Pawnees—and they is Pawnees—likely to come 'crost that crick. You in wild country, boy . . . you may as well get bloodied."

"Do it, Kirby," his father said. "And watch yourself. Don't hesitate a second to shoot. Those savages won't show you any mercy, so you do the same for them."

Kirby, a little pale around the mouth, took up the heavy Sharps and the box of tubes, reloaded the rifle, and made himself as comfortable as possible on the rear slope of the slight incline, overlooking the creek.

"Not there, boy." Preacher corrected Kirby's position. "Your back is open to the front line of fire. Get behind that tree 'twixt us and you. That way, you won't catch no lead or arrow in the back."

The boy did as he was told, feeling a bit foolish that he had not thought about his back. Hadn't he read enough dime novels to know that? he chastised himself. Nervous sweat dripped from his forehead as he waited.

He had to go to the bathroom something awful.

A half hour passed, the only action the always-moving Kansas winds chasing tumbleweeds, the southward-moving waters of the creek, and an occasional slap of a fish.

"What are they waiting for?" Emmett asked without taking his eyes from the ridge.

"For us to get careless," Preacher said. "Don't you fret none . . . they still out there. I been livin' in and round Injuns the better part of fifty year. I know 'em better than—or at least as good as—any livin' white man. They'll try to wait us out. They got nothing but time, boys."

"No way we can talk to them?" Emmett asked, and immediately regretted saying it as Preacher laughed.

"Why, shore, Emmett," the mountain man said. "You just stand up, put your hands in the air, and tell 'em you want to palaver some. They'll probably let you walk right up to 'em. Odds are, they'll even let you speak your piece. They polite like that. A white man can ride right into near-abouts any Injun village. They'll feed you, sign-talk to you, and give you a place to sleep. Course . . . gettin' out is the problem.

"They ain't like us, Emmett. They don't come close to thinkin' like us. What is fun to them is torture to us. They call it testin' a man's bravery. If'n a man dies good—that is, don't holler a lot—they make it last as long as possible. Then they'll sing songs about you, praise you for dyin' good. Lots of white folks condemn 'em for that, but it's just they way of life.

"They got all sorts of ways to test a man's bravery and strength. They might—dependin' on the tribe—strip you, stake you out over a big anthill, then pour honey over you. Then they'll squat back and watch, see how well you die."

Kirby felt sick to his stomach.

"Or they might bury you up to your neck in the ground, slit your eyelids so you can't close 'em, and let the sun blind you. Then, after your eyes is burnt blind, they'll dig you up and turn you loose naked out in the wild . . . trail you for days, seein' how well you die."

Kirby positioned himself better behind the tree and quietly went to the bathroom. *If a bean is a bean,* the boy thought, *what's a pea? A relief.*

Preacher just wouldn't shut up about it. "Out in the deserts, now, them Injuns get downright mean with they fun. They'll cut out your eyes, cut off your privates, then

slit the tendons in your ankles so's you can't do nothin'
but flop around on the sand. They get a big laugh out of
that. Or they might hang you upside down over a little
fire. The 'Paches like to see hair burn. They a little strange
'bout that.

"Or if they like you, they might put you through what
they call the run of the arrow. I lived through that . . .
once. But I was some younger. Damned if'n I want to do
it again at my age. Want me to tell you 'bout that little
game?"

"No!" Emmett said quickly. "I get your point."

"Figured you would. Point is, don't let 'em ever take you
alive. Kirby, now, they'd probably keep for work or trade.
But that's chancy, he being nearabout a man growed."
The mountain man tensed a bit, then said, "Look alive,
boy, and stay that way. Here they come." He winked at
Kirby.

"How do you know that, Preacher?" Kirby asked. "I
don't see anything."

"Wind just shifted. Smelled 'em. They close, been easin'
up through the grass. Get ready."

Kirby wondered how the old man could smell anything
over the fumes from his own body.

Emmett, a veteran of four years of continuous war, could
not believe an enemy could slip up on him in open daylight. At the sound of Preacher jacking back the hammer
of his Henry .44, Emmett shifted his eyes from his perime-
ter for just a second. When he again looked back at his
field of fire, a big, painted-up buck was almost on top of
him. Then the open meadow was filled with screaming,
charging Indians.

Emmett brought the buck down with a .44 slug through
the chest, flinging the Indian backward, the yelling abruptly
cut off in his throat.

The air had changed from the peacefulness of summer
quiet to a screaming, gun-smoke-filled hell. Preacher looked
at Kirby, who was looking at him, his mouth hanging open

in shock, fear, and confusion. "Don't look at me, boy!" he yelled. "Keep them eyes in front of you."

Kirby jerked his gaze to the small creek and the stand of timber that lay behind it. His eyes were beginning to smart from the acrid powder smoke, and his head was aching from the pounding of the Henry .44 and the screaming and yelling. The Spencer Kirby held at the ready was a heavy weapon, and his arms were beginning to ache from the strain.

His head suddenly came up, eyes alert. He had seen movement on the far side of the creek. Right there! Yes, someone, or something was over there.

I don't want to shoot anyone, the boy thought. *Why can't we be friends with these people?* And that thought was still throbbing in his brain when a young Indian suddenly sprang from the willows by the creek and lunged into the water, a rifle in his hand.

For what seemed like an eternity, Kirby watched the young brave, a boy about his own age, leap and thrash through the water. Kirby jacked back the hammer of the Spencer, sighted in on the brave, and pulled the trigger. The .52-caliber pounded his shoulder, bruising it, for there wasn't much spare meat on Kirby. When the smoke blew away, the young Indian was face-down in the water, his blood staining the stream.

Kirby stared at what he'd done, then fought back waves of sickness that threatened to spill from his stomach.

The boy heard a wild screaming and spun around. His father was locked in hand-to-hand combat with two knife-wielding braves. Too close for the rifle, Kirby clawed his Navy Colt from leather, vowing he would cut that stupid flap from his holster after this was over. He shot one brave through the head just as his father buried his Arkansas Toothpick to the hilt in the chest of the other.

And as abruptly as they came, the Indians were gone, dragging as many of their dead and wounded with them as they could. Two braves lay dead in front of Preacher; two braves dead in the shallow ravine with the three men;

the boy Kirby had shot lay in the creek, arms outstretched, the waters a deep crimson. The body slowly floated downstream.

Preacher looked at the dead buck in the creek, then at the brave in the wallow with them . . . the one Kirby had shot. He lifted his eyes to the boy.

"Got your baptism this day, boy. Did right well, you did."

"Saved my life, son," Emmett said, dumping the bodies of the Indians out of the wallow. "Can't call you boy no more, I reckon. You be a man now."

A thin finger of smoke lifted from the barrel of the Navy .36 Kirby held in his hand. Preacher smiled and spat tobacco juice.

He looked at Kirby's ash-blond hair. "Yep," he said, "Smoke'll suit you just fine. So Smoke hit'll be."

"Sir?" Kirby finally found his voice.

"Smoke. That's what I'll call you now on. Smoke."*

Smoke came back to the present when Shorty Robinson nudged his arm with a canteen. "Don't you want no water, Jensen?"

Smoke took the canteen, wiped the spout off, then took a deep swallow. It tasted as good as anything he'd ever swallowed.

*The Last Mountain Man

13

Smoke drank his fill of the water, sleeved moisture off his lips, and passed the canteen over to Shorty Robinson.

"Here ya go, Shorty."

"Thanks, Smoke," the little man said as he upended the canteen and gulped the rest of the liquid down.

Dynamite Dick leaned over and whispered to Smoke, "Jensen, you think there's any way we can get the drop on the marshal?"

Smoke shook his head, a slow grin appearing on his lips. "Having the Hanging Judge waiting to put a noose around your neck isn't dying fast enough for you, Dick? You want to go to hell a little faster?"

"What's that supposed to mean?"

"Just that Tilghman has a reputation of never having lost a prisoner, though I hear tell he's had to bring a few in dead who didn't start out that way," Smoke said. "You want to commit suicide, go ahead. But me, I'd rather take my chances with Judge Parker. At least a couple of men have survived going before him. . . . None have tangled with Tilghman and lived to tell about it."

Dynamite Dick looked disgusted. "I figgered you for more sand than that, Jensen." He looked over at Shorty and Jonathan Mayhew. "Either of you gents got the guts to try it with me?" he asked.

Both men just shook their heads.

Dick slapped his thigh. "Yellow sons of bitches," he muttered.

Tilghman walked around the wagon, a slight smile on his face as if he'd heard what the men had said. "You'd be smart to listen to Jensen, Bodine," he said. "That way you might live to make it to Fort Smith."

Dick scowled and Tilghman laughed. "All right, men, break's over. Get back in the wagon and we'll get on our way."

Two hours later, when the wagon was halfway across an open prairie with no cover other than the saw grass that grew to knee height, Tilghman pulled back on the reins and jumped down off the hurricane deck. He walked around to the back of the caged area and pulled a long, brass spyglass out of the saddlebags on his horse.

Putting the glass to his eye, he aimed it at the horizon and braced his arm against the side of the wagon to steady his gaze.

Smoke looked out between the bars and could see a cloud of dust, which looked to be about six or seven miles distant.

"Company coming, Marshal?" he asked.

Tilghman nodded without taking the glass from his eyes. "Yeah, an' I don't much think they're friendlies."

"Indians or outlaws?" Smoke asked.

Tilghman looked at him. "Probably a little of both. We've had some reports of some renegade Mescalero Apaches ridin' with some cattle rustlers who've taken to hidin' in the Nations. This is their stomping grounds so I'd bet it's them."

"They got any reason to be mad at you?" Smoke asked.

"Other than the fact they don't much like anybody with a star on his chest, not that I know of," Tilghman replied.

Smoke craned his neck to look on all sides of the wagon. "Doesn't seem to be any place nearby to make a stand."

Tilghman glanced over his shoulder at an outcropping of rock almost five miles ahead of them. "That's the closest, but I don't think I stand a Chinaman's chance of makin' it, leastways not while pullin' this wagon."

Dynamite Dick looked up. "You could always leave the wagon an' take off on your hoss, Marshal," he said with a hopeful glint in his eye.

Tilghman reached in his breast pocket and pulled out a large square of tobacco. Taking a long-bladed knife from a scabbard on his belt, he sliced off a quarter of the square and put it in his mouth. He chewed for a moment, looking off toward the dust cloud, then leaned over and spat a brown stream of tobacco juice into the dust of the trail.

"Yep, I reckon I could, if I's a mind to."

"Then you're gonna leave us an' run for it?" Shorty Robinson asked, not looking as happy about the prospect as Bodine had been.

"Nope," was Tilghman's short answer.

He stepped to his horse and pulled a bright yellow-sided carbine out of a rifle boot next to the saddle. It was an 1873-model Winchester, the one called the Yellow Boy.

He jacked a shell into the firing chamber, placed a box of cartridges on the edge of the wagon next to him within easy reach, and settled in to fight the outlaws.

Smoke made his way within the wagon until he was next to the marshal. "If you want some help, Marshal, I'd be glad to oblige."

Tilghman smirked. "Yeah, but then that'd kind'a be like askin' the fox to guard the henhouse, wouldn't it, Jensen?"

"Have it your way, Marshal. Just don't let your stubbornness get you killed."

The group of outlaws, rustlers, and murderers crested a small ridge and their leader, Zachary Stillwell, held his hand up, bringing them to a halt. Jaime Gonzalez, his second in command, shaded his eyes with a hand, peering through the heat haze to the wagon in the distance.

"What you make of it, Zach?" he asked.

Zachary smiled grimly. "Why, Jaime, it looks like one of

those wagons the U.S. marshals use to take prisoners over to visit the Hangin' Judge in Fort Smith."

George Hungry Bear, a Mescalero Apache renegade, said, "That mean no gold or silver."

Zachary shook his head. "No, but there's usually only the one marshal with the prisoners. It wouldn't be too much of a chore to take him out and maybe get us some more men to ride with us."

Jaime looked around at the men riding with them. "Why for we need more men, Zachary? We got ten now."

"You want to hit that payroll train comin' into Fort Worth next week, don't ya?"

Gonzalez nodded. "Yes. I hear it carry over a hundred thousand dollars."

Zachary smiled. "Then we're gonna need a couple'a extra guns."

"That mean less money for us," Hungry Bear observed.

Zachary shook his head. "Not necessarily. Nobody says they have to survive the robbery. What happens to 'em after we got the gold won't matter to nobody but them."

Gonzalez and Hungry Bear looked at each other and grinned. "Then, let us go free some prisoners," Gonzalez said, whipping the rump of his horse with a short whip he carried on his left wrist.

The ten riders spread out in a line as they galloped toward the wagon, pistols and rifles in their hands, whooping and hollering like Indians on the warpath.

Tilghman calmly leaned to the side, spat in the dirt, shifted his chaw to his left cheek, and took deadly aim. The explosion of the Yellow Boy kicked back against his shoulder, and seconds later one of the attackers threw his arms in the air and catapulted backward off his mount.

Tilghman jacked another shell in the chamber and muttered, "That's one down."

"Nice shooting," Smoke observed as he watched through the bars.

Tilghman managed to get two more bandits before

Zachary Stillwell got smart and pulled his men back out of rifle range.

"What now, Zach?" Gonzalez asked. "We lost three men already, and we ain't got nothin' to show for it yet."

Stillwell motioned with his arm. "Two of you men circle around to the left, an' another two circle to the right. Stay out of range until I give the signal, then start advancing in on the wagon afoot. That'a way you'll make less of a target. Sooner or later, we'll get 'em, 'cause he cain't watch all sides at the same time."

An hour later, when all the men were in place surrounding the wagon, Stillwell held his pistol in the air and fired a single shot.

The men began to creep up on the wagon, keeping low, and keeping up a steady stream of fire at the marshal, who moved quickly back and forth, snapping off shots when he got a glimpse of a head or a rifle barrel, but not hitting anything.

After a second bullet pinged off a bar and ricocheted around inside the wagon, Smoke said, "You got to give it up, Marshal, else we're all going to be picked off."

Tilghman sighed. "You're right, Jensen. I don't have no cause to put you men in danger any longer."

"Get on your horse and hightail it out of here," Smoke said.

"Uh-uh, I ain't leavin' you men to no desperadoes. Maybe they'll be content with me an' let you men go free."

Tilghman stepped out in the open, put his rifle in the dirt, and raised his hands over his head.

Within a few minutes, the remaining seven outlaws were gathered around the wagon. "Keep a gun on the star-packer," Stillwell told Gonzalez, who held his Colt pointed at Tilghman's belt buckle.

Stillwell walked up to the cage and peered through the bars. "What have we here?" he asked with a grin on his face. "Some bad desperadoes?"

He got the key to the cage from Tilghman's pocket and

opened the door, standing back and wrinkling his nose as the four men climbed out.

"Whew, but you're a ripe bunch of monkeys," he said.

"You would be too if'n you'd rode a hundred miles in the back of that hot box," Dynamite Dick Bodine said, grinning.

"And who might you be?" Stillwell asked.

"My handle's Dynamite Dick Bodine."

Stillwell's eyebrows raised. "The train robber?"

"Yep, one an' the same."

Stillwell nodded. "Good, we're plannin' a little job an' your experience will come in mighty handy."

"Be glad to oblige you, mister," Dick said, moving over to stand with the outlaws.

"And how about you?" Stillwell asked the others.

"Them two ain't nothin' but a card sharp an' a street fighter," Dick said, pointing to Mayhew and Robinson, "but that big galoot over there's Smoke Jensen."

Stillwell stared intently at Smoke. "*The* Smoke Jensen?"

Smoke looked steadily back at the outlaw. "One and the same," he said drily.

Stillwell walked up to stand nose-to-nose with Smoke. "I can use a man with your experience. You interested in joinin' up with us?"

Smoke grinned, but his eyes remained flat. "If it'll get me out of this cage, I am."

Stillwell inclined his head toward Mayhew and Robinson. "What 'bout them? You think they'll be any good to us?"

Smoke shrugged, glancing around at the dead bodies scattered among the scrub brushes and saw grass nearby. "It appears to me you just lost three or four men. I'd think anybody dangerous enough to be in the company of the marshal over there would be an asset to whatever you have planned. Anyway, what've you got to lose? If they don't work out, you can always get rid of them later."

Stillwell laughed and slapped Smoke on the shoulder. "I like the way you think, Jensen."

Smoke pointed at a large canvas bag lying up on the

hurricane deck of the wagon. "You mind if I get my guns? The marshal's got them stored in that bag there."

"Go ahead," Stillwell said, turning his attention back to Marshal Tilghman. "I've got some business with the marshal here."

Smoke hurriedly grabbed his belt and holsters along with his large Bowie knife and scabbard out of the sack. He strapped the guns on in their usual manner, right one butt back, left one butt forward, and stuck the knife and scabbard onto the rear of the belt.

He pulled both guns and opened the loading gates, checking to make sure they were still loaded—they were, six and six.

Stillwell pulled his gun and approached Tilghman, grinning. "I've never kilt a U.S. marshal before," he said, "but there's a first time for ever'thing."

Smoke spoke up. "Hold on, Stillwell. That may be a type of trouble you don't want."

Stillwell glanced back over his shoulder, a scowl on his face. "What do you mean, Jensen?"

Smoke shrugged. "It's just that whenever a U.S. marshal is killed, his friends never give up hunting down the men who did it. And more often than not, they end up getting their men."

"Yeah, but if we don't get rid of 'im, he'll just do the same thing," Jaime Gonzalez said, still holding his pistol pointed at Tilghman's gut.

"Not necessarily," Smoke said. "What if we break the wheel on that wagon, and leave the marshal afoot out here in no-man's land? That way it'll look like he broke down and lost the horses and died of thirst when they find his body . . . if the coyotes and wolves leave anything to be found at all."

Stillwell looked doubtful. "I don't know . . ."

"Plus," Smoke added, "it'll be more fitting for the son of a bitch to die slow and painful-like. A bullet's too easy for him."

Tilghman's eyes narrowed as he stared at Smoke, his expression looking as if he thought maybe he'd misjudged the mountain man after all.

George Hungry Bear snorted through his nose as he laughed. "Jensen think like Indian. It be good to see how the lawman dies."

Stillwell smiled, as if that decided the matter. "All right. Hungry Bear, go over there and break the wheel on that wagon an' unhitch those hosses. We'll take all three of 'em with us until we reach the next town. Should be able to sell 'em for a little somethin' for our trouble."

"Better unload the marshal's pistol and leave it with him. Wouldn't do for him to be found without any iron on him. By the time he reloads it from his belt cartridges, we'll be out of range," Smoke said.

"Good idea," Stillwell said, nodding toward Gonzalez to indicate he should do as Smoke said.

While Gonzalez was busy unloading the marshal's pistol, Smoke stepped up to put his face close to the marshal's. "Thought you were going to see me hang, did you?" he asked, winking at Tilghman where no one else could see. He cut his eyes toward the outcropping of boulders and trees in the distance. "You be careful where you step out here, Marshal. You never know what kind'a snake is going to be in front of you."

Tilghman gave a slight nod to show Smoke he understood. "Yeah, Jensen," he said, his voice bitter. "I wouldn't want to step on any of your relatives."

Smoke laughed and swung up on the marshal's bay horse. He tipped his hat as the others mounted up also. "See ya' around, Marshal," he said, smiling.

"I hope so, Jensen, I hope so," Tilghman said, his face grim.

Gonzalez threw the marshal's Colt in the dirt twenty yards away, and Stillwell and his gang put the spurs to their horses, leaving Tilghman standing in a cloud of dust.

He walked over to his gun, brushed the dirt off, and reloaded it with cartridges from his belt.

He watched the men ride off out of sight and shook his

head. "I hope you know what you're doing, Jensen. You're playin' a mighty dangerous game."

He pulled his hat down tight, grabbed a half-full canteen of water from the ruined wagon, and started walking toward the only shelter in sight.

He figured he had about four or five miles to walk in boots that weren't designed for walking just to get out of the sun and wind. *Damn,* he thought, *some days it just don't pay to get outta bed.*

14

Cal and Pearlie were sitting in Aunt Ida's Boarding-house having breakfast when Marshal Heck Thomas approached their table, a grim look on his face.

Pearlie looked up from his plate of bacon, eggs, wheat cakes, and sliced peaches. "Howdy, Marshal," he said. "Pull up a chair and we'll treat you to some good home cookin'."

Thomas shook his head as he pulled out a chair, and signaled Aunt Ida to bring him some coffee. "You boys might not be so generous when I tell you the news."

Cal put his fork down, a worried look on his face. "Why? What's the matter, Marshal? Weren't you able to get in touch with Judge Parker?"

"Oh, I got in touch with him, all right."

"Then why the long face?" Pearlie asked, stuffing another forkful of wheat cakes in his mouth.

"'Cause he said what I overheard Gibbons say don't amount to a hill of beans in a court of law."

"What?" Cal exclaimed. "But you heard him admit that Smoke didn't shoot that outlaw."

"That's right, Cal, but the judge says that don't count under the law. Seems Gibbons's written statement will stand until and unless he says he lied while under oath."

Pearlie waved his fork in the air. "Then, that's no problem,

Marshal. We'll just traipse on over to the hotel where that tinhorn is stayin' and make him tell the truth."

"I only wish it were that easy, Pearlie," the marshal said as he poured a tablespoon of sugar into his coffee and took a tentative sip.

"Believe you me, Marshal," Pearlie persisted, "Cal an' me can be mighty persuasive when the need arises."

Thomas smiled. "I don't doubt it, Pearlie. Remember, I know from experience just how persuasive you an' Cal are." He hesitated, then said, "I might as well come right out with it. I went over to Gibbons's hotel myself, just to brace him with what I heard an' see if he'd agree to amend his statement."

"What'd the bastard say?" Cal asked.

Aunt Ida interrupted the conversation by appearing at the marshal's elbow, a stern look on her face.

"You gonna order some food or just sit there slopping down my coffee?" she asked.

The marshal chuckled and said, "Sure, Aunt Ida, you know I always eat here when I'm in town."

She was somewhat mollified, and her expression softened.

"I'll have three hens' eggs, scrambled with sweet cream, half a pound of bacon, fried crisp, an' a short stack of those wheat cakes Pearlie's wolfin' down."

"That's what I like 'bout you, Marshal," Ida said. "You eat like a man, not like some greenhorn from back East."

As she turned to go, she winked back over her shoulder. "I'll even throw in some of those tinned peaches for you since you been such a loyal customer."

An impatient Pearlie said, "Go on, Marshal, What'd the bastard say?"

Thomas looked at Pearlie. "Nothin'. Seems he must've heard about our little eavesdropping session the other night, 'cause he packed his bags an' took off during the night."

"Took off?" Cal asked. "How'd he do that? He came in on the train with us."

"I asked the desk clerk who was on duty when he left. He said Gibbons had a surrey he'd rented from the livery stable." The marshal smiled grimly. "Guess the tinhorn don't like to ride horses."

"Did the clerk say which way he headed when he left town?" Pearlie asked.

The marshal cocked an eye at Pearlie. "Why? You figgerin' on goin' after him?"

"Marshal Thomas, Smoke Jensen is not only the best friend Cal and me got, he's the best man we know. We aim to clear his name if we have to follow that son of a bitch all the way to San Francisco."

Thomas sighed. "Well, the clerk said he headed northwest outta town, toward Jacksboro."

"Jacksboro?"

"Yeah. It's another cow town 'bout twenty miles from here. Not as big or as famous as Fort Worth, but every bit as cantankerous. If you go there after Gibbons, you'd better ride with your guns loose. The place is a haven for every footpad and murderer in the area, and they don't exactly take to strangers, 'specially if you're not someone riding the owl-hoot trail."

Pearlie glanced at Cal. "Finish those eggs, Cal. We got places to go an' we're burnin' daylight sittin' here."

Thomas held up a hand. "Pearlie, let me warn you. If you do manage to find Gibbons an' get him to admit he lied, you got to do it in front of a peace officer or it won't count in court. The deputy sheriff of Jacksboro is an old friend of mine. Name's Johnny Walker. You tell him you're workin' with me on this murder an' he'll be more than glad to help. You get him to put in writin' that Gibbons changed his testimony, an' I'll be able to get Judge Parker to listen."

Pearlie stood up and grabbed his hat. He held out his hand to Thomas. "Thanks for your help, Marshal. We'll let you know soon's we find Gibbons an' get him to talk."

Thomas took Pearlie's hand. "*If* you get him to talk," he said.

"Oh," Pearlie replied, "the sumbitch'll talk, all right, or he'll never talk to anyone again."

Thomas grinned. "Now, Pearlie, don't go doin' nothin' rash. I don't want to have to come after you on another murder charge."

"Don't worry none, Marshal," Cal said with a grin. "I'll keep Pearlie under control."

Thomas shook his head and began to eat his breakfast. "Go on an' get outta here, you two, 'fore I come to my senses and arrest you both."

15

After riding for ten miles, Zachary Stillwell held up his hand, signaling the men following him to halt.

"This looks like 'bout as good a place as any to make camp for the night," he said, walking his horse up to a copse of cottonwood trees next to a small stream. "This is liable to be the only water 'tween here an' the next town."

Smoke got off Marshal Tilghman's dun, which he'd been riding, and hitched the animal to a branch of one of the trees.

Stillwell's gang now consisted of eleven men, counting the three he'd rescued from Tilghman's cage along with Smoke. The mountain man was busy planning on how he could get away with an extra horse for the marshal without having to kill most or all of the outlaws. He wasn't particularly concerned with saving their lives, being as how they weren't men he respected, but in any gunfight, especially when the odds were so heavy against him, there was a chance he'd lose. And, he reasoned, if he lost, it would also mean the death of a man he did respect, Marshal Bill Tilghman.

George Hungry Bear went about building a campfire, while some of the others broke out cooking utensils and slabs of fatback bacon and dried pinto beans. Smoke took a deep pot down to the stream to fill it with water to cook the beans, noticing that Stillwell followed him.

As he squatted next to the slowly moving water, Stillwell built himself a cigarette and watched as Smoke filled the pot.

"You know, Jensen, I heard a lot about you over the years."

"That so, Zach?" Smoke answered, glancing back over his shoulder at the man standing behind him.

"Yeah. I heard you was 'bout the fastest man alive with a short gun, an' I also heard you never hesitated to send anybody who drew down on you to Boot Hill."

"You heard right, Zach. A man calls the dance on you, someone has to pay the band, and so far, it hasn't been me."

"But what's got me worried, Smoke, is that I never heard nothin' 'bout you bein' a robber. You had some paper on you over the years, mostly for murder of men who goaded you into it, but you were never wanted for robbery or rustlin' or nothin' like that."

Smoke put the pot down on the ground and stretched his back, rubbing his buttocks where Tilghman's saddle had made them sore.

"You're chewing on something, Zach, so why don't you just spit it out and say what's on your mind?"

Smoke noticed Stillwell's hand was resting near the butt of his pistol.

"I was just wonderin' why you agreed to join us on our little trip to take down a train," Stillwell said.

Smoke smiled, using the distraction to turn sideways so Stillwell wouldn't see him loosen the rawhide hammer thong on his right-hand Colt.

"Well, Zach, if you'll remember, I didn't have a whole hell of a lot of choice in the matter. It was either ride with you and your men, or stay with the marshal and get my neck stretched by Judge Parker in Fort Smith."

"So you're sayin' you don't want to help with the train?"

"What I'm saying, Zach, is that I'll ride with you to the next town. Then I'll make my mind up whether to stay the course or not."

"That don't exactly clear my mind on you, Jensen."

"I don't really give a damn about your mind, Zach. That's just the way it is." Smoke inclined his head toward Stillwell's Colt. "Now you can either draw that six-killer on your hip you're playing with and go to work, or get out of my way so we can get some dinner cooked."

Stillwell's face blanched at the ominous threat in Smoke's voice, as if he knew he was seconds away from death. "I didn't mean nothin' by what I was sayin', Jensen," he said quickly, moving his hand so it wasn't near his pistol. "I just wanted to make sure you was on our side."

Smoke bent and picked up the pot of water. "Whose side did you think I was on, Zach? The marshal who was taking me to be hung?"

Stillwell gave a shaky laugh. "No, I guess not."

"Good. Then move aside so I can get us some beans cooking. I'm so hungry my stomach thinks my throat's been cut."

After a supper of fried bacon, pinto beans, and some pieces of jerked meat, washed down with boiled coffee and some whiskey a few of the outlaws had in their saddlebags, the men spread their ground blankets near the fire and stretched out to sleep.

Like most men riding the owl-hoot trail, they didn't take the saddles off their horses, but just loosened the belly straps in case they had to make a quick getaway if trouble arrived.

Smoke waited until midnight, when the coals of the fire were almost completely out, before he made his move. He gathered his blanket and moved to Tilghman's horse.

Drawing his Bowie knife, he made the rounds of the gang's horses, quietly cutting each belly strap almost all the way through.

When he was done, he took the reins to one of the horses that had been pulling Tilghman's wagon, along with the marshal's horse, and slowly walked away from the camp.

The moon had set so the night was dark, illuminated only by starlight, as he made his way across the prairie grass back toward where they'd left Marshal Tilghman.

He was still walking, almost a hundred yards from camp, when the sharp crack of a stick behind him made Smoke turn around.

Stillwell stood twenty feet away, a pistol in his hand, his teeth gleaming dully in the faint starlight.

"I knowed you wasn't to be trusted, Jensen," he said. "Now bring them cayuses back to the camp an' we'll see what we're gonna do with you."

Without another word, Smoke drew and fired all in one fluid motion, crouching as he did so. His gun went off at the same time as Stillwell's, and he heard the buzz of the slug as it passed through the brim of his hat.

Stillwell's head snapped back, a black hole appearing in the center of his forehead as the back of his head exploded in a fine red mist, with brains and bone and blood flying around the exiting bullet.

Smoke swung into the saddle and spurred Tilghman's horse into a gallop, hanging on to the reins of the wagon horse so it would follow.

Stillwell's gang jumped out of their bedrolls at the sound of the shot and made for their horses. They didn't know what was going on, but they knew it meant trouble. As they climbed into their saddles and started to ride away, one after the other hit the dirt as the cut belly straps gave way and they tumbled to the ground.

Smoke smiled at the sight, looking back over his shoulder at the confused melee the men made, scrambling around on foot trying to catch horses running wild with fear.

"That ought to keep them off my back trail until I can get to Tilghman," Smoke muttered as he leaned over the saddle horn and rode as fast as his horse could run.

* * *

It was full morning before Smoke arrived at the outcropping of rock and boulders where he'd indicated Tilghman should wait for him.

"Yo, Marshal Tilghman," Smoke called as he approached the hillock, still leading the horse behind him.

He stopped the horses seventy-five yards from the boulders, well out of pistol range, just in case the marshal was feeling trigger-happy after the events of the day before.

Tilghman stuck his head up from behind a rock, his pistol in his hand.

"That you, Jensen?" he called.

"Yeah," Smoke called back.

"You alone?"

Smoke smiled. He was sitting on a horse out in the open, with nothing around for miles.

"You see anyone else, Marshal?" he answered.

Tilghman stood up on top of the boulder. "Then come on in."

Smoke shook his head. "Not while you're holding that Colt. Throw it down on the ground."

"Now why should I do that?" Tilghman asked, not moving to release the gun.

"Because if you don't, I'll just turn these horses around and head on back to Fort Worth by myself, leaving you an awfully long walk back to town."

Tilghman considered his options for a moment, discovered he really didn't have any, and finally threw his pistol off the outcropping.

Smoke walked the horses up to the base of the hillock and got down out of the saddle. He picked Tilghman's Colt up and dusted the dirt off it while the marshal climbed down from his perch on the boulders.

When he got down, he walked over to Smoke. "Why'd you ask for my gun?"

"I didn't know just what sort of frame of mind you'd be in, so I figured better to be safe than sorry."

The marshal's eyes narrowed as he saw the hole in Smoke's hat. "You have some trouble with that outlaw?"

Smoke nodded. "Yeah, Stillwell wasn't too keen on the idea of me bringing you your horse back."

"You kill him?"

"I didn't stop to check, but unless he can live without half his skull, yeah."

"What about the others?"

"I left them on foot chasing down their mounts, with no belly straps to keep the saddles on."

Tilghman looked off in the distance, toward where Smoke had left the outlaw gang. He nodded, as if thinking to himself. "Then I guess I'll just have to go after them then."

"Marshal, there are nine hard cases out there. Don't you think you ought to get some help before you try to apprehend them?"

"In this job, Jensen, a man learns not to rely on getting others to help him."

"Well, it's your funeral."

Tilghman shrugged. "That possibility comes with the badge. You gonna give me my pistol back?"

Smoke stared at the marshal. "If you give me your word not to try and arrest me before I have a chance to clear my name."

"I don't make deals with murderers, Jensen. You should know that."

"I'm not a murderer, Marshal. I just need a little time to prove it."

Tilghman rubbed his chin whiskers. "I guess I owe you that, at least. Tell you what, Jensen. I'll go after the others first, but once I have them in custody, I want you to know I'm coming after you."

Smoke nodded. "Fair enough, Marshal."

He climbed down off Tilghman's horse and handed him his pistol. "Your rifle's still in the boot, and all your ammunition is in your saddlebag."

"What about you?" Tilghman asked.

Smoke inclined his head toward the wagon horse standing nearby. "I'll ride that one on into Fort Worth. I've got to have a word with that tinhorn who lied about seeing me shoot the Durango Kid."

"There ain't no saddle on that bronc," Tilghman said.

"It's better than walking," Smoke said. "Besides, I'm used to riding without a saddle. It won't be a problem."

Tilghman reached his hand out. "Good luck, Jensen. I hope you find the proof you're looking for, 'cause after all you've done, I'd sure hate to be the one to put a rope around your neck."

Smoke shook his hand. "Me too, Marshal."

Tilghman climbed into his saddle and touched the brim of his hat. "One way or another, Jensen, I'll be seein' you."

Smoke nodded as Tilghman jerked his horse's head around and trotted off toward the outlaw band.

16

Louis Longmont took Sally Jensen's elbow and helped her up the steps to board the train. As she stepped aboard, she dropped her purse and he bent to pick it up.

"Whoa, Sally. What do you have in here, stones?" he asked, a quizzical expression on his face.

She smiled slightly and opened the purse for him to look inside. Nestled there was a chrome-plated Smith and Wesson .36-caliber short-barreled pistol.

He glanced up at her. "You planning on robbing this train?"

"No," she answered, "but if anyone thinks they're going to hang Smoke Jensen without having to first deal with his wife, they are sadly mistaken."

Louis looked back over his shoulder as Monte Carson kissed his wife Mary good-bye. Both men were accompanying Sally on the train ride to Fort Smith, Arkansas. They were planning on appearing as character witnesses for Smoke when he came to trial before Judge Isaac Parker. Sally, however, was planning on doing more than that in the event it became necessary. She intended to break Smoke out of jail if the judge refused to listen to reason and sentenced him to hang.

After they'd gotten seated and the train began to move, Louis opened a window next to his seat and took out one of his trademark long, black stogies. He raised his eyebrows at Sally to see if she minded, and she shook her head.

He scratched a lucifer on his pants leg and put the fire to the cigar, inhaling deeply and blowing the smoke toward the open window.

"Do you think the judge will listen to us and believe Smoke is innocent?" Sally asked Monte.

The lawman slowly shook his head, a worried expression on his face. "Not from what I've heard. The word is Judge Parker is a man who believes fully in the law, spelled with a capital L. If he's got a witness who says he saw Smoke shoot a man in the back, then the judge is gonna sentence him to hang, no doubt about it."

"But, Monte, you and Louis both know if anyone says that about Smoke they must be lying," Sally protested.

He nodded. "Of course we know that, Sally. The trick is going to be to convince the judge the man, whoever he is, must be lying for some reason known only to him."

Sally patted her purse, giving Louis a knowing look. "Well, if the man is in Fort Smith, and he intends to lie about my husband, then I might just have to have a word with him before the trial."

Louis grinned. "We'll *all* have a talk with him, Sally, and don't you worry. If he's lying, Monte and I will make him admit it, one way or another."

At that moment, Cal and Pearlie were riding slowly into the city limits of Jacksboro, Texas. Jacksboro, though much smaller, was a town not unlike Fort Worth and twenty-odd miles to the northwest. Built around the cow business also, but on a much smaller scale, the town consisted mostly of cattle pens, butchering houses, hotels, brothels, saloons, and eating establishments.

The streets were awash with horses, buckboards, children, dogs, and men and women. Many people were walking up and down the wooden boardwalks that lined the dirt streets.

"Jimminy," Cal said as he looked up and down the streets wide-eyed. "I ain't never seen so many people in one place at one time just rushin' around in a hurry like."

Pearlie nodded, following Cal's gaze. "Yep. They all runnin' round like they got to be someplace in a hell of a hurry. Wonder what the rush is all about."

"How do you 'spect we'll ever find Gibbons in all these people?" Cal asked. "There must be twenty or more saloons an' gamblin' houses."

"We'll just have to start at one end of the town an' make our way up an' down the streets till we find the bastard," Pearlie answered. "Sooner or later, he'll show up. Tinhorns cain't hardly stay away from the poker games. They like a man with a powerful thirst for liquor. They always find someplace to get what they need."

"You want to start now?" Cal asked, eyeing the sun, which was nearing the horizon in the west.

"Naw. Let's find a hotel and grab some grub an' maybe a hot bath. My butt cheeks feel like they done growed to this saddle, an' I'm afraid I smell worse'n some of those beeves walkin' down the street over yonder," he said, inclining his head to where a couple of punchers were slowly driving ten head of cattle right down the middle of Main Street.

After they'd gotten rooms at the Star Hotel on Main Street, and partaken of a hot bath in the communal bathing room on the third floor, the boys went to the nearest restaurant and sat down to have some dinner.

The diner was called the Hofbrau, and was run by a heavyset German woman who spoke with a thick, almost guttural accent. Pearlie had to ask her several times what the different items on the menu were, and he finally just let her decide what he should have—"as long as there's plenty of it," he added as she walked toward the kitchen.

After stuffing themselves on pot roast, German potato salad, and two slices of Dutch apple pie, washed down with a pot of coffee that was so strong Cal said he didn't think it needed a cup, they made their way toward the deputy sheriff's office, just off Main Street.

When they walked through the office door, the first thing Cal and Pearlie noticed was the large number of iron-barred cells in the rear of the building, almost all of which were filled with prisoners.

"Seems like the deputy sheriff does a right smart business in this town," Pearlie observed.

Most of the men appeared to be cowboys, probably just off cattle drives, who looked as if they'd partaken of too much cheap whiskey and not enough food.

"Can I help you gents?" a tall, lean man asked from the side of the room. He was sitting behind an oak desk, scarred with numerous spur marks, with his feet up on the edge of the desk and a long, black cigar protruding from his lips. He was dressed in black pants, with a black vest over a boiled white shirt, and had a thin string tie in a bow at his neck. He had a long, handlebar moustache that reminded Cal of pictures he'd seen of Marshal Wyatt Earp in Tombstone, making Cal wonder if the resemblance was calculated on the deputy sheriff's part.

"Howdy," Pearlie said, striding up to stand before the desk.

The deputy sheriff nodded, his eyes watching Cal and Pearlie closely as if he were trying to figure out if they were here to cause him some sort of problem.

"Somethin' I can help you with?" the deputy asked again.

Pearlie nodded. "Are you Deputy Sheriff Johnny Walker?"

The man nodded, his right hand resting on the butt of his Colt, ready for trouble.

"U.S. Marshal Heck Thomas told us to look you up," Pearlie said. "He said you might be able to help us find a man."

For the first time, Walker gave a slight smile. "Ole Heck said that, did he?"

"Yes, sir," Cal said.

"Well, who is this man an' what's he wanted for?" Walker asked.

"His name's Gibbons, an' he's a tinhorn gambler," Pearlie said. "He gave a false statement to Marshal Thomas 'bout a killin' in Fort Worth; then he skipped out of town."

Walker's face assumed a dubious expression. "You mean Heck sent you all the way down here just to look for a man who's only offense was lyin'?" He laughed and sat up in his chair. "Hell, if I was to arrest ever' man in town who lied, there wouldn't be room for 'em all in the jail. Most of the men in Jacksboro are guilty of somethin' a whole lot worse at some time in their lives. That's why they end up here 'stead of Fort Worth or some bigger town."

Pearlie's voice got a little harder. "This man lied about a friend of ours . . . said he back-shot a man outside a saloon. Now our friend's on his way to Fort Smith to be hanged."

Walker pursed his lips. "Well, now. That's a horse of a different color. And Heck knows this man was lyin' when he said that?"

"Yes, sir," Cal declared. "He overheard the man admit he'd lied, but before he could get him to change his statement, Gibbons left town."

"Why don't Heck just tell the judge the story? That ought to take care of the matter."

"The judge in question is Judge Isaac Parker," Pearlie said. "You ever dealt with him?"

"Oh," Walker said, leaning back in his chair, "that do make it difficult. Ole Judge Parker is a stickler for the legal niceties bein' followed, all right."

"Sheriff," Pearlie said, a bit impatient. "Will you help us? Marshal Thomas said he'd consider it a personal favor."

"Sure, boys. Just let me grab my hat an' we'll get started lookin' for this tinhorn."

As he accompanied them out the door, Walker asked, "What kind'a fellow is this Gibbons? High-class or low-class?"

"What do you mean?" Pearlie asked.

"Well, is he likely to go for a high-stakes game, or try to find one with less money at stake?"

Pearlie glanced at Cal. "I'd figure him more for the high-stakes game. He dresses real nice, an' the night he saw the gunfight he'd been at one of the best saloons in Fort Worth."

"Then we'll start at the north end of Main Street. That's where all the 'gentlemen' gamblers tend to congregate." Walker smiled. "The whores are prettier up there too."

Pearlie grinned. "That should be his sort of place then, 'cause he do appreciate pretty ladies."

"That's how we trapped him into admitting he'd lied," Cal added.

"Oh, tell me 'bout it," Walker said.

As they turned the corner onto Main Street and proceeded northward, the boys told Walker how they'd paid a whore to get Gibbons to incriminate himself.

Walker nodded appreciatively. "Yep. Seems there's a woman behind the downfall of most men, that or liquor, or both."

When they got to the end of the street, he pointed to several brightly lit establishments. "That there's the Lucky Lady, an' over there's the Double Eagle an' the Cattleman's Palace. Those'd be the ones to start with."

"Which one has the most women in it?" Cal asked.

"Son," Walker said, "this is a cow town. They all chock-full of women."

Pearlie pointed. "The Lucky Lady is the closest. Let's try there first."

As they walked through the batwings, the drone of conversation and laughter dimmed for a moment as the patrons saw the star on Deputy Sheriff Walker's vest, then continued unabated when they saw he was just in to look around.

A couple of the girls smiled and waved at Walker, showing he was no stranger to the establishments, and he waved back, a grin on his face.

Pearlie and Cal pulled their hats down low over their faces so Gibbons wouldn't recognize them if he happened to look their way, and they began to weave among the many tables of cardplayers, searching for the man they were after.

It took them over half an hour to ascertain he wasn't in the Lucky Lady, while the deputy stayed at the bar helping himself to a glass of beer, watching them as they searched.

When they were done, he downed the last of his beer and said, "Well, we can try the Cattleman's Palace next. It's right down the street."

Pearlie chuckled. "It's funny, but the Cattleman's is the name of the hotel we stayed in over in Fort Worth."

"Not so funny when you think about it," the deputy said. "Can't throw a stick in either town without hittin' a cattleman, so it's only natural to put the name on places you want them to come to."

17

Smoke rode slowly toward Fort Worth, but his conscience wouldn't let him be. *Damn it,* he thought, *the marshal doesn't know what he's getting himself into. Those nine men are hard cases who won't give up without a fight.* He shook his head, thinking. *Nine against one is tall odds, even for a man as good with a gun as Tilghman is supposed to be.*

"Horse," he finally muttered to the animal he'd borrowed from the marshal, "we gotta turn around. I couldn't live with myself if I let the marshal go it alone and he got himself killed."

He pulled the mount's head around and began following the marshal's horse's prints toward the outlaw band. As he rode, he checked his pistols one at a time, making sure they were loaded up six and six, and then he filled his pockets with extra cartridges, just in case the upcoming battle lasted longer than he expected.

Smoke stayed well back, just barely keeping Tilghman in sight on the horizon. He knew if the man knew Smoke was coming to help, he'd try and talk him out of it by saying it was his job, not Smoke's, to corral the desperadoes.

No matter. Smoke intended to help only if it looked like the marshal needed it. If he was doing all right by himself, Smoke would stay out of sight.

* * *

It was almost dusk when Smoke saw the marshal up ahead get down off his horse and run crouching to get behind a small copse of trees near the stream where Smoke had left Stillwell's band of men.

"Come on, horse," Smoke said, putting the spurs to the bronc he was riding and circling around to the west of where the marshal was stalking the outlaws. He wanted to come at them from out of the setting sun if he had to intervene, using every advantage he could in the face of superior numbers.

Just as Smoke reached the edge of the small trickle of water, downstream from the bandits, he heard Marshal Tilghman shout for the men to put down their weapons and come out with their hands up.

"Fat chance," Smoke said to himself. "They're gonna come out, all right, with hands filled with iron and guns blazing."

He knew men like those he'd ridden with, men used to riding the owl-hoot trail, wouldn't give up without a fight, and most probably a fight to the death.

Sure enough, seconds later as Smoke was getting down off his horse and creeping up the stream toward the men, he heard a volley of gunshots ring out from the group, answered by the booming explosion of Tilghman's Winchester Yellow Boy.

The group of outlaws hunkered down behind the boles of cottonwood trees and in the shelter of the bank of the small stream they were camped next to.

Jaime Gonzalez, who'd taken over leadership of the bandits after Stillwell had been killed by Smoke, glanced over at George Hungry Bear, lying on his stomach behind a fallen log next to him. "Damn it," he shouted, "I thought that marshal was out of it."

"That Smoke Jensen must've gone to help him after killin' Zach," Hungry Bear yelled back.

"You think we can make the hosses?" Gonzalez said, referring to their horses, which they'd tied to another group of trees fifty yards away.

"And do what?" Hungry Bear answered. "Ride them without saddles?"

"I thought you Injuns were good at that," Gonzalez said with a smirk.

"Hell, Jaime, I was raised on a reservation. I ain't never ridden bareback in my life, an' I don't intend to start now. We got the white eyes outnumbered. We just have to send some of the men sneakin' around behind him an' all this'll be over in a little while."

Gonzalez looked to the other side, where the three men they'd rescued from Tilghman were huddled together behind a large, double-trunked cottonwood.

"Hey, Dynamite Dick," he shouted, "how about you and your friends making your way off to the side an' come at the marshal from behind?"

Bodine yelled back, "We ain't got no guns, remember? The marshal took 'em from us when we was arrested."

Gonzalez pulled an old Walker Army Colt from his second holster and pitched it over to Bodine. "Take this," he said.

Bodine leaned out from behind the tree to pick up the pistol, and a slug from Tilghman's Yellow Boy almost took his head off.

"Jesus," he yelled, ducking back behind the tree with the gun in his hand. "Hell, Jaime, this thing must weigh four pounds," he said, hefting the Walker in his hand.

"You want me to hold it for you?" Gonzalez said sarcastically.

"What about us?" Jonathan Mayhew yelled.

Gonzalez nodded at Hungry Bear, who scooted back to his saddlebags, pulled out a couple of older-model Army revolvers, and threw them over to the men with Bodine.

"Make your shots count," he said. "We ain't got a whole lot of extra ammo."

Mayhew took one of the Armys and handed the other to Shorty Robinson. "I hope you're better with this than I am," Mayhew said.

Robinson expertly flicked open the loading gate and checked the rounds. "Yeah, I guess you tinhorns are more used to derringers than real guns," he opined.

He added, "This works the same way. . . . You get close enough it don't matter where you hit him, he'll go down."

Gonzalez leaned back and shouted at Brooks Sullivan, a cattle rustler who was riding with Stillwell's gang. "Brooks, you an' Willy Jackson sidle on downstream until you get outta sight of the marshal, then crawl on up the hill until you behind him. When Bodine an' his men are ready on the other side, give a whistle an' we'll all charge at once from all different directions."

Brooks nodded and tapped Jackson on the shoulder, pulling him backward down toward the stream behind them.

They crouched down so they'd have the cover of the shallow banks and began to wade downstream, looking back over their shoulders to make sure the marshal couldn't see them.

Once they'd rounded a corner out of sight, they straightened up and began to move faster. "That god-damned lawman ain't gonna know what hit him," Brooks said, glancing at Jackson.

He stopped talking when he saw Jackson's eyes widen in fear, staring ahead of them down the stream.

Brooks jerked his head around in time to see a tall, broad-shouldered man standing there, his hands hanging at his sides.

"Howdy, gents," the man said, "remember me?"

"Smoke Jensen!" Brooks exclaimed.

"This ain't your fight, Jensen," Willy Jackson said, his voice trembling a little. "Why don't you just ride off an' mind your own business?"

"It's a little late for that, boys. I've anted up in this game. . . . You want to call my bet or fold?"

"Call!" Brooks shouted, and grabbed for his pistol as Willy Jackson did the same.

Smoke's Colt appeared in his hand as if by magic, cocked and spitting lead before the other two men cleared leather. His first slug took Brooks in the center of his chest, knocking him backward to land with his arms outflung on his back in the icy water of the stream.

A split second later, his second slug entered Willy Jackson's open mouth, punching out his two front teeth and continuing on to blow out the back of his neck, almost decapitating him in the process.

Willy spun around, finally managing to get his pistol out of his holster, but never living to pull the trigger. He fell face-down almost on top of Brooks Sullivan, their blood mingling to stain the clear water of the stream a crimson color.

Smoke hesitated long enough to punch out his empties and reload before continuing his journey upstream.

"What the hell was that?" Gonzalez yelled when he heard the shots from downstream.

Hungry Bear started to shake his head, then ducked as a slug from Tilghman's Yellow Boy slammed into the log he was behind and showered his face with splinters and wood dust. "Shit!" he yelled to Jaime. "We gotta get outta here or he's gonna pick us off one by one."

Just as he said it, one of the other men, Sam Best, a gunman from Tombstone who'd left town at the urging of Wyatt Earp, jumped to his feet and began to run toward the horses.

He'd only gotten twenty yards when his left knee was blown out by a slug from Marshal Tilghman. After he fell to the ground screaming, he tried to crawl the rest of the way, until another bullet took off the back of his head.

Gonzalez peered to the side, seeing that Bodine and Mayhew and Robinson were almost in position to fire on Tilghman's back.

He raised his head slightly to see better, and a bullet from Tilghman hit him exactly dead center in his Adam's apple, tearing a fist-sized hole in his throat. He grabbed his neck with both hands, trying to scream, but finding he had no vocal cords to make a sound with. He gurgled and strangled for a moment on his own blood, until a second shot blew out the left chamber of his heart on its way through his chest. He dropped like a stone, dead before he hit the ground.

Hungry Bear lowered his head and began to chant a death-prayer in his native tongue. He'd never believed in the old ways, but figured if he was going to die, it wouldn't hurt to try to appease the old ones' gods, if they existed.

Finally, he rolled to the side, seeing Roy Bailey, an eighteen-year-old who fancied himself the next Billy the Kid, hiding in a mulberry bush next to a cottonwood off to the side. Bailey, evidently not as brave in a gunfight as he'd thought, had not shown himself since the marshal had attacked.

"Bailey," Hungry Bear whispered hoarsely, "climb up in that tree you're hiding behind an' see if you can get a shot at the marshal."

"But," the kid said, terror in his voice, "what if he sees me?"

"Then he'll shoot you dead, you yellow-belly," Hungry Bear angrily replied, "but if you don't do what I say, I'll kill you myself!"

Slowly, being careful to remain out of sight, the young man began to climb the tree, his Henry thrown over his back on a rawhide strap.

Just then, Dynamite Dick Bodine and Shorty Robinson jumped to their feet from twenty yards behind Marshal Tilghman and began firing their pistols.

Shorty Robinson's second shot took Tilghman in the fleshy part of his left arm, knocking his rifle from his grasp and spinning him around and saving his life.

Bodine's first shot barely missed the marshal when he spun to the side from the impact of being shot, and as was common with the Walker Colts, the second shot exploded in the firing chamber, taking Bodine's first two fingers of his right hand off at the first knuckle.

As Bodine grabbed his hand and fell screaming to the ground, Tilghman drew his pistol and fired from his position lying on his back, hitting Shorty Robinson in the belly, doubling him over as he grabbed at the hole in his stomach, trying without success to keep his intestines in.

Jonathan Mayhew started to point his pistol at the marshal, had second thoughts, and threw it to the ground, raising his hands over his head. Evidently, he figured he had a better chance with Judge Parker than with the angry-eyed lawman, who was drawing a bead on his face.

"I give up, Marshal," Mayhew shouted. "Please don't kill me!"

"Lie down on your face an' spread your hands out, Mayhew," Tilghman growled. "An' if you reach for that pistol, you're a dead man!"

Hungry Bear looked up at Roy Bailey, hidden in the branches of the cottonwood, his rifle cradled in his arms. "You got a shot?" the Indian asked.

"Naw," Bailey replied, "he's lying down an' I can't get a bead on him."

"Wait a minute," Hungry Bear said, "I'm gonna go out there with my hands up. When he shows himself to arrest me, you plug him good. You understand?"

"Right. You get him to stand up, an' I'll take him down," Bailey replied, more brave now that he knew he couldn't be seen.

"Marshal," Hungry Bear shouted without raising his head up.

"Yeah?" Tilghman replied.

"You've kilt all of us 'cept me. I'm gonna throw my gun out and give myself up."

"Then come on, but don't try nothin' fancy, or I'll drill you through an' through," the marshal replied from his position on the ground.

Hungry Bear pitched his pistol over the log and stood

up, his hands held high over his head. He stepped over the log and began to walk toward where Tilghman lay.

When Hungry Bear was out in the clear, away from his gun, the marshal stood up, motioning with his Colt for Mayhew to follow him toward the Indian.

Mayhew and George Hungry Bear stood in front of Marshal Tilghman, their hands up. "You men are under arrest," Tilghman said, reaching behind his back to pull out some manacles to put on their wrists.

A sudden shot rang out from the direction of the grove of trees near the stream, and Tilghman whirled around, crouching, pointing his pistol toward the sound.

A body, still holding a Henry repeating rifle, fell from a tree to land with a resounding thump on the hard-packed dirt. Roy Bailey squirmed once, calling out for his mamma; then he quivered for a moment and died, still holding his rifle.

A tall, dark figure stepped from the cover of the trees, his hands above his head. "Don't shoot, Marshal," the man called. "It's Smoke Jensen."

As Smoke approached, the marshal shook his head, grinning. "Jensen, I thought you was on your way to Fort Worth."

Smoke shrugged, lowering his hands and holstering his Colt. "I was, but I thought you might need a little backup."

"That you I heard shootin' over downstream a while back?"

Smoke nodded. "Yeah. A couple of the gang were on their way to sneak up on your back. I let 'em know that wasn't appreciated."

Tilghman laughed. "Yeah, I heard how you told 'em, with a .44, it sounded like."

"You need some help with that arm?" Smoke asked, noticing the marshal's wound.

"If you could keep a gun on these galoots, I'll tie it off with my bandanna. Then we can get 'em on their horses for the ride back to the wagon."

"No problem, Marshal." Smoke glanced around. "You ought to have enough broncs to pull it the rest of the way."

"Yeah, an' you can get back on your way to Fort Worth to finish your business there."

As Smoke started to ride away, the marshal added, "Jensen, I want you to know I'm grateful for what you did here today."

Smoke nodded.

"But, Jensen, I've never let my personal feelin's interfere with my work as a U.S. marshal. Even though you probably saved my life by doin' what you did, if you're still wanted for murder when I get to Fort Smith, I gotta tell you, I'll be comin' after you, just like any other wanted man."

"I appreciate the warning, Marshal, and I would expect nothing less," Smoke said.

"Just wanted you to know not to expect any special treatment 'cause of today."

"Don't worry about it, Marshal. I'm going to get this mess cleared up so there won't be any need of you having to track me down."

"I hope so, Jensen, for your sake, 'cause I always get my man, one way or another."

18

As he rode toward Fort Worth, Smoke realized he had to do some heavy thinking. It wasn't going to be enough to get that tinhorn who said he'd seen Smoke shoot the Durango Kid in the back to recant his testimony. Smoke was going to have to find the culprit who did the shooting to really clear his name. After all, he'd been the one found standing in the alleyway over the dead man's body.

Smoke began to go through various possibilities in his mind. Murders weren't all that uncommon in the West, especially in cow towns like Fort Worth. Bumping a man's arm at a bar, stepping on his toes, or even stealing a whore he was wooing was often grounds for senseless killing and violence. But to cold-bloodedly shoot a man in the back spoke of a hatred more intense than that usually occasioned by a barroom fight or an imagined insult.

He figured it had to be someone with a powerful hate, or a real good reason to see the Kid dead, who did him in. As he thought back over the events of that night, he remembered the Kid had said they'd only just gotten to town with their beeves the night before, so it would be unusual for him to have made such a deadly enemy so quickly.

Smoke nodded as he continued to think it through. That meant the most likely suspects were the men riding with the Kid. One or more of them would probably have reason to want the outlaw dead. "Money or women," Smoke muttered to himself, thinking extreme violence usually had one or the other of those two ancient motives behind it.

"Now all I have to do is track down the men who were riding with the Kid and find out which one of them had the most reason, and the opportunity, to shoot him dead," he said in a low voice to the back of his horse's head. "I just hope they're still in town," he added, thinking it would be difficult if not impossible to trail them if they'd gone on their way without telling anyone where they were headed.

In Jacksboro, Cal and Pearlie had failed to find the gambler Gibbons on their first night of searching.

"I'm sorry, boys," Deputy Sheriff Johnny Walker said after trailing them through most of the saloons along Main Street. "I got to get back to my duties, but I'll tell you what. You find that galoot, see if he's willin' to change his story, an' I'll write it all down for Marshal Thomas, and I'll even send a wire to Judge Parker over at Fort Smith."

"Thanks, Sheriff," Pearlie said. "If we find him, I'll guarantee he'll tell the truth."

"I hope so, boys, 'cause if he don't change his story, I'm afraid the hangin' judge is gonna live up to his name with your podna."

After the deputy sheriff left them at the lobby of their hotel, Cal asked, "What now, Pearlie? You want to walk around the rest of the night an' see if'n we can find Gibbons some more?"

"Naw," Pearlie said. "If he was gonna gamble tonight, he'd already be at the tables. Maybe he was so tired he took the night off to get some rest."

"Or maybe he found hisself a girl to spend the night with," Cal said.

Pearlie nodded. "That's a possibility. I suggest we get some shut-eye an' start out first thing in the mornin'. If we don't find him by lunchtime, we can take a nap an' be fresh an' ready to try again tomorrow night."

"I just hope we're not too late for Smoke," Cal said in a low voice, a sorrowful expression on his face.

"Don't you worry none 'bout Smoke," Pearlie said. "He's been in plenty worse situations than this. He can take care of himself."

"It's not Smoke I'm worried about," Cal said as they climbed the stairs toward their room. "It's that Hangin' Judge. From what I hear, he's a mite too anxious to use that rope of his."

As soon as Smoke got to Fort Worth, he went to the Cattleman's Hotel, where he'd left Cal and Pearlie.

He walked up to the desk clerk. "Can I have my key?"

The man looked up from his register, a startled look on his face. "But . . . but I thought you were on your way to Fort Smith." It was the same snooty dandy that had been on duty when Smoke and the boys first arrived.

Smoke smiled reassuringly. "New evidence came in, Jason, so Marshal Tilghman let me go. Now, I'd like to get to my room, get a bath, and catch a little shut-eye, after I talk to my friends."

Jason shook his head. "Your friends left the other day."

"Left?"

"Yep. They were asking all over town about that gambler fellow—I can't bring his name to mind—and then they heard he went to Jacksboro, so they went after him."

"Oh. Well, has my suite on the top floor been rented out?

"No, sir."

"Then give me the key and see if you can get the bath boy to heat up some water."

"But it's the middle of the day," the dandy said, his face aghast at the idea of anyone bathing before darkness came.

"Jason," Smoke said, his patience wearing thin. "I haven't bathed in almost a week. Get the water hot and give me a key before I come across that desk and teach you how to do your job!"

"Yes, sir, Mr. Jensen," Jason said, sleeving sweat off his forehead with the back of his arm as he handed the key across the desk to Smoke.

After his bath, Smoke slept the rest of the afternoon, getting up just after sundown. He dressed in clean clothes, electing to wear black trousers, a white shirt under a black vest, and no coat, since the cool spring nights were mild.

He ate a hearty dinner at the Cattleman's Hotel, then went looking for the Kid's friends. He knew the Kid and his men had liked the Silver Dollar, for that was where he'd first met them, so he headed there to begin his search.

He eased through the batwings and stepped to the side, as was his habit, observing the room for possible danger before entering. He didn't know if Cal and Pearlie had talked with Marshal Heck Thomas, or even if the marshal was still in town, but he didn't want to meet up with him until he'd had a chance to do some looking around.

He saw no one familiar, so he made his way to the bar and ordered a mug of beer. It looked to be a long night of searching, so he stayed away from whiskey.

He took his mug and leaned back with his elbows on the bar, looking for the women who'd been entertaining the Kid and his friends the night of the killing.

Building himself a cigarette, he drank and smoked slowly, waiting for one or another of the women to show themselves.

Finally, while on his second beer, Smoke saw one of the women come down the stairs, her arm around the waist of a drunken cowboy.

He got the bartender's attention and nodded at the girl. "What's that lady's name?" Smoke asked.

The man chuckled. "She ain't exactly a lady, but her name's Dolly."

Smoke grinned. He glanced at the barman. "Seen Marshal Thomas around lately?"

"No, thank goodness. Word is he's ridin' around to all the local ranchers, askin' some questions 'bout stolen beeves." The man began wiping the bar down with a soiled rag. "Good thing too. Ever' time he comes in here I lose business. Ain't nobody likes to drink and carouse with a U.S. marshal lookin' over their shoulders."

Smoke threw a coin on the table and touched his hat. "Thanks for the information."

The man raised his eyebrows. "You want to . . . talk to Dolly?"

Smoke nodded. "Yeah. I'm going to go over to that table in the corner. Why don't you send her and a bottle of whiskey over?" he said, adding another coin to the one on the bar.

"Yes, sir," the man said, sliding the coins into his pocket.

Smoke carried his beer to the table and took a seat, his back to the wall, just in case the Kid's friends happened to come in. He was relieved he didn't have to worry about running into Marshal Thomas for a while. It made things a whole lot simpler.

After a few minutes, he saw the bartender whisper into Dolly's ear. She glanced his way, smiled, and disengaged herself from the grasp of the drunken cowboy. Grabbing the whiskey bottle and a couple of glasses from the barman, she began to walk toward Smoke, grinning and waggling her hips as she moved through the crowd.

She took a seat next to Smoke at the table, sitting so close their hips touched.

"Howdy, cowboy. Max over at the bar said you asked for me special."

"That's right," Smoke said.

She deftly pulled the cork from the bottle and poured them both drinks, hers slightly heavier than his.

Clinking glasses, she said, "Here's to a good night, an' a mornin' without a hangover."

Smoke touched glasses and took a small sip of his whiskey.

Dolly leaned over and whispered in his ear. "You want to drink for a while, or just head on upstairs?"

"Let's talk for a while," Smoke said.

She raised her eyebrows. "Well, mister, a drink'll buy you a little time, but for serious talk, it's gonna cost you more than that."

Smoke pulled a double eagle gold coin from his shirt pocket and placed it in her hand.

Her eyes widened. "Twenty dollars? Hell, cowboy, for that much you get all night."

Smoke laughed. He knew the going rate for all night was closer to five dollars, but he didn't say anything.

He kept the conversation to generalities until Dolly had downed several drinks. He was hoping to get her drunk enough to not be suspicious when he began asking her questions about the Kid and his men.

After a while, she stared at him. "I don't remember entertainin' you before, mister, an' believe me, I'd remember you."

"No, we haven't met before."

"Then why'd you ask for me? Somebody give you my name?"

It was the perfect opening for Smoke. "Yeah. I saw you with some men several days ago. A tall man dressed in black, a Mexican with three fingers on his left hand, and two other gents."

"Oh, them," she said, a chill in her voice.

"You remember them?" Smoke asked.

"Sure," she said, shrugging her shoulders. "The only one in the group who was willin' to spend any money went an' got himself shot before I could get him upstairs."

"Oh?" Smoke asked, pretending to be surprised.

"Yeah. An' the other galoots were so cheap they thought buyin' me an' Suzie a few drinks entitled them to take liberties, if you know what I mean."

Smoke nodded.

"We finally told them how the cow ate the cabbage," she said, slurring her words a little. "If you wanna play, you gotta pay."

Smoke laughed out loud. He was beginning to like this

Dolly. She was plainspoken, but had more personality than most women in her line of work.

"Have they been back?" Smoke asked, an innocent expression on his face.

"Naw," she said. "When they found out we wasn't givin' it away, they kind'a lost interest. Said they had to sell some cattle 'fore they could spend that kind'a money on whores," she added, an insulted look on her face.

"You know where they are now?" Smoke asked.

Her eyes suddenly became sharp, showing she wasn't as drunk as she'd been pretending to be.

"Oh, so this isn't 'bout you an' me, it's 'bout them cowboys, ain't it?"

Smoke figured he had nothing to lose by being truthful. "Yes, it is."

Her expression became shrewd. "What's it worth to you if I can find out where they're stayin'?"

"You can keep that double eagle and I won't make you earn it."

She smiled, looking him up and down. "Now, who said I'd mind earnin' it with you?" she asked.

He shook his head. "You can keep the coin and I'll give you another just like it, if you let me know next time you see them, or can find out what hotel they're staying at."

She grinned. "Now you're talkin'. Where're you stayin', cowboy?"

"The name's Jensen, and I'm at the Cattleman's Hotel."

She raised her eyebrows at the mention of his hotel, which was about the swankiest in town.

"Well, I'll start askin' around. I should hear somethin' by tomorrow night."

He put his hand over hers. "Dolly, be careful. These men are dangerous. Don't let them find out you're asking around about them."

She bent down and pulled the hem of her dress up, exposing a garter on her leg holding a double-barreled derringer. "You think they're dangerous, honey, you ain't seen Dolly at work!"

19

Cal and Pearlie, after sleeping most of the afternoon, arose just before sundown and went to a local eatery for dinner. Pearlie, as usual, ate enough for two men, while Cal, who was worried about Smoke, hardly touched his meal.

"You got to put some vittles in your gut, Cal," Pearlie said as he stuffed a large piece of corn bread in his mouth. "You cain't do Smoke no good if'n you're famished."

"I'll eat when we get that statement from Gibbons," Cal replied sullenly. "I just don't have no appetite, thinkin' of Smoke in that jail in Fort Smith."

"All right then," Pearlie said, "let's get to it."

He paid their bill and they walked out onto Main Street. "Where do you think we ought'a try next?" Cal asked.

"Well, we tried all the highfalutin places last night, an' didn't see hide nor hair of the galoot," Pearlie drawled. "Maybe he's short of cash an' cain't afford the high-stakes games. Tonight, let's hit the places down by the Mexican quarter. Maybe we'll find him there."

They turned left on Main and walked five blocks, then took another left toward the cattle yards where the lower-class part of town was. Its residents were mainly Mexicans, blacks, and working-class whites, and the area had several cantinas and bars that were downright dangerous to enter.

According to Johnny Walker, even he didn't go into the area at night unless backed up by at least two other deputies. As they walked, Cal and Pearlie both loosened the rawhide hammer-guards on their pistols, ready in case of trouble.

In the third place they entered, which had the unlikely name El Gato Negro, The Black Cat, they found their man. The saloon was made of adobe and had a low ceiling and dirt floors. With the few lanterns and hazy, smokey air, it was hard to see more than ten feet in front of your face, but the boys recognized Gibbons's flashy yellow and black plaid coat from across the room.

"There the sumbitch is," Pearlie growled, loosening his Colt in its holster. "You sidle on around to get between him an' the back door, an' I'll ease on up to him from the front."

"Pearlie," Cal said, staring at the table Gibbons was sitting at.

"Yeah?"

"Watch your back. Those men he's playin' with look awful hard to me."

Pearlie nodded. Cal was right. At the table with Gibbons were two Mexicans with long, handlebar mustaches, both wearing large Colt Army pistols on their belts and knives in scabbards stuck in their pants. A huge, six-foot-tall black man wearing an undershirt and pants held up with a rope was the fourth man at the table.

Cal moved through the crowd of drunken men until he was standing in front of the rear door, the one leading back to the privy in the alley behind the saloon. He leaned back against the wall next to the door and let his hand rest on the butt of his pistol, sweating nervously as he watched the milling crowd in the small room.

Pearlie walked over to stand behind and to the side of Gibbons, out of sight of the gambler. He noticed most of the money and poker chips at the table were piled in front of the tinhorn, and that the other men at the table were staring at Gibbons with ill-concealed anger.

Gibbons must have known he was in over his head, for when he turned and saw Pearlie standing beside him, he grinned nervously and greeted Pearlie like an old friend.

"Why, Pearlie, how're you doing?" he asked, turning in his chair to face him.

Pearlie nodded at the pile of money in front of Gibbons. "Pick up your winnin's, Gibbons," he said in a low, hard voice. "We got to talk."

"Gladly, my boy, gladly," the gambler said, taking off his hat and raking the bills, chips, and coins into it.

"Wait a minute, *señor,*" the Mexican next to Gibbons said harshly. "The gringo has won all our moneys. He cannot leave."

Gibbons held out his hand in a placating manner. "Don't worry, Jose," he said. "I'm just goin' out to the privy to relieve myself and talk to these gentlemen for a moment. I'll be right back."

"You better, mistuh," the large black man said, "or I'll cut you up real good."

Pearlie noticed the man had a machete stuck through the rope in his pants.

Gibbons nodded, smiling and grinning as sweat ran down from his forehead to drip off his chin.

"Come on, Pearlie, let's go out back and settle this."

Pearlie followed him out the back door, picking up Cal on the way. Once outside, he grabbed Gibbons and swung him around. "Are you gonna change that lyin' statement you gave to Marshal Tilghman, or am I gonna have to beat the shit outta you?" Pearlie asked.

Gibbons held up his hands, palms outward. "Pearlie, I'll sign anything you want if you'll get me out of here. These men are not very gracious losers, and I'm afraid they plan to do me bodily harm if they don't win their money back."

A soft sound from behind him made Pearlie turn around. The Mexicans were standing there, both with large pistols in their hands. One of them held up a pair of aces. "You left these behind you, *señor,*" he said to Gibbons. "They fell out of your coat when you left the table."

"Why," Gibbons said, his voice quavering at the sight of the cards, "those aren't mine!"

"Lying gringo," the Mexican said, letting the hammer down on the pistol. It exploded, sending a .44 slug slamming into Gibbons's chest, flinging him backward to land half in the privy, his head resting against the seat.

Both Mexicans turned their pistols on Cal and Pearlie, who were standing there openmouthed at the suddenness of the violence.

"Please be so kind as to not move, *señors*," one said while the other walked over to Gibbons's dead body and removed his hat. The man emptied the money out of it and set it gently back down on Gibbons's skull.

"*Adios, señors*," the other said, and they took off running down the alleyway.

"Goddamn!" Pearlie exclaimed, bending over Gibbons to check for signs of life. Finding none, he grabbed Cal and pulled him down the alley away from the direction the Mexicans took. "Let's get the hell out of here before someone comes out and accuses us of killin' Gibbons," he said, breaking into a run.

"But . . . but what about Smoke?" Cal said, jogging beside Pearlie as they rounded a corner.

"We're gonna have to find some other way to clear him," Pearlie said. "'Cause Gibbons sure as hell ain't gonna change his statement now."

Pearlie and Cal walked back over to Main Street and entered Deputy Sheriff Johnny Walker's office. As usual, Walker was sitting back in his chair with his feet up on his desk, sipping coffee out of a stained mug.

"Howdy, boys," he said, smiling. "You find that tinhorn yet?"

Pearlie nodded. "Yeah, we found him. Trouble is, a couple of Mexes put a .44 slug in his chest. He's lyin' in the privy out behind the Black Cat Cantina."

Walker pursed his lips, staring at Pearlie. "I don't suppose there're any witnesses to say you boys didn't do it, are there?"

Cal shook his head. "Sheriff, you know we needed him to save our friend's life. We wouldn't've killed him."

After a moment, Walker nodded. "I suppose that does make sense."

"Are you gonna go over there and check it out?" Pearlie asked.

"You say you're sure he's dead?"

"Deader 'n a stone," Pearlie said.

Walker shrugged. "Then I don't see no sense in botherin' about it tonight. I'll amble on over there at first light in the morning."

"Sheriff," Cal said, "after the gunshot, no one even came out of the cantina to see what was happenin'."

The deputy laughed. "No, I don't s'pect they did."

"Isn't that a little strange?" Pearlie asked.

"You boys know how many men get killed in that area ever' night?"

The boys shook their heads.

"Enough so's it not nothin' anybody over there gets too excited about. Hell, they'll probably go on using the privy too, after movin' him to the side a bit, an' not even say nothin' about it."

"What do you suggest we do now?" Pearlie asked.

"Seems to me, your only chance of helpin' your friend is to find out who really killed the man in Fort Worth. Was it me, I'd go back there and see what I could dig up."

Pearlie looked at Cal. "He's right, Cal."

"Then let's go," Cal said. "Smoke don't have too much time left."

20

Sally, followed by Monte Carson and Louis Longmont, walked right by the clerk guarding the door to Judge Isaac Parker's chambers.

"Hey, miss, you can't do that . . ." the young man began, starting to rise from his chair.

Sally, without pausing, turned steel-hard eyes on the boy and pointed her finger at him. "Sit!" she said, putting her hand on the door and pushing it open.

The young clerk stared openmouthed at Louis and Monte as they followed Sally into the room. Louis glanced back over his shoulder with a sympathetic look at the man. "Women," he said, and shrugged as he walked into the room.

Parker looked up from his desk, tilting his head to see over the half-glasses on his nose. "What is the meaning of this interruption of my work?" he asked imperiously.

Undaunted, Sally strode right up to the front of his desk and stood there, staring down at the judge. He was in his mid-thirties, dark-haired, and wore a dark gray suit coat and vest over a white shirt and black bow tie. His face appeared stern and his visage was serious, and Sally thought to herself, *Here is a man who thinks he is doing God's own work. He'll be pompous and take himself too seriously, I'll bet.*

"My name is Sally Jensen, and I've come to talk to my husband."

The judge shook his head and leaned back in his chair. "I don't handle visitation of prisoners, ma'am. You'll have to speak to the Superintendent of Jails. Didn't my clerk inform you of that fact?"

"I'm afraid the young man didn't have a chance to inform us of anything, Your Honor," Louis said.

Parker cut his eyes to Louis. "And just who might you be?" he asked.

Louis gave a short bow. "I'm Louis Longmont, Your Honor. Pleased to make your acquaintance."

Parker's eyes roamed to Monte Carson, who took off his hat and held it in both hands in front of him. "I'm Monte Carson, Judge. Sheriff of Big Rock, Colorado."

Parker steepled his hands under his chin and glared at the group standing in front of his desk.

"I presume you all have some reason for being here?"

"We've been to the Superintendent of Jails, Judge Parker," Sally said, "and he said there is no one in jail by the name Smoke Jensen."

"Ah, so you're Smoke Jensen's wife," Parker said, his eyes softening a little. "I've heard a great deal about your husband, especially in the last couple of weeks."

Sally held her chin up high. "Then you know Smoke couldn't possibly have shot a man in the back."

The judge leaned forward. "I notice you didn't say your husband couldn't possibly have shot the man, just that he didn't do it in the back."

Sally looked at the judge as though he was a simpleton. "Of course he could have shot the man, given adequate provocation. My husband is a famous shootist, Judge, and this is the West. On occasion, men come up to Smoke to try and get a reputation, or to prove their bravery. Most times, he can talk them out of trying his hand with a gun, but sometimes it just isn't possible and he has to kill them. He regrets it, but he simply does not instigate confrontations, and he is so proficient with firearms that he does not need to shoot anyone in the back."

"I see," the judge said, leaning back in his chair. "So your husband has killed many men, Mrs. Jensen?"

Sally's eyes became flat, and she gave him a look that would curdle milk. "As have you, Judge Parker."

Parker looked offended. "Surely you're not comparing me to a gunfighter?"

"No," Sally said simply, "a gunfighter shoots in self-defense and puts his own life on the line, while you hide behind those law books on your shelves and make your judgments with no risk to yourself." She hesitated. "But the end result is the same, one man left alive, one man left dead."

Sally regretted her words almost immediately. She could tell by the hurt look on the judge's face that he was wounded by her accusation, and remembered hearing that he often shed tears when sentencing a man to die by hanging.

He looked off out his window, which overlooked the scaffold in the distance on which so many men had died by his pronouncements.

"Please, Mrs. Jensen, take a seat," he finally said, waving his hand at a group of chairs near his desk.

Sally, Louis, and Monte sat down, waiting to see what Parker had to say.

After a moment, he spoke, his eyes soft now with none of their former arrogance. "First of all, Mrs. Jensen, I'll tell you what I tell all of the men I sentence to hang. It is not me that is killing these men, it is the law, the law they broke when they murdered or raped or robbed someone. I am only its instrument, carrying out the justice demanded by the men who wrote the laws in the first place and by the society which demanded a code of conduct that, if broken, must be punished."

"I know that, Judge Parker, and I apologize if I offended you. But you must also realize that I am fighting for my husband's life. He's a man I know as well as one can know another human being, and I *know* that he could not have done the crime of which he is being accused."

"Then he will be set free, Mrs. Jensen. On that you have my word."

"Excuse me, Judge," Louis interrupted, "but it is not as simple as that. You and I both know that innocent men have been convicted of crimes they did not commit. That is a fact, and that is what we aim to prevent if we can help it."

Before the judge could respond, Monte leaned forward in his chair. "Judge, we heard someone had given testimony that he saw Smoke shoot the man in the back. Is that true?"

Parker looked at a stack of papers on his desk and thumbed through them looking for a copy of the wire he'd received. "Ah, here we are," he said, holding up a telegram. "You are right, sir, there is such a testimony on record." He read further for a moment, then added, "However, Marshal Heck Thomas says he has evidence the man was lying in his statement and is taking steps to get it revised."

The three visitors looked at each other, relief on their faces. "There, Judge, I told you so," Sally said.

He held up his hand. "Hold on a moment, Mrs. Jensen. As I told Marshal Thomas in a reply to his telegram, the original statement will hold if the witness does not recant his testimony. That is the law."

"So, even though a sworn peace officer of this court tells you the witness is lying, you're still going to rely on perjured testimony?" Louis asked, disgust in his voice.

The judge spread his hands. "I have no choice, Mr. Longmont. As I said, it is the law."

"Then the law is in error," Louis said angrily.

Sally, trying to head off a confrontation, said, "May we see my husband, Judge Parker?"

"Oh, I thought you knew," he answered.

"Knew what?" Sally asked.

"There has been some delay in his arrival here. Marshal Bill Tilghman was bringing him, along with three other miscreants, overland by caged wagon, and he has failed to arrive on schedule."

"What has happened to them?" she asked, a worried look on her face.

"I do not know, Mrs. Jensen. We have received no word from either Marshal Tilghman or any other law enforcement officers concerning these prisoners."

"Well, what are you doing about it?"

The judge looked uncomfortable, and wouldn't meet Sally's eyes as he replied, "Mrs. Jensen, you have to realize, our U.S. marshals each cover thousands of square miles of wilderness territory. They go out alone, and come back alone. We simply do not have the manpower to provide them with adequate backup. They are, in a very real sense, on their own out there."

"Do you really expect me to just sit here and wait to hear if my husband is alive or not?" Sally asked, rising from her chair.

For the first time in the meeting, the judge grinned, slightly. "No, Mrs. Jensen. After meeting you, I am quite sure that is the last thing a lady such as yourself would do."

He bent his head and scribbled a quick note. "If you will give this to one of the marshals in the main office, one of them will show you on a map the route Tilghman would most likely take to bring your husband here from Fort Worth."

He leaned back, still smiling. "And then, you may go out to meet him, or to see what might have befallen him on the trip here."

She took the note and turned without another word, hurrying out the door.

Louis took the time to tip his hat at Judge Parker. "Thank you for your courtesy, sir."

Parker's eyes remained on Sally's back as she left the room. "She is quite a woman, isn't she?" he murmured, almost as if to himself.

Louis smiled. "She is that, all right!"

"This Jensen fellow may or may not be a murderer, but

after meeting his wife, I'd say either way, he is one of the luckiest men in the world."

Louis nodded. "You are right, Judge. They just don't make them like Sally Jensen very often."

Louis paused when he got to the door. "In fact," he added, looking back over his shoulder, "I'm quite sure she is unique among women."

After Louis and Monte and Sally had gone, Parker got a fresh sheet of paper and began writing a telegram to be sent to Marshal Heck Thomas in Fort Worth.

"Marshal Thomas, I have come to believe you may be correct in proposing Jensen's innocence. Spare no expense in investigating the aforementioned affair. I want to get at the truth in this matter."

He signed it at the bottom and called in his clerk to get it sent at once.

21

Dolly, the prostitute Smoke had talked to about the Durango Kid's men, waited until the bartender began to shut the Silver Dollar Saloon down before making her move.

She checked the loads in the derringer in her garter, then made her way down Main Street to the Star Hotel. She knew the men who'd been riding with the Durango Kid were staying there, but hadn't mentioned the fact to Smoke Jensen, thinking she might be able to get more money from the men by not telling of their whereabouts than from the big, handsome cowboy who'd braced her in the saloon.

Dolly, on her own since the age of fourteen when her stepfather raped her and then threw her out of the house, had learned the hard way that a girl had to take care of herself, because sure as hell no one else was going to do it.

When she stepped through the door of the Star, the clerk, dozing at the main desk, woke up and scowled at her. "We don't allow no whores in here," he said in a nasty tone of voice.

Dolly glared at him for a moment, then forced herself to smile. After all, the one thing she'd learned in her years earning a living on her back was that a smile would get most of what she needed from most men.

"Excuse me, sir," she said, laying it on thick, "I have

personal business with some of your guests. I am in possession of information they urgently need. I'm sure they would be most . . . upset if you kept me from seeing them."

"What guests?" the man asked suspiciously.

"Misters Juan Gomez, Jack Cummings, and Bob Gatling," she answered sweetly.

Evidently the man knew whom she was talking about and didn't want to anger them. As he remembered, they were indeed hard-looking men.

"Top of the stairs on the left, Rooms 302 through 304," he said, immediately laying his head back down on the desk and resuming his nap.

Dolly climbed the stairs, looking around at the lavish furnishings of the elegant hotel. It wasn't often . . . Hell, it was never that she got to see such opulence. She felt sure she'd been right in her decision not to tell the tall man about where these men were staying. If they could afford this hotel, then they could afford to pay her a lot of money to keep their secret. The thought she'd be walking into danger never entered her mind. In her profession, danger was an everyday occurrence and was accepted as the price of doing business.

She knocked on the door to Room 302, fluffing her hair a bit to make herself appear more attractive.

A gruff voice, slurred a bit by too much alcohol, called out, "Who is it?"

"A friend," Dolly answered in as sweet a voice as she could manage.

After some rumbling noises inside, indicating the man was putting on his pants and boots, the door opened a crack. One eye peered out, checking the corridor behind Dolly to make sure she was alone before opening the door fully.

Three-Fingers Juan Gomez opened the door and stepped out into the hall, a Colt hanging from his right hand. "What do you want? I didn't order no girl."

"I have some information I thought you might like to

have," Dolly said. "It concerns your friend who was killed the other night."

"Yeah? What is it?" he asked.

Dolly glanced up and down the hall. "I don't believe you'd want me to go into it out here in the corridor where just anyone could overhear."

Gomez considered this for a moment, then stepped aside, letting her into his room. She crossed the small space and took a seat in a chair by the window, arranging her skirts as she sat so she could get to her derringer quickly if the need arose.

"All right, tell me," he said gruffly, flopping on the bed, putting his feet up, and crossing his hands behind his head as he lay back against the pillows.

"Well," Dolly said, dropping her gaze demurely, "the information is rather important, and I was hoping you'd offer to pay me for my trouble in bringing it to you at such a late hour."

Gomez smiled cruelly. "I ain't payin' you nothing, girl. Now you tell me what you got to tell me or I'll just have to beat it outta you."

Dolly smiled, causing Gomez to assume a worried expression. He wasn't used to women not being afraid of him when he threatened them.

"I'm sorry, sir, but I've already been offered twenty dollars for the information from another fellow. If you don't want to pay, that's fine."

She started to get up from her chair. "I'll just go to this other gentleman and sell him what I know."

Gomez was off the bed and across the room in a flash. He grabbed Dolly by the throat, his eyes wild with anger. "Don't you go threatenin' me, you little whore!" he screamed. "Now, you gonna tell me or do I have to hurt you?"

Without taking her eyes off Gomez's face, Dolly reached under her skirt and brought out the derringer. She thumbed back the double hammers with a loud metallic click, and stuck the twin barrels under the point of Gomez's chin.

"Just how do you plan to hurt me, sir, with what little brains you have scattered all over the ceiling?" she said in a calm, low voice.

Gomez's eyes rolled downward and he released Dolly's throat, holding his hands high above his head. "Be careful with that . . . miss," he stammered. "It's liable to go off."

She smiled into his eyes. "If it does, you'll never hear it, Pancho," she said derisively.

She pushed him back and walked over to his bed, where he'd laid his Colt. She picked it up and let the hammers down on the derringer. "The Colt makes a much nicer hole than that little popgun, don't you think?" she asked.

Gomez didn't answer. He couldn't take his eyes off the barrel of the Colt, which was pointing at his groin.

"Perhaps I'm talking to the wrong man," Dolly said. "Why don't we wake your friends up and see if they might be more reasonable about paying me for information that is vital to your survival?"

She put the gun under her overcoat and followed Gomez as he went to the adjoining rooms and managed to get his friends awake. They all gathered in Curly Bob Gatling's room. The three men sat next to each other on the bed, while Dolly sat across the room in a chair, the big Colt resting on her lap.

"Now, gentlemen, what am I bid for what I know?"

The three looked at each other. Finally, Curly Bob said, "We can give you twenty dollars."

She smiled and shook her head. "I told the Mex here I've already been offered twenty dollars and I wouldn't have had to go to all this trouble. No, gentlemen, you're going to have to sweeten the pot a little to ante up in this game."

The men put their heads together, whispering quietly among themselves for a moment, then looked back at Dolly. "We might be able to get forty dollars together, but that's all we got. We got some beeves for sale, but we ain't got the money for 'em just yet."

Dolly pursed her lips, thinking. Forty dollars was all right, especially if it was all they had. After all, she reasoned to herself, there was nothing to keep her from selling the same information to the man who called himself Smoke after she'd made her deal here.

"All right," she said, "get it."

The men fumbled in their pockets, finally having to go to some saddlebags lying on the dresser to get the money together. Curly Bob took the handful of crumpled bills and reached across the room to hand it to Dolly. She took the bills without taking her hand off the Colt.

"Now, just what is so all-fired important that we'd be willin' to pay forty dollars to hear?" Rawhide Jack Cummings asked, the first time he'd spoken since Dolly entered the room.

"Two things," Dolly said. "Word on the street is that Marshal Heck Thomas is going around to all the local ranchers checking up to see if anyone sold you those beeves you're wanting to sell. So, if you plan to get rid of them and get out of town, you'd better hurry."

"What makes you think our cattle are stolen?" Gomez asked, trying to assume an innocent expression.

"Oh, please," Dolly said, laughing. "I've been entertaining cowboys for years now, and if you three ever earned a dime herding or selling beeves, I'll eat this here Colt."

Curly Bob chuckled. He was beginning to like this woman. She knew how to read men. "What else do you have for us?" he asked, smiling at her.

"There's this tall, good-looking gent, goes by the name Smoke Jensen, asking around town about you boys." She raised her eyebrows. "Seems he wants to meet with you in the worst way."

"Jensen?" Gomez asked. "I thought the marshal arrested him an' hauled his ass off to Fort Smith."

"Must have been a quick trip," Dolly observed.

"What's he want with us?" Rawhide Jack asked, puzzled.

"Says he wants to talk with you boys about finding out who killed your friend, the Durango Kid."

"That don't make no sense," Curly Bob said. "I thought Jensen killed him."

Gomez, who'd begun to sweat at the mention of Smoke Jensen, stood up. "That all you got to say?" he asked, his voice rough.

"Yes, for now," Dolly replied, also standing up and moving toward the door. "However, if I hear anything else, I'll be sure to give you gentlemen a chance to buy it. That is, if you live long enough to sell those beeves you've got stashed at the edge of town."

Gomez took a step toward her, but Dolly eared back the hammer on the Colt. "Now, Pancho, don't do anything stupid, all right? I'd hate to wake everyone in the hotel up by blowing your guts all over the wall."

Gomez stopped and backed up, sweat pouring from his forehead.

Dolly cocked her head. "I can see that the idea that Smoke Jensen wants to talk to you about your friend's death has upset you."

She glanced at Curly Bob and Rawhide Jack. "Perhaps you gentlemen better have a talk with your friend here before Smoke finds you. It appears to me he might know more than you do about who shot the Kid."

Dolly opened the door and stepped out into the hall. "I'll just leave your pistol in the next room on my way out. But, gentlemen, don't try and come after me for a little while, because I may just stand out here in the hall to see if anyone tries to open this door. Good morning, gents, I'll see you later."

After she eased the door shut, Curly Bob stepped around to stand in front of Gomez.

"Just what the hell did she mean about you knowin' somethin' 'bout the Kid's murder?"

When Gomez's eyes shifted back and forth and he refused to meet Curly Bob's gaze, Gatling knew Dolly had been right.

"Out with it, Three-Fingers. What did she mean?"

Gomez whirled around. "I don't know what she's talkin' about. She's just some crazy whore!"

Curly Bob stepped over to the bedpost where his holster was hanging. He pulled out his pistol and pointed it at Three-Fingers Gomez.

"We been ridin' together a long time, Three-Fingers. It'd be a shame for me to have to drill you 'cause you tryin' to feed me some bullshit."

Gomez wilted, sitting on the edge of the bed with his head in his hands. "I just couldn't stand it no more," he moaned. "The Kid always ridin' me 'bout me being Mexican, tellin' me I wasn't gonna get my fair share of the money from the beeves, me havin' to stay over on the west side of town an' all."

Rawhide Jack stood up and began to pace the room. "So, you tellin' us you shot the Kid in the back?"

Gomez looked up, his face red with shame. "I don't know what came over me, boys. When the Kid went out in that alley to brace Jensen, I snuck out the back door to see if he'd get shot. 'Fore I knew it, my six-gun was in my hand an' I shot him in the back. All that anger just kind'a boiled outta me an' I shot him deader 'n shit."

"Goddamn it, Three-Fingers, we was partners," Rawhide Jack said angrily.

"You was partners," Gomez answered. "Remember, the Kid said I wasn't gonna get a fair shake when we divvied up the money."

Curly Bob held up his hands. "All right, it's over and done with now, an' I gotta agree with Gomez. The Kid did ride him awful hard."

"Yeah, but now we not only got this Marshal Thomas on our back trail, we got Jensen to worry about," Rawhide Jack said.

Curly Bob nodded. "That's true, but I think I see a way outta our troubles." He glanced at Gomez. "Three-Fingers, didn't you say you met a *vaquero* up from Mexico over at the cantina wanted to buy our beeves the other night?"

Gomez looked up, hope in his eyes. "Yeah, only he wasn't offerin' as much as the Kid wanted."

"Well, thanks to you, the Kid ain't around no more to object, is he?"

"No," Gomez admitted, "an' bein' as how we're only splittin' the money three ways 'stead of four, it'll be almost the same amount to us anyway."

"That's about the first smart thing you've said since I met you," Curly Bob said. "Now, my idea is to sell those beeves to the Mex as fast as we can to get some ready cash so we can hightail it outta Fort Worth."

"That might get the marshal off our backs, but what about this Jensen feller?" Rawhide Jack asked.

"We might just have to use some of Three-Fingers' share to buy us some insurance," Curly Bob said, a grim smile on his face as he stared down at Gomez.

"While we're over at the cantina makin' our deal with the Mex, we'll see if we can't find some hard cases who might want to earn some spendin' money by takin' Jensen out."

"What do you mean, out of my share?" Gomez asked.

Curly Bob pointed the gun at Gomez. "It was you who caused him to be on our backs; it's only fair you pay to get him off them."

Gomez nodded, knowing he didn't have a hell of a lot of choice in the matter.

22

Three-Fingers Gomez led Curly Bob Gatling and Rawhide Jack Cummings to the cantina where he'd first talked to the vaquero from Mexico who wanted to buy their beeves. The cantinas stayed open all night, not closing early like the more upper-class establishments in the wealthier part of town.

As they entered the cantina, the men had to strain to see through the thick clouds of cigar and cigarette smoke that hung in the air like a morning fog. The smell of stale beer and whiskey and vomit was strong enough to make their eyes water, and the noise of drunken Mexicans and blacks laughing and talking in loud voices made their ears ring.

"You see your man?" Curly Bob asked, having to put his lips close to Gomez's ear to be heard over the din.

Gomez looked around the room, finally seeing the buyer in a far corner sitting at a table with two Mexican whores and two other cowboys.

He pointed, then led the way across the room toward the man.

"Señor Trujillo," he said. *"Buenas noches."*

The *vaquero* looked up through bleary, bloodshot eyes. "Ah, my friend Gomez. How are you this fine evening?" he said, only slurring his words slightly.

Three-Fingers pulled up a chair from a nearby table

and sat next to Trujillo. "I'm fine. I have reconsidered your offer and wonder if you still want to buy our cattle."

"*Sí*," Trujillo said, his eyes becoming more alert. "But I can only pay what we discussed before."

"That's fine," Gomez said, "as long as we can make the deal tonight."

"Why the rush, *señor*? Sit, drink, and enjoy the company of the fine *señoritas* here at the cantina. We can talk business later."

Gomez shook his head. "No, Señor Trujillo. It must be tonight. My compadres and I must be on the trail early in the morning."

Trujillo's eyes narrowed with suspicion. "You have trouble, no?"

"We have much trouble, *señor*, and if we don't sell you those cattle tonight, you won't be able to buy half the number from anyone else with what you have to spend."

Trujillo nodded. "All right. Make out a bill of sale and I will give you the moneys."

Gomez looked over his shoulder at Curly Bill, who nodded. Gomez pulled out a piece of paper, and wrote he was selling the cattle to Trujillo and listed the price. When he pushed the paper across the table to the Mexican, Trujillo grinned, grabbed a leather wallet from inside his coat, and handed it to Gomez. He stuck out his hand and they shook on the deal.

Gomez got up from the table and walked to the bar, followed by Curly Bob and Rawhide Jack. He counted the money in the wallet, ordered tequila all around, and when the drinks arrived, leaned back against the bar and surveyed the other inhabitants of the place.

"Now," Gomez said, "we've got to find some men willing to take money to get rid of Smoke Jensen."

Curly Bob took a deep drink of the tequila, made a face, and said in a hoarse voice, "That shouldn't be too hard from the looks of the men here."

Rawhide Jack, after seeing the effect the tequila had on Curly Bob, took a tiny sip, then put the glass back down on the bar without finishing it. He pointed to a table in a far corner of the room, occupied by six men who were all wearing pistols in holsters tied down low on their thighs. Two of the men had bandoliers of rifle shells criss-crossed on their chests.

"Those gents look the type," he said.

"Why don't you go have a word with them?" Curly Bob said to Gomez. "I think it'd go better if you went alone. You'll probably have to speak Mex to 'em anyway."

Gomez nodded and started toward the men, but Curly Bob grabbed his arm.

"Don't offer 'em more'n you have to. We need some of that money to travel on."

He stared at Curly Bob for a moment, then reached over to the bar and grabbed the bottle of tequila, taking it with him to the table.

Curly Bob watched as Gomez sat at the men's table and began pouring them all drinks from the bottle of tequila.

"Man knows how to bargain," Rawhide Jack said.

"You know, Rawhide, I been wonderin' if we might not ought'a think 'bout moseyin' on down the road alone. Could be that stickin' with Gomez is gonna get us hanged right along with him if that Jensen feller comes after us."

Rawhide Jack's eyes strayed back to Gomez. "You might be right, Curly. We'll just have to play it by ear. One thing, though, from what I heard 'bout Jensen, if he do come after us, it would be good to have an extra gun along. I'd hate to face him without a whole lot of firepower."

"There is that to consider," Curly Bob said.

After a few minutes, Gomez and two of the men at the table got up and walked out the door.

Curly Bob and Rawhide Jack followed.

Gomez talked in a low voice to the men, then pulled out the leather wallet Trujillo had given him and counted out a number of bills. He handed them to the men, who grinned, stuffed the bills in their coats, and went back into the cantina.

"Well?" Curly Bob asked.

"It is done," Gomez answered. "I described Jensen to them, said they couldn't miss him bein' as how he's 'bout the biggest man in town."

"They gonna do it?" Rawhide Jack asked.

"Yeah. They said for us to stay outta sight until tomorrow evening an' they'd hunt him down and put a window in his skull." Gomez grinned. "I told 'em he'd probably be over at the Silver Dollar talking to Dolly, tryin' to find out where we were stayin'."

Curly Bob nodded.

Gomez looked at him, his eyes flat. "I told him as long as they were doin' it, I'd pay an extra fifty dollars if Dolly happened to get caught in the cross fire."

"Why'd you do that?" Rawhide Jack asked.

"'Cause she's figured out I gunned down the Kid. I don't want her talkin' to no lawmen after we're gone."

"We gonna wait around to pay 'em after it's over?" Curly Bob asked.

"Hell, no," Gomez answered with a grin. "I'm hightailin' it outta town tonight. I ain't waitin' around to see how it all turns out."

"Where you figuring on headin' to?" Rawhide Jack asked.

Gomez scratched his chin for a moment, then smiled. "I think I'll head down south, toward Galveston. Might just catch me one of those steamboats and take a little cruise on around to the East Coast."

"That's not a bad idea," Curly Bob said, looking at Rawhide Jack. "Even if Jensen does survive the fracas with the Mexes, he'll never be able to track us on a boat."

Rawhide Jack thought for a moment, then shook his head. "I'm afraid I'm gonna have to pass, boys. The one time I was on a boat, I got so sick I like to puked my guts out."

Gomez looked at him suspiciously. "Well, what are you gonna do?"

"I'm gonna head on over to Jacksboro. I heard that's where a lot of fellers go when they on the run from the law, or somebody else who might be huntin' 'em. I figure the town's big enough to get lost in for a while, 'specially if'n it's full of other men on the hideout too. After all, Jensen ain't gonna be lookin' for me. I didn't kill nobody."

Gomez started to say something, his face red with anger, but Curly Bob grabbed his arm. "Come on, Three-Fingers. Rawhide's right. Makes better sense if'n we split up anyhow. If Jensen does come lookin' and askin' around, he'll be lookin' for three men ridin' together, not two."

"All right," Gomez admitted. "But you better keep your mouth shut about what you know, Rawhide, or it won't only be Jensen come lookin' for you."

Curly Bob glanced at the horizon, where specks of light could be seen.

"Come on, boys. It's gettin' on toward dawn an' I want to be in the saddle 'fore sunup."

The three men walked rapidly back to the hotel, split the rest of the money, and packed their bags, then headed to the livery stable where they'd left their horses.

They paid off the boy at the stable and rode out to the edge of town.

They sat there for a moment, looking at the two roads leading away, one south, one north.

"Adios," Gomez said, sticking out his hand to Rawhide Jack.

Jack took it and smiled. "Good luck, boys."

Curly Bob grinned. "Luck don't hardly have nothin' to do with it, Rawhide. You ride with your guns loose, you hear?"

Rawhide waved and started his horse up the north trail while Gomez and Curly Bob turned south toward Galveston.

23

Sally and Monte and Louis were less than ten miles out of Fort Smith when they saw a man riding a wagon coming toward them in the distance.

Sally spurred her horse into a full gallop and raced toward the man.

As she pulled the horse to a stop, she noticed the man was holding a Winchester Yellow Boy cradled in his arms, the hammer cocked.

She grinned. "Are you Marshal Tilghman?"

He glanced over her shoulder at Monte and Louis, who were just arriving, and moved the rifle a bit so it covered all three.

"Yeah."

She inclined her head at the rifle. "Are you expecting trouble, Marshal?"

"Expectin' it or not, it usually seems to find me. Who are you an' what can I do for you?"

"My name is Sally Jensen, and I was told you were bringing my husband to Fort Smith to stand trial for murder."

Tilghman nodded and seemed to relax just a bit. "I was."

"What do you mean, was?" Sally asked, moving her horse a little to the side so she could see in the back of the cage. "Isn't Smoke with you?"

"No, ma'am," Tilghman answered shortly.

"Well, where is he?"

"On his way back to Fort Worth, I 'spect."

"Marshal," Sally said, her exasperation clearly showing in her voice. "Would you please tell me what's going on?"

"Mrs. Jensen, why don't you get down off that horse and climb up here on the hurricane deck with me? That way I can tell you while I keep this wagon headin' toward Fort Smith. I'm already a couple'a days late an' I'd kind'a like to keep movin'."

Sally jumped down off her horse, handing the reins to Monte Carson, and climbed up on the wagon with Tilghman.

He snapped the reins and got the wagon moving, setting his rifle in the boot next to his feet while he drove.

"Now, Marshal, what about my husband?"

"I'm fixin' to tell you the damnedest story you ever heard, ma'am," the marshal said, grinning as he glanced sideways at her.

Sally shook her head. "Marshal, if you knew Smoke like I do, you'd know nothing you can say about him will surprise me."

Half an hour later, when Tilghman had finished telling Sally about the confrontation with Zachery Stillwell and his gang, and Smoke's subsequent rescue of the marshal, Sally just nodded.

"That's just like Smoke. He never could stand to see an underdog get beaten without joining in to help."

The marshal glanced at her as if he didn't much like being called an underdog, but then shrugged as if he knew what she'd meant by it.

"So, you *do* believe my husband's innocent of the charges against him, don't you, Marshal?"

Tilghman thought on it for a moment, then slowly nodded his head. "Yes, ma'am, I do. I just can't see a man who did what your husband did for me bein' a back-shooter."

He paused to build himself a cigarette, holding the reins between his knees while he put the tobacco in paper and licked it. Striking a match on the side of the wagon, he lit the cigarette, turning his head to the side to blow the smoke away from Sally.

"Course, you understand that it don't much matter what I think 'bout Smoke. Under the law he's still a wanted man an' I got to bring him in, soon's I get these galoots to the jail in Fort Smith."

Sally nodded. "I understand you have to do your duty, Marshal Tilghman, but it is good to know you don't truly believe Smoke is capable of shooting a man in the back."

"No, ma'am. I think that gambler fellow Gibbons was lyin' when he said he saw Smoke do it. I just don't know why . . . yet."

"So, you intend to question the gambler more about his accusations?" she asked.

"Yes, ma'am. I do. In fact, that's top of my list of things to do, once I get Smoke back in custody."

"You plan to head back to Fort Worth as soon as you drop these prisoners off at the jail?"

"Well, that's a mighty long ride, ma'am. I'll probably take the day to rest up, take a bath, an' get some shut-eye 'fore I try to ride all the way back there."

Sally thought for a moment. "Marshal, doesn't a train run between Fort Smith and Fort Worth?"

Tilghman looked at her. "Yes, ma'am. The Southern Pacific makes a daily run down there."

"How about if we all go by train? We'll get there much sooner, and you can sleep while the train's taking us there."

Tilghman frowned. "That'd be a right nice idea, ma'am, 'cept the U.S. Marshals Service don't pay for no train rides. They expect us to use horses to get back an' forth."

"Oh, for heaven's sake, Marshal. I'll pay your fare. It's important for me to find Smoke before someone else tries to arrest him and causes him to do something that might get him in more trouble than he's already in."

Tilghman smiled at her and slapped the reins to get the horses to move faster.

"You're right intent on takin' care of your man, ain't you, ma'am?"

"You're damned right, Marshal. So get those horses moving, because we're burning daylight."

"Gid'yup!" the marshal yelled at the horses, grinning as they took off at a slow lope, pulling the wagon as fast as they could.

Cal and Pearlie were riding southeast down the trail toward Fort Worth, talking about what they were going to do when they got there.

"Our only chance now is to talk to the men with the Durango Kid on the night he was killed. Maybe they'll know somebody who might have had it in for the Kid enough to shoot him in the back like that," Pearlie said.

The road from Jacksboro to Fort Worth was narrow and not much traveled, so Pearlie and Cal took notice when they saw a lone rider approaching them from a distance on the trail.

"Looks like we got company coming," Cal said.

"Yeah," Pearlie answered. He pulled a pocket watch from his pants pocket and looked at the time. "Hell, it's almost noon. Why don't we stop for a bite to eat? Maybe he'd like to join us."

Cal looked at Pearlie. "Don't tell me you're offerin' to share your grub with a stranger."

Pearlie shrugged. "Why not? 'Fore we left, I had that German lady fill my saddlebags with enough food for three or four men for the trip."

Cal laughed. "Well, since you usually eat enough for two, that don't leave a whole lot for him an' me."

"You'll just have to make do," Pearlie said. "Besides, I

want to see what the news outta Fort Worth is, see if this man's heard anything 'bout Smoke or the killin'."

Cal and Pearlie pulled their horses off the trail, and Cal began to gather some rocks to make a fire while Pearlie got his saddlebags off his horse and began to unload the sack lunches the lady at the Hofbrau had prepared for them.

He had a package of cold fried chicken, a container of German potato salad, and three cans of sliced peaches spread out on his ground blanket when the man on the horse pulled abreast of them.

Cal had the water in the coffeepot boiling, and was just adding in spoonfuls of coffee when he looked up to see the man slow his horse.

"Jimminy," Cal whispered to Pearlie, "that's one of the galoots was at the table with the Durango Kid the night he was killed."

Pearlie nodded, turning his back to the man so he wouldn't hear. "Be careful and keep your hand next to your gun in case he recognizes us," Pearlie said. "I'm gonna invite him to sup with us."

"They were all pretty drunk that night," Cal said. "I doubt he'll remember us, since it was the Kid did all the talkin' to Smoke."

"Just keep your guns loose," Pearlie said, "just in case."

He straightened up and turned to face the man on the trail. "Howdy, mister. We're just about to take a noonin'. Care to join us?"

Rawhide Jack, tired and dusty from being up all night and on the trail all morning, welcomed the chance to get out of the saddle and take a break.

"Don't mind if I do, mister," he called, turning his horse's head off the trail to ground-rein it next to Cal's and Pearlie's mounts under a nearby tree.

Jack dusted off his butt and stretched as he walked over to the fire. "You gents headed toward Fort Worth?" he asked.

"Yeah," Pearlie said. "We've just come from Jacksboro, on our way to see the big city."

Jack squatted next to the fire and took the cup of coffee Cal handed him with a nod of thanks. "Boy, this sure smells good after sucking in trail dust all day."

"You comin' from Fort Worth?" Cal asked, an innocent expression on his face.

"Yep."

Pearlie lay on his left side on the edge of his ground blanket and began to eat the chicken. "Got some fried chicken here, if'n you want some," he offered.

Jack's eyes lit up. "Sure do," he said, sitting cross-legged across from Pearlie. "I'm so hungry I'd almost trade my hoss for some."

"Dig right in," Pearlie said, winking at Cal, who stayed over by the fire so he'd be behind Jack.

As Jack ate, he stared at Pearlie for a moment. "You look kind'a familiar. I ever seen you before?"

Pearlie shook his head. "Nope, not that I recollect."

"How 'bout some of that tater salad?" Jack asked.

Pearlie handed the bowl over to the man and continued to munch on a chicken leg.

"How're things in Fort Worth?" Pearlie asked. "Plenty of action there?"

"'Bout all you could want, an' then some," Jack said with a grin. "Prettiest girls I ever seen in all my born days."

"What hotel you stay at?" Pearlie asked.

"The Star, but it's kind'a expensive for my tastes," Jack answered. "There's plenty more won't take all your drinkin' money to let you have a bed."

Pearlie laughed, shifting his body a bit so he could get at his pistol quickly if need be.

"Is it pretty rough over there? We heard the other day a man got back-shot outside one of the saloons."

Jack's eyes dropped and his face became more serious. "There's some trouble, if you go to the wrong places. Were I you, I'd stay in the nicer saloons. Not so much gun-play there."

"How 'bout that cowboy got shot?" Cal called from behind him. "You see it?"

Jack swiveled his head to glare at Cal. "Why you so interested in one shootin'? Hell, there was three men killed in gunfights the week I was there."

Suddenly, Jack stiffened and he stared harder at Cal. "You look mighty familiar to me too. I know you boys from someplace."

Pearlie eased his pistol out of his holster and had it pointed at Jack when he turned back around. "Yeah, we do know you, mister. We were sittin' with Smoke Jensen the night your pardner, the Durango Kid, got hisself shot dead."

Jack's hand moved toward the gun in his holster, until Pearlie thumbed the hammer back on his Colt. "I wouldn't do that if'n I were you, mister, 'less you wanna meet up with the Kid sooner than you planned to."

"Goddamnit," Jack said, slumping where he sat. "I knew I'd seen you boys before. I just couldn't remember where."

Cal eased up behind Jack and lifted the man's pistol from his holster, then moved around to sit across from him.

"Now, you gonna tell us what you know about that night, or are we gonna have to make you tell us?" Pearlie asked, his voice low and hard, his eyes flat and dangerous.

"Hell, you were there too," Jack said. "You know as much about it as I do."

Pearlie shook his head. "No, sir, I don't think so. Our friend Smoke Jensen has been accused of shootin' the Kid in the back, an' we know for a fact he wouldn't do somethin' like that. Now, you know the Kid better'n we do, so you probably know who had reason to shoot him."

Jack stared at the ground before him. "I don't know nothin'," he said sullenly.

Pearlie winked at Cal. "Cal," he said, "go add some wood to the fire, get the coals nice an' hot."

Cal winked back. "Yeah?"

"Then get that brandin' iron outta my saddlebags. I can see we're gonna have to do some powerful persuadin' to get this man to talk."

Jack's eyes flicked up. "What? What do you mean, branding iron?"

Pearlie shrugged. "We're out here twenty miles from nowhere. Won't nobody hear you scream, an' I *do* intend to get the truth outta you, one way or another."

"Wait just a minute," Jack pleaded. "You can't just go around brandin' a man to make him talk."

Pearlie glanced down at his pistol, pointed at Jack's chest. "Oh? Well, Mr. Colt here says I can do just about anything I want to do out here."

"But if I tell you who shot the Kid, he'll kill me."

Pearlie's heart beat faster at the man's admission he knew who had shot the Durango Kid. "And if you don't tell me, you'll spend the next couple of hours in more pain than you can imagine."

Jack's face fell and he slumped again. "All right. It was Three-Fingers Gomez who shot the Kid."

"Who is Three-Fingers Gomez?" Pearlie asked.

"He was the Mex sittin' with us that night at the Silver Dollar."

"Why'd he shoot the Kid?" Cal asked from behind Jack.

"The Kid had been ridin' him pretty hard all week, makin' him stay down in Mexican Town, not lettin' him have a fair share of the money we were gonna get from selling our cattle."

"Your cattle?" Pearlie asked with scorn. "You mean the cattle you stole?"

"Yeah, that's what I mean," Jack answered, completely defeated now.

Pearlie pointed at the chicken on the ground blanket. "Go on an' eat your fill, mister, 'cause when you finish you're gonna go back to Fort Worth with us an' clear our friend's name."

"But then the marshal will put me in jail."

Pearlie shrugged again. "Better'n being branded, ain't it?"

24

Smoke walked around Fort Worth, checking with the desk clerks at most of the hotels near the center of the city. He figured the Durango Kid and his cohorts would probably have stayed somewhere near the Silver Dollar Saloon, where he'd first seen them. The problem was, none of the clerks would tell him if men fitting their description were staying at their hotels. They all said it was against hotel policy, but Smoke thought they just didn't want any trouble in their places.

Finally, discouraged that he'd ever find the men unless he ran into them on the street or in a saloon or bar, he returned to the Silver Dollar, hoping Dolly had been able to find something out about their whereabouts.

He bought a mug of beer from the bartender and told him if he saw Dolly, to send her over to his table. He found one that was empty in a corner of the room, where he could sit with his back against the wall, as usual. He did this both out of long-standing habit, and because he wanted to keep an eye out for the three men as well as for Marshal Heck Thomas. He didn't know if Thomas would believe that Tilghman had let him go or would try to re-arrest him.

He was on his second beer when he saw Dolly at the bar, talking to the bartender. She glanced over at him, stared a moment as if trying to decide whether to speak to him or not, then finally shrugged and walked over to his table.

"Hello, Dolly," Smoke said. "Grab a seat."

"Uh, Mr. Jensen, I'm a working girl. I got to keep circulating or the boss man will get mad."

"That's all right. I guess you don't have any news for me anyway."

She looked down at him, noticing he was looking discouraged. She stepped around the table and pulled up a chair next to him. "Listen, Smoke, if you'd like to . . . hire my services, we could go up to my room and talk for a while."

He smiled at her. "Don't think I'm not attracted, Dolly. You are a right handsome woman. But I'm a married man who loves his wife very much. I have never strayed and I'm not about to start now." He hoisted his beer glass to her. "So, thanks, but no."

Dolly was touched. She'd been with hundreds of men, a lot of them married, and she respected a man who wouldn't think of cheating on his wife. It was something she didn't often see.

She chewed on her lip for a moment, thinking about what she should do. "You really want to talk to those men, huh?"

He looked into her eyes. "Dolly, I'm a wanted man, wanted for a murder I didn't commit. If they can't help me clear it up, then in all likelihood, I'm going to hang for something I didn't do."

He took another drink of his beer. "It's either that or go to running for the rest of my life. Either way, my life is over if I don't discover who did kill the Durango Kid."

Dolly made up her mind. She glanced over her shoulder to see if anyone could hear her, then leaned over close to Smoke. "I know where they're staying," she whispered.

Smoke was about to ask her where when, out of the corner of his eye, he saw something that didn't make sense. He turned his head to see four Mexicans enter the saloon. The men were hard-looking gunnies, all wearing pistols tied down low on their legs, two of them carrying rifles.

The Silver Dollar was a high-class saloon right in the center of the wealthiest part of Fort Worth. Men like this just didn't come here to drink or to gamble. The hair on the back of Smoke's neck stirred when he saw them stand in the doorway, looking around as if searching for someone. He knew instinctively it was him they were looking for.

"Dolly," he said urgently, "get the hell away from here!"

"What?" she asked with a surprised expression on her face.

When one of the men in the group saw him and said something to the others, pointing his finger in Smoke's direction, Smoke shoved Dolly aside and flipped the table up on its edge, ducking behind it.

The first man drew a pistol and started walking toward Smoke, firing at the table as he approached.

Smoke drew his right-hand Colt and rolled to the side just as several slugs punched their way through the thin wood of the table. He came to rest on his stomach and aimed and fired in one fluid motion. His first bullet took the Mexican in the forehead, blowing the top of his scalp off and showering surrounding tables and gamblers with blood and brains.

Women started screaming and men began to shout and dive for cover as the remaining three Mexicans opened fire.

Smoke hit the second man in the stomach with his second shot, doubling him over just in time for Smoke's third bullet to enter the top of his head and shatter his skull, dropping him like a stone to land face-down in spilled beer and spit and peanut shells.

The other two men began to fire their rifles, shooting and jacking the levers and shooting again. Bullets pocked the wooden floor on all sides of Smoke as he rolled again, first one way, then the other, trying to escape the fusillade of slugs.

As the room filled with heavy layers of gun smoke, making it difficult to see, Smoke leaped to his feet and jumped up on a nearby table, hoping to see over the low-lying cloud of smoke.

He could barely make out the two men, their large Mexican sombreros just visible sticking up out of the smoke.

Whipping out his left-hand gun, Smoke began firing with both hands as rapidly as he could cock and pull the triggers.

The sombreros jerked twice each, then disappeared as the men dropped out of sight into the smoke.

Smoke stepped down off the table and walked toward the men, his guns held waist-high in front of him.

He stepped over the first two bodies, seeing they were dead as dirt, and kept walking, blinking his eyes against the acrid sting of the cordite and smoke in the air.

The third man was lying on his back, open eyes looking upward as if they were trying to see the hole in the center of the forehead that Smoke's .44 had drilled there. He too was dead.

The fourth man was on his stomach, crawling on hands and knees toward the batwings of the saloon, moaning and cursing in Spanish, his left arm dragging behind him, a trail of blood on the floor between his legs as he crawled.

He'd dropped his rifle, so Smoke used the toe of his boot to kick the man over onto his back. The right side of his head had a deep furrow in it, all the way down to where bits of brain could be seen in the hole.

Smoke knelt next to the man, cocked his Colt, and put it against the gunman's nose. "Who paid you to do this?" he asked.

The bartender ran up holding a shotgun in his arms, and squatted next to Smoke in time to hear the man say, "Gomez . . . *hombre* with *tres* fingers . . . paid us to kill Smoke Jensen."

Smoke looked at the barman. "You hear that?" he asked.

The bartender nodded. "Gomez, he said."

Smoke looked back down at the man, whose eyes became unfocused as blood began to pour from his ear.

"Amigo," Smoke said, "whatever he paid you, it wasn't enough."

The man tried to smile, choked once, and died.

25

Smoke stood up and took a deep breath. His heart was hammering and his mouth was dry from the excitement of the gunplay. *No matter how many times this happens,* he thought, *it doesn't get any easier to kill a man.*

He glanced down at the hunks of flesh and blood that only minutes before had been living, breathing human beings, with hopes and aspirations just as real and poignant as those of anyone else in the saloon. No matter the men had taken money to end another's life. They were still men with souls and minds that to them were the most important things in the world. It was no small thing to take all that a man is or ever hopes to be and change it in the blink of an eye to a lifeless pile of meat, cooling rapidly in the spring evening.

He looked around at the shambles of the saloon, the overturned chairs and tables, men and women coming out from their hiding places, horrified, scared looks on their faces, some openly weeping at the terror they'd experienced just moments before.

He saw several other lifeless bodies scattered around the room, three men and one woman who hadn't moved fast enough to get out of the way of the murderous onslaught of the four hired killers. People who were dead in some small way because of him and who he was. That also was not an easy thing to live with.

He glanced over to the table where he'd been sitting, looking to see if Dolly was all right, and saw her legs sticking out from under an overturned table in the corner. He holstered his pistols and rushed to her side.

She lay there, curled in a fetal position, with blood on her chest just below her right shoulder. He gently touched her face and her eyes opened, cloudy with pain and suffering.

"Dolly," he said in a low voice as people began to gather around. "You doing all right?"

She gave the sarcastic smile he'd grown to appreciate over the past two days and shook her head slightly. "No, I'm not all right. I've been shot, you big blockhead."

He grinned back at her. With his practiced eye, he examined her wound. There was no bright red liquid pumping from the hole in her chest, and there was no foam on her lips or bubbling in her breathing. Evidently, the bullet had missed her lung. She would most probably survive if infection didn't set in and if she could get medical help soon.

Smoke looked up at a gambler standing over them. "Go and get a doctor . . . now!" he ordered, and the man turned and ran from the room.

The bartender came over and squatted next to Dolly, taking her hand in his. "Don't worry none, Dolly," he said. "We've sent for the doc."

She glanced at him and whispered thanks, then looked back at Smoke.

"Mr. Jensen, I gotta tell you something."

"What's that, Dolly?" Smoke asked.

"The other night, after you were here, I went to see those men you were looking for."

Smoke didn't say anything, but merely nodded. He'd suspected as much.

"You see, I knew where they were staying, but I wanted

to see if they'd pay me more not to tell you than you would to know."

He put his hand on her cheek. "Don't worry about it, Dolly. Just rest until the doctor gets here."

She shook his hand off, an earnest expression on her face. "No, I gotta say this, just in case . . . well, just in case."

Smoke nodded. "Go on."

"When I was talking to them, I got the idea that the Mexican—name of Gomez, I think—had something to do with the death of that man they're saying you shot."

"He tell you that?" Smoke asked skeptically.

She grinned, and there were specks of blood on her teeth, not a good sign.

"Yeah, but only 'cause I took his gun away from him and he didn't have much choice."

Smoke remembered something about the night of the killing. "Do you know what kind of gun it was?" he asked.

Dolly's forehead wrinkled in puzzlement at the question. "Sure, it was a Colt . . . a Navy model."

Smoke nodded. That made sense, since the gun that'd been used to kill the Kid was a smaller caliber than the .44 most men carried, and most of the Navys were .36-caliber.

He put his hand back on her cheek. "Thanks, Dolly. By telling me that you may have saved my life."

She leaned her face into his hand, then her expression got serious. "Now, you go on and get outta here before the law gets here, Smoke, or you won't be able to go and find those men."

She was right, Smoke thought. The town sheriff or maybe even Marshal Thomas would be there shortly after hearing all the commotion.

He glanced up at the bartender. "Will you stay with her?"

The man nodded and squeezed her hand. "Sure, mister. But like she says, if you're gonna git, you better git fast."

Smoke stood up just as Sheriff Billy Jackson walked

through the batwings and began to look around, a pistol in his hand.

The bartender inclined his head toward the rear of the room. "Out the back door 'fore he sees you. I'll make sure he knows you had nothin' to do with all this."

Smoke touched his shoulder. "Thanks, and make sure the doc takes good care of Dolly. Tell him to spare no expense and I'll make sure he gets paid."

"Will do," the barman said.

As the sheriff began to question the people in the saloon, Smoke ducked his head and made his way slowly out the back door. Once in the alleyway, he moved at a fast pace toward his hotel room, knowing the sheriff would soon be there to get his side of the story of the gunfight at the Silver Dollar Saloon. He couldn't afford to be detained, either by the sheriff or by Marshal Thomas if he happened to be in town.

Just before he got to the hotel, he saw three riders coming up Main Street. Two of the figures looked familiar, even at the distance they were down the street.

Cal and Pearlie, he thought. *Thank God, I can use some help in this business.*

He stepped into another darkened alley and whistled softly as they came abreast of his position.

Pearlie jumped at the sound and whipped his pistol from its holster, twisting in the saddle and pointing it at the barely seen figure in the darkness.

"Who is it?" he said in a harsh voice.

"Smoke," Smoke called softly.

"Smoke!" Cal said, jerking his horse's head around and trotting his animal over near the alley. "We got good news for you."

Smoke inclined his head at the man in the saddle next to Pearlie. "Who's that?" he asked.

"That's Rawhide Jack Cummings," Cal answered, looking back over his shoulder. "He's one of the men who were ridin' with the Durango Kid."

"What're you doing with him?" Smoke asked.

"That's the news we got to tell you," Cal answered.

Smoke looked around, up and down the street. "We need to talk, but I can't go back to the hotel. The sheriff's gonna be there looking for me shortly."

Cal thought for a moment, then said, "Why don't Pearlie an' me get some new rooms? You can keep this galoot covered an' bring him up the back stairs after we get settled."

Smoke nodded. "That sounds good. I'll just take him down the alley behind the hotel, and you can call down to me and tell me what rooms you're in."

Thirty minutes later, Smoke took Rawhide Jack up the back stairs to rooms on the same floor as his old room, but down the hall a ways.

Once they were all gathered together, Cal and Pearlie quickly filled him in on their tracking of Gibbons to Jacksboro and his subsequent death at the hands of the disgruntled poker players.

Smoke nodded. "I never figured him to last long in the business of card-sharking. He just wasn't good enough at it to fool anyone for very long."

He cut his eyes over at Rawhide Jack, who was sitting in a chair by the window, a hangdog expression on his face. "Tell me about this one," Smoke said, pulling his makings out of his pocket and building himself a cigarette.

As he took a deep puff and tilted smoke out of his nostrils, Pearlie told him about how they'd trapped Rawhide Jack on the way to Jacksboro.

"And he says he knows who killed the Durango Kid?" Smoke asked.

"Tell him, Jack," Pearlie said.

"You go to hell!" Jack said defiantly. "I've done all the talkin' I'm gonna. You won't dare do nothin' to me here in town."

Smoke grinned, but the smile never touched his eyes. "Mister," he said in a voice as hard as ringed steel, "I've just killed four Mexican *bandidos* that said you boys paid them to gun me down. Now," Smoke added, taking the cigarette out of his mouth and looking at the glowing red end, "I'm not much one for torture, but I *do* aim to get at the truth. After killing four men, putting a few minor burn holes in your hide don't sound too bad to me."

Rawhide Jack stared at the cigarette and sweat popped out on his forehead.

"You wouldn't dare," he said, though the fear on his face belied his false bravado.

"Pearlie," Smoke said as he started to get up out of the chair, "take your bandanna and tie it around Jack's mouth. We wouldn't want to disturb the other guests with his screaming."

When Pearlie got up off the bed, Jack held up his hands. "No, now hold on a minute. I guess it won't hurt none to tell my side of it."

Smoke sat back down and crossed his legs. "Go on," he said, leaning back in his chair.

"The Kid, Curly Bob Gatling, Three-Fingers Gomez, an' me, we rustled some cattle from some Injuns over in the Nations a couple of weeks back. After we changed the brands, we drove 'em here and stuck 'em in a corral at the edge of town, plannin' on sellin' 'em and usin' the money to pay our way out to California."

Smoke nodded, finishing his cigarette and stubbing it out on the bottom of his boot.

"While we was tryin' to find a buyer, the Kid kept raggin' on Gomez, treatin' him like dirt an' tellin' him he wasn't gonna get an even share of the loot 'cause he didn't do the same amount of work in the drivin' an' brandin' of the beeves."

"So, the Kid was the leader of your gang?" Smoke asked.

Rawhide Jack frowned. "We wasn't no gang nor nothin'. Just a few men tryin' to make a livin'."

"Go on," Smoke said, a disgusted look on his face.

"Well, when the Kid called you out and followed you out of the saloon, while we were all watching the front of the place, Three-Fingers Gomez snuck out the back door. He said he didn't know what came over him, but when he saw the Kid standin' there, he just drew his pistol and plugged him in the back. When everybody else ran out the front door to see what had happened, he came back in the rear door and just walked on out the front with all the other onlookers."

"And that's when Gibbons, pissed off 'cause you'd humiliated him on the train, must've got the bright idea to get back at you by claimin' he saw you do the shootin'," Pearlie said to Smoke.

Just then, they heard a pounding coming from down the hall and a loud voice yelling, "Come on out, Jensen, we know you're in there!"

"It's time to tell your story to the sheriff, Jack," Smoke said, getting up from his chair. "And if you don't, then either I or my friends here will kill you dead before you can get out of town."

"But they'll arrest me for stealin' those beeves," Jack said, his eyes wide with fright.

Smoke walked up to him. "I don't care about the cattle. You can leave that part out, for all I care. But you'd better be real clear when you tell them Gomez admitted to you he shot the Kid in the back, or you're a dead man as sure as I'm standing here." Smoke paused. "You can also tell him that Gomez was the one hired the Mexicans to shoot me down."

He gave a small smile. "After all, Gomez isn't here to dispute your story."

Rawhide Jack nodded, his mind working over the possibilities that he might get out of this with his hide intact. Finally, he looked up and nodded. "All right," he said, knowing he really didn't have any other choice.

It was almost midnight by the time Fort Worth Sheriff Billy Jackson had the stories all straight. He'd taken Smoke, along with Rawhide Jack, Cal, and Pearlie, over to his office under armed guard.

True to his word, Rawhide Jack told the sheriff the

same story he'd told Smoke, leaving out the part about the rustled cattle.

Jackson finally leaned back in his chair and told his deputies to give Smoke and Cal and Pearlie their guns back. "An' lock that sumbitch up in a back cell till I can talk to Marshal Thomas 'bout him in the morning," he added.

After Rawhide Jack was escorted to a cell, Smoke asked the sheriff, "When is Marshal Thomas due back in town?"

"I don't know," the sheriff said. "Right now, he's out traipsin' around to all the ranches in the area lookin' for some beeves stolen from the Indian Nations a few weeks back."

"Was anyone hurt in the theft?" Smoke asked.

The sheriff nodded. "Yeah, seems three young braves was gunned down. Evidently, they never stood a chance."

Smoke's face became hard. "Sheriff, Rawhide Jack left out some details in his story. You might want to ask him about some cattle he and his friends sold to a Mexican *vaquero* night before last. If you hurry, you might even be able to catch up with the herd before it gets to Mexico."

"You mean that sumbitch . . . ?"

Smoke nodded. "And, if you get a chance to talk to Marshal Thomas, would you be sure to tell him I'm innocent? I don't want him out looking for me on the old warrant."

"Will do, Mr. Jensen. And thanks for your help, boys. I know the marshal will be glad to get this cleared up."

"Come on, Cal, Pearlie," Smoke said, standing up and grabbing his hat. "We need to get some shut-eye if we're gonna head down to Galveston after Gomez and Gatling."

"Why don't you boys let the law handle this?" Sheriff Jackson asked.

"'Cause the law doesn't move fast enough to catch them before they sail off to God knows where," Smoke said. "And since I have to go down that way to the King Ranch anyway, I might as well kill two birds with one stone."

The sheriff laughed. "I sure as hell wouldn't want you on my back trail, Jensen."

Smoke's face was serious when he said, "No, Sheriff, I don't believe you would."

26

Smoke came instantly awake to a light tapping at his hotel room door. Reaching over, he pulled his Colt from its holster hanging on the bedpost and walked on tiptoe over to the door.

When he eased it open, his heart began to beat wildly. Sally was standing in the hall, smiling demurely at him.

"Is this the room of the famous gunfighter Smoke Jensen?" she asked, a teasing tone in her voice.

Smoke grinned widely and stepped back to let her enter.

"How did you get up here?" he asked. "I would have bet that Jason fellow at the front desk wouldn't approve of a woman calling on a male guest in his hotel."

"He didn't," Sally said, her lips curling slightly, "until I showed him this." She opened her purse and let Smoke see the shiny surface of her short-barreled Smith and Wesson.

He slammed the door closed, threw his gun on the bed, and wrapped his arms around her, hugging her so tight she almost couldn't breathe.

"When did you get here?" he asked without letting her go.

"Less than an hour ago. Monte and Louis and I came in on the train from Fort Smith with Marshal Tilghman.

We went straight to the sheriff's office and he told us you were here in the hotel."

Smoke stepped back. "What time is it? We've got to get on the train to Houston."

Sally smiled and began to remove her clothes. "Don't worry, we've got hours yet before the train leaves. Plenty of time for us to . . . say hello."

Later, a much refreshed Smoke and Sally joined their friends along with Marshals Bill Tilghman and Heck Thomas at breakfast in the hotel dining room.

It took a while for everyone to tell their part of the story, but by the time Pearlie was on his second helping of everything, all were up to date.

Over final cups of coffee and cigars and cigarettes, Tilghman asked Smoke, "What do you plan to do now?"

Smoke took a sip of his coffee, then leaned back in his chair. "I plan on taking the Cottonbelt train down to Houston, and from there heading on over to Galveston to see if I can head off Gomez and Curly Bob Gatling before they get on that steamer."

Tilghman glanced at Thomas, pursing his lips as if trying to think of a way to say what was on his mind. "You know, it ain't your job to do that, Smoke."

When Smoke started to speak, the marshal held up his hand. "And technically, you're still wanted for the murder of Jim Slade, the Durango Kid."

"What?" Smoke exploded. "You know I didn't do that. You've got the testimony of a U.S. marshal that the witness was lying, and the testimony of the killer's partner that he admitted he shot the Kid."

Tilghman gave a slight smile. "I know all that, but the fact of the matter is you've been formally charged with the crime. It don't matter what I know, but what the court rules after considering all the evidence. You're gonna have to go before Judge Parker and be declared not guilty before the charges can be dropped."

"That's bull . . ." Smoke said, then paused and glanced at Sally sitting next to him. "Dung, and you know it!" he went on.

Tilghman shrugged. "Yeah, I know it is. But I'll tell you what. If Heck here agrees," he said, glancing at his friend, "I don't see any reason why you can't stop by Fort Smith on your way back to Colorado. After you get your beeves from the King Ranch, you gotta drive 'em pretty near there anyway to get 'em home."

Smoke stared at the two marshals. "You'd trust me to do that?"

Tilghman and Thomas looked at each other and nodded. "Sure," Tilghman said.

"What are you two going to do about Gomez and Gatling?" Smoke asked.

"Well, our first job is to get those beeves back the *vaquero* bought from the Kid's partners. So, Heck's gonna take a few deputies and get on the trail after 'em."

"And what are *you* going to be doing?" Smoke asked.

"Why, I plan to book passage on the Cottonbelt too," Tilghman answered.

"That's why you're so ready to trust me to come back to Fort Smith," Smoke said. "'Cause you're going to be right by my side the whole time."

"Well," Heck Thomas said, "truth of the matter is, we'd kind'a hate to have to chase Gomez an' Gatling all the way to the East Coast. Be much easier if they just happened to still be in Galveston when Bill here gets there."

Tilghman looked directly into Smoke's eyes. "And I would trust you to keep your word, Smoke. You've proven that to me on several occasions already."

Monte pulled a pocket watch out of his coat and announced, "If we're gonna catch that train, we'd better get a move on."

Smoke hired a private car on the Cottonbelt so the group could all stay together on the two-day journey down to Houston. From Houston, they'd have to either rent or buy horses for the fifty-mile trip down to Galveston, since the train didn't go that far.

As they sat at tables in the car, drinking brandy, Monte, Louis, Cal, and Pearlie played with a deck of cards. Pearlie was anxious to show Louis what he'd learned from Smoke about the game of poker. Louis just grinned, figuring he'd show Pearlie a few things he hadn't yet learned.

Bill Tilghman, Sally, and Smoke sat at a table alone, talking about the past.

"It must be exciting work, Marshal," Sally said, "spending all your time hunting dangerous men."

Tilghman nodded. "It is, Mrs. Jensen. Human beings are about the most dangerous game there is to hunt. One of the few animals who'll shoot back at the hunter."

As he spoke, Smoke's mind went back to the time he'd hunted down the men who'd killed his father . . .

After meeting up with Preacher, Smoke's father, Emmett, told Preacher that he was going out looking for the three men who killed Smoke's brother and stole some Confederate gold. Their names were Wiley Potter, Josh Richards, and Stratton. Emmett went on to tell Preacher that he was going gunning for those polecats, and if he didn't come back, he wanted Preacher to take care of Smoke until he was grown up enough to do it for himself. Preacher told Emmett he'd be proud to do that very thing.

The next day, Emmett took off and left the old cougar to watch after his young son. They didn't hear anything for a couple of years, time Preacher spent teaching the young buck the ways of the West and how to survive where most men wouldn't.

During that time, Smoke became about as natural a fast draw and shot as Preacher had ever seen, the boy spending at least an hour every day drawing and dry-firing the twin Navy Colts he wore.

Two years later, at Brown's Hole in Idaho, an old mountain man found Smoke and Preacher and told Smoke his daddy was dead, and that those men he'd gone after had killed him. Smoke packed up, and he and Preacher went on the prod.

They arrived at Pagosa Springs, Pagosa being an Indian term for healing waters, just west of the Needle Mountains, and stopped to replenish their supplies. Then, they rode into Rico, a rough-and-tumble mining camp that at that time was an outlaw hangout.

Smoke built a cigarette as his mind wandered, lighting it and taking a deep puff, remembering how it had been for the young boy and his old friend in those rough and rowdy days . . .

Smoke and Preacher dismounted in front of the combination trading post and saloon. As was his custom, Smoke slipped the thongs from the hammers of his Colts as soon as his boots hit dirt.

They bought their supplies, and had turned to leave when the hum of conversation suddenly died. Two rough-dressed and unshaven men, both wearing guns, blocked the door.

"Who owns that horse out there?" one demanded, a snarl in his voice, trouble in his manner. "The one with the SJ brand?"

Smoke laid his purchases on the counter. "I do," he said quietly.

"Which way'd you ride in from?"

Preacher had slipped to his right, his left hand covering the hammer of his Henry, concealing the click as he thumbed it back.

Smoke faced the men, his right hand hanging loose by his side. His left hand was just inches from his left-hand gun. "Who wants to know—and why?"

No one in the dusty building moved or spoke.

"Pike's my name," the bigger and uglier of the pair said. "And I say you came through my diggin's yesterday and stole my dust."

"And I say you're a liar," Smoke told him.

Pike grinned nastily, his right hand hovering near the butt of his pistol. "Why . . . you little pup. I think I'll shoot your ears off."

"Why don't you try? I'm tired of hearing you shoot your mouth off."

Pike looked puzzled for a few seconds; bewilderment crossed his features. No one had ever talked to him in this manner. Pike was big, strong, and a bully. "I think I'll just kill you for that."

Pike and his partner reached for their guns.

Four shots boomed in the low-ceilinged room, four shots so closely spaced they seemed as one thunderous roar. Dust and birds' droppings fell from the ceiling. Pike and his friend were slammed out the open doorway. One fell off the rough porch, dying in the dirt street. Pike, with two holes in his chest, died with his back against a support pole, his eyes still open, unbelieving. Neither had managed to pull a pistol more than halfway out of leather.

All eyes in the black-powder-filled and dusty, smoky room moved to the young man standing by the bar, a Colt in each hand. "Good God!" a man whispered in awe. "I never even seen him draw."

Preacher moved the muzzle of his Henry to cover the men at the tables. The bartender put his hands slowly on the bar, indicating he wanted no trouble.

"We'll be leaving now," Smoke said, holstering his Colts and picking up his purchases from the counter. He walked out the door slowly.

Smoke stepped over the sprawled, dead legs of Pike and walked past his dead partner.

"What are we 'posed to do with the bodies?" a man asked Preacher.

"Bury 'em."

"What's the kid's name?"

"Smoke."

A few days later, in a nearby town, a friend of Preacher's told Smoke that two men, Haywood and Thompson, who claimed to be Pike's brother, had tracked him and Preacher and were in town waiting for Smoke.

Smoke walked down the rutted street an hour before sunset, the sun at his back—the way he had planned it. Thompson and Haywood were in a big tent, which served as saloon and cafe, at the end of the street. Preacher had pointed them out earlier and asked if Smoke needed his help. Smoke had said no. The refusal had come as no surprise.

As Smoke walked down the street, a man glanced up, spotted him, then hurried quickly inside.

Smoke felt no animosity toward the men in the tent saloon; no anger, no hatred. But they'd come here after him, so let the dance begin, he thought.

Smoke stopped fifty feet from the tent. "Haywood! Thompson! You want to see me?"

The two men pushed back the tent flap and stepped out, both angling to get a better look at the man they had tracked. "You the kid called Smoke?" one said.

"I am."

"Pike was my brother," the heavier of the pair said. "And Shorty was my pal."

"You should choose your friends more carefully," Smoke told him.

"They was just a-funnin' with you," Thompson said.

"You weren't there. You don't know what happened."

"You callin' me a liar?"

"If that's the way you want to take it."

Thompson's face colored with anger, his hand moving closer to the .44 in his belt. "You take that back or make your play."

"There is no need for this," Smoke said.

The second man began cursing Smoke as he stood tensely, legs spread wide, body bent at the waist. "You're a damned thief. You stolt their gold and then kilt 'em."

"I don't want to have to kill you," Smoke said.

"The kid's yellow!" Haywood yelled. Then he grabbed for his gun.

Haywood touched the butt of his gun just as two loud gunshots blasted in the dusty street. The .36-caliber balls struck Haywood in the chest, one nicking his heart. He dropped to the dirt, dying. Before he closed his eyes, and death relieved him of the shocking pain by pulling him into a long sleep, two more shots thundered. He had a dark vision of Thompson spinning in the street. Then Haywood died.

Thompson was on one knee, his left hand holding his shattered right elbow. His leg was bloody. Smoke had knocked his gun from his hand, then shot him in the leg.

"Pike was your brother," Smoke told the man. "So I can understand why you came after me. But you were wrong. I'll let you live. But stay with mining. If I ever see you again, I'll kill you."

The young man turned, putting his back to the dead and bloody men. He walked slowly up the street, his high-heeled Spanish riding boots pocking the air with dusty puddles.

After Smoke shot and killed Pike, his friend, and Haywood, and wounded Pike's brother, Thompson, he and Preacher went after the men who killed Smoke's brother and stole the Confederates' gold. They rode on over to La Plaza de los Leones, The Plaza of the Lions. It was there they trapped a man named Casey in a line shack with some of his *compadres*. Smoke and Preacher burnt them out by setting the shack on fire, and captured Casey. Smoke took him to the outskirts of the town and hung him.

After the hanging, the sheriff of the town put out a flyer on Smoke, accusing him of murder and offering a ten-thousand-dollar reward.

Preacher advised Smoke they should head up into the mountains and go into hiding, but Smoke said he had one more call to make. They rode on over to Oreodelphia, looking for a man named Ackerman. They didn't go after him right at first. Smoke and Preacher sat around doing a whole lot of nothing for two or three days. Smoke wanted Ackerman to get plenty nervous. He did, and finally came gunning for Smoke with a bunch of men who rode for his brand . . .

At the edge of town, Ackerman, a bull of a man, with small, mean eyes and a cruel slit for a mouth, slowed his horse to a walk. Ackerman and his hands rode down the street, six abreast.

Preacher and Smoke were on their feet. Preacher stuffed his mouth full of chewing tobacco. Both men had slipped the thongs from the hammers of their Colts. Preacher wore two Colts, .44's. One in a holster, the other stuck behind his belt. Mountain man and young gunfighter stood six feet apart on the boardwalk.

The sheriff closed his office door and walked into the empty cell area. He sat down and began a game of checkers with his deputy.

Ackerman and his men wheeled their horses to face the men on the boardwalk. "I hear tell you boys is lookin' for me. If so, here I am."

"News to me," Smoke said. "What's your name?"

"You know who I am, kid. Ackerman."

"Oh, yeah!" Smoke grinned. "You're the man who helped kill my brother by shooting him in the back. Then you stole the gold he was guarding."

Inside the hotel, pressed against the wall, the desk clerk listened intently, his mouth open in anticipation of gunfire.

"You're a liar. I didn't shoot your brother; that was Potter and his bunch."

"You stood and watched it. Then you stole the gold."

"It was war, kid."

"But you were on the same side," Smoke said. "So that not only makes you a killer, it makes you a traitor and a coward."

"I'll kill you for sayin' that!"

"You'll burn in hell a long time before I'm dead," Smoke told him.

Ackerman grabbed for his pistol. The street exploded in gunfire and black powder fumes. Horses screamed and bucked in fear. One rider was thrown to the dust by his lunging mustang. Smoke took the men on the left, Preacher the men on the right side. The battle lasted no more than ten to twelve seconds. When the noise and the gunsmoke cleared, five men lay in the street, two of them dead. Two more would die from their wounds. One was shot in the side—he would live. Ackerman had been shot three times: once in the belly, once in the chest, and one ball had taken him in the side of the face as the muzzle of the .36 had lifted with each blast. Still Ackerman sat in his saddle, dead. The big man finally leaned to one side and toppled from his horse, one boot hung in the stirrup. The horse shied, then began walking down the dusty street, dragging Ackerman, leaving a bloody trail.

Preacher spat into the street. "Damn near swallowed my chaw."

"I never seen a draw that fast," a man said from his storefront. "It was a blur."

Later, the editor of the paper walked up to stand by the sheriff. He watched the old man and the young gunfighter walk down the street. He truly had seen it all. The old man had killed one man, wounded another. The young man had killed four men, as calmly as picking his teeth.

"What's that young man's name?"

"Smoke Jensen. But he's a devil."*

Smoke came out of his reverie as Sally asked him a question.

*The Last Mountain Man

"What did you say, dear?" he asked.

"Daydreaming, huh?" she said.

"Yeah. Just sitting here gathering wool, thinking about old times like some old codger on a porch in his rocking chair," Smoke said.

Across the table, Tilghman nodded. "It's a disease common to all of us who live by the gun," he said. "Sometimes, the memories of those times when your life hangs by the thread of who's the quickest with a six-killer are overpowering."

27

Sally poured tea for herself and stirred in some sugar.

"That's an interesting way of putting it, Marshal Tilghman," she said. "How did you get in the marshaling business anyway?"

Tilghman added a dollop of brandy to his glass and took a sip, thinking on how to put it.

"When I was about eight or so, my father went off to fight in the Civil War, and my older brother, Richard, became a drummer boy. I was left alone as the 'man' of the place. Let me tell you, it was quite a job for a boy of eight to help keep food on the table, plow the fields with an old mule, bring in the crops, and take care of my mother at the same time."

Sally nodded. "I can see it must have made you mature quite early."

"Yep, an' it didn't help any when my dad came back from the war blind and my brother married and moved away."

"What'd you do?" Smoke asked.

"The only thing I could do. I kept workin' the farm and takin' care of Mom and Dad. Then, after they died—this was in the summer of '72—I got work as a professional buffalo hunter. I'd become a pretty fair hand with a rifle, shotgun, knife, an' pistol during my years takin' care of the farm, so the work kind'a came natural to me."

"I've read stories about the old buffalo hunters, Buffalo Bill Cody and Wild Bill Hickok, but I've never met one," Sally said. "What was the life like?"

"Well, that summer of '72, me an' a group of men made a camp near where the Kiowa and Bluff Creeks come together, 'bout fifty miles from Dodge City. We built a dugout large enough for all fourteen of us, and one for the horses an' mules too. After a while, we'd just about shot all the buffalo for miles around, so we moved southward and made another similar camp on the Kiowa Creek. Now, just south of there was the Cimarron River on the edge of the Gloss Mountains, home of the Cheyenne."

Tilghman stopped to pull a cigar out of his pocket and put a lucifer to it, while Smoke refilled his brandy glass.

"Now, the Cheyenne just naturally resented us white men comin' in an' shootin' up all their buffalo. One day, when we got back from an afternoon of shootin' damn near ever'thing in sight, we found the camp destroyed . . . tents shredded, equipment smashed, and everything just generally torn up."

Sally glanced at Smoke, her mouth open. "Did you then leave the area?"

"The other men wanted to, but I was a young buck, full of piss an' vinegar." He paused, his face reddening. "Excuse me, ma'am. Sometimes my mouth forgets I'm in the presence of a lady."

Sally laughed. "Marshal, I've lived among cowboys too long to be offended by earthy language. You go ahead and tell your story in your own words. It's a fascinating tale of the old West."

"Yes, ma'am. Like I said, to me the attack was a personal insult, an' I wasn't about to stand for it. So, after the others took off, I hid in some tall prairie grass near the camp, figurin' the Injuns would come back to see what we'd done."

He took a drag on his cigar, a sip of his brandy, and continued. "Sure enough, I'd only been there a couple'a hours when three of 'em came back. One of 'em had a rifle, but the other two only had these long, nasty-lookin' knives. When they saw me, they charged right at me, whoopin' and hollerin' to beat the band. Guess they figured it'd scare me off like the others."

"And did it?" Sally asked, forgetting all about her tea and letting it get cold untouched on the table before her.

"No, ma'am. I let the hammer down on my shotgun, and a full double load of buckshot hit the lead one in the stomach, killin' him right away. The second one, seein' my gun was empty, ran up at me with that big knife in his hand, figurin' on gettin' my scalp. I clipped him hard under the chin with the butt of the shotgun and knocked him on his . . . uh, down in the grass, unconscious. The third one jumped on my back, intent on cuttin' my throat, an' we wrestled around a bit 'fore I was able to turn that knife into his own throat."

"What happened to the one you knocked down?" Sally asked.

Tilghman chuckled. "Oh, when he got up an' saw what'd happened to his friends, he took off runnin' an' never looked back."

"I'd venture a guess that you had no further problems with the Cheyennes on that hunt," Smoke said.

"Nope," Tilghman replied. "As a matter of fact, a few days later we had the best hunt of the year at that particular spot."

"So the other hunters returned after you'd gotten rid of the Indians?" Sally asked.

"Yeah. They showed up the next day, all carryin' their big Sharps buffalo rifles, ready to do some shootin'."

"What caliber Sharps did you use?" Smoke asked, interested, since he'd had lots of experience with the gun called the Sharps Big Fifty, a .52-caliber weapon, when he was up in the mountains with Preacher in his early days.

"Oh, I didn't use a Sharps," Tilghman replied. "I used a shotgun."

"What?" Smoke asked, astounded. "How on earth could you kill a buffalo with a shotgun?"

Tilghman laughed. "You sound just like my old huntin' partners. They asked the same question."

"Well?"

"I made some special loads for my shells. Instead of buckshot, I substituted a single lead slug in the shell."

"Why did you do that?" Sally asked.

Tilghman glanced at Smoke. "Smoke will know what I mean when I say I didn't much like the way the Sharps kicked. I was afraid it'd knock me off my feet or give me a broken shoulder."

"And did it work?" Smoke asked, thinking back to the times he'd had to put a poultice on his shoulder after firing his Sharps Big Fifty.

"Only too well," Tilghman replied. "The best thing was, I could fire while ridin' my pony, without having to jump down an' fire from the ground like my partners. In less than half an hour that first day, I'd bagged a dozen buffalo. I guess the number I got total that year was over four thousand, while the combined total of all my partners taken together was less than half that."

"Did they finally see the light?" Smoke asked, smiling at the innovation of this marshal.

"Oh, yeah. 'Fore long, all of 'em wanted to use shotguns 'stead of Sharps."

Sally tasted her cold tea, made a face, and got up to make herself another cup. When she returned to the table, she asked, "What did you do after you gave up buffalo hunting, Marshal?"

"When the buffalo got scarce, sometime around '75, I rode on over to Dodge City, just to see what was goin' on. I met Charlie Basset, who was sheriff of Ford County, an' he asked me if I'd consider bein' his deputy."

Tilghman shrugged. "Heck, I didn't have nothin' else goin' on, an' I'd never been a lawman before, so I said I'd give it a shot."

"Wasn't Dodge City very . . . rough back then?" Sally asked.

"Yes, ma'am. On my second day on the job I had a run-in with a local gunman named Texas Bill. When he saw my shiny new badge, he stepped in front of me on the board-walk and blocked my path. I told him, 'You'll have to turn your guns in or leave town. It's a new ordinance.'"

"Did he draw on you?" Smoke asked, enjoying the tales of towns he'd been in himself.

"Not then. He just said, 'Never heard of it. If you want 'em, come an' take 'em from me.'"

"Did you?" Sally asked.

Tilghman smiled at the memory. "Being new to the job, I didn't quite know what to do. It seemed a small thing to shoot a man over, so I just slugged him."

"You knocked him out?" Smoke asked, laughing.

"Yeah, an' then two of his buddies jumped on me an' I had to knock them out too. Once they was all out cold, I just got some citizens to help me carry 'em to jail."

"Those were certainly rough times in Dodge," Smoke said.

"You're right, Smoke, an' it went from bad to worse. In early '76, Mayor Dog Kelly, who owned the Alhambra Saloon, wired Wyatt Earp over at Wichita to come to Dodge an' take over from the town marshal. Old Dog had heard a bunch of Texas cowboys were on their way to Dodge an' he didn't think Bat Masterson an' I could handle it alone."

"So that's how Wyatt got to Dodge?" Smoke asked. "I always wondered."

Tilghman nodded. "Uh-huh, an' he brought Neal Brown an' Bat's brother, Ed, with him."

"I assume everything went all right and you were able to control the cowboys," Smoke said.

"Yes, but it weren't easy. Back then the town was full of toughs, men like Doc Holliday, Ben Thompson, and even the worst of 'em all, Wes Hardin. After a while, Bat Masterson was elected sheriff of Ford County an' hired me to stay on as his deputy."

"And how was that?" Smoke asked.

"It was all right, but I soon tired of it an' homesteaded me a few hundred acres, built me a cabin, an' married a widow woman named Flora Robinson. I partnered up with Neal Brown an' just took life easy for a while."

Smoke wanted to ask more about the wild days and times Tilghman had lived in, but noticed Sally trying to stifle a yawn across the table.

He took a final drink of his brandy, and stood up. "Well, Marshal, this has been most interesting, but I see my wife is about to fall asleep at the table. We'd better call it a night."

Tilghman glanced at Sally, a chagrined look on his face. "Sorry, ma'am, hope we haven't bored you to death with all this man talk about the past."

"Oh, no," Sally protested. "It was very interesting and exciting, but as you know, Marshal, we've been on trains for the better part of three days and I am just exhausted." She stood up and held out her hand. "I hope we'll be able to continue the stories tomorrow."

"I'm done wore out talkin' 'bout myself, ma'am, but maybe you can get Smoke to tell us some of his adventures up in the mountains back before white men came here," Tilghman said, shaking her hand.

She looked at her husband. "Getting Smoke to talk about himself is like pulling teeth, but I'll try. Good night, Marshal."

"Good night, ma'am."

28

The private car the group was riding in was divided into three parts; private sleeping quarters for Sally and Smoke, a bunk room for the other men, and the main part of the car.

After Sally and Smoke retired, Tilghman walked over to the poker table, where Louis Longmont was giving Cal and Pearlie and Monte Carson a lesson in cardsmanship.

"You boys have markedly improved your skills at poker," Louis said with a grin. "It took me almost two hours to clean you out."

They'd been playing with poker chips that came with the car, not for real money, but losing still stung the boys. "I've just never seen such a run of luck," Pearlie complained, throwing his last hand down on the table.

Cal shook his head. "I don't believe luck had nothin' to do with it, Pearlie," he said. "If I remember correctly, you had just as many good hands as Louis. You just didn't win as much with 'em as he did."

Monte smiled approvingly. "That's the most important lesson you can learn about poker, Cal. Luck may determine who wins a particular hand, but at the end of the night, luck has nothing to do with who has the most chips."

Louis nodded. "The sheriff's right, boys. You got to know when to hold them and when to fold them, when to bet big and when to ease into a hand to make the most money from your luck when it hits."

Pearlie frowned. "I guess I still got a lot to learn then."

Louis smiled. "Don't feel too bad, Pearlie. You didn't learn to handle a cow pony or a mean steer overnight. It took you a lot of years and a lot of sore behinds before you could stay in the saddle in the middle of a stampeding herd, didn't it?"

"You got that right, Mr. Longmont."

"Well, the same is true of any other skill, even poker. You have to get your butt kicked a few times before the lessons sink in, but then you don't forget them."

"Gentlemen," Tilghman said, "I'm gonna hit the hay. It's been a long day, an' tomorrow don't figure to be any shorter. Good night."

The other men agreed and all decided to hit the bunks.

As Bill Tilghman lay there, images from his past kept flicking through his mind, brought on by his retelling the story of his early days to Smoke and Sally. As he finally dozed off, the images turned into dreams. He occasionally moaned in his sleep as the recollections were reenacted in his thoughts . . .

After Tilghman left Dodge City, he met up with Chris Madsen and Henry "Heck" Thomas, and they all hired on to bring law to the town of Perry, where they became known as the "Three Guardsmen." One of their first duties had been to track down the members of the Doolin Gang, headed by Bill Doolin.

One night, on patrol with Heck Thomas, Tilghman noticed a crude dugout cabin several hundred yards off the trail they were riding.

"Heck," he said, pointing with his head, "there's a place I ain't never seen before. You hang here while I go check it out."

He pulled the head of his bay around and walked it through the light underbrush to the doorway of the dugout. The night was wild, with heavy winds and light rain moving almost sideways in the gale.

Tilghman knocked, then pushed the door open and stepped inside, taking off his hat and flinging water off it to the floor. When he looked up, he noticed in the dim light of a lantern hung from a nail on the wall that both sides of the interior were lined with bunks, covered with hanging blankets.

At the end of the room, a large river-stone fireplace was blazing, sending out welcome waves of heat into the room. In the center of the open space between the bunks, a man sat with a Winchester rifle across his lap.

"Howdy," Tilghman said, brushing more water from his slicker. "I'm lookin' for Bee Dunn's place. How far is it from here?"

"That's for you to find out," the man replied sourly.

"Well, I's just passin' by with my fightin' dog and thought maybe I could get Bee to match a fight," Tilghman said, keeping his voice light and calm. "He told me a while back he thought his dog could beat mine."

Tilghman, every lawman instinct in him crying out danger, noticed the man's eyes flicking to the sides to look at the bunks on either side of the room.

"I done tole you to find it on your own," the man growled.

"All right, I'll do that, but this fire sure feels good," Tilghman said, rubbing his hands and stamping his feet in front of the blaze, using his movements to cover his looking at the bunks. He noticed the tips of several rifle barrels sticking out from behind the blankets, all aimed at him.

"I guess I'll be goin'," Tilghman said from his place near the fire. "Which way does a fellow go to get out of here?"

"The same damned way he came in."

Without betraying the terror he felt, Tilghman calmly backed toward the door, jamming his hat back down on his head. "Well, adios, stranger. I'll just let myself out an' see if I can find the Dunn place on my own."

The man in the chair didn't answer, but his hands were tight on the rifle in his lap and his eyes were cold and hard as he watched Tilghman back out the door.

As fast as he could, Tilghman rode back to the trail where Heck was waiting.

"What'd you find out?" Heck asked.

"I couldn't see much, it was too dark," Tilghman replied. "But one thing's sure. There's a passel of men hidin' out in there, an' we're gonna need help to bring 'em in."

They rode over to Pawnee and enlisted the help of Chief Deputy John Hale, who formed a posse. When they got back to the cabin, the only occupant left was the man in the chair.

"What's your name, mister?" Tilghman said after they'd disarmed the man of his rifle.

"Will Dunn," the man replied, still in a surly mood.

"Where are the men who were hidin' here when I was here before?" Tilghman asked after checking the bunks and finding them empty.

"The outlaws is already gone. An' you would be too, lawman, if Bill Doolin hadn't kept his men from shootin' you in the back as you left."

"What do you mean?" Heck Thomas asked.

"They was all here, ever' one of Doolin's gang . . . Bill Doolin, Red Buck, Charley Pierce, Tulsa Jack, and Little Bill Raidler. Old Red Buck sure wanted to kill you, Marshal," Dunn said to Tilghman, smiling as if he agreed with the sentiment. "He was all ready to shoot you in the back, but Bill Doolin stopped him by grabbin' his gun hand."

"Why'd he do that?" Tilghman asked, a puzzled expression on his face.

Dunn snorted, "Doolin said Bill Tilghman is too good a man to be shot in the back." He shook his head. "Red Buck was plenty peeved off at being stopped. . . . He must have a powerful hate for you, Marshal."

Tilghman felt a chill up his spine at the close call he'd had, but it wasn't to be his last by a long shot.

Bill Tilghman groaned and turned over in his bunk, the near miss in his dreams leading him to his next encounter with Bill Doolin . . .

A few months after the cabin incident, Bill Doolin and his gang held up the express station at Woodward and made off with over ten thousand dollars. Will Dunn, who was being left free but kept on a short leash by the lawmen, informed Tilghman that Doolin and some of his men were supposed to meet up at his brother Bee's place in the next few days.

Tilghman, Heck Thomas, and a posse rode over to the Bee Dunn Ranch. Tilghman dragged Bee out to stand in front of the posse.

"Dunn," Tilghman said, his face right up against Bee's, "you're gonna be arrested and tried as an accomplice if you don't help us capture Doolin and his men when they arrive."

"But they'll kill me, Deputy," Dunn protested.

Tilghman shrugged. "Better'n spending the next twenty years caged up like an animal," he replied.

Dunn finally nodded, broken.

Tilghman staked the posse out around the ranch, hidden and waiting for the outlaws to show up.

On the third night, Bitter Creek Newcombe and Charlie Pierce rode up to the corral.

When they got close enough, Heck Thomas stood up, his Winchester in his hands. "Hold on, boys. Put them hands up and give it up now, you hear?"

Newcombe and Pierce hesitated only a moment before they jumped from their horses to the ground. They pulled six-shooters and began to charge at the sound of Heck's voice, firing wildly into the darkness as they ran.

Heck and Bill calmly aimed and returned the fire, not bothering to duck. As lead slugs whistled around their heads, the two lawmen continued to pull triggers and fight the bucking of their rifles, trying to hit the crouching, running figures barely outlined against a night sky.

Newcombe was the first to fall, two slugs hitting him almost simultaneously, one in the face and the other in the chest. He was stopped in midstride as if he'd run into a brick wall, falling dead on the cold hard ground.

Pierce slowed when he saw his partner fall, and it got him killed. When he hesitated, both Tilghman and Thomas fired, killing him where he stood.

"Damn," Heck said, standing over the bodies. "Now Doolin will never come back to this place."

Tilghman nodded. "Yeah, but I'm gonna get him anyway. I heard he's got a hidin' place in the Osage Nation." He glanced at Heck. "You game to go up there after him with me?"

"Hell, yes," Heck replied.

They headed for the ranch in the Indian Nations a few days later, finding it just where they'd been told it would be. They rode quietly up to the wooden structure, their guns loose and ready for trouble.

As they approached the ranch house, a man walked around the corner, his head down, not seeing the lawmen. Tilghman recognized him as Little Bill Raidler, a longtime member of the Doolin gang.

"Halt, Raidler. This is Bill Tilghman talkin'," Tilghman called out, jacking a shell into his Winchester.

When he heard the lawman's voice, Little Bill whirled around and drew, firing his gun. The slug passed within inches of Tilghman's head and he returned fire, striking Raidler in the right wrist and shattering the bone as the gun whirled away in the sunlight.

They doctored Raidler up as well as they could and took him to Guthrie, where he was placed under arrest. He would say nothing about the whereabouts of Bill Doolin.

After a few more unsuccessful attempts to locate

Doolin, Tilghman was about to give up when he got word Doolin's wife was in Winfield. Tilghman went to the Winfield post office to see if there'd been any mail delivered to her from her husband. The postmaster told Tilghman that Mr. Doolin was in Eureka Springs, Arkansas. He said the outlaw had gone there to visit the hot springs to ease his rheumatism.

Tilghman was on a stage the next day, headed for Eureka Springs. The coach he was riding pulled into Eureka Springs on December 5th. Tilghman went directly to the Basin Hotel. He checked in and left his rifle and baggage there to go in search of Bill Doolin.

As he walked through the lobby, Tilghman saw Doolin calmly sitting on a couch, reading a newspaper. When Doolin glanced up to see who was walking by, Tilghman turned his head and moved away.

Then he stopped for a moment, wondering if he should approach the wanted man in the crowded lobby, fearing innocent people would get shot if there were gunplay.

What the hell, he finally thought, *I been chasin' him all over creation. Can't let him get outta my sight now.*

Tilghman pulled his Colt and walked back to stand directly in front of Bill Doolin.

"Bill Doolin, you are under arrest," Tilghman said.

Doolin assumed an innocent look, glancing around at the people in the lobby, who had stopped to see what was going on.

"What's the meaning of this?" he asked, spreading his hands as if he had nothing to hide.

"I'm Deputy Marshal Tilghman," Bill said.

Doolin stood on hearing Bill's name and reached into his coat, trying to get to one of the pistols he wore in shoulder holsters under his coat.

Tilghman grabbed his arms and the two began to wrestle in the lobby, Bill knowing if Doolin got a gun out, there would be lead flying everywhere.

One of the hotel clerks came running up.

"What's going on here?" he asked.

As they struggled, Tilghman gasped out, "Get his guns out from under his coat while I hold him. I'm a marshal."

The clerk stepped gingerly around the wrestling men, trying to get at the guns under Doolin's coat. He managed to get the coat open, but Doolin growled, "I'm gonna kill you, kid!"

The clerk turned and ran from the room without a backward glance.

This put Tilghman at a disadvantage. Now that Doolin's coat was open, he was more likely to get to his guns sooner or later.

Tilghman gritted his teeth, released Doolin, and stepped back, whipping his Colt out of his holster before Doolin could draw.

"I'll shoot you, Bill, if you go for that gun!" Tilghman said, his voice low and hard and mean.

Doolin hesitated, as if figuring out whether he had a chance or not, then finally relaxed. His shoulders slumped and he hung his head as Tilghman leaned forward and removed two pistols from shoulder holsters under his coat.

The next day, Tilghman and Doolin boarded a train headed back to Oklahoma Territory.

With the arrest of Doolin in his dreams, the images faded and Bill Tilghman finally sank into a deep and dreamless sleep.

29

The next morning, after they all ate a breakfast of day-old biscuits and fried chicken, topped off with canned peaches that Sally had brought along on the train, the card game resumed among Louis, Cal, and Pearlie, while Monte joined Smoke and Sally and Bill Tilghman for another round of stories.

With the details fresh in his mind from his dreams of the night before, Bill was persuaded to tell the tale of his wrestling match with the famous outlaw Bill Doolin.

When he'd finished, he glanced at Smoke. "I hear tell you've had some righteous adventures yourself, Smoke. Ever wrestled a bad man to the end?"

Smoke smiled. "There were a few times," he said modestly.

"Tell him 'bout the time with the Sundance Kid an' his gang, up in the mountains," Monte urged, having been told the story by Smoke's old mountain man friend Puma Buck.

"Well . . ." Smoke hesitated, clearly embarrassed.

"Go on, dear," Sally said. "We'd all like to hear it to help pass the time away."

"The Sundance Kid was this young man who thought he was a bad hombre," Smoke started. "During a fight a year before, I'd cut his left ear off to make a point, hoping to save his life by getting him out of the gunfighting business."

"I take it the lesson didn't work," Tilghman said, smiling.

Smoke shook his head. "No, in fact it just made matters worse. Humiliated by the experience, the young man went down to Mexico and recruited a gang of toughs to come back up to Colorado and teach me a lesson. One thing led to another, and before long we were all up in the high lonesome in a fight to the death . . ."

Smoke was loaded for bear. He had his two Colt .44 pistols, a knife in his scabbard, a tomahawk in his belt against the small of his back, a Henry repeating rifle in one saddle boot, and a heavy Greener ten-gauge shotgun on a rawhide thong over his shoulder. He was ready to hunt, and to kill anything that got in his way.

He rode through thick ponderosa pines, making no sound that could be heard from more than a few feet away. By late afternoon he'd located the party of gunmen looking for him. Unused to traveling in the mountains, they were making so much noise they were easy to find.

Smoke stepped out of his saddle, leaving his horse ground-reined for a quick getaway should it be necessary, and slipped down a snowy slope toward a ribbon of trail the gang was following.

As the last man in line came abreast of his hiding place, Smoke took a running jump and leapt on the rider's horse behind him. Before the startled man could make a sound, Smoke slit his throat with his knife. Smoke pulled the dying man's gun from its holster and a knife hidden beneath the man's mackinaw as the outlaw slumped over his horse's withers.

He pushed the dead body out of the saddle, and threw the knife at the next rider in line. The blade buried itself in the gunman's back, causing him to arch forward, screaming in pain.

Smoke thumbed back the Colt's hammer and began to fire. Two more of Sundance's hired killers were mortally wounded before any had time to clear leather.

Smoke whirled the dead man's horse in a tight circle and galloped into the brush, leaning over the saddle to avoid low-hanging branches and limbs.

Sundance's gang jerked their reins and tried to turn around to give chase, but the trail was narrow and all they managed to do was to get in each other's way. Two men were knocked from their mounts, one sustaining a broken arm in the process.

Only minutes after the attack began, Smoke had disappeared and the gun hawks counted four dead and one injured, while not a shot had been fired at the mountain man.

Sundance was furious as he rode among his followers. "Goddamnit! You worthless bastards didn't fire a single round!" He leaned to the side and spat on one of the bodies lying in the dirt. "Hell, I thought I was ridin' with some tough gun slicks." He shook his head in disgust. "I might as well have hired schoolmarms, for all the help you galoots have been."

"Fuck it!" yelled Curly Bill Cartwright. "I'm gonna kill that son of a bitch!" He filled his hand with iron and spurred his horse into the brush after Smoke.

Three other men pulled guns and started to follow Cartwright.

"Hold on there," yelled Sundance. "That's just what Jensen wants us to do." He waved the gang toward him. "Circle up and get ready in case he comes back. We'll stay here and see what happens. Maybe Cartwright'll get lucky."

Lightning Jack chuckled. "I doubt that, Boss. He's goin' into Jensen's territory now, an' I'll bet a double eagle he don't come out."

A loud double explosion came from the forest, startling the outlaws' mounts, causing one of the Mexicans to begin shooting wildly toward the noise while shouting curses in Spanish.

The gang waited expectantly, every gun trained on the spot where Smoke and then Cartwright had entered a stand of dense trees. After a few moments the sound of a horse moving through brush could be heard.

The men cocked pistols and rifles as a horse walked out of the trees onto the trail. In its saddle was the decapitated body of Curly Bill Cartwright. His head and upper shoulders had been blown off by a double load of ten-gauge buckshot. A tree branch had been stuck down the back of his shirt and his feet were tied together under the animal's belly to keep him upright in his saddle.

Lightning Jack spoke quietly. "You think maybe Jensen's sending us a message, Boss?"

Sundance said, "Shit! I want to kill that bastard so bad I can taste it!"

Perro Muerte walked his horse over to Sundance. "What now, *jefe*? We go into trees, or stay on trail?"

Sundance said, "Stay on the trail. If we can locate his camp we can keep him from gettin' to his supplies and ammunition. Sooner or later, he'll run low and then we can take him." He pointed to Jeremiah Gray Wolf. "Take the point, Gray Wolf, and see if'n you can find some tracks or sign showing which way his camp might be."

Moses Washburn spoke in a low voice to Bull. "I don't like this, Bull. I don't like it one bit."

Bull shook his head. "Me either, partner, me either."

Jeremiah Gray Wolf leaned over his saddle and began to walk his pony up the trail, followed twenty yards back by the rest of the group.

After a quarter of a mile, he held up his hand and called over his shoulder, "I've found some tracks. Let's go."

The Indian straightened in his saddle and spurred his mount into a trot, disappearing around a bend in the trail. The others drew weapons and followed him from a distance.

Sundance rounded the bend and stopped short when

he saw Gray Wolf's pony standing riderless by the side of the trail, grazing on the short grass partially hidden by melting snow. "Shit," he whispered under his breath. He hadn't heard a sound, not even a call for help.

When the rest of his men rode up to him, Sundance slowly urged his horse forward, scanning trees and brush on either side for a sign of Gray Wolf.

From behind him, Sundance heard a sharp intake of breath, and the words *"Madre de Dios,"* spoken in a hoarse whisper. He turned to see Perro Muerte crossing himself and staring up at a nearby tree.

He followed Perro Muerte's gaze, and found Jeremiah Gray Wolf hanging from a limb, a rope around his neck, his legs still kicking, quivering in death throes. The half-breed's bowels had let loose and the stench was overpowering.

Sundance held his bandanna across his nose and rode over to examine the area under the body. Horse tracks showed that Smoke had probably roped the man while hiding in the tree, then dropped to his horse, pulling Gray Wolf out of his saddle by a rope he'd looped over the branch.

Bull said, "He never knew what hit him."

"Shut up!" yelled Sundance. "Come on, Jensen can't be more'n a few hundred feet away. Let's go!"

The group cocked their weapons and started to follow Sundance up a steep slope past the tree with the body hanging from it. It was a steep grade, covered with loose gravel and small stones, and they were only about halfway up the incline when a gunshot from above caught their attention.

They looked up to see Smoke standing next to a large pile of boulders, grinning, holding something in one hand and a smoking cigar in the other. He cried, "Howdy, gents," and put his cigar against the object in his other hand. As a fuse began to sputter and sparkle, he dropped the bundle amongst the rocks and ducked out of sight.

"Holy shit, it's dynamite," yelled Moses Washburn as he jerked his reins and tried to turn his horse around. The men all panicked and reined their horses to turn in different directions, running into each other, knocking men and animals to the ground.

The explosion was strangely muffled and it didn't sound very loud, yet the pile of boulders shifted. Slowly at first, then with gathering speed, huge rocks rolled and tumbled, racing down the slope, bounding as they descended toward the trapped riders milling about on the trail.

A huge dust cloud enveloped the area, covering screaming men and horses as rocks crushed bones and flattened bodies and ended lives.

When dust had settled, the only men left alive were Sundance, Lightning Jack, Bull, and Perro Muerte. The slide had killed four Texas gunfighters and Moses Washburn, who could only be identified by a black hand showing from beneath a huge boulder. Nothing but his hand was visible.

In the sudden quiet of dusk, the remaining men could hear the sounds of Jensen's horse in the distance galloping up the mountain.

"Moses," Bull said through gritted teeth, "I'm gonna kill him for you."

Sundance took a deep breath, looking around at all that was left of his band. "Okay, boys. He's headed straight up the mountain. There ain't much cover up there, an' there ain't nowhere to run to once he gits to the top."

He pulled his pistol and checked his loads. "Let's go git him!"

The moon had risen and, in a cloudless sky, it made the area as bright as day. Smoke was hidden in his natural fortress, leaning over the edge, peering below through his binoculars, waiting for Sundance and his men. It was time to end it, and he was ready.

There was movement below, and Smoke could see Bull and Perro Muerte crawling on hands and knees off to his right. They were going to try to inch up the slope, using small logs and rocks on that side for cover. Smoke grinned, remembering tricks Cal had devised for just that eventuality.

Smoke waited until they were halfway up the incline. Bull, panting heavily in thin air, motioned for Perro Muerte to stop so he could catch his breath.

Smoke worked the lever on his Henry and sighted down the barrel. "Hey, Bull!" he cried.

The big man squinted in semidarkness, trying to see where Jensen's voice was coming from, hoping to get off a lucky shot. "Yeah, whatta ya want, Jensen? You wanna know how I'm gonna kill you?"

Smoke grinned. "No, I was just wondering if you'd noticed all those gourds and pumpkins down there."

Bull and Perro Muerte glanced around them, and saw for the first time a number of small squash and pumpkins resting on the ground. Bull looked up the slope. "Yeah, what about it? You hungry?"

Smoke laughed out loud, his voice echoing off surrounding ridges. "Did you ever wonder, you ignorant bastard, how gourds could grow on bare rock?"

Bull's eyes widened in horror and he opened his mouth to scream as he realized the trap they had fallen into.

Smoke squeezed his trigger, firing into the pumpkin directly in front of Bull and the Mexican. Molten lead entered the gourd, igniting black powder. The object exploded, blasting hundreds of small stones hurtling outward. Bull and Perro Muerte's bodies were riddled, shredded, blown to pieces. They died instantly.

Below, Sundance sleeved sweat off his forehead and turned to Lightning Jack. "Maybe we ought'a head down the mountain and come back later, with more men."

Lightning Jack looked at the gunfighter with disgust. "You low-down coward. You got over thirty good men killed lookin' fer yore vengeance. You ain't backin' out now."

Sundance dropped his hand to his Colt, but froze when a voice behind them said, "Hold it right there, gents."

Lightning Jack and Sundance turned to see a small, wiry man in buckskins pointing a shotgun at their heads. "Ease them irons outta those holsters and grab some sky."

As they dropped their pistols to the ground, Puma called out, "Hey, Smoke. I got me a couple of polecats in my sights. What do you want me to do with 'em?"

"Bring 'em up here."

Puma pointed up the hill with his scattergun. "Git."

As the outlaws struggled uphill, the mountain man, more than twice their age, walked nimbly up the slope with never a misstep, nor was he breathing hard when they reached the top.

Smoke stood there, hands on hips, shaking his head at Puma. "It's easier to tree a grizzly than to keep you ornery old-timers out of a good fight."

Puma nodded. "Yeah, I'd rather bed down with a skunk than miss a good fracas." He cut his eyes over at Smoke. "You want me to dust 'em now, or just stake 'em out over an anthill?"

Sundance's eyes widened. "You wouldn't do that . . . would you, you son of a bitch?"

Smoke pursed his lips, rubbing his chin. "Well, I'm feelin' real generous tonight. How about you boys picking your own way to die? Guns, knives, fists, or boots, it makes no difference to me."

Lightning Jack grinned, flexing his muscles while clenching his fists. "You man enough to take me on hand to hand?" He inclined his head toward Puma. "Winner goes free?"

Smoke removed belt and holsters, took a pair of padded black gloves out of his pants, and began to pull them on. "Puma, if this loudmouth beats me, take his left ear as a souvenir and let him go."

Puma grunted and spat on the ground. "How 'bout I take his topknot instead?"

"Wait a minute . . ." began Lightning Jack, until Puma jacked back the hammers on his shotgun, shutting his mouth for now.

Smoke stepped into the middle of a level area at the top of the plateau. He bowed slightly and said, "Let's dance!"

Lightning Jack worked his shoulders, loosening up. "Any rules?"

Smoke grinned, but his eyes held no warmth. "Yeah, the man left alive at the end is the winner."

"Just the way I like it. Say good-bye to your friend, mountain man."

The two men circled slowly, bobbing and weaving and throwing an occasional feint to test their opponent's reflexes. Lightning Jack suddenly rushed at Smoke swinging roundhouse blows with both arms. Smoke ducked his chin into his chest, hunched his shoulders, and took two heavy blows on his arms. He grunted with pain, and thought, *This man can hit like a mule!* As Jack drew back to swing again, Smoke unloaded two short, sharp left jabs, both landing on Jack's nose, flattening it, snapping his head back hard enough so that Puma could hear his neck crack.

Jack shook his head, flinging blood and snot in the air, a dazed look on his face. Smoke stood, spread-eagled, his fists in front of him, waiting patiently.

After a pause Jack sleeved blood off his lip and felt his flattened nose. He glared at Smoke, hate in his eyes. Growling like an animal, he advanced toward the mountain man, pumping his arms while swinging his fists.

Smoke stepped lightly to one side and swung a left cross against Jack's chin, stopping him in his tracks. Smoke followed with a straight right to the middle of his chest, knocking him backward, rocking him back on his heels. Another left jab to the forehead to straighten him up, and then a mighty uppercut to his solar plexus, just under his sternum, lifted him up on his toes before he fell to one knee. Jack remained there a few moments, catching his breath.

He looked up at Smoke, blood pouring from his ruined nose. He grinned wickedly, then snatched a slender knife from his boot and rushed at Smoke with the blade extended.

Smoke took the blade in the outer part of his left shoulder, bent to his right, and swung with all his might. His fist hit Jack in the throat, crushing his larynx with a sharp, crunching sound. The knife slipped from Jack's numb fingers and he fell to his knees, grabbing his neck with both hands. A loud, whistling wheeze came from his mouth as he tried to pull air in through his broken trachea, and his eyes widened, bugging out like a frightened frog. His skin turned dusky blue, then black as he ran out of air. His eyes glazed over and he died, falling on his face in the dirt.

Smoke took the knife handle in his right hand, closed his eyes and set his jaw, and yanked it free with a jerk. He staggered at the pain, then straightened, a steely glint in his eye as blood seeped from the wound to stain his shirt.

Puma started toward him, but Smoke waved him away. "Not yet, Puma. We got one more snake to stomp 'fore we're through."

Sundance stuttered, "But I'm not much good with my fists. I ain't no prizefighter."

"You fancy yourself a gunfighter?"

"Yeah, and I'm a hell of a lot better'n I was last time you bushwhacked me, Jensen. I been practicing for years."

Smoke, his left arm hanging limp at his side, bent down and picked up belt and holsters. "Buckle this on for me, would you, Puma?"

Puma placed the guns around Smoke's waist and snapped the buckle shut, then tied the right-hand holster down low on his thigh. Smoke slipped the hammer-thongs off both guns, using his right hand, stepping over to the center of the plateau. "Give the lowlife his pistols, Puma, then watch your back. Sundance is famous for shooting people from the north when they're facing south."

Sundance put his hand on the handle of his Colt. "You're gonna die for that, Jensen."

The two men squared off, thirty yards apart, hands hanging loose, fingers flexing in anticipation. "You called this play, Sundance. Now it's time for you to pay the band. Fill your damn hand!"

Sundance snarled and grabbed for his pistol, crouching and turning slightly sideways to give Smoke less of a target. Smoke waited a second, giving the gunfighter time to get his gun halfway out of his holster. In a move that was so fast Puma blinked and missed it, Smoke cleared leather and fired. His bullet took Sundance in the right wrist, snapping it, flinging his Colt into the dirt.

Sundance howled, cradling his right hand with his left, hunched over, tears running down his cheeks. "Okay, you bastard. You win," he sobbed.

Smoke shook his head. "No, I don't think so. You've got another gun and another hand. Use 'em."

Sundance looked up in astonishment. "My left hand against your right? That ain't fair!"

Smoke shook his head, twirled his right-hand Colt once, and then settled it in his holster. "I'll cross-draw my left gun, if that's more to your liking."

Sundance's lips curled in a tight smile. The cross-draw wasn't a speed draw. No one could beat him with a cross-draw, even left-handed, he thought. "Okay. It's your call, Jensen."

He stood up, threw his shoulders back, and went for his iron.

Smoke's right hand flashed across his belly, drawing and firing again before Sundance could fist his weapon. This time, Smoke's slug took the outlaw in his left shoulder, shattering it while spinning him around to land facedown on the ground.

Smoke looked at Puma. "Bring me a rope from that bag over yonder."

He took the rope from Puma, formed a large loop, and passed it over Sundance's arms to tie it around his chest. He dragged the sobbing, sniffling gunman across the plateau to the edge of the cliff on the east side of the clearing.

"Help me lower him down onto that ledge down there, Puma."

"What . . . what are you doing? No . . . no . . . please . . ."

The two mountain men lowered the crying outlaw twenty feet down the side of the sheer cliff, letting him down gently on a three-foot ledge that stuck out over a drop of two hundred feet.

Smoke leaned over the edge and called down. "I'm gonna do something for you that you never did for your victims, Sundance. I'm gonna give you a choice of the way you want to die. You can lay there on that ledge and slowly starve to death, or you can jump and fall two hundred feet so you'll die quick. It's all up to you."

"Wait, you can't do this to me. It ain't right . . ."

Smoke and Puma slowly walked away, ignoring cries from the coward below. Neither one much cared how he chose to die, just so long as he died, and that was a certainty.

"You want me to fix up that there shoulder?" Puma Buck asked as they reached the horses.

"Naw," Smoke replied. "Just get me home to Sally. She's a lot more gentle than you are, you old grizzly."

Puma smiled. "Yeah, Lord knows we don't want nobody to treat you rough, Smoke Jensen."*

Tilghman shook his head. "Smoke, that makes my little fracas seem like a Sunday school outin'."

Smoke shrugged. "Bill, things were a lot different back then, and especially up in the high lonesome. The only rules were there were *no* rules."

Vengeance of the Mountain Man

30

When the train pulled into the station at Houston, Smoke's group exited and got their baggage from the baggage car.

"What now?" Tilghman asked. "Do we head for Galveston right away?"

Smoke glanced at Sally, who was stretching and trying to get the kinks out caused by two days on a rough-riding railroad car.

"If it's all the same to you, Marshal, I think we could all do with some good cooking and a night in a fine hotel," he said.

Sally grinned in relief. "Yes, please. One with a hot bath and a soft feather mattress."

Tilghman grinned. "I guess another day won't make much difference. I hear it's almost fifty miles to Galveston, and to tell you the truth, I don't hanker to spend another couple of days in a stagecoach right now."

They went to the biggest hotel they could find, one called the Capitol Hotel. The proprietor told them the beautiful building had once been the capitol building of Texas, until the government was moved to Austin.

"All I want to know," Sally said, "is do you have a bath with hot water?"

The desk clerk looked offended. "But of course,

madam. The Capitol has all the modern conveniences, as well as a first-rate dining room."

Pearlie's ears picked up at the mention of a dining room. "Forget about the bath, just show me where the grub is," he said with relish.

Sally gave him a stern look. "Pearlie, if you plan to eat with us, you *will* take a bath first. After all," she said, a look of mock earnestness on her face, "cleanliness is next to godliness."

"Yeah, but starvation isn't," Pearlie moaned, picking his bags up and trudging up the stairs while the others laughed at his woebegone expression.

The next morning, after all were well rested and well fed, Smoke hired a special stage just for them for the two-day journey to Galveston.

As they boarded the stage, the station master warned, "Y'all be careful now. There's been reports of Mexican *bandidos* stoppin' some of the coaches."

"I don't believe we have to worry about that," Smoke said with a grin. "We have the famous U.S. Deputy Marshal Bill Tilghman with us."

The stationmaster frowned and leaned over to spit tobacco juice in the dirt. "Yeah, well, I'm sure the *mexicanos* will be impressed when they shoot you full of holes."

As they bounced and rumbled over the trail from Houston toward Galveston, Sally noticed the sparkling gold badge Tilghman had pinned on his shirt under his vest.

"That's a very interesting badge you have there, Mr. Tilghman," she said. "It looks almost as if it's made of gold."

"It is," Tilghman answered shortly.

"Man," Monte observed, "I've gotta get me a job with the U.S. Marshals Service if they're givin' out badges made of gold now."

Tilghman laughed. "No, Monte. It didn't come with the job. Back when I was first appointed, a group of my friends had a blacksmith hammer this one out of two twenty-dollar gold pieces. It's a bit gaudy for my taste, but"—he shrugged—"what could I do? I didn't want to insult my friends."

"They must've really appreciated what you were doin' for them," Cal said from the seat opposite.

Tilghman shook his head. "Let me tell you something about law enforcement, Cal. The average citizen appreciates what you're doin' for him only so long as it doesn't inconvenience him in any way. But as soon as you tell him he can't walk his horse on a boardwalk or carry a gun inside the town limits, suddenly you're not so popular anymore."

Smoke was about to add he'd lost a lot of so-called good friends when they found out he was a gunfighter, but he was interrupted by the sound of distant shots and the driver yelling "Whoa" to the horses pulling the stage.

Pearlie leaned his head out the window, his hand holding his hat to keep it from blowing off. He ducked back inside, his hand going for the butt of his pistol.

"Uh-oh," he said, looking from man to man in the coach, "looks like trouble up ahead."

"What is it?" Smoke asked, unhooking the rawhide thongs on his twin Colts as the other men did the same.

"Looks like about ten or fifteen men on horseback in the middle of the road ahead, just sittin' there with rifle butts restin' on their thighs."

Sally pulled her purse around, opened it, and withdrew her short-barreled .32 Smith and Wesson. She arranged her frock coat to cover it as she stuck it in the waistband of her dress.

When the stage ground to a halt, the brake making a high-pitched squealing sound as it slowed the steel-rimmed wheels to a stop, everyone piled out of the stage, looking ahead at the group of men sitting on their horses in front of the team pulling the stage.

The driver already had his hands above his head.

"We ain't carryin' no gold," he called to the man at the front of the pack, the evident leader.

He was a broad-shouldered Mexican, squat bordering on fat, Mexican with crossed bandoliers of shotgun shells on his chest and a sawed-off Greener in his hands.

"*Buenos dias, señores e señoritas,*" he said, pulling his large Mexican sombrero off and sweeping it before him in an elaborate bow. "I am El Gato," he added, then said in English, "That means mountain cat."

"We understand Mex," Tilghman said, his voice hard and unfriendly. "What do you want?"

"Why, nothing much, *señor*. My compadres and me," he said, sweeping his arms out to point at the men riding with him, "are poor *vaqueros*, who want nothing more than a few pesos to feed our hungry children."

As he spoke, Monte, Louis, Smoke, Cal, and Pearlie slowly edged sideways to be away from Sally so when the shooting started, as they all knew it would, she wouldn't be in the direct line of fire.

"You men will get nothing from us," Tilghman said, letting his hands move closer to his pistols.

"Aw, *señor,* that is most unfriendly," El Gato said, opening his mouth in a wide grin, exposing blackened stubs of teeth.

"Where are you from, mister?" Tilghman asked.

"Just across the border, *señor,* a place called Piedras Negras. Why do you ask?"

"I just wondered if they didn't have dentists where you come from," Tilghman said, trying to goad the man into action.

The smile faded from El Gato's face. "As I said," he went on, twisting in his saddle to look around at his men, "the *señor* is not being friendly."

"You've got five seconds to get out of the way an' let this stage proceed," Tilghman said, moving his vest so El Gato could see the golden badge. "I'm a U.S. marshal, an' I'm orderin' you out of the way."

El Gato's voice became harsh and he frowned as he leaned over the saddle horn. "You do not order El Gato," he growled. "Can you not see I have fifteen men to your six?"

"I know the odds aren't fair," Tilghman replied scornfully, "but we just don't have time for you to go an' get more men."

El Gato's eyes widened in amazement and he started to lower the barrel of his shotgun.

Smoke's group all drew at one time, with Louis's and Tilghman's pistols firing a split second after Smoke's, and Cal and Pearlie's a split second after theirs.

Smoke and Tilghman both aimed for El Gato, figuring without their leader, the other *bandidos* wouldn't be as brave. El Gato took two slugs before he could aim his shotgun, one in the forehead and the other in the belly. He grunted as his head snapped back and he somersaulted over his horse's rump to land face-down in the dirt of the road.

His men managed to get off two wild shots before the fusillade from Smoke's friends tore into them, knocking them off their horses like a hurricane wind whipping through the coastal plains grasses.

Horses snorted and crow-hopped at the tremendous explosion of all the guns. Men yelled and screamed in pain, and still the guns kept firing.

Sally, only a second slower than the men, had her .32 in her hand and knocked two of the bandits out of their saddles before they could clear leather.

Monte got three men, Cal two, and Pearlie three within seconds of beginning the dance. Smoke and Tilghman whirled to the side and accounted for the rest.

As the giant cloud of gunsmoke and cordite slowly drifted away on the Texas breeze coming in from the Gulf of Mexico, bodies could be seen lying sprawled all over the landscape, some still moving in pain or trying to crawl away on hands and knees, dripping blood to mix with the dirt and form a scarlet mud that reeked of death.

"Should we finish them off, Marshal?" Pearlie asked.

Tilghman shook his head. "No, just take their weapons and scatter their horses. If the coyotes and wolves don't finish them, the buzzards will."

The stagecoach driver coughed and choked, and finally leaned over the side of the stage and vomited several times.

"What's the matter?" Tilghman asked him, walking to the side of the coach. "You hit?"

When the purple-faced man could finally speak, he said, "Hell, no! When all the shootin' started, I plumb swallowed my chaw of tobaccy. Damn near killed me!"

Tilghman laughed and walked over to Smoke, who was making sure Sally was all right.

"Yes, dear," she said, making a face. "But I ripped my dress pulling out my Smith and Wesson, and I didn't pack my sewing kit."

Smoke shook his head and turned to watch Cal and Pearlie and Monte move among the wounded men, picking up their guns and shooing their horses away.

Louis walked up to Smoke and Tilghman and grimaced. "Damn," he said, a disgusted look on his face.

"What is it, Louis?" Smoke asked as Tilghman looked on.

"Now there are two men who are *almost* as fast on the draw as I am."

Smoke chuckled, glancing at Tilghman. "Do you think we should just let him go on in his delusion?"

Tilghman smiled. "Sure, why not? I've always said, it's not who's the fastest on the draw that counts, it's who puts his lead where it needs to go that counts most in a gunfight."

"By the way, Marshal," Smoke asked, "you mind telling me why you shot El Gato in the stomach instead of the chest or head?"

"We have a sayin' in the Marshals Service, Smoke. Two in the belly an' one in the head sure makes a man dead."

He grinned. "I was just startin' on the belly when you beat me to the draw an' put one in his head."

Smoke and Louis laughed.

"That's pretty good, Marshal," Louis said.

"And true too," Smoke added. "I've seen men take so much lead they'd sink if they tried to swim, and still manage to get off a few rounds before they died."

Tilghman nodded. "I made a deal with myself the day I went into bein' a lawman. If I ever have to shoot, I'm gonna shoot till the job gets done. It's the only way to survive."

"Amen," Monte said from behind him.

31

The stagecoach pulled up at a large dock, bustling with activity. Across the bay, dim outlines of Galveston Island could be seen through sea mist hanging low over the warm salt water. There were wagons lined up for the ferry carrying all manner of agricultural goods, but most prevalent were the many bales of cotton, stacked one or two to a wagon.

"My goodness," Sally observed. "This place looks busier than Dallas."

The stage driver leaned to the side and spat his ever-present tobacco juice onto the salt grass alongside the road. "It is, ma'am. Up north, all they talk about is cattle, but down here, 'cept for the King Ranch, of course, cotton is king."

After waiting in line for some time, the stage was finally allowed on the ferry and they made the short trip across the bay without incident, though Pearlie refused to get out of the coach and walk around the ferry as the others did.

"If God'd wanted man near this much water," the cowboy said from his seat inside the stage, "He'd've made us with webbed feet like ducks."

Finally, they made their way to downtown Galveston, which was just a few blocks from the beachfront, and Sally was amazed to see large, fine homes comparable to any she'd seen on her travels to visit her family in New York City.

The group disembarked at the stage depot, where there was another group of people waiting to make the trip back to Houston, it being a common destination for the well-to-do to travel to for both business and pleasure.

Smoke paid off the driver, and they proceeded to the Galvez Hotel, which was on a bluff overlooking the breaking waves of the Gulf of Mexico and the pure white beaches of the island.

"Let's get some grub and make some plans on how to find Gomez and Gatling," Smoke suggested.

"That sounds good to me," Pearlie piped up from the rear of the group.

Cal looked at him. "The mention of food always sounds good to you, Pearlie," he observed drily.

Down on the waterfront, Three-Fingers Gomez and Curly Bob Gatling, just awaking from a night of revelry in the red-light district of Galveston, gathered for breakfast at a small diner frequented by seamen.

The Albatross was a small, single-roomed shack made of what looked like driftwood and old lumber washed up on shore during storms, and was just up the beach above the high-water line of seaweed, set back in the sand dunes.

Its main attraction wasn't the cuisine, which was plain but adequate. It was the wide selection of liquors and beers that were served at all hours, breakfast being no exception.

As the two men leaned over their food in the dimly lit diner, Three-Fingers Gomez said, "When did they say that ship would be sailin'?"

"Tomorrow," Curly Bob Gatling answered as he shoveled runny scrambled eggs into his mouth, washing them down with coffee so black and strong he could almost chew it.

"Damn," Gomez said, glancing out the window at the many ships moored in Galveston Harbor. "With all them boats out there, you'd think they'd have some goin' our way 'fore then."

Gatling shrugged as he held up his cup to show the waiter he wanted a refill. "They do, but most of 'em are freighters, an' they don't carry but a couple'a passengers each. I got us in line to get the first places available."

When Gomez grunted gloomily and began to eat his food, Gatling asked, "Why are you so jumpy? Why not just sit back and enjoy the nightlife here? Hell, they got more good-lookin' women here than I ever seen before, an' we finally got some spendin' money in our pockets from sellin' those beeves."

"It's just that I got this here itch on the back of my neck, like somebody's on our back trail. I can't enjoy myself for lookin' back over my shoulder to see who might be there."

Gatling leaned back and lit a cigarette, blowing the smoke toward the ceiling, where it mingled with clouds of smoke from the other patrons in the place.

"One thing I've learned after all my years ridin' the owl-hoot trail, podna, is that you can't think about what may be behind you. If you do, you soon go crazy in the head."

Gomez shook his head. "How do you stop?"

"You got to live one day at a time. . . . You got to figure you're gonna take a dirt nap soon enough, so worryin' about it don't do no good. When it happens, it happens."

Gomez finished his eggs and coffee and pushed the plate away from him on the table.

"That's easy for you to say, Curly Bob, but you didn't put that bullet in the Kid, an' you don't have that Jensen feller on your trail."

"What do you mean by that?" Gatling asked hotly. "We're partners, ain't we? If they after you, that means they after me too. When it comes right down to it, if Jensen's still alive, which I doubt, he ain't gonna just come up to us an' say, 'Which one of you shot the Kid?'" He shook his head. "Nope. He's gonna just show up an' start blazin' away with those big Colts of his, so I got as much to lose as you, Three-Fingers."

Gomez glanced across the table and smiled. "I know, Curly Bob. You are a good friend, and I know I can count on you if push comes to shove."

"That's right!" Gatling said, nodding his head and grinning. "Now, we got twenty-four hours till we set sail for the East Coast, so let's see how many women we can bag, an' how much whiskey we can drink, between now and then."

After settling in at the Galvez and cleaning up from their dusty journey from Houston, the group met at the Galvez Restaurant, where they dined on red snapper, speckled trout, fresh blue crabs, and oysters on the half shell, along with fried potatoes, coleslaw, and corn bread.

Pearlie eyed the oysters skeptically. "I don't know 'bout eatin' those things," he drawled from the end of the long table in the dining room.

He picked up an oyster shell and held it under his nose, sniffing.

"Don't smell it, Pearlie," Sally said, "eat it." She took a shell in her hand, poured some red sauce on it, and tipped it up, letting it slide down her throat in one gulp.

Pearlie watched her through narrowed eyes. "What's it taste like?" he asked.

"Delicious," Sally said, a pleased expression on her face. "I haven't had food this good since New York."

Pearlie was thinking, but had the manners not to say, that he wasn't sure he wanted to eat food that looked like something he'd hawked up from the back of his throat.

"They say," Louis Longmont said as he tipped a shell and swallowed the shellfish, "that oysters are good for your nature."

"Nature?" Pearlie asked. "They ain't nothin' wrong with my nature."

"What's nature?" Cal asked innocently, his eyebrows raised.

As the men at the table laughed, and Sally blushed,

Monte said, "It's something somebody your age don't have to worry none about, Cal."

"How about you, Monte?" Louis asked. "Are you going to partake of one of the sea's best delicacies?"

Monte shook his head. "No, Louis. My nature don't need no stirrin' up, not with Mary a thousand miles away." He smiled. "Though I might see if I can take some back to Big Rock with me."

As Smoke wolfed down a quick half-dozen of the oysters, Sally glanced at him and leaned over to whisper in his ear, "Go easy on those, big fellow. You don't need any help with your nature either. It's fine just as it is."

After they finished the meal, Sally went to browse the shops along the waterfront next to the hotel, and the men went to the shipping offices at the Port Authority.

While Tilghman and Smoke went in to talk to the clerk, Monte and Louis and Cal and Pearlie strolled along the beach, picking up shells and enjoying the balmy day.

A half hour later, Smoke and Tilghman emerged, smiles on their faces.

"What did you find out?" Louis asked.

"Yeah," Monte said. "We asked around out here an' word is there's more'n a hundred bars and saloons and houses of ill repute along the wharf. Ain't no way we're gonna find two men among all those, not unless we get awful lucky."

"We got lucky," Tilghman said. "The clerk in there went through the records for us an' found a Juan Gomez an' Robert Gatling scheduled to sail out on the *Sea Sprite* tomorrow morning to Georgia."

"I can't believe they're still here," Pearlie said. "They had a two- or three-day start on us."

"There again, we got lucky," Smoke said. "The clerk told us the ships were backed up and running late due to some storms in the Gulf. There hasn't been a ship out of here for the past four days, or they'd probably be long gone."

"So what's the plan?" Monte asked.

Smoke shrugged. "I'm going to relax and spend the day with Sally, shopping and seeing the sights. It isn't often we get to make a trip like this together. Then tomorrow, at dawn, Marshal Tilghman and I are going to get on the ship early and be waiting for the two killers when they board."

"What about us?" Cal asked, a disappointed look on his face.

"You'll be our backup," Marshal Tilghman said. "You'll cover the roads to the ferry and the area around the ships' loading docks, just in case they decide to leave Galveston instead of boarding the ship, or in case they get by us."

Louis nodded and cracked his knuckles, stretching his fingers. "Well, while you play dutiful husband, Smoke, I'm going to check out the various gaming establishments along the shore here and see if Texicans can play poker any better than the men in Colorado."

Pearlie smiled. "You mind if Cal an' I tag along, Louis? I want to try out what you taught us on the train, see if'n I can win some money."

Louis laughed. "Not at all, Pearlie. How about you, Monte?"

Monte shrugged. "Sure, why not? Beats hanging around the hotel missin' my wife."

Smoke nodded and left, going to look for Sally. He wanted to see if the oysters really *did* make a difference.

The next morning Smoke and Tilghman, followed by Louis, Monte, Cal, and Pearlie, walked through a fog so thick you could cut it with a knife. The sun wasn't quite up, but the eastern clouds were beginning to turn a brilliant orange and red and yellow on the horizon.

When they got to the dock where the *Sea Sprite* was moored, Tilghman stationed the other men around the area as a precaution, and he and Smoke walked up the gangplank.

A burly sailor, his massive arms covered with tattoos, started to stop them, but backed off when Tilghman pulled his vest back and showed him his gold badge.

They went to the quartermaster and asked him which cabin was assigned to Gomez and Gatling.

"Number three," he said, and led them down a long, dark, dank corridor to the room, which he opened for them.

The cabin was incredibly small, and both Tilghman and Smoke had to duck their heads, not being able to stand erect in the tiny enclosure.

"We can't wait for 'em here," Tilghman said. "No room to maneuver in case they resist."

"You're right," Smoke said. "Let's get settled up on deck. We can brace them there when they come aboard."

They searched the upper deck until they found the right place to hide, just behind the opening to the belowdecks area. It was a small, raised wooden structure that would keep them concealed until the two men were well on board. Then they could step out and arrest them.

Smoke and Tilghman settled down, sitting on coils of rope as thick as Smoke's arm, and smoked and talked of western things until it was almost eight o'clock.

Tilghman peeked over the wooden structure, and could see several people making their way toward the ship. "Time to get ready."

Smoke smiled. "Strike up the band?" he asked.

Tilghman grinned back. "Start the dance," he added.

Three-Fingers Gomez and Curly Bob Gatling strolled up the gangplank. Gomez was smiling and whistling, and Gatling laughed. "See, partner?" Gatling said, nudging Gomez with his elbow. "I told you we didn't have nothin' to worry about. Jensen's dead, an' we're on our way to Georgia."

Smoke and Bill Tilghman stepped out from behind the

entranceway to the cabins, their hands hanging next to their pistol butts.

"The reports of my death have been greatly exaggerated," Smoke drawled, a grim smile on his face.

"Goddamn!" Gatling exclaimed, stopping dead in his tracks and dropping the duffel bag he had slung over his shoulder.

He glanced at Gomez, who shook his head.

"I knew it," he said morosely. "I told you I felt someone on our trail."

"Juan Gomez and Robert Gatling," Tilghman said in a formal tone of voice, "I'm a U.S. deputy marshal and I arrest you for the murder of Jim Slade, known as the Durango Kid."

Gatling held out his hands. "I didn't have nothin' to do with the Kid's murder," he said, a whining note in his voice.

"But you *did* conspire to have Smoke Jensen murdered by paying some *vaqueros* to kill him, didn't you?" Tilghman asked.

"Shit!" Gatling said.

"I think you boys have a date with George Maledon," Tilghman said grimly.

"Who's this Maledon feller?" Gomez asked. "I don't know no Maledon."

"He's known as the prince of hangmen," Tilghman said. "He is the chief executioner for Judge Isaac Parker, the man who's gonna judge you boys."

Gomez began backing away, his hands near his pistol. "I ain't gonna get my neck stretched for killin' a snake like the Durango Kid. It ain't fair," he said, sweat breaking out on his forehead.

"It ain't fair to be shot in the back either," Smoke said, "but the Kid didn't have any choice in the matter, and neither do you, Gomez."

"Yes, I do!" Gomez said, going for his gun.

Gatling did the same, crouching and slapping at his holster.

Smoke and Tilghman drew in the same instant, guns coming up and firing almost simultaneously, twin explosions that shattered the peaceful morning and caused seagulls to wheel away from the ship, keening and screeching in fear.

Gomez flung his arms backward, his pistol still in its holster, as the molten lead from Smoke's Colt punched a hole in his chest and exploded his heart. He whirled around and fell facedown on the deck of the ship, smashing his nose and breaking three of his front teeth. . . . But he felt no pain. He was dead before he hit the deck.

Tilghman's slug took Gatling in the gut, his gun also still in its holster, and doubled him over, so that Tilghman's next shot entered the top of his head and drove him to his knees. He stayed in the bent-over position for a few seconds, as if giving up a prayer for his sins, before he toppled over to sprawl on the deck, leaking blood and brains over the hardwood planks.

Smoke took a deep breath and sighed as he put his Colt back in its holster.

Tilghman just let his hand drop to his side, shaking his head at the waste of human life he'd seen.

Tilghman turned his head and stared at Smoke. "I'd always heard you were fast enough to snatch a quarter off a snake's head and leave change 'fore he could strike. I guess I heard right."

Smoke laughed. "I think you beat me by a split second, Marshal."

Tilghman shook his head. "No way, Smoke. It was a dead heat."

"Remind me never to draw against you, Bill," Smoke said.

"Don't worry, mountain man, I will!"

32

Smoke and everyone said their good-byes to Marshal Bill Tilghman at the ferry on the mainland side of the Bay of Galveston. He was heading back north to Arkansas to file his report on the murder of the Durango Kid, while Smoke and his friends were heading south to Corpus Christi and the King Ranch.

Smoke stuck out his hand. "Marshal, it's been a pleasure knowing you."

Tilghman took his hand and shook it. "Same here, Smoke. I'll be sure and clear your name with Judge Parker an' let him know it was all a mistake."

"So, I don't need to stop by there on my way back to Colorado?"

Tilghman smiled and glanced at Sally. "No, I don't think so. Besides, from what I hear, the judge would just as soon not have to face Mrs. Jensen again. It seems she made quite an impression on him at their last meetin'."

Smoke raised his eyebrows. "Oh, is that so?"

"Yeah," Tilghman said, laughing. "He said something about how he'd rather face a mad dog than another woman like her takin' up for her man in his court."

Smoke smiled at Sally. "She does have a rather . . . forceful way about her when her dander's up," he said.

"I resent that," Sally said, her face reddening. "I just told him the truth, that Smoke Jensen would never shoot anyone in the back."

"Oh, it's not what you said, Miss Sally," Tilghman said, "it's how you said it. You see, the judge, he kind'a feels like he's the king of his courtroom, an' he's not used to someone gettin' in his face like you did. It upsets his equilibrium somehow."

"Well," Sally said, standing up straight, "the only king in my world is Smoke, and the judge will just have to accept that fact."

Smoke and his group of friends spent an enjoyable week at the King Ranch near Corpus Christi. Sally was much impressed by the modern way Richard King and his foreman used new scientific methods to improve the breed of cattle known as Santa Gertrudis. She hounded the poor foreman for several days, inquiring about bloodlines and breeding methods and feed and the amount of meat they could expect from their shorthorn crosses with the Gertrudis bulls, until by the time they'd taken the bulls to the train yards for shipment to Colorado, he was glad to see her go.

While Sally was inquiring into the breeding and care of the new breed, Richard King took Smoke, Cal, Pearlie, Monte, and Louis hunting on his thousands of acres of prime land.

Smoke, after killing a Texas mule deer, allowed as how he'd never seen a deer so big.

Pearlie and Cal were more impressed by the number of quail and doves they killed. Especially Pearlie, who said he'd never tasted anything so good as quail barbecued over a mesquite fire.

"So, you like them better than the oysters?" Louis asked as he gnawed meat off one of the small birds next to the campfire.

King glanced at Pearlie. "You didn't care for our oysters?"

Pearlie shook his head. "Not enough so's you could tell," he answered.

"That's the first thing I ever saw ole' Pearlie wouldn't eat," Cal said.

"I done tole you, ain't nothin' wrong with my nature," Pearlie said defensively.

King laughed. "Well, out here on the ranch, we have another kind of oyster you might like better."

Pearlie gave him a funny look. "If you're talkin' 'bout mountain oysters, we got those up in Colorado too, an' they're not too high on my list of things I like to eat either."

Smoke looked at him. "But, Pearlie, you always said you liked the stew that Puma Buck made for us when we stayed up in the high lonesome with him that winter."

Pearlie turned his head to stare at Smoke. "You don't mean . . ."

"Yep," Smoke said. "One of the prime ingredients was deer testicles, or mountain oysters as you call it. Where do you think they got the name?"

Pearlie made a face and got up from the campfire. "Excuse me, gentlemen," he said. "I think I'll go wash out my mouth."

As the men all laughed, Cal said, "Pass me another one of them quail quick, 'fore Pearlie comes back an' eats 'em all up."

33

Back at the Sugarloaf, Smoke and Sally leaned on a fence, watching the Santa Gertrudis bulls as they discovered the delights of Smoke's shorthorn cows in a large pasture out behind their cabin.

Sally smiled. "Well, I can see the Santa Gertrudis bulls seem to take to our shorthorn cows just as well as the ones back on their home range."

"Sally," Smoke said, "bulls are just like men. They don't much care who the filly is when they get in the mood, just as long as she's ready and willing."

Sally cut her eyes at Smoke, giving him a look. "Are you speaking from experience, Mr. Jensen, sir?"

"Uh . . ." Smoke stuttered, knowing he'd made a tactical mistake of major proportions.

"Go on, answer me," Sally said, turning to stare at him with her hands on her hips.

"Uh . . . why, no, Sally," he answered weakly. "Just commenting on most men . . . in general, I mean. Of course, I only have eyes for you, dear."

She nodded, not smiling. "Uh-huh."

"By the way," Smoke said, taking her by the arm and leading her toward their cabin, "I want to talk to you about those oysters we had. They had the strangest effect on me."

She smiled up at him, putting her arm around his waist and her head on his shoulder. "I noticed, dear. I noticed."